Dream Sacrifice

Book III of the Oneiroi Trilogy

L. W. Phillips

DRAGON SCALES PRESS

Dream Sacrifice

Book III of the Oneiroi Trilogy

Copyright © 2024 L. W. Phillips

Cover Art by Rowan Magennis

First published in the United States of America.

ISBN: 979-8-9876482-5-4 (Paperback)

ISBN: 979-8-9876482-6-1 (Hardcover)

This book is a work of fiction. Any reference to historical events, real people, or real places are used fictitiously. Names, characters, and places are products of the author's imagination.

10 9 8 7 6 5 4 3 2 1

Designed with Atticus

To Joanna and Kellie
For helping my dreams come true!

"Man is the noblest of all animals. Separate him from law and justice and he is the worst." ~Aristotle

Trigger Warnings

Know Your Triggers Before Reading

Dream Sacrifice is a work of fiction that may contain triggers in the written word for some readers. Triggers are but are not limited to, the following: graphic language, consensual intercourse, sexual assault, abduction, confinement, battle scenes, and death.

PLAYLIST

WHAT WAS IN MY EAR WHILE WRITING

1. *The Death of Peace of Mind* by Bad Omens

2. *Whatever It Takes* by Imagine Dragons

3. *Awake* by Godsmack

4. *I Appear Missing* by Queens of the Stone Age

5. *Angel* by The Weekend

6. *Believer* by Imagine Dragons

7. *The Louvre* by Lorde

8. *Demons* by Imagine Dragons

9. *My Name is Human* by Highly Suspect

10. *Everybody Wants to Rule the World* by Lorde

11. *I'll Follow You* by Shinedown

12. *Send Me an Angel* by Highly Suspect

13. *Love-Hate-Sex-Pain* by Godsmack

Prologue

Millions of years ago, God created all manner of beings who lived among one another—until they could no longer live together in harmony. The more power a being possessed, the higher up the proverbial food chain they were, and that left humans and all other mortal beings at the bottom of that chain.

Instead of feeling blessed with what they had, immortals dominated humans, causing chaos and havoc. Keeping humans in a constant fear by making them pawns in games between gods, angels, and creatures.

Because of this imbalance, God banished all immortal beings to separate realms. Guardians were the only ones allowed to pass between these realms; after all, they were the upholders of mankind. However, many rules applied. They could only stay in the human realm long enough to *fix* the problem, and they were never to get involved with a mortal, especially intimately. Revealing their true nature was forbidden, and performing *magic* in front of a mortal was prohibited.

Deities did not always abide by the rules. Chaos always resumed when a god became willful in the mortal realm, even if it took a millennium for their anarchy to catch up with them. This caused heartache and often death to all the parties involved. Frequently, children were the product of such disobedience.

Sometimes, a god or goddess would be on the receiving end of the turmoil wreaked by their peers. In such events, a quorum would gather to debate whether a deity would be granted permission to live amongst the mortals. This happened only three times with the Greek Pantheon. Angelia, the daughter of Hermes and Aphrodite, was one particular goddess who had permission. Zeus was all too happy for his granddaughter to leave Olympus. Only none of the gods of the Greek Pantheon knew why she was granted sanction. It was not spoken of, buried in secrets and politics. Unfortunately, after a thousand years, her presence amongst the mortals started causing problems because she chose to procreate.

Another of those instances was a considerable cover-up of Zeus' indiscretions, which left his child and grandchild in the mortal realm, living as humans—until a dream god stumbled on his enchanting granddaughter, and the truth reared its ugly head.

The third was one of an Oneiroi, a dream god of the Greek Pantheon. Because of his obligation and sacrifice in lending his abilities to Zeus' coverup, he was granted a home in Athens, Greece. However, he was not allowed intimate knowledge of mortals.

These three gods were granted permission to circumvent the rules, which is one reason we have gods and demigods walking among humans in the mortal realm in the twenty-first century.

But what about other beings and creatures? Surely, one does not honestly believe only the Greek Pantheon initially broke the rules. Indeed, there are others if gods and demigods walk in the mortal realm. Right? What about creatures? Not all immortals are gods. Who or what else walks among us?

It's been two weeks since he took me. One week went to physical healing. The second was the need for mental healing, which never came.

Amanda wrote in her journal. She had no one she could talk to or who would or could understand. As hopeless as she felt, she decided to go to South Africa with her father after graduation. Maybe a change of scenery and no gods would help her mental state. Or at least help her sleep better. The dark circles grew larger and darker every time she looked in the mirror. It was the end of the first week she'd been back at school, and every day, a student or a teacher asked her if she was okay. She always told them she just felt a little under the weather. Fortunately for her, Kallisto had stopped asking. Nicole begged her to let Phobetor help her sleep. She wanted nothing less. Allowing a god, even one she once trusted, to help her would not happen. They didn't get it. She didn't want anything to do with any of them. Not the Oneiroi, not her mother, not even Kallisto. The only one she trusted was her dad, who left for Africa that morning. He would return for graduation in a few weeks, but until then, she would do her best to avoid everyone for her sanity.

"No! Please, no!" Amanda screamed.

With rancid breath, Phobos whispered in her ear, "You will never be his. Not only have I been here," he raked his claws intimately down her body, "one day my father will be, and your dream god will hate you for it."

She woke on her stomach, her head on her journal, and the feeling of Phobos' hand—no—his paw wrapped around her neck. How could she still feel his giant claw after waking? She touched her neck, then wiped away the tear trailing down her cheek. With the memory fresh in her head, she swore she could still hear the low chuckle he gave while defiling her.

Chapter I

Africa

"Just a doppelganger. It's been two months, and I'm still just a doppelganger," Amanda informed her reflection. The day before her second kidnapping, her demigod abilities were released from her grandmother's concealment. What a shock it was to one day be a mortal and the next a demi-god. It was a lot for her to take in, especially since she had no abilities, unlike her cousin, Nicole.

Angelia was her maternal grandmother, better known as the Greek goddess, who never told her daughters or grandchildren that they were descendants of the infamous Zeus himself. Amanda was the *king of the gods'* great-great-grandchild. Her three cousins, Nicole and her five-year-old twin brothers, were the other unsuspecting winners of the powerful lineage.

Nicole's abilities began to manifest before their grandmother released them from the concealment she had them under. However, they were minuscule. She was a dream bender and became even more badass once her concealment was removed. It was pretty cool, actually. Her cousin could control not only her dreams, but if taken by an Oneiroi to another's dreams, she could also walk their imaginings, no matter the being's abilities or status. Piss her off, and you could be in a great deal of pain when you woke because the love of her life was the Greek god of nightmares—the middle Oneiroi, Phobetor. She could imagine almost anything she wanted to—and control it. In her dreams, she reigned supreme, even against the three Oneiroi.

Unfortunately for Amanda, she just looked damn good. Her grandmother, Angelia, was the daughter of Hermes and Aphrodite. Angelia got her godly good looks from her mother, not that Hermes looked unsavory. None of the gods did. They were all extraordinary-looking and—hot. However, Aphrodite was the elite in terms of looks and sensuality, and Angelia, her daughter, looked just like her. Their eye color was the only difference—and Amanda was Angelia's doppelganger. "Spitting image," her Aunt Kellie from Tennessee once said.

When the concealment was undone, Amanda's beauty intensified. She had always been gorgeous and still looked like herself, but now—she was—luminous.

It's taken a long time to get over everything the first part of the year dealt her. But she had finally started coming out of the fog. It helped to distance herself from the gods who had invaded her personal space, even if she had to distance herself from her best friend, Kallisto. She wouldn't lie; that was hell. However necessary. That proved easier once she left for South Africa with her dad after graduation.

Begging wasn't usually in her repertoire, but she needed to get away, and what better way than to go to another continent with the only ordinary human left in her life? Not that the gods couldn't get to her if they wanted. Hell, they could watch her from those damn orbs she despised. But she felt safer than she had in a long time.

Her dad ran the biology department of the local university in Hawaii and was the lead marine biologist on a three-month grant to study great white sharks off the coast of Africa and the reason running from her problems was possible. Unfortunately, he spent days at a time on a ship, and she didn't see him a lot, but he still provided her with the means to finally get away before she started college in the fall. Until then, she spent her days reading at the camp or shopping in the city.

Occasionally, she spoke to Kallisto, but things had changed, whether either of them wanted it to or not. After a decade of friendship that was more like sisterhood, it had only taken three immortals to sever the ties that bound their relationship. Ares, the god of war who kidnapped them both last January; Phobos, who took her two months ago and brutally abused her; and *Phantasos*—she didn't want to think about him. Not wanting to was one thing—actively doing it was another. Her thoughts often strayed to him. The look in his eyes when he wiped the dagger on Phobos' shirt sleeve after ripping it back out of the lion's heart, effectively killing the god who had tormented her and her cousin, terrified her. She was grateful but couldn't forget the haunting look in his black eyes. Would he be scarred from the life he took on her account?

It was her first time seeing Phantasos in what she could only think of as his battle state. She refused to believe the wings and fangs were his natural form, manifesting the look of a Greek god only in her presence. His look in that form was beyond striking. There weren't words she could use to describe him that weren't too mundane.

"Okay, Amanda," she chastised herself. "Get off your ass and go see Annika."

She grabbed her backpack and cell phone and took off to the street market, where she would meet Annika, whom she had met the first week she was in South Africa while shopping. The two of them immediately hit it off. They loved the market, books, watching people, and being silly. It was an easy friendship with laughs and no drama—no gods. No Kallisto.

As she approached the market, she noticed Annika standing outside the entrance, excitedly waving something.

"It came in yesterday," Annika held up the book she'd ordered.

"Great. Don't ask me questions about it. I'm not a spoiler of literature," Amanda grinned. "Are you looking for anything in particular?"

"No. Not really. If I find something I can't live without in the States, I'll get it," Annika spoke with a British accent. She had gotten into Harvard in hopes of becoming a cardiologist one day. Crazy smart and very pretty, she stood only five feet tall and had long, black curly hair with eyelashes you could see a mile away.

"I'm looking for a vibrant scarf and maybe something for my dad. He's coming ashore today or tomorrow, and I can't wait."

"Well, vibrant will not be a problem," Annika waved her hand around, emphasizing the bright colors of the market. Oranges, blues, reds, and purples were everywhere. The ambiance those colors invoked made shopping in the markets inviting and entertaining.

"True," Amanda laughed. It wasn't just the bright colors that allured her. The aroma of the spices, purses, blankets, and friendly faces made the markets Amanda's favorite thing to do on the weekends. She could and often did visit them for hours.

After a couple of hours of shopping, she found the perfect scarf. They ate, sat, and did what she thought most fun—people-watching and gossiping.

"So, tell me more about this book you're writing," Annika said as she sipped from her berry shake.

"I haven't really written much since I've been here," Amanda admitted. Actually, she'd never written anything down. The book was a white lie she'd told her new friend. She needed some way of expressing what she'd been through, and there was no way she could tell her the truth.

"Well, you have to promise me I will be the first to read the finished product. I can't wait to find out if Angie hooks up with the third god."

Amanda spat her drink out in shock.

"Are you okay?" Annika laughed.

Cleaning her reddened face from soda, Amanda responded, "Why would you think those two would ever be a thing?"

"Isn't it obvious?" Annika looked confused. "I thought that's where the book was going."

"No. Angie hates him, and I'm pretty sure he hates her. It's getting late. I better get back since Dad will be in soon, if not already," Amanda said while she hastily gathered her spoils and threw them in her backpack.

"Did I say something wrong?" Annika asked.

Amanda exhaled and reminded herself that her new friend didn't know her unrealistic stories were not made up.

"No…not at all. I just forgot Dad was coming in early, and I haven't seen him in two weeks. Since I've only been here three and a half, it feels like forever."

It dawned on Amanda that she had told Annika earlier that morning that her dad would be in today or tomorrow—*Shit!* She thought.

No wonder Annika didn't look convinced. "Call me when he goes back out, and we can hang out more. I won't leave for two more weeks. You?"

"I'm not sure. My friend is trying to get me to visit her in Greece before I return to Hawaii. I haven't decided yet."

"Greece? Sign me up," Annika smirked, then waggled her eyebrows. "Grecian men equal beautiful men."

Amanda laughed and waved, "See ya soon."

Three more weeks and she would have to make some decisions. Before school was out, she sent late admissions requests to a couple of mainland universities, hoping she could get out of Hawaii for a while. Her mother had called a couple of days before, letting her know she had received a letter stating she had gotten into the University of Southern California. That phone call rocked her world. Yes, she wanted and needed to get out of Hawaii. She needed to separate herself from her best friend. Not because she didn't love her but because of the baggage Kallisto came with. Amanda accepted the offer to USC, but would she be happy jumping into a new life? Three weeks—she had three weeks to make her mind up.

Amanda stopped right before she was free of the market. She felt the heavy weight of someone watching her. It wasn't the first time since she'd been in Africa that she felt the watcher, the god—but it had been a couple of days since the last disturbing incident. Unfortunately, she, unlike her cousin, couldn't tell who the watcher was. Was the being friend or foe? She turned in a complete circle and looked for the deity. No one stood out to her. Deciding to face the being if he or she materialized, she continued her walk to the campsite. She was confident Ares wasn't the pursuer since he was still in mourning. She thought most likely it was Kallisto or one of the Oneiroi—*Phantasos*. She closed her eyes briefly, thinking of the stunning yet infuriating god.

The thought of the eldest Oneiroi took her musings down the path of her friend Annika's opinion of the *book* she was writing. How she thought the heroine and the third god would ever get together was beyond her.

Back at the campsite, Amanda stretched across her bunk with a book she picked up at the airport on her trip to South Africa. She had read a lot since the last abduction. Books took her mind away from the memories, away from the terror and torture she endured, and into a fantasy world. She made sure she steered clear of mythology—no stories of the gods. After a few minutes of reading, she felt the watcher fade away. Was it him?

Two and a half months. That's how long it had been since he plunged the Atlantean dagger into Ares' son, Phobos. Since he killed Nicole's year-long tormentor. The one who kidnapped Amanda instead of Nicole. The one who scared her face with his claw. Two and a half months since he spoke to Zeus and made a deal with the King of the Underworld. Phantasos had trained and meditated every day since, preparing for the day Ares would avenge his son's death. The day Ares would come for him and—*her*. When he was not training, he watched—*her*. He had tried to stay away, but unfortunately, since the day he met her, he had not been capable of staying away. He lasted just over a month before he broke. Between her smart mouth and those brilliant blue eyes, she was irresistible. Unfortunately, the witty sarcasm had subsided since her time in the basement with the lion-shifting deity. Visible scars were not the only things she left that basement with. Phobos had broken a part of her.

Phantasos was pained by Amanda's refusal to acknowledge him. He knew she recognized a deity watching her. The old Amanda would have called him out on it. The girl curled up on a makeshift bed reading a book did not. This new Amanda refused to yell in protest and demand that her watcher materialize. Not that he would. He, too, had changed since taking Phobos' life. Zeus gave him no choice but to change.

After he killed Zeus' grandson, the king of the gods summoned him to his throne room. It was the first time Phantasos had seen the king in a rage. A rage directed at him because directing it at himself would be counterproductive. After all, it was the god king's fault. He chose to allow Ares and his sons to torment others.

"You killed my grandson!" Zeus shouted and hit the floor with his staff hard enough to cause a fissure in the marble floor, running from his throne to the painting of his daughter, Thia, on the opposite side of the room.

"Your grandson tortured and tormented two of your great-great-granddaughters and the husband of your grand-daughter. He would have killed Amanda," Phantasos yelled back, not caring if the god-king before him struck him down with lightning.

Zeus shook with anger. His voice was deep, and his accent thick with grief. "You should have brought him to me."

"He had gone mad. There was no saving him. Ask Aphrodite and Hermes," Phantasos responded. "If you will not believe me, believe Aphrodite. She loved her son but knew he had to be put down. He was an animal."

"No matter. Ares will come for you. May the best god win. I will not stop him from ending your existence."

Zeus turned his back to the Oneiroi, and Phantasos vanished from Zeus' throne room.

After days of contemplation, he decided he needed help protecting the ones he loved. That was when he made a deal with Underlord himself. Once he agreed with Hades' terms, he knew he had made a deal with Hades. The dark king now owned him. He had all three Oneiroi in his grasp. *Zeus had better be careful.*

Chapter II

Training

Reading became Amanda's escape. She'd always loved to read, but now, it was an obsession, consuming a book or two a day if she mixed physical and audiobooks. Romantasy was her favorite, combining her rom-com and high fantasy loves. The only problem was that no fantasy could top her life, so she started reading billionaire romances the week before and found them entertaining and no truer fantasy. She loved a great enemies-to-lovers, where the man fell hopelessly in love with the financially embarrassed woman who hated him—causing him to work exceptionally hard to win her approval and adoration. *Seriously, how many billionaires fell for the broke girl who hated him?* About fifty pages into her *fantasy* novel, she heard the calls of the camp hands—*He's back.*

"Dad!" Amanda shouted and waved over the commotion of everyone working to unload the boat and greet the crew. This was the university's first return vessel. She saw her dad, Alaric, look for her, and when their eyes met, she knew his exploration had been a success. The gleam in his eyes told her all she needed to know; the grad students and professors would celebrate tonight.

"Hey, honey." Alaric grabbed his daughter up and spun her around. "We did it. We tagged two female great whites and one male."

"That's awesome. How big were they?"

"One female was about twelve feet, and the other was just over fifteen. The male was eleven and a half," Alaric gleamed as he spoke. "I wasn't expecting us to tag on our first outing, but we did, and it was great."

The animated look across her father's face made her heart happy. It was the first time she felt excited and truly happy since before the basement.

"Did you get in the cage?" Amanda asked. This was what worried her the most. Her father, submerged in a cage, waiting for giant sharks to get close enough to touch—*scary AF.*

"Yes, and it was the most amazing adrenaline rush ever. I have pictures," Alaric grinned. "I tagged the smallest female. Mark tagged the other two."

Mark was the professional diver and scientist assigned to the university research team. He lived in South Africa, was twenty-six years old, and was drop-dead gorgeous. With his shoulder-length dark hair, emerald eyes . . . and oh, the muscles, he was what the old Amanda would call eye candy. *Damn.* Not to mention highly intelligent. He finished his Ph.D. last December, right after his twenty-sixth birthday. *How can someone be so attractive and so damn smart?* She couldn't help but admire him from afar since he was quite intimidating.

Yes, she had been around literal Greek deities, but there was something about a mortal man who looked like Mark. Add in the age difference and his scientific brain, and he was on another plane of existence. She also knew how crazy it was to think of their age difference and not that of the gods. It had to be that the gods looked younger. Mark looked twenty-six and was mortal. She expected immortals to be otherworldly.

At that moment, she realized she compared Mark to the gods and not to the boy she was dating before she got on the plane to Africa. Lucky for her, she and Kai made a deal—they could date other people while she was away for the summer. If they wanted a more permanent relationship when she returned to Hawaii, they would discuss it then. If not, they would continue as before she left—*friends with some perks.* Honestly, she thought she would never want a serious relationship after all she had gone through since January. Long story short, she was free to date, and she thought a roll in the sand with Mark would give her South African summer the edge it needed to help her forget—*him*— and by him, she didn't mean Kai. Unfortunately, she was sure Mark would not be interested in her almost nineteen-year-old self.

"I can't wait to hear all about it," Amanda said as she and her dad walked to the tents.

"I'm going to get a much-needed shower. I'll tell you all about the trip when I'm done. Then, we'll have a good time eating fresh seafood by the fire with the crew." Alaric kissed her on the top of her head and ducked into his tent to gather clothes. The showers were a good walk up the beach to the public facilities, so she had time to kill.

As soon as Amanda turned to walk back to the boat, where she would offer her help, she felt it—the watcher, for the second time in one day. Usually, the stalker watched at most once a day. Many days, there wouldn't be any invisible spectating. *Today—twice? Weird.*

※———※

Phantasos continued with his training. He'd only watched Amanda for a few minutes. Watching her any longer would cause that pain in his chest to rear its head—the one he insisted on ignoring. He would wait a few more days to check in again;

he knew Kallisto had Morpheus checking on her, too, even though she held the ability to do it herself now. It hurt her too much to see her vibrant best friend turn into an introvert.

He wielded short swords, long swords, daggers, and magic during training. Sometimes, he worked with Hermes on the training fields of Olympus and occasionally in the Underworld with Hades since the Underlord now had an invested interest in Phantasos staying alive. Mostly, he trained alone, fighting with practice dummies and meditating. To beat Ares, he needed his mind in the right place. The god of war would be the most challenging opponent he would ever encounter. Unlike the last time he fought Ares, the god will be at full strength, and the fight would be to kill—Zeus had given his permission. That meant he had to kill the god of war or die.

"Phantasos, how are you, brother? I hoped I would catch you here," Phobetor said as he appeared at the edge of his training room.

"Damn it, Phobetor. Is this payback? I have daggers in my hands. I could have cut your throat," Phantasos grumbled.

"Actually, this is payback for all those times you popped in without notice or invitation. And you would need to move faster to cut my throat, old man," Phobetor mocked his brother, hoping to ease the perpetual scowl across Phantasos' brow.

"Really? Here," Phantasos tossed Phobetor a short sword. "Let me see what damage you can do, little brother."

The two gods circled each other before they launched themselves into a graceful but lethal dance. Thousands of years of training and fighting together made them equals in the ring. The only way one would win was if the other made a grave mistake. After twenty minutes of sparring, Phantasos had Phobetor on the ground with what would have been a killing blow.

"Damn. Hermes teach you that?" Phobetor asked.

"No. Hades did," Phantasos answered as he helped his brother up from the mat.

"Are you ever going to tell me and Morpheus what Hades has over you?"

"Nope," Phantasos answered, taking a long drink of water and then pouring the rest over his head.

"Why not? You know what our deals with him are," Phobetor said, following suit with his water. Twenty minutes of god-sparring produced a lot of sweat.

"I am not ready to discuss anything with anyone. Now, fight me or leave," Phantasos ordered and raised his daggers.

"Fine, but if I win this round, you must answer my questions," Phobetor insisted.

"Why are you here, Phobetor? I know you did not come to train with me."

"I just wanted to visit. Nicole is shopping with her mother, and Morpheus is at some art thing with Kallisto. Why they are still working at the gallery for Hermes beats me," Phobetor answers as he ducks Phantasos' quick slash to his head.

"I guess when your fiancé is a god but has been a mortal all her life, you do mortal things," Phantasos said as he spun and kicked Phobetor's legs out from under him. "Looks like I will not be answering any questions today."

Phobetor flipped to his feet and tackled Phantasos. "Not so sure about that."

Phantasos used power to throw his brother from him and into the wall. He leered and stalked toward Phobetor like a wild animal. He felt his fangs lengthen and his eyes turn. He felt his control slipping.

"Brother, it is me—Phobetor. We are sparring. Snap out of it." Phobetor had no choice; he returned the power and encased his brother in a mental nightmare.

Phantasos dropped his daggers and grabbed his temples. "Okay, stop! I am okay," he grunted.

"What happened to you?" Phobetor asked as he waved his hand and released him from the visual sense.

"You bastard. I get that I was off the rails, but did you have to give me that vision?"

"I gave you a nightmare of regret. I thought it better than your biggest fear," Phobetor answered.

"Apparently, they are the same."

"What happened? Why did you go all battle god?"

"I am not sure. I felt the shift, but I had no control over it."

"You need to speak to someone about this. Have you been to see Amanda since that night?"

Phobetor did not have to state which night; he knew the one his brother referred to. "No. And I do not plan on it. I saw the fear in her eyes—her fear of me. She has always hated me, and that is for the best, but to fear me." He heard the pain in his voice. "I refuse to see that look again—ever."

"Well, maybe you should rethink that. She has decided to go to the mainland for school instead of going with Kallisto to university in Hawaii. She has also decided not to go to Greece to visit Kallisto's grandmother."

"I know all this," Phantasos acknowledged. That is another reason I should stay away. She does not want anything to do with the gods, including Kallisto. She needs time."

"I honestly believe you are the only one who will be able to get through to her," Phobetor said.

"Now, you are the one going mad. She despises me."

"Maybe so, but you are also a challenge—one she cannot resist proving wrong. You need to confront her," Phobetor said as he downed some water. Look, she does not hate you. She never has. I will see you soon, brother. Stop isolating yourself, and come see us." Phobetor vanished with the last word.

A challenge. Zeus knows that is what I have always wanted to be.

Chapter III

Possessive

Phantasos could not stop thinking about what Phobetor said about Amanda. He had no idea why his brother thought he should challenge Amanda. Maybe to provoke her into going to school with Kallisto instead of the mainland? What his brother failed to understand was that it would not be him who convinced her. He thought it was good that she was getting away from the gods, and going to school with Kallisto would keep her around them—including him. He would not risk it.

All thoughts of the blonde caused his curiosity to build, and he caved. After a long hot shower, he decided to check on her again. What he found made him smile—at first.

She sat beside her father on a boulder covered by a colorful blanket before a small bonfire. Many large rocks with laughing people circled the fire, and from what he gathered, they told tales of their recent adventures at sea. He watched Amanda's face as Alaric told his story of cage diving with sharks. Personally, the sea was not Phantasos' idea of a great time. He lived under Zeus' rule, not Poseidon's. However, if he lived through his battle with Ares, he might have to plead to the god of the sea for refuge. He was sure Zeus would have his head if Ares did not take it.

Seafood, tall-tales, and alcohol were the recipe for what Phantasos saw that made him stop smiling. It was obvious to him that Amanda had too much to drink. She was of drinking age in South Africa–she was not in the U.S. So, it did not take much for her to be a little too indulged.

◆——··——◆

Is he looking at me? Yep, I think he's looking at me. Dizzying thoughts spun through Amanda's head as she listened to everyone's adventures. She felt someone watching her, well, two *someone's.* Her godly watcher was back, three times in one day, and someone more corporal—Mark. At first, she thought she was overthinking his interest—until he winked. She smiled back. No way was she going to let her dad see her interest in the man he called a colleague, so she would wait until the camaraderie ended and everyone was safe and snug in their tents to make her move. Channeling the old Amanda, she decided Mark would be her escape.

It wasn't ten minutes after their wink-and-smile exchange that Mark decided to wander over and talk with her dad. He sat so close to her that she felt the heat radiating off his skin. He made her very aware of his presence when he leaned over her slightly every time he addressed her father. Anytime Alaric turned to laugh at the antics of the students, Mark would convey interest with his body language and eyes. When the slight breeze changed directions, she could smell his aftershave, a woodsy scent that made her mind whirl with anticipation. *Damn, he looked good.* Before long, his leg was touching hers as they conversed, bare thigh to bare thigh. *Damn.*

When her father excused himself and went to speak with the vessel's captain, Mark turned to her and whispered in her ear, "Meet me at the rock bend later?"

Amanda nodded in answer. Trying to keep from doing a happy dance, she turned and asked the closest person when the next trip to sea would be. The response surprised her. Three days was all the time she would have with her dad before he sailed again. *Well, that sucks.*

Two more drinks, and it was time to head to the tents. Alaric bid her goodnight and turned toward his shelter, and she to hers. Amanda waited ten minutes then poked her head out of her tent. The only people she could see were a couple making out by the water. Admittedly, she was a little dizzy from the alcohol—not being used to it—but she refused to let that deter her from meeting up with Mark.

Holding her shoes, she sprinted from her tent, keeping to the shadows. Luckily, clouds partially covered the three-quarter moon, helping with concealment. It only took a few minutes to get to the bend, and as promised, Mark stood against the rocks with his arms and ankles crossed, waiting.

"I wasn't sure you would come," Mark said, grinning as she approached.

"Have you not heard? I'm always up for a challenge."

⸎————⸎

That was all Phantasos could take. When Amanda informed the mortal that she was always up for a challenge, what Phobetor said hit him square in the chest, and he would be damned if that prick *challenged* her. Amanda made it less than a meter from the asshole before he appeared by her side.

Three things happened in succession. The asshat let out an unmanly scream, Amanda said a few unwomanly four-letter words directed at him, and he hit the mortal man in the face with his fist.

With a wave of his hand, Phantasos froze the man in place as he writhed on the ground. Then turned to Amanda and asked, "What in Hades do you think you are doing?"

"Me? What am I doing?"

"That is what I asked. What are you doing here with that," Phantasos pointed at Mark's still body. He felt his anger build. Being so close to Amanda made his senses run wild. The mortal on the ground made him manic.

"I'm trying to get laid. What do you think I'm doing with him?" Amanda crossed her arms over her chest and glared at him.

That was the wrong thing to say. Phantasos' eyes went from baby blue to swirling crimson. He closed them and tried to calm his rising temper. It took a full minute, which felt more like ten, and when he opened them, he saw it on Amanda's face—fear. What he never wanted to see crossed her face again. *Well, too damn late. I refuse to let her fuck this prick.*

Phantasos stepped right up to her, chest to chest. "You are not going to fuck him—ever."

He watched Amanda bristle. Apparently, his words removed all traces of fear and exchanged them with anger.

"That's none of your damn business." She spat. "Besides, what's wrong with him?" Amanda pointed at the man lying at their feet, frozen. "He's an intelligent man with a future. You didn't have a problem with me fucking Kai, and he's a teenager with a future as a surfer."

Phantasos' eyes went red . . . again. This time, he did not hide them from her. He saw the fear flash over her face, but to her credit, she did not back down.

"I have been away. Had I known you were engaging in sexual acts with mortal men, I would have returned sooner."

"Why?" Amanda asked, raising her chin.

Phantasos turned away from her to think. "Because you are better than that. You need time to heal and not jump in bed with—anyone," he said, turning back to face her.

"Again, that's none of your business. Now, fix him," Amanda said, pointing to Mark's still body.

Phantasos waved his hand, and Mark disappeared from the sandy ground.

"What did you do? Where did he go?" Amanda's sounded frantic as she spun around, looking for the scientist. "Please say you didn't hurt him or, worse, rapture him to some unknown realm."

There it was again—fear. Amanda's voice was full of fear, and he put it there. He was pissed at her, but he hated hearing the terror in her voice.

"Relax. I sent him to *his* designated tent. He will not remember anything and think he had more to drink than he thought."

He saw relief cross Amanda's face before she squared her shoulders and glared at him.

"Why are you here, Phantasos?"

"I told you. You are not ready for . . . *him.*" Even he heard the drip of hate in his acknowledgment of the man Amanda was about to indulge in.

"Leave me alone. I'm here," Amanda gestured around her, "to get away from all of you. Just go."

Phantasos not only saw the pain in Amanda's eyes but felt it radiate off her in waves. *She is serious.*

"Even Kallisto?" he asked.

"Yes. Even her. I'm done. I want out," Amanda confirmed and shook with sadness.

They stood toe to toe with only the sound of waves crashing in the background. He had to give it to her, afraid or not, she never looked away from his eyes. He supposed it was so he could see her pain and the truth of her words. So, he watched as tears began to trail from her eyes to her chin. It was never supposed to be this way. With everything in him, he took her chin between his finger and thumb and looked past his reflection and past the tears to where her fantasies once lay. They were no longer there.

"I am truly sorry, ἄγγελος. I will go, and I will never bother you again." Then he vanished.

⸭—ⅲ—⸬

Amanda lowered herself to the ground with her arms wrapped around her middle. The tears that trickled down her face in front of Phantasos were nothing to the ones that flooded her hands and the ground beneath her as pain rocked through her body. Memories of before and after Greek deities invaded her life raced through her mind. The reflections of her sister-like relationship with Kallisto wrecked her. They caused blows of pain so deep she could hardly breathe. After she worked through those memories, others surfaced. Phantasos' sarcasm and his need to protect her, mixed with her mild hatred and in-credulous attraction for him, started the waterworks up again. The agony she felt was the pain of loss. It was at that moment she knew she would never be able to let them go. Kallisto was her sister—her family. You don't leave your family. Phantasos, ironically, made her feel safe. If he was out of her life, would she ever feel safe? If Ares wanted her—hiding wouldn't stop him.

Amanda continued sitting on the sand until the sun peeked out from the ocean. It rose like a giant. She made her way to the water and splashed her face enough to remove the streaks of dried tears, then walked back to camp.

After her breakdown, Amanda decided two things. First, she wanted to go to sea once with her dad. She needed more time, and she really wanted to see a great white. Second, she would book a ticket to Greece.

Chapter IV

Boarding

Amanda only got an hour of sleep before everyone in the camp began to stir. "Coffee. I need coffee," she mumbled as she stumbled from her shelter.

"Thank you," she said to Mark when he handed her a cup of java outside her tent. She found it interesting that he stood only feet from the entrance to her tent.

"No problem. Uh, I just wanted to say I'm sorry if I was out of line last night."

Amanda stood frozen at his words. *Shit. He's not supposed to remember.* She called on her inner actress and manifested a confused look.

"I'm not sure I know what you mean," she responded.

"Did I not say anything off-kilter around the fire last night?" Mark asked, his face masked with hope.

"I don't believe so. I mean, we all had a little too much to drink, but I don't recall anything unusual. Why?" Amanda asked. She wanted to know what he remembered.

"Well, I guess I just dreamt it. Anyway, enjoy your coffee."

Mark winked at her before he walked off toward the other crew members.

Weird.

About ten minutes later, her father walked up, holding two cups of coffee. "I see you already have a cup."

"I do, but I could use more. I didn't sleep well," Amanda admitted.

"Why not?" Alaric asked.

"Don't know." Amanda changed the subject before he used his *dad* superpowers on her and sensed the lie. "I was wondering if you would let me go out with you guys on your next trip. It's a bucket list thing, plus I could spend more time with you." She grinned, blowing cool air across her hot coffee before taking another sip.

"I'm not sure about that," he answered. "There's only one bathroom, one shower, and no turning back if you happen to get seasick or just hate it."

"You know I don't get seasick, and I'm not afraid of a little stink. As long as it comes off when we return." She grinned over her cup at her father.

"In that case, I guess you can. And you're in luck. This trip is only three days long."

"Why's that?" Amanda asked.

"We're testing new equipment. If it works, we'll need to come in and prepare for an extended trip at sea. If it doesn't work, we'll need to offload it and put the older equipment back aboard.

"Thanks, Dad. When do we leave?"

"Day after tomorrow. Early."

"I can't wait."

Amanda hugged her dad and texted Annika to see if she wanted to meet and people-watch. She also wanted to tell her new friend that she would be going to Greece after all. The night before, she'd thought a lot about Kallisto and the rest of her family and friends and decided she needed to face her life head-on and stop running from it. Even if she no longer wanted to be around the gods, she needed to explain to Kalli why she felt that way.

◆——■——◆

Phantasos exploded. Instead of immediately leaving Amanda on the beach, he watched her to make sure she stayed out of trouble and out of the asshole's tent. He looked on as she fell completely and uncontrollably apart. Unable to help her because she loathed him. So, he spent most of the night wrecking his gym. Not one piece of equipment, furniture, or weaponry was where it should be. He flung everything in his path, every muscle bunched in rage. Not because he was mad at Amanda, but because he hurt her to the point that the light left her eyes. The sarcastic, beautiful, formidable woman he first met was no longer there, and he had as much to do with her transformation as the gods who tormented and tortured her.

"Are you done?" Morpheus called to him from across the gym.

"What are you doing here?" Phantasos unkindly asked while he picked up a large display case full of weapons he had thrown over on its side.

"I came to see how you are doing."

"As you can see, I am great. Now . . . leave," Phantasos grumbled as he physically repaired his gym to its previous glory.

"Why are you picking that up when you can . . ." Morpheus asked and waved a hand, mimicking using his powers.

"Because I still have energy that needs dispelling," Phantasos answered his youngest brother.

"I see. Well, how about we go spar? Fists only, that way, you can release whatever this is," Morpheus gestured around the room as he spoke, "and we can discuss what happens next."

"What do you mean, what happens next?"

"I mean, make plans for when the mourning period for that asshole Phobos is over."

Phantasos went completely still. He knew his brothers would want in on the bloodshed. He just thought it would take a little longer since the mourning period for the gods was quite lengthy.

"If I wanted or needed my brothers to help me fight my battles, I would have asked," Phantasos snapped at Morpheus as he righted another large piece of gym equipment without grunting.

"Since you see no need in us asking to intervene, we decided not to ask and just force our involvement. We are the Oneiroi, a team, brothers . . . You will not fight this alone. Accept that this way, we can prepare rather than go in without a plan," Morpheus smiled and crossed his muscular arms over his chest.

Phantasos stopped, closed his eyes, and wished for a spark of patience. He wanted to be alone, but his brother had a different idea. Deciding to appease his brother for the moment instead of arguing with him, he nodded and then said, "Fine. Get Phobetor and meet me back here. I will put the ring back while you get him."

⬥ⱅ⎯⎯ⱅ⎯⎯ⱅⱅ⬥

Two days later, Amanda boarded the vessel that would take her to experience the monsters of the deep—the great whites that she and her father shared a love of. Nervous excitement radiated from within her. She tapped the rail and waited for the captain to take her on the thrill ride. The anticipation of danger had always been Amanda's favorite buzz. She reveled in the excitement that stimulated an exhilaration bordering on insatiable. She never got enough of feeling the thrill brought on inside her. She always needed more, except when introduced to the gods.

That was when the light went out of her eyes. The one everyone harped on after Ares raptured her last January. It wasn't just the once when he kidnapped her and Kallisto . . . no. . . he had taken her a couple of times before. That deadly thrill became a nightmare. Today was different. The anticipation of seeing deadly, great white sharks was in no way the same as taunting a god. The excitement was there, but her dad would be with her. He always made her feel safe.

"Well, well, well. I guess the rumors were true. The daughter of the great Professor Alaric Fanel will be going out to sea with us."

Mark sauntered to Amanda's side with a grin so wide he looked as if he could eat her whole. Not that she would complain. He was more than handsome. However, her father was on this ship . . . this small ship . . . with them. Therefore, she would not be acting on her more basic instincts.

"Yes. I begged. I can't wait to see live great whites. When I was a little girl, Dad and I watched *Shark Week* together every time it came on, and for us, that was often because we had them all recorded. Sometimes, Dad, my best friend, and I would curl up on the sofa on Saturdays and watch them all day and night. He would act like he had enough of sharks by midafternoon, but we would beg to continue, and he would feign irritation. I know this because I always saw him grin and wink at my mother."

"Sounds like he's a good dad."

"He's the best. How about you? How did you start this kinda stuff?" Amanda asked.

"I've always been fascinated with large bodies of water, especially the oceans. I don't remember not wanting to go out to sea," Mark relaxed against the railing as he spoke.

"So, you became a scientist of the deep. I have no idea what I want to do with my life. If I decided to be what I always wanted as a little girl, I would marry a prince and live in a castle," Amanda said, looking out at the waves as she did.

"Maybe Prince Charming will sweep you off your feet one day. I suppose you would have to move, though. I don't know of many castles in Hawaii," Mark grinned.

"True. Well, I better go find my father. He needs to see I'm here."

"I hope you enjoy yourself, Amanda," Mark said as he raised off the rail and walked to the other side of the boat.

The feeling Mark projected was thick and gave her chills. The look in his eyes was different from two days ago. The last time she spoke to him was when he gave her coffee and an apology. Something seemed off, but Amanda couldn't put her finger on it. Most likely, it was her imagination. After all, she remembered what they were about to be up to when *you know who* showed up.

"Dad!" Amanda yelled at her father over the crash of the waves. Winds started about thirty minutes after they sailed from port. The boat's rise and fall wasn't bad, but she had to hold the rails to keep from falling. Her father seemed not to have that problem. He walked a straight line toward her, without using the railing. *Show off.*

"I just looked into the lady's quarters to see if you were there. I'm glad you're here." Alaric gave her a side hug since one of her arms held a death grip on the rail. "We normally have a little sailing party with a few drinks and cheers, but everyone is getting ready for the rain. It wasn't supposed to hit until late this evening."

"Well, maybe we can do that after the storm," Amanda suggested. "I want to experience everything."

Alaric grinned at her. "I would like for you to go to the kitchens or your barracks while we prepare for the storm. After it's over, I'll come for you."

"Okay. I'll go to my quarters and wait."

Amanda kissed her father on the cheek and placed one hand over the other along the railing as she made her way to the stairs leading to the female sleeping quarters. A storm of any kind, mild or tempest, was not what she had in mind. She hoped it would be over soon so she could enjoy the experience of the deep-sea and shark-watching. Plus, the added benefit of taking her mind off the parts of her life that were hanging in the balance.

CHAPTER V

SIRENS

FINALLY, ALARIC KNOCKED ON the cabin doors, signaling all was well and they could go on deck. Everyone was relieved to find the storm was more wind than anything. There was still a slight breeze, but Amanda no longer felt the need to apply a chokehold to the railing. As promised, champagne and wine were passed around, and songs were sung. She watched her dad in his element. Instead of telling *dad jokes,* her father participated in telling scientific *nerd* jokes. It was the type of joke that if she did get the punch line, it wasn't funny. If she rolled her eyes anymore, they would be in danger of getting stuck. *Bless him* was the southern endearment her mother used when her dad worked a room. A ship with equally nerdy academic types caused her to *bless them all* as they told stories and puns. It warmed Amanda's heart to watch him accomplish his dreams, even if his jokes went over her head.

After her overindulgence in beverages a couple of nights ago, Amanda didn't feel the need to treat herself . . . at all. So, unlike most of the crew, she nursed only one glass of champagne the entire evening. After a couple of hours of eye-rolling, the hair on the back of her neck stood on end as a tingle ran from her nape to her lower back. It wasn't the normal deity intrusion. She wasn't sure it was a deity at all. *Mortal?* Determined to find the creeper, Amanda leveled her eyes and scanned the ship. Nothing. She didn't see anyone looking at her. *Weird.*

"Dad," Amanda tapped her father on his shoulder. "I'm going to bed. Thank you for bringing me out here. You know I'm not a morning person. So, I'm going to do the mature thing and get some sleep so I can wake up with you and the crew—since you crazy scientist types believe morning starts while it's still dark out."

"Very mature of you, daughter," Alaric laughed. "If you need anything, text me. Breakfast is at 4:45."

"You nerds are insane. 4:45 should only come in the PM. Love you, Dad."

Amanda was making her way back to her cabin when a very faint, strange trill pricked her ears. It was so weak that she wondered if she had heard anything at all. She stopped before entering her room and listened intently. *Nothing. Great! Now you're hearing shit.* She thought, turning the handle to her room.

It only took a few minutes to ready herself for her dreaded bed, where she usually spent hours trying to make herself fall asleep. Every night was the same. The quieter her surroundings became, the louder her mind sounded. Tonight, she battled with herself over whether returning to Hawaii was the right thing to do. Why she tried to fall asleep was beyond her. Most of the time, she woke with sweat coating her flesh from the nightmares her noisy thoughts insisted on conjuring. She thought more than once to call on Phobetor to settle her mind and rid her of the terror that plagued her dreams, but she refused to reach out to the Oneiroi. Not as long as she could keep from it. Unless the nightmares made her vomit like they had for weeks after Phobos took her.

The cabin door opened, and her two roommates staggered in, giggling and hushing each other. She looked at her watch to find it was just after midnight. Apparently, the party had ended. Both girls fell asleep moments after crawling into their bunks, leaving Amanda with her blaring thoughts once more.

Just as sleep latched onto her, she heard the distant trills of women singing. Beautiful singing. Voices that sent euphoric feelings through her body. She sat up in bed to see if her roommates were equally affected. They continued to sleep. The song intensified, as the number of women singing must have doubled. Amanda slipped on her robe and climbed the stairs to the abandoned deck. Her ears controlled her feet. Slowly, she made her way to the side of the ship. Where giant rocks appeared in the middle of the ocean. Where the mountain of boulders came from, she didn't know, but atop them were odd creatures singing. They had beautiful feminine faces and the bodies of large birds—*eagles, maybe? Another nightmare.*

Their song was about the beauty below the surface of the water. She desperately wanted to see that beauty—no, she *needed* to see it. The thought passed through her mind just as a hand snaked around her waist. She knew without looking that it was Mark.

"Beautiful doppelganger, don't you want to see the beauty they sing of?" Mark's seductive voice sent an icy chill down her spine.

"I do," Amanda heard herself respond as she leaned the back of her head against his chest. Her voice sounded meek and far away to her own ears.

"Then jump," he encouraged.

"But they're so far away. I don't want to swim that far."

"You don't want them. You want to see the beauty under the waves. The beauty they sing of," he stroked his hand up and down the curve of her waist as he whispered into her ear. She felt feather-light touches from his lips from his whispers and heard herself groan in delight.

"Will you go with me?" she asked her father's second.

"I'll come later," he replied.

Amanda closed her eyes and listened to the song the sirens sang. Mark's voice continued to caress her ear. The sea called to her. She needed to explore the splendor of the deep waters that the beauty of the magnificent creatures sang about. *I want to see,* she thought while she closed her eyes and enjoyed the ambiance.

"Stop this," a loud booming voice rose above the siren song, blasting Amanda out of the trance. Immediately, Mark's hand fell to his side, releasing her. She turned to him and saw his eyes were glassed over. He wasn't himself. She watched as he turned, his movements stiff and mechanical, and walked away.

Next, she searched for the booming voice to find the most gorgeous man she'd ever seen hovering above the waves. His heavily muscled, almost naked body dripped with seawater. His skin looked sun-kissed under the moonlight, and his eyes—Aqua—were the same as Kallisto's—were the *same eyes as Zeus,* she thought. The god before her had to be Poseidon. He could be no other with those mesmerizing eyes and that straight, refined nose. If his eyes hadn't given him away, his sheer size and the trident he held in his right fist would have.

On either side of him, four others rose from the water, only their head and torsos showed—two women and two men. *Gorgeous.*

"Kill the sirens," Poseidon ordered the four without looking at them.

With a nod from each, they dove under the water, and large fishtails broke the surface in their wake.

"Oh shit. Are those—"

"Merpeople? Yes," the larger-than-life, very wet god smirked.

Damn, he's beautiful.

"And you are, Poseidon?" Amanda's question was more a statement of fact, but he answered her anyway.

"Yes. And you are Angelica's doppelganger. Hermes great-granddaughter."

"How do you know that?" Amanda's senses started coming back, and she realized her predicament. Even though the god of the seas removed the sirens' danger, he was also a potential threat. One she had no way of stifling. There was no combat power in *looking good*.

"The cluster brewing on Olympus has reached us all. Besides, you look identical to your grandmother," Poseidon hovered closer to the ship as he spoke. His grin wasn't at all comforting. It looked forced and sensuous.

Instinctively, Amanda took two steps back from the railing. "Why are you here?"

"If you move any closer to her, you will regret it."

Amanda's back stiffened at the new voice behind her. *His* voice—Phantasos—*thank the gods.* Better to be with the danger you know than the terror you don't.

"Phantasos," Poseidon smirked as he verbally acknowledged the Oneiroi, not taking his eyes off Amanda. "What brings the god of fantastical dreams to the middle of the ocean?"

"Oh, you know. Making fantasies come true," Phantasos moved behind Amanda and wrapped a possessive hand around her waist, splaying his fingers across just under her belly button. Electricity ran through his fingers when he touched her. Momentarily, he wondered if she felt the jolt. He had his answer when he felt her shiver.

"So, is the doppelganger the reason you and Ares are quarreling? It all makes sense now. Let me guess. He wants what you have. Wait—do you have her?" Poseidon's grin widened, still not taking his eyes off Amanda.

"Ares kidnapped Amanda, and months later, his son, Phobos, took her." He felt her stiffen at the gods' names. "They both tortured her, and I killed Phobos for it. That is the reason Ares wants my death. She belongs to no one," Phantasos answered.

"Well . . . your posturing states otherwise," Poseidon's mouth twitched, and he pointedly looked at Phantasos' hand, which was wrapped possessively around Amanda.

Before he opened his mouth, Amanda jumped in with an explanation.

"He's protective. My best friend, your niece, is to wed his brother. She would have their heads if anything happened to me. Not to mention what my grandmother would do," Amanda finished, not moving from Phantasos' hold, knowing he was the lesser of the two evils.

"I am not here to harm you. I admit—I was curious about the demi who had Olympus in such an uproar—especially one without power. When I heard the sirens calling for you, I decided to show myself. Those hideous creatures would have eaten you and your friend alive," Poseidon explained as he continued to watch Phantasos' hold.

"Thank you for helping me," Amanda said.

"See Phantasos. She knows how to treat a god of power. Now that I have an idea of what is happening on my brother's mount, I will take my leave. It was good to meet you, Amanda," Poseidon started to descend into the water and stopped just before his torso fully emerged. "Phantasos—enjoy your fantastical creations." Poseidon disappeared into the black depths with those last words and a parting wink.

◆———◆◆———◆

Once the sea swallowed the king of the waters, Amanda turned on Phantasos, effectively removing his hand from her waist. "Why are you here, Phantasos?"

"Well, that is a fine way to thank me."

"I thought you weren't going to come around anymore?" Amanda crossed her arms over her chest, realizing she was in nothing but a nightshirt, robe, and fuzzy socks.

"I felt your fear. And before you ask, I am not sure how. When I looked on, I saw Mark in a trance walking away from you and, to my horror, Poseidon. He is not a god to challenge. He may come across as endearing, but he is more ruthless than either of his brothers," Phantasos answered.

"I guess a thank you *is* in order then. So, thanks. Now I'm going back to bed," She turned to walk away, flushed from the memory of Phantasos' hand splayed across her stomach and how he tightened his hold when Poseidon said she belonged to him.

"Not so fast, ἄγγελος," Phantasos grabbed her arm and spun her back to face him. An electric current ran from his hand down her spine. If he was affected, he didn't show it. "What was Mark doing out here?"

"He tried to get me to jump into the water," Amanda answered.

Phantasos' body went ridged, and his fists clenched. "He wanted you to jump into the water?"

Yes, but his eyes were glassed over. He wasn't in control of himself. I'm unsure what controlled him, but I bet he won't remember anything in the morning."

"Sirens can control mortals and many immortals and make them do their bidding, but humans must be amenable to such intrusions. Something is off about that man. You need to stay clear of him," Phantasos' words were stern, but his hold on her was gentle and warm.

"Might I remind you, I do whatever the hell I want," Amanda jerked her arm from Phantasos' hold and glared up at him. *Damn, he smelled good.*

He stepped toward her—his chest pressed to her robe. "You continue to think that, ἄγγελος, but we both know that is not completely true," Phantasos snarled. He looked feral as his nose flared, making the hair on the back of her neck stand on end. Could he smell her arousal? *Shit, I hope not.*

Amanda refused to let him intimidate her, even though the memories of his battle persona pushed their way to the surface of her mind. "I don't care what Kallisto or Morpheus asked you to do. You don't have any control over me. Thank you for stepping in, but if I want to see Mark or anyone else, I will."

Amanda stepped around him and walked toward the barracks. Thoughts of the last few minutes ran through her head, and the one that stuck was rather minor in the large picture. She stopped and turned back to face the Oneiroi, who had not moved from where she left him. "By the way—what does ἄγγελος mean?"

Phantasos cocked one brow, smirked, then vanished.

Amanda looked to the sky and yelled, "Prick!" She thought she heard laughter.

Chapter VI

Sharks

Amanda was exhausted. After returning from her brush with one of the most powerful Greek deities and the newfound knowledge that there were such creatures as sirens and mermaids, it took another hour to fall asleep. Her mind bounced from one crazy occurrence to another. Oddly enough, the one that made the biggest impression was the lingering weight and warmth around her waist and arm. That warmth stayed with her until she finally drifted to sleep. Two and half hours later, she was awake and on deck for breakfast and lots of coffee.

"Hey, Dad," Amanda raised her coffee cup to her dad in greeting. "I found some ambrosia and bagels. Unfortunately, they only had cups for it and no IVs."

"I asked for caffeinated IV lines to be packed for the trip. I was told they weren't in the budget," Alaric winked. He took her cup from her hands and sipped her *ambrosia*. "Damn, that's good."

"Hey, get your own." Amanda playfully swatted at her father and took her cup back.

"You ready to see some great whites? Alaric grinned down at her. "I hope this equipment works and you get to experience some cool events."

"Just being out here is cool, Dad." Amanda kissed her father on his cheek. "Thank you for bringing me."

"Alaric," Amanda tensed at Mark's voice. She and her father turned to see him coming toward them. "The team has everything ready. If you're ready, I'll have them chum the water."

Amanda noticed Mark didn't even acknowledge her. *Odd.* The memory of Phantasos' warning popped into her mind.

"Go ahead. I'll be there in a minute," Alaric said.

"Gross! Can I come?" Amanda scrunched her nose and then grinned. "I want to see them when they hit. Even if you're luring them with stinky dead fish parts and blood."

Alaric laughed. "Sure. But if you throw up, do it overboard."

Thirty minutes later, Amanda was in awe. There were sharks everywhere. Unfortunately, none were the infamous great whites, but the ones swarming mesmerized her. She had never seen anything like it—a shark-feeding frenzy.

"Let's head around the bend and chum there," Alaric turned to Mark, who recorded the coordinates and what types of sharks were enjoying a free morning meal.

Alaric looked to Amanda, "Where we're going is about four miles that way," he pointed to the boat's starboard side. "We tagged one over there last time."

"Can they not smell the blood from that far away?" Amanda asked.

"Three miles, maybe a little more, yes—however, four is a little far. Plus, they know better than to swim that far to fight for scraps."

"Hey, boss?" One of Alaric's crew members yelled from across the boat.

"Excuse me, honey. I'm needed." Alaric kissed Amanda on the top of the head and headed toward the sailor, who needed guidance.

Amanda couldn't help but watch the joy on her dad's face as he all but skipped across the ship. He was truly in his element.

Even though the sharks they just left behind vying for blood and bone hadn't been the kings of the sea, she could tell he was excited to see them. Smiling at her father's retreating back was when she first heard it. Someone called to her from . . . *No! Surely not.* She looked around and made sure no one on the boat was calling her. Then she closed her eyes in resignation. The voice, which called again, came from the water.

Leaning over the side watching the ship cut through the ocean, she saw it . . . a half-man, half—*fish* was keeping pace with the boat just below the water's surface. *Damn, it's fast.* Again, she looked around, hoping no one else had seen the disturbing sight before her. Amanda had hoped last night had been a dream, but of course, it wasn't. Not only had Poseidon, sirens, and merpeople spoken with her when she should have been asleep, but it seemed the King of the ocean wanted her to know he watched during the day as well. *Why?* She had no clue.

It also meant that Phantasos had been on that deck with his arm around her waist. It didn't seem like avoiding her best friend of a decade was a deterrent from the gods. Apparently, they were everywhere. The merman sped away, leaving Amanda staring into the blue depths, waiting for another mythical being to emerge.

In less than half an hour, the crew chummed the ocean again. This time, it proved successful. The male great white they had tagged sailed through the air, catching a large dead fish before it could hit the water. His jaws extending, reaching for its prey mid-jump, were the most powerful things she had ever witnessed. No wonder her father was in love with the massive creatures. Every inch of the white shark emitted power.

"That was unreal," Amanda shouted as a chaos of cheers went up around her. The size and fluid moments of the giant of the deep were mesmerizing. Several smaller sharks, types Amanda didn't know, slapped at the water's surface, causing a flurry of madness, but the great white swam in giant arcs, picking off the larger fish the crew threw, and again jumped from the water, capturing another in his jaws. As scary as the huge man-eater was, instead of fear, she was captivated.

"Cage is ready, sir," a crew member shouted above the ruckus. Amanda turned to see her father in his diving gear.

"You're not going down there with those things, are you?" Amanda pointed at the frenzy just feet away.

"Of course I am. Who do you think uses that cage?"

"I don't think I can watch this?" Amanda admitted to her father, who was stepping into the shark cage. Tears of fear stung her eyes.

"It's all good. I have to move now, though. They will let me down on the opposite side of the boat.

"Who's going down with you?" Amanda asked her dad.

"Me," Mark announced. He had walked up behind her without her knowledge. It was the first time he had spoken to her all morning.

"Please be safe, Daddy." Her use of Daddy instead of Dad proved how nervous she was. The only time he was *Daddy* was when he was slaying the monsters under her bed when she was little.

Mark entered the cage, and the crew lowered the two men down to the opposite side of the boat, where the frenzy was quickly ending. That many scavengers cleaned up the bloody mess rather quickly. Amanda could see the fin of the Great White further out than before, still circling the craft as it waited for more.

The crew member Amanda knew as Max approached her with a large screen. It looked a lot like an iPad, but it was larger, and on its screen, she could see the feed from her father's ocean camera. He held up a gloved thumb before it, showing he was good. She watched as several fish swam by, and, *shit*, there it was. The giant her dad so loved. Fear caused her hands to sweat as Max explained everything the shark and her dad were doing. She watched as the shark came right up to the bars, seemingly as interested in the men as they were in it. She saw the tag they had managed to attach to the beast on their last voyage.

"That tag," Max pointed at the screen, "will tell us the shark's habits. Where it goes, the depths it travels down to, the temperature of the water, and mating habits. We hope to learn more about them and help maintain their existence," he informed Amanda as she watched her father cage dive with a great white.

"That is scary as shit but so damn cool," Amanda said, her voice was shaky but filled with awe. Her dad just went up in points on the cool scale. "My dad is a badass!"

"What the hell?" Max's eyes went wide. "What is that?" He pointed to a spot on the screen. Amanda froze, but all she saw were shadows.

"I don't see anything," another crew member, whom Amanda couldn't recall her name answered Max's wide eyes.

"I could have sworn I saw a face," Max gaped at the shadows.

"Okay, Max. No more late nights of fun followed by early mornings of work for you," the lady patted him on the back and walked away.

Amanda hoped whatever Max saw was not recorded. She had a feeling the face was that of the unwanted merman she had seen earlier.

Chapter VII

Bunkmates

Waking up well before sunrise had left Amanda exhausted by the end of the day. She couldn't keep from yawning as she and the crew sat around the deck, discussing the day, each recounting stories of their prior adventures at sea. Mark told a remarkable story about a humpback whale he encountered a few years prior while diving. The thought of such a large animal made gooseflesh spring up on Amanda's arms as she imagined one swimming just below the surface of the water she was floating on.

During Max's tale of the shark bite he sustained when he was in his early twenties—why he would ever continue in his career of shark observation was insane to Amanda—she thought she heard a voice. A whisper in the wind as she tried to make sense of Max. There it was again, her name, followed by, *come see me tonight.* Fear and anticipation flowed through her veins, followed by the feeling of being watched. Poseidon or Phantasos was her guess. In truth, the king of the ocean was intimidating, but curiosity had always been her downfall.

What the hell's wrong with me? I don't want anything to do with the gods, and now I'm wondering about the world Poseidon possesses. While Amanda warred with herself, the crew continued with their adventure telling.

"Are you okay, honey?" Alaric asked her.

Amanda blinked rapidly, dispelling the enchantment she was under, thinking about the craziness of her interest. "Sorry, Dad. Just off in my own little world, thinking about the amazing day I've had."

"I'm so happy you were able to see a little into my world today. I hope tomorrow is as amazing. It looks like the new equipment worked, so we'll gather more intel tomorrow for around this area, and then we will head to another location late tomorrow afternoon."

"Your world is amazing. Who knows, I may change my major and follow in your footsteps," Amanda said as she yawned.

"Tired?" Alaric laughed at her gaping mouth.

"You people are killing me with these crazy ass hours. I think I'm going to head on to bed." Amanda kissed her dad's cheek, just as she had every night before she went to bed for as long as she could remember—each of her parents always received a kiss on their cheek before she went to sleep. No matter how old she became, that one act remained the same, and it was her way of showing her parents that she was forever their little girl.

Leaving the crew to their antics, Amanda went below deck. As she set her watch to wake her at 2:00 AM, a shift in the air made her spin on her heels.

"What the hell? For someone who was not going to bother me anymore, I sure am seeing a lot of you," Amanda glared at Phantasos. He was decked in another D.F.O. t-shirt—*is that all he ever wears?* This one boldly exclaimed, *No Need to Argue When I'm Always Right.* Amanda arched a well-manicured eyebrow at the shirt and the god who wore it. "Really?"

Phantasos looked down at his shirt and smirked. "Really."

Taking a pissed-off stance with her arms crossed, Amanda asked, "Why are you here, Phantasos? And was that you watching me on the deck?"

"I am here because 2:00 AM is a little early for shark watching. And yes, it was me watching."

"So? Why do you care what time I set my watch for?"

"Because I assume the early rising, which you hate doing, is because of the whisper you received from Poseidon. You are not going to him," Phantasos' voice was stern. His stance mirrored Amanda's—both unmovable and stern.

"That is none of your business." Amanda lowered her arms and looked away from Phantasos' baby blue eyes. He didn't fight fair with those eyes. Turning from him to her nightshirt on the bed, she continued, "I have no idea why you continue to try and control me."

"I told you before. Kallisto would be very upset if something were to harm you, especially someone from our world. Poseidon is the opposite of safe." She could physically feel him, even with her back to him and at least a meter separating them. His presence consumed the room.

"So, you're protecting me so Kallisto won't get upset? Well, as you can see, I'm okay. I don't plan on going anywhere with any god, much less Poseidon."

"Not intending and it happening are two different things. He cannot be trusted," Phantasos said.

Amanda turned to face the imposing god. He continued to stand, rooted to the same spot where he materialized. She began busying herself around the small space between bunks, gathering everything she needed to prepare for bed. Twice, she accidentally bumped into the wall of muscle, and twice, she tried to conceal her reaction to the electricity that ran from the bottom of her spine to the top of her head. *Is it getting hotter in here?* She picked up a piece of paper from the little table between the bunks and fanned herself.

"Well, I'll be on the deck at two. I suppose if you *need* to keep me safe for *Kallisto's sake,* you had better set an alarm. Now, you should vanish," Amanda waved her hand at him, shooing him away. "My bunkmates will be coming to bed soon, and a man they've never seen popping up on a ship in the middle of the ocean will be a little suspicious."

"Two it is. I will be watching until then."

Before Amanda could object, Phantasos was gone.

"Asshole," she said to the ceiling of her room. "Don't watch me change." She could have sworn she heard a chuckle.

Amanda, frustrated at Phantasos' heavy-handedness, had trouble falling asleep. She heard the other ladies come in, not as intoxicated as before but louder than she thought completely necessary. It took them forever to quieten down. During that time, she wondered what Phantasos thought about the college girls' blatant descriptions of Mark and another crew member named Junior. Since they thought she was asleep and alone, their wonderment was not PG—hell, it wasn't PG-13. It tickled Amanda to think about the torture Phantasos was going through listening to the girls' verbal wishes for Mark and Junior. *I'm sure he will say something to me about it.* She thought.

Finally, after a giggling description of Mark that made Amanda blush, she turned over so they could see that she was, in fact, not asleep.

"So sorry we woke you," Marcy apologized but didn't look the least bit apologetic.

"No worries. I was having trouble falling asleep anyway," Amanda said as she reached for her water bottle. "So, you two like Mark? How well do you know him?"

"We just met him here," Lindsey replied. *I think her name is Lindsey. I need to do better.*

"I did, too. You have one thing right—he is hot!" Amanda admitted. All three girls giggled. "I haven't met Junior yet."

"He's from South Africa but attends school in Hawaii with us. Do you have a boyfriend back home," Marcy asked.

"I wouldn't say a boyfriend. I date a guy. We were exclusive until summer. We decided to reconnect after summer break if we haven't found ourselves otherwise entangled," Amanda laughed and sipped her water. "Sorry, I haven't had a lot of time to hang out. When we get back, we should go to the street market. I have a good friend I met there. We can hang out before you go back out on the boat," Amanda said. Even she was amazed at how much she was talking. This was how she was before the beginning of her senior year of high school—the snarky social butterfly who always had a quip.

"You won't be coming back out with us?" Marcy asked.

"Probably not. I may be going to Greece before I head home. Can't decide."

"What's to decide? Go to Greece, girl!" Lindsey exclaimed.

"I love Greece, but it's with my best friend, and we aren't as close as we once were. Anyway, enough of that. I need to get some sleep. You people with these early ass morning hours are killing me. I love to sleep in late and go to bed even later," Amanda said while she fluffed her pillow the best she could with what they gave them and plopped her head back down, effectively stopping the conversation about boyfriends and best friends. After all, Phantasos was listening.

⁕⸺⸱⸺⁕

Phantasos' eyes almost rolled clear to the back of his head. Why in the hell did he decide to stick around? If he had to hear one more word about Mark's V-line, a term he had never heard but was able to discern its meaning from the women's comments, he would materialize and make the girls sleep—after, he showed them a real V-line and then wiped their memory.

His anger increased at Amanda's comment about her boyfriend. She had been fucking Kai while he was working on a plan and training to meet Ares in the not-so-far future. Images of her under the prick turned into a constant loop in his brain. This prompted a glass of Isabella's Islay. He rarely indulged in the expensive pick-me-up; cheap whiskey would do the trick, but he was Phantasos. He drank from Isabella's Islay when life's best or worst things happened. In the last year, he had drunk more than ever before. It was now down to a quarter full decanter, and he had six months to finish it. So, finding out Amanda was fucking another man after he found out she was a demigod, well—that was a good enough reason for him. The second he discovered Amanda's lineage, he felt like The Fates had kicked him in the nuts. *This calls for two glasses.* It took a god a lot more than a mortal to become intoxicated, but he finally smiled with two three-finger glasses of Isabella. Not drunk, but—okay with interacting with Amanda twice in one night after conversations of men's V-lines and talk of that prick Kai—Phantasos closed his eyes and regrouped.

It was almost two o'clock and time to meet the demigod that was causing him to drink exceptionally expensive whiskey. He had trouble staying levelheaded without the presence of another man, let alone a formidable god, which would test his self-control. He knocked back the rest of his high-priced amber liquid and prepared for what was about to happen.

Phantasos materialized on the deck of the ship, concealing himself just in case someone was still there. With a wave over the vessel, he placed everyone but Amanda into a deep sleep and braced himself for the blonde to join him because the first glimpse of her, every damn time, took his breath.

Chapter VIII

Poseidon

Amanda finished dressing for her second audience with the king of the ocean. Phantasos' warning of how Poseidon wasn't trustworthy ran through her thoughts. *What the hell can Poseidon possibly want with me?* Honestly, were any of the deities of the Greek Pantheon trustworthy? They seemed to all work off their own agendas, and if and when they were finally willing to rectify their indiscretions, it would be hundreds, if not thousands, of years before they acknowledged them. She supposed when you're immortal; time means nothing.

She rubbed at her face and took a deep breath before opening the door to the deck. She was in South Africa to escape the immortals and their incessant drama. The last few weeks had been god free and awesome, but it had not gone unnoticed that Amanda had spoken with two deities in the last several days and came face-to-face with two creatures she thought only lived in fairytales. The realization that her life would *never* be the same as it was before Kallisto's dad went missing hit her in the gut.

"Well, I see you're going to come with me no matter my wishes," Amanda glared at Phantasos, who stood outside the door looking—*amused?* She would never admit it to him, but she was thankful he was with her as she faced Poseidon.

"What are you smiling about," she asked the ancient Greek.

"Just thinking how good annoyance looks on you," Phantasos smirked, falling into step with her as she made her way to the ship's starboard side.

"Well, thank you. I always look good since I'm always annoyed when you're around. Have you been drinking?" Amanda could smell the whisky since the breeze was insistent on bringing not only the smell of alcohol to her but also the god's natural essence. *Damn!* He smelled masculine with the underlying scent of Olympus—*lavender and honeysuckle*—a heady combination.

"Yes, I have. Why?"

"I've just never smelled alcohol on you before," Amanda stopped at the railing and refused to look at her companion. "Plus, you were smiling."

Before the two started their usual banter, Poseidon materialized on the ship beside them.

"Shit!" Amanda jumped and screamed, not expecting the larger-than-life god to be *on* the ship. "Human here. You could've literally scared me to death."

"Almost human," Poseidon's mouth twitched.

Amanda's mouth went dry at the god's proximity. He was muscular and tanned, and the only hair he possessed was the long, wavy hair on his head. She could tell this because he was naked. Every rounded muscle shined from the saltwater clinging to him under the moonlight. The only thoughts she could muster were *what Marcy and Lindsey would say about his V-line,* and *the anatomically correct statues were not generous enough*, as her face heated. He looked no older than thirty—if that. But Amanda knew he was thousands of years old.

Phantasos glared at the god and stepped in front of Amanda, effectively blocking her view. "Put some damn clothes on."

Amanda turned her reddened face away from the giant of man. It wasn't that he presented a bad sight, quite the opposite; it was just that he was *naked*. Not something she was accustomed to seeing in public, and especially not in front of another . . . *man*.

"Oh, yes. I forget how mortals, particularly those from the far West, tend to be narrow-minded when it comes to the human body." With a thought, Poseidon donned a silk chiton. "Better?"

"Much," Amanda said and walked out from around Phantasos. "Why did you want to see me?"

"Why would I not? Look at you. You are absolutely stunning," Poseidon bit the inside of his cheek as he looked at her from top to bottom and back up, caressing her body with his eyes at specific junctures that reddened her face for the second time in minutes.

Amanda felt Phantasos tighten at the god's blatant desire, so she spoke before he could, not wanting him to rub the king of the sea the wrong way to protect *Kallisto's bestie.*

"Well, thank you, but that's no reason to summon me. You're a god and surrounded by beauty all the time. What's the real reason you summoned me?"

"Beauty, yes. But surely you know that you are more beautiful than most, if not all, those goddesses. However, yes, I did want to speak with you. I am rather curious."

"Well, get on with it then," Phantasos interjected with a snarl. "She needs to sleep."

"You're not my keeper," Amanda scowled at Phantasos and nodded at Poseidon. "Please continue."

Poseidon looked from Phantasos to Amanda, "Interesting."

"Is there something I can do for you?" Amanda questioned. Again, Phantasos' posture cued her in that she had spoken the wrong words. "What I meant to say," Amanda took note of the heated gaze Poseidon looked at her with and continued, "is that he is correct. My father wants me up three hours earlier than what's normal for me on a weekday, so yes, I need to wrap up this little impromptu meeting, if you please."

"Are you working for my brother? Not the arrogant ass, but the broody recluse one," Poseidon looked at Phantasos and not at her.

"Working for?" Phantasos' eyebrows shot up. "I do not work for anyone. I am hardly a common god. Why?"

"It is rare for Hades and me to visit one another. When I say rare, we have not seen each other in over three millennia, yet Hades showed up at my home last night after my visit with you?" Poseidon turned his head slightly and looked at her. "He asked me if I would keep an eye on you while you were on the water. When I asked him why he was asking me to protect a demigod with no power, he spewed something about how close he and Hermes were and how your great-grandfather was concerned after your two abductions. When I told him you had a guard dog, Hades asked if I meant you." He then looked at Phantasos. "You see," Poseidon continued even though Amanda opened her mouth to speak, "he was lying. He and Hermes are closer than, say, he and Ares, but for my brother to leave the Underworld to seek out protection for a human girl, well, something is up, and I am—*curious*."

⊰•—••—•⊱

Phantasos did not like where the conversation was going. He especially did not want Amanda to think Hades was at all involved with him. Using Hermes as a reason to watch over her was better than her learning he had asked him to—maybe even better than the reason he kept giving her, *Kallisto's best friend.*

While it was true that they were best friends, and if something happened to Amanda, Kallisto would definitely be devastated, that was not the reason he watched over her. Deep down, he knew the reason, but he refused to bring it to the surface of his thoughts—or, gods forbid—speak it aloud.

"I have no idea why Hades wants to keep her safe. Maybe it is because she keeps getting kidnapped by your other brother's immediate family," Phantasos snarled at the god, who watched Amanda as he spoke. *He is pissing me off.* Phantasos thought.

"Possibly. However, I do not think so. Did you hear the part where Hades left the Underworld? You, my dear, are an anomaly I plan on figuring out." Poseidon spoke directly to Amanda, which made the hair on Phantasos' arms rise and his canines lengthen. *Shit, Amanda's going to see me like this.* Phantasos had never lost control of his battle form. EVER. *What the fuck?*

"An anomaly? Hmm—I've been called worse," Amanda glared at Poseidon.

"You need to leave. I will protect her," Phantasos spoke low, almost a growl, and he could feel his eyes start to shift. *Where the hell is my control?* He felt Amanda stiffen by his side and refused to look at her—of all the things for him to lose control over. The one thing he knew made her fear him.

"There is something strange going on here. Yes, you are stunning, but that is no reason for the entire Pantheon to go mad. Put your fangs away, Oneiroi. If I truly wanted her, you could not stop me."

Phantasos stepped in front of Amanda. "Never underestimate a man with something to lose, old man. Now leave before this gets messy." Phantasos struggled to keep his wings from coming out.

"Very interesting," Poseidon's menacing smile spread across his face as he looked from Phantasos to Amanda. "Amanda, if you need me, all you have to do is say my name. I do believe Greece is in your future plans. I will send a horse if you need."

"How do you know that?" Amanda peeked out from around Phantasos' unyielding body.

Poseidon cocked his head and said, "I am one of the three. I know more than you think. I do not fare well when I am left in the dark. Good to see you, Phantasos. You might want to get ahold of yourself before you meet up with someone not as forgiving as I am," with that, Poseidon vanished.

Phantasos closed his eyes and willed them back to baby blue instead of the red he knew they were. After a moment, he felt his irritation subside, his eyes lightened up, and his fangs retreated. When he turned around, Amanda had started back to her barracks.

"Amanda," Phantasos called to the infuriating woman. She chose to speak with Poseidon, even though he had warned her about him. Why did she have to be so obstinate?

❖▬────▪▪▪────▬❖

At Phantasos' call, Amanda stopped but refused to turn around. She had no desire to see the fanged creature. Red eyes, fangs like the fabled vampire, wings like a giant bird of prey, or worse, like a black-winged angel of death. *Was that what fallen angels looked like?* She couldn't decide if the *alter ego* of the annoying deity behind her scared the shit out of her or poked at her carnal side. She preferred he left her alone, and she got a few hours of sleep, but nope, she had stopped and was waiting. *Why?* She had no idea. Obviously, her brain was not running the show. *Sleep deprivation?*

"We need to talk about this," Phantasos closed in behind her.

"I have nothing to say to you. You heard Poseidon. Unless you know why Hades is acting as possessive as you and apparently Kallisto since she sent you, then I'm going back to—Dad?"

"Hey, honey. I heard voices. Thought I would check things out. Phantasos? What has you out in the middle of the ocean?" Alaric addressed her and the dream god, who was now only a few steps behind her.

"I was watching over your daughter. Kallisto is concerned," Phantasos responded, and Amanda could not help but roll her eyes in irritation at his words.

"I appreciate that, but surely, out here in the middle of nowhere, she's safe," Alaric addressed Phantasos.

"Everything's okay, Dad. Phantasos just wanted to relay some information. I made it clear that I'm not ready to reconnect with their world," Amanda said to her father. Turning, she finally looked at the god, now only an arm's length from her. She was thankful that he was back to normal, for a god, anyway. "Thank you for the concern, Phantasos. Please let Kalli know that when I'm ready, I'll call her. And that I don't need a bodyguard." She turned and walked to her dad, kissed his cheek, and continued below deck.

✦———✦

Phantasos looked pointedly at Alaric. "Your daughter has a way of not listening to reason. Please understand. Just because you are not on land, danger from gods and creatures still exists. There are as many in the water as there are anywhere else."

"I apologize. Your world is not one I'm used to. All I know is my daughter has not been the same in many months. I blame your kind for that. I finally saw a spark of the old Amanda this week. I want to keep adding sparks to her eyes," Alaric said. "That will be hard to do if gods continue to pop up."

"Just try to convince her that she does need watching over. I do not trust Ares to abide by traditions and not come for her as retaliation on me. He knows how I—well, let us say—Ares is incredibly astute and exceptionally conniving. She needs protection."

Alaric rubbed his hands over his face and inhaled deeply. "I understand, and I'll speak with her. It's just that she's in a lot of emotional pain. I've never seen my daughter broken. It's not easy to watch."

"You may call on me or my brothers if you need assistance. Take care, Alaric. I am being called." Phantasos bowed slightly at the waist in respect to Amanda's dad and vanished. It did not go unnoticed that Alaric should still be asleep.

Chapter IX

Guest

Phantasos walked into the sitting room of Phobetor's Grecian home, where he was summoned. "I was just speaking with Amanda's father. He found us on the deck of his ship right after Poseidon disappeared, leaving me with red eyes and fangs."

"What the fuck? I have so many questions." Phobetor responded to the odd visual. "What the hell does Poseidon have to do with anything? And why were your fangs out?"

"Last night, sirens coaxed Amanda and one of her shipmates from their beds. Apparently, the crew member was there to help Amanda overboard if she refused to dive in on her own. The sirens' song lured her, but their control over her was not quite as strong as that of the crewman. Fortunately, Poseidon appeared and vanquished the dangerous femme fatales, and I saved Amanda from him. That bastard earth-shaker looked at her with too much interest."

"What did they all want with Amanda?" Phobetor asked.

"Sirens always want to piss off the gods, and I assume they felt the presence of a demi. Poseidon claimed he wanted to meet the demi who was causing a stir on Olympus. You and I both know he would bed her if given half a chance. He is a lot like his brother," Phantasos snarled the last words.

"That would be a political nightmare," Phobetor interjected.

Phantasos ignored the remark since politics had not come close to entering his mind. "Poseidon called for Amanda again tonight. I went with her, to his irritation. He said that Hades came to see him—the first time in thousands of years—concerned about Amanda's welfare."

"Why does the god of the Underworld care what happens to Amanda?" Phobetor furrowed his brow in confusion. "Hades never leaves his post."

"That may have something to do with the outcome of my meeting with him. He offered to help watch over Amanda and keep her safe in exchange for a *favor* at his discretion. No questions asked. I made the deal," Phantasos admitted.

Phobetor paced before Phantasos, clearly considering the news. "I understand why he made that particular deal with you. What I cannot grasp is why he would visit with his brother after so long to discuss a demigod. In addition, he left the Underworld to do it. Something is not adding up." Phobetor stopped pacing, "We should confront Hades. What does he know that we do not?"

"Hades now has the Oneiroi in his pocket. None of this can be good. Maybe a better question is, what does he want with us, and what does Amanda have to do with it?" Phantasos looked at the floor as if it would provide the answers. "Sorry. I came in and laid all that out, forgetting you summoned me."

"Yes. This justifies the reason and need for why I called. We need to convene with Morpheus and the ladies. I do not enjoy Olympus politics and refuse to allow them to harm Nicole. She has been through enough. Morpheus and I intend to help you with Ares—" Phobetor held up a hand to stop the interruption he was about to get. "He and I wanted the six of us to meet and discuss the future. Do you think Amanda would meet with us?"

"I doubt it. She is not the same person I met six months ago. Some of her banter has returned, but her eyes are heavy with pain. She hates all gods to the point she rarely speaks to Kallisto. Maybe we should meet with Kallisto and Nicole and see if they can convince her to speak with us," Phantasos said.

Memories of how she looked pinned to Phobos' chest with his clawed hand around her throat, blood, and tears streaming down her face, assailed him. Since that night, Phantasos has woken up with the scene playing on repeat. The other scene that made him weak was how she looked at him in his battle form. After months of pushing his feelings aside, to find out The Fates Three had fucked him over with their warnings, and now she feared him. He wanted their heads on a spike alongside Ares'.

"I am meeting with the others later, and I will explain what we have learned and have the girls meet with Amanda. If two of the big three are concerned with Amanda's well-being, she needs to be with us," Phobetor said.

"Agreed. Let me know what you find out."

"I am glad you came clean about Hades. I understand you want to keep your distance from Amanda, but she is a large part of this. You need to come to terms with how you feel."

"She is an enigma. The Fates screwed me over, and I have no clue why. Hades is eager to keep Amanda safe—more so than my asking him should prompt—and Poseidon is curious about her. Not to mention, the god of war has been infatuated with her since he first laid eyes on her *before* the removal of the concealment. What will he do now that the concealment has been lifted? There is more to Amanda than we know, and I am afraid to find out what," Phantasos admitted to his brother.

"We all have crosses to bear. Amanda is yours, whether you are ready to admit it or not," Phobetor smirked. "No one ever said love was easy."

Phantasos' eyes shot to look at his brother. "Love is a little overboard, brother. She is more like a pain in my ass who cannot stay out of trouble. A curiosity I have in common with Poseidon," Phantasos scowled and vanished.

Phantasos heard his brother chuckle as he entered the entrance hall of his Olympian mansion. Home was the only place he could truly be himself, whoever that was. He sauntered to his bedchamber, which consisted of three large rooms with six-meter ceilings that were conjured to swirl with the same sky wherever Amanda was. If she was under a stormy sky, thunder and lightning lit his space, night showed all the stars she could see, and day was as beautiful or not as what she witnessed. His chambers were his secret, ones he would never allow his brothers to see. He could not stop thinking about her when he met her at the Gallery of the gods seven months ago, so he summoned his world to imitate hers. The only time his ceiling had not mimicked hers was when she was raptured to another realm. His ceiling was completely black when he was at his home, and she was in another realm. Here in his bedchamber, he could admit, only to himself, that he had it bad.

Stripping, he jumped into an almost unbearable hot shower. He needed the pain of the scalding water to wash away the memories of her face the first time he picked her up from the floor, her eyes swollen shut as blood ran from her nostrils caused by the hands of Ares. Then, the time he witnessed the agony in her eyes as the Phobos had her pinned to his chest, blood running from a cut the beast had marked her face with. The dirt mixed with blood and tears had torn at his heart. He wanted to wash away the look on her face each time she saw his fangs, his eyes swirling red, and the one time she saw his wings. He tilted his face to the searing water, needing it to rid the memory of the mingled look on her battered face of appreciation and horror as he plunged a dagger into the beast's heart and then cleaned the blade on the dying god's clothes.

He wished his brain would allow him to muse over her beauty and sarcastic banter; instead, his mind was always plagued with her pain, tears, and fear. Memories of the blood that marred her beautiful, flawless skin that Ares and Phobos stained with their abuse. Mostly, it was her mental state that tortured his thoughts. Will the Amanda he met in that gallery ever return to him and her friends and family? He stood under the blistering water with both hands pressed to the wall, his head hung. If anyone were to see him, they would see defeat.

Phantasos left his washroom with a towel wrapped low around his hips. Watery footprints marked his way to his bedroom, where he heard a female voice.

"Seems the god of fantasies is in a mood."

"What in Hades' name are you doing in my house—in my bedchamber?" Phantasos growled. "You have some nerve coming here after what you and your sisters did to me. Did you know Amanda and Nicole were demigods?" Phantasos snarled at the auburn-haired Fate, slinging the questions plaguing him. The middle sister sat on his sofa with one leg crossed over the other; a gold stiletto bobbed up and down as if excited to be there. She looked him up and down and smiled.

"I wanted to speak with you about Amanda," Atropos answered only one of his questions. *Typical.*

Chapter X

Realization

"Well? Did you find out anything?" Morpheus asked Phobetor as soon he materialized in Morpheus' Hawaiian home, where Nicole, Kallisto, and the youngest Oneiroi awaited his return. Everyone met in Hawaii since it was easier for Nicole. She had yet to learn to de- and re-materialize.

"Yes. Glad you are sitting down," Phobetor walked to the bar and poured amber liquid into a whiskey glass. Rolling the newfound information around in his head. "When Phantasos answered my summons, he had come from the ship where he just met with Amanda and Poseidon."

"Say that again," Morpheus suggested, blinking rapidly.

"Apparently, that was their second time to be in the presence of the earth-shaker," Phobetor knocked the amber liquid back in one swallow.

"Start at the beginning," Kallisto said as she looked at Nicole's shocked face. Nicole was still coming to terms with the fact that all the Greek legends of old were real.

Phobetor went through the first visit as Phantasos told it. He stopped only twice to confirm to both girls that, yes, mermaids and sirens were as real as Pegasus. The awe on their faces made him grin. It was the reason for Poseidon's second visit that had them all stumped and quiet.

"Hades left the Underworld to ensure Amanda was kept safe, and Poseidon offered his divine horses if she needed them. Assuming she would go to Greece before she returned here," Morpheus summed up everything in one statement.

Everyone sat with their foreheads creased in bewilderment. Morpheus stood and paced, just like Phantasos would have if he had been with them. "Why?" Morpheus asked on his third lap around the room.

"When Phantasos went to see Hades, he made a bargain." All three groaned. "He pledged one favor if Hades would protect Amanda," Phobetor dropped the bomb.

"Let me get this straight. He has me in his back pocket for freeing Kallisto's father, you for letting you out of Tartarus early, and now Phantasos for protecting Amanda," Morpheus said as the blood drained from his face. "Hades has the complete power of the Oneiroi at his beck and call—Fuck!" Morpheus said what they all thought. Hades' possession of his power and the Oneiroi powers made him the most powerful deity in the Greek Pantheon.

"Yes," Phobetor agreed with his brother's assessment.

"What does that mean exactly?" Kallisto asked.

"It means Hades' vendettas are now the Oneiroi's if he so chooses," Phobetor answered. "He has the collective power to cause more harm to the Greek Pantheon than any other god before him."

"We need Phantasos and Amanda here," Morpheus resumed pacing. "Hades is up to something. Ares is after our brother, and Amanda's name continues to be at the center of conversation on Olympus."

"Why does Hades want the Oneiroi? He's been gathering y'all for a long time," Nicole asked in her sweet southern dialect that made Phobetor hold back a smile. She had come a long way since the first time he entered her dream state.

"That is one of the questions we need to answer, but we need Phantasos and Amanda to construct a plan," Phobetor answered.

⁕———⁕

Amanda tossed and turned the remaining two hours of sleep she should be getting. Unfortunately, she would have another day with no sleep and dark circles. Phantasos, mermaids, sirens, and Poseidon were the forethought of her mind. She would be returning to shore before nightfall, and her mind wondered what would happen next. She knew she should call Kallisto. What would she say to her best friend of a decade? That question alone explained Amanda's new outlook on all things. Never had she been nervous about talking to the one person who always understood her. Kallisto had been her person—her sister. They shared their secrets, their struggles, and achievements. But, with Kallisto came a lot of pain. Not only was her best friend surrounded by gods, she was one. Not just any god, either. She was the granddaughter of Zeus, Ares's niece, and Phobos's first cousin.

She wiped her tears with her blankets. Just thinking about Kallisto brought so much emotion to her chest. It felt like her heart was breaking all over again. She knew Kallisto could not help her heritage and understood she wasn't to blame. However, with Kallisto came the gods—all of them. She needed to be free of the deities that wreaked her world. Staying close friends with Kallisto would be the opposite of what she needed. Yet the pain of losing her sister was almost as painful as anything she had endured, possibly more. After all, physical scars heal faster than emotional trauma. Dealing with her emotional trauma had been more difficult without Kallisto to lean on.

⁌——⁍

"Again—you dare to enter my home," Phantasos snarled.

"I knew you would be angry, but really, do you have to bear those ghastly fangs at me? We both know you are no match for me or my sisters. I do not owe you an explanation, but I felt you needed one. So, calm down and have a drink with me." With a twirl of Atropos' index finger, two glasses of ambrosia appeared.

"Fuck you," Phantasos said softly but with threat.

"Now, now, Phantasos. Either hear me out, or I will leave. If I leave, you will never understand."

He closed his eyes and fought back the anger. After several clenches of his fists and deep breaths, Phantasos opened his baby blue eyes, and his teeth returned to normal. He took the offered drink and reluctantly sat across from the middle Moirai after he donned a white linen shirt and jeans.

"Was that so hard?" She taunted.

"Get on with it. I am barely hanging on to my civility," he groused.

"There is something about Amanda that gives us pause. My sisters and I thought it would be best if you stayed away from her. Yes, we knew she and Nicole were demigods, but Amanda is more human than Nicole. We contemplated whether the trace of blood that allowed any godhood was missing."

"You are not making sense," Phantasos swirled the ambrosia around in the flute.

"Exactly. By birth, by blood, Amanda is a demigod. However, she does not feel like one. She does not have a god signature we can detect, and my sisters and I collectively know everything," Atropos answered.

"If that is so, then why does she look exactly like her grandmother? Why did the sirens come for her? How did Poseidon know she was on that boat?" Phantasos stood and walked to the window that overlooked his koi ponds.

"Had you not been with her just days before? Were you not watching over her? It was your signature that led them to her."

Phantasos spun around to see the sadness on Atropos' face. It hit him like a wrecking ball. Amanda was better off without the watchful eyes of the gods, including Kallisto—*including him.*

"Believe what you want about me and my sisters, but we did not want you to fall for her. You did not need another heartache. She is predominantly human, so much so that she does not carry the signature of a god or even a demigod. The best way to keep Amanda safe is to stay away from her. She will never be able to defend herself against our kind. You and her family placed a bounty on her head that she cannot run from."

"What about Ares?" Phantasos asked.

"As long as she stays away from all gods, and they away from her, he should not bother with her. However, should is a big word with little meaning. Should not does not mean he will not," Atropos answered.

"So, we are supposed to sit back and see if he finds her? That is not reasonable," Phantasos said, turning back to the window as he thought about what Atropos had said.

"Remember, Phantasos—my sisters and I see all. She is in danger. Stay away from her. Do not push her to visit Kallisto."

"But—"

"That is all I needed to say. Remember, our warnings have a purpose," Atropos faded from sight and left Phantasos in stunned silence. He needed to look in on her, she was struggling.

◆—◆—◆

"Do you need me to help you sleep?"

Amanda was not surprised by the god's quiet voice. After all, she felt him the second he started watching her and somehow knew when he was physically present before he spoke.

"No. Why are you here, Phantasos?" She refused to allow him any control over her body or mind—no matter if he had saved her life twice. He was an ass and only around because Kallisto asked him to be.

"You are exhausted, and I could feel your struggle to sleep. Seems you need help."

"Shh, you might wake my roomies," Amanda whispered a warning and turned over to see the outline of the Greek deity. She had to admit he was a fine specimen. *Damn it, Amanda, get ahold of yourself.* She mentally reprimanded herself. *Damn, I'm tired.*

"They will not wake. I made sure of that before I materialized. Now, let me help you," the right side of Phantasos' mouth curved into a smirk.

"Why?" Amanda glared at him, knowing he had read her thoughts. She yawned, proving her exhaustion.

He stood there in all his godly glory, ignoring her question. *Ass.* His grin now stretched to both sides of his mouth.

"Your chivalry should only extend to Kallisto asking you to keep me safe. Not helping me sleep."

"Let this be my last act of kindness. I am going away for a long time. Plus, I thought about it. You are right to keep yourself away from all gods, including Kallisto," Phantasos was now close enough that Amanda could touch him without effort and smell him.

"Excuse me? First, you admit I'm right. Did hell freeze over? Second, you believe I should stay away from all gods, including Kalli? What changed your mind?" Amanda pushed her pillows against the iron headboard and raised herself to see the confusing god better. It was Phantasos' wide eyes and clenched fist that reminded her that she was only in a very thin, lacy camisole and matching panties. With a blush and grown, she pulled the sheet to her chest.

"I do not know about the weather in hell or what that has to do with anything, but I think the creatures and Poseidon found you because they could sense that I had been around you recently."

"Okay," Amanda rubbed her eyes. "Why do you think I should stay clear of Kallisto?"

"The Fates believe the more gods are around you, the more others will follow."

Amanda could tell Phantasos was choosing his words carefully, making her mind go into overdrive. "Well, I don't know if that is true or not, but whether I go around Kallisto or any of the gods is my decision and not that of the women who speak in riddles and enjoy messing with the lives of everyone," Amanda knew The Fates had warned Phantasos away from her. She blamed them for the cruel way he often acted in her presence.

"I have no doubt you will do as you wish. Since I said you are right, that means you staying away from the gods is something you and the Moirai agree on."

Amanda thought for a moment and decided to table the argument about her seeing the gods since she agreed. Now, she wanted to know where he had been going for so long.

"Where are you going for a long time?"

"To prepare for the future," Phantasos looked defeated, and if she didn't know better, he looked sad.

"Will I ever see you again?" Amanda choked out the question she needed to ask but didn't want him to overthink it.

"Unfortunately, unlike The Fates Three, I cannot predict the future. However, I do not intend on bothering you again."

Those words made her feel like a hot knife slammed into her heart. The feeling was so powerful that she looked down and grabbed her chest. "So that's a no. I won't see you again."

"Most likely not," Phantasos said so low she could barely hear him.

Amanda threw back her sheet and jumped from the bed. All rational thought left her head, and the pain in her chest controlled the anger that poured from her.

"Fine. I knew the only reason you came around was because Kallisto asked you to," Amanda stepped around the god and grabbed her robe. "I guess since the weird sisters made yet another *warning,* you finally have a reason to leave forever." *Those damn wenches were the cause of every—*

Before Amanda's thought was complete, Phantasos had jerked the robe from her hands and had her pressed against the wall beside her bed, the same way he had pinned her at the gala over six months ago.

"I need to get something straight with you. Never have I watched over you because I was asked to. I did it because I wanted to. The fucking Fates know the future, and I refuse to be the reason you are tortured ever again. Do you understand me?" Phantasos' voice came out so low and deep that Amanda could feel the vibration from his chest down the length of her body.

She slowly nodded in answer, stunned at his admission.

"I have kept myself from you to protect you. When you see me, it is from weakness. When I cannot stand it any longer, I materialize. You, Amanda, are my weakness, and I refuse to be your downfall."

Phantasos pressed his lips to hers. *Warmth, so warm, so soft...*she opened to him. They became a frenzy of lips, tongues, and hands. He pulled away from her mouth and began to devour her neck. Chills ran down her spine and took over, burning between her thighs. She was so consumed with it that she wrapped a leg around his hip, bringing him closer. Phantasos groaned in her ear and pressed harder. He stroked her through the thin layer of fabric, and they both moaned. Seconds later, Phantasos lowered her back to the floor and backed away.

❖——••——❖

"Why did you stop?" Amanda asked, breaths heavy with need.

She was so beautiful. Not because she was Aphrodite's great-granddaughter but because she was Amanda. Her lips were swollen and red. He could see that her legs were shaking, much like his own. Pulling away from her was the hardest thing he had ever done. Leaving her would be even harder. It might kill him.

"I refuse to fuck you against a wall in a small room with two others sleeping a meter away. Even if they are in a deep Oneiroi sleep."

He watched, still breathing heavily, as she donned the robe he had dropped at her feet. *Life is so unfair,* Phantasos thought.

"I suppose you're right. I hope you figure your future out. When you decide to stop listening to those three bitches and realize you can't change destiny, come back." Amanda brushed his arm as she passed to climb back into bed. "Be careful,

Phantasos. Ares is a bastard, and he will kill you if you are not prepared."

Phantasos reached for her and wiped the traitorous tear slowly rolling down her face. He looked at his finger where her tear sat. Then, he rubbed it between his index finger and thumb and closed his eyes. "Goodbye, Amanda."

The air shifted, and Amanda knew Phantasos had vanished. The middle of her chest felt like it had been eviscerated, a raw throbbing pain that nothing could heal. Honestly, what the hell was she thinking? Didn't she hate the gods, especially that grumpy, cynical one? According to her body's reaction, hate was not in the equation, *but wasn't there a fine line between—nope, not finishing that thought.*

Chapter XI

Friendship

Amanda woke late with puffy, raw eyes and dried tear streaks lining her face. Phantasos had put her to sleep after all. So that meant she cried during her sleep. She closed her eyes, touched her lips, and remembered the feel of his warm, soft lips and the strength of his tongue tangled with hers. She made it to the shower, where she allowed more tears to fall. It wasn't just Phantasos, even though he was the catalyst that started the torrent of sobs. The limbo her life was in, the emotional distance between her and Kallisto, and the pain of feeling like the family outcast—all of it—came crashing down on her as she stood under the spray of hot water.

Once she got on deck, Amanda aimed to hunt down some coffee and find her father to apologize for last night. She saw him talking with Mark and Junior. *The girls must be drooling, having both v-lines huddled in one spot.*

"Morning, Dad."

"Amanda, glad you could join us," Alaric smirked and looked at his wrist. "You mean afternoon? Gentlemen, if you would excuse me. I would like to talk with my daughter."

That doesn't sound pleasant, Amanda thought.

"Look, Dad, I'm sorry about last night. I know—"

"What exactly do you know, Amanda?" Alaric cut her apology off mid-explanation. He looked at her with the stern eyes of the father she saw only when he was dismayed with her choices. Those eyes made her want to crawl back into bed and cover her head. She and her mom often got into heated debates about—well, everything—but she and her dad were tight. Rarely did he get upset with her, and she found that she didn't like it. She felt like a disobedient child. *I suppose I am.*

"That you don't want me around the gods."

"Then why did I see you with that overly possessive dream god and some half-dressed one on the deck of my ship?" Alaric looked sick. "When I walked out on that deck and saw those two, I thought, for a second, that my heart stopped. From my viewpoint, Phantasos had taken a stance against that giant of a man, and I had no idea if either of them would take you away—again."

"I'm so, so sorry, Daddy. That giant of a man was Poseidon, and he saved me the night before last."

Alaric stopped her before she could continue. "Saved you from what?" She could've sworn her father's voice dropped two octaves.

"Sirens. They called for me, and I unwillingly went. He stopped them," Amanda whispered, just in case she was overheard. "Anyway, I know all this is a shock. It is to me, too. But Poseidon wanted to see me again. He's one of the big three, and I felt like I had to go. Phantasos found out and wouldn't let me go alone. That's it. I promise. You can trust Phantasos."

Amanda watched her father take deep breaths, clearly trying to calm his anger and panic. She knew he was counting. It was what he taught her to do—count backward from ten before reacting. That was one of the few times he had given her his stern eyes. She was twelve, and Cindy Snow made fun of Kallisto's *strange* eyes. She hit Cindy square in the nose, causing a scene in the gym and her three days in detention. Alaric gave her instructions on holding back her temper. The memory flitted through her head, causing pain in the pit of her stomach. She missed her best friend.

"Did you ask the gods to come out here?" Alaric finally spoke with controlled anger. His voice was still deep and menacing. He was definitely in protection mode.

"No. I promise. Apparently, Kallisto and the Oneiroi watch over me. I feel them sometimes, but I don't interact."

"I suppose extra bodyguards won't hurt," Alaric reached for her and wrapped her in his arms. He smelled like home and safety. "I just don't know who to trust with my baby girl."

✦———••———✦

Kallisto stood in her grandmother's kitchen doorway, filled with sunlight and memories, and watched her YiaYia roll phyllo dough. After their meeting, she and Morpheus returned, and she asked him to go and keep Phobetor company while she hung out with the most amazing woman she knew.

"You could help," Zenovia glanced at her through her absurdly long lashes. Kallisto still had a hard time imagining her YiaYia in love with the king of the Greek Patheon, but it was their love story that she valued most—a forbidden love like her own.

"Okay. Where do you want me?" Kallisto smiled at her grandmother, washed her hands, and began rolling dough alongside her. "How many pans of Baklava are you making for the party?

"I thought I should make four pans. If your mother gets her way, there will be many people in attendance. Enough small talk. I have a feeling you need an ear." Zenovia said, not taking her eyes off her work, knowing without having to look.

"I need advice," Kallisto continued rolling phyllo. She had made the tasty pastries with her grandmother since she was a little girl. The familiarity of the ritual soothed Kallisto's anxiety. For over two months, she had felt out of sorts. The truth was, she was on the borderline of depression. Ever since Amanda's last abduction and her best friend's spiral into someone she didn't know.

"It must be important if it's taken you over four weeks to finally get up the nerve to talk to me about it."

"You sound as if you know what I want to say," Kallisto glanced at her grandmother.

"You have been brooding ever since you landed. I assume it has nothing to do with you landing in your favorite place. After the ordeal two months ago, I suppose you have a lot going on in that head of yours. Plus, your mom told me you've been moping around. Something about Amanda not wanting you around?"

"I understand why; it just hurts so bad," Kallisto said, dropping the dough she was rolling and began to cry. With flour-covered hands, Zenovia wrapped herself around her and allowed her to cry until she couldn't anymore. By the time the torrential downpour was over, and she was spent, they huddled on the floor against the island in the middle of the kitchen.

"Oh, YiaYia, your dough is too tough now. I'm so sorry." Kallisto rose from the floor and held out a hand to her grandmother.

"Don't you worry about that. I'll make more," her grandmother said, walking to the sink where they washed up. Zenovia took two mugs from the cupboard and made each one a hot cup of tea, Kallisto's favorite. Sitting around the small kitchenette, Kallisto wrangled the nerve to finally discuss all the pain she was in—something she had not done, not even with her mother or Morpheus.

"Amanda has always been the strong, sarcastic, witty one—a force to be reckoned with. When we were in junior high, she stood up to this creep of a boy who decided he didn't like me being taller than he was, so, he tripped me in the hall. Amanda declared that she was about to kick his ass right before she threw her books to the ground and proceeded to . . . kick his ass," both women laughed. "Now she is a shell of that person. She's definitely sad and depressed, but it's more than that. She's . . . lost. And because I am not just any god but the granddaughter of Zeus and niece of her tormentor, she doesn't want my help or my shoulder. We've been connected at the hip since elementary school," Kallisto sipped her tea as two tears slipped down her face. "Other than you, Mom and Dad, she has been my constant through everything. It's like I've lost a limb or a couple of limbs."

"She *will* come around. In the meantime, you need to show her you're not giving up. You haven't seen her in a month. It's time you fight for your best friend. I believe you are probably the only person who can get through to her." Zenovia spoke over the rim of her herbal goodness.

"I remind her of the gods. Hell, I *am* one—a powerful one of the Pantheon she fears," Kallisto's voice conveyed trepidation and fear over her best friend's mental state.

"Yes, you arc. But that's not all you are. You're still the friend she spent at least one night every weekend with. You are the one she protected when you could not protect yourself. Look, honey, Amanda loves you deeper than any sister and truer than any friend I have ever seen. She's in pain, but she's had a month. It's time *you* fought her battles and protect her from whoever wants to harm her. Between you and the Oneiroi, she will be fine."

"You're right, YiaYia. Will you give me a few hours before you start your dough? I know we'll be pushing it, but if I try really hard, hopefully, you will have six hands instead of two. I'm going to South Africa, and I'm begging her to hear me out."

Chapter XII

Reunion

It wasn't hard for Kallisto to find Amanda. It had nothing to do with god signatures; the connection of nail polish, movie nights, and vaulted secrets guided her to the docked ship, where she saw Amanda walk down the ramp to the wooden pier with a girl on either side. She looked happy, sending a twinge of pain and jealousy through Kallisto. She knew her emotions were silly, well, the jealousy anyway. The pain, however, was certainly warranted. With a quick prayer to God and for the first time ever, Kallisto walked toward her best friend with dread.

Stopping about twenty meters from Amanda, Kallisto framed her mouth with her hands and called to her best friend, "Amanda!"

⊹⊱────⊰⊹

Amanda stopped dead in her tracks. Her bunkmates slowed and asked if she was okay or that's what she thought they were saying. She knew that voice like it were her own. With her eyes downcast to the old wood decking of the ramp, she shook her head for her new friends to go on without her. She then said a silent prayer that the voice she heard was not the best friend she found herself estranged from. *It can't be. I'm not ready.* Even though it was only her name, she knew that faintly accented petition. Amanda closed her eyes and readied herself. Lifting her head toward the call, she saw her. Raven hair, full lips, and the aqua eyes that marked her as the goddess she was. *Kalli.*

Emotions of all calibers slid over her body like a punch to her gut. Amanda's first instinct was to run to her chosen sister, but the fear of the woman before her won out. The fear of what came with being her friend. Slowly, she made her way to Kallisto, and the trek was harder than she had ever imagined. Each step toward the girl she'd spent over a decade confiding in and protecting made the anxiety she'd managed to relax a little clamp back down on her like a vise. Deep breaths through her nose only managed to make her chest feel heavier. When she was a meter from the aqua-eyed goddess, she realized tears were streaming down her face and Kallisto's.

Kallisto reached for her, and she felt herself flinch. The movement did not go unnoticed, for they stared at each other for what felt like minutes.

"Please, Amanda. Please." Kallisto begged.

Hearing her best friend's plea, Amanda embraced her friend tightly. They both fell to the ground, wrapped in each other's arms, and cried ugly tears.

◆━━━◆

"So, it seems we cannot get enough of each other," Phantasos said as he knocked back another drink.

"We thought while Kallisto went to see Amanda, we would have a talk with you," Morpheus looked unpleased with his arms crossed in Phantasos' doorway to his veranda. "Should you not be working out or something instead of drinking your sorrows away?"

"Did you say Kallisto went to see Amanda?" Phantasos asked with a look of nervousness, ignoring his brother's question.

"Yes. Is that a problem?" Phobetor interjected.

Phantasos closed his eyes, desperately trying to calm his emotions to all things Amanda. "The Fates say the gods and creatures are popping up around Amanda because of *our* signatures, not any of her own. Not even they can feel her godhood. *We* are the ones that caused her attacks. Me, you—fucking all of us," Phantasos' voice rose with each sentence and ended with him throwing his glass against his marble home.

"When did you speak with The Fates?" Morpheus asked.

"Atropos decided to invade my privacy and told me they knew she was a demi the entire time, but because she was mostly mortal with no signature, I needed to stay clear of her."

"Damn." Phobetor said.

"My sentiments exactly," Phantasos went back into his mansion, knowing the other Oneiroi would follow. "Morpheus, you need to go get your goddess. Staying away from Amanda will crush Kallisto, but we all must stay away from her."

"Are you listening to yourself?" Morpheus gestured up and down at his eldest brother. "You have had enough Ambrosia. For all gods and creatures to stay away from Amanda, her own family would have to leave her. That is not going to happen."

"*I* refuse to be the reason she is harmed again! I cannot be the reason her blood flows down her cheeks, her wrists are bound, and her ribs are bruised," Phantasos yelled in Morpheus' face since he was now standing toe-to-toe with him, pointing at himself. z

"The closer you are to her, the better you can protect her," Morpheus yelled back.

Phantasos glared at Morpheus, "You saw her both times, brother. How could you ever think I would allow myself to be the cause of her torture?"

"At least you will be there if it happens. How will you deal if you find out she has been taken again and you were not there to prevent it or help her?" Phobetor interjected.

"Her family needs to heed the warning given by The Fates. Protecting Amanda is far more important than visiting with her. Knowing their presence would rain Tartarus down, how could they go near her?" Phantasos' anger poured from the bunching of his muscles and the crimson eyes he sported. With tight lips and fangs, he announced, "I am going away for a while. Stay away from Amanda. That goes for your women, too." Phantasos vanished, leaving his brothers in his home.

⊕━━━━⊕

Sitting on the beach with Kallisto, overlooking the vast ocean, Amanda asked the question that she burned to know. "How's Nicole? Has her powers grown?"

"They have. She can control any dream she's pulled into now. It used to be extreme emotion that allowed that trait. Now, it's natural for her and by command. She can also travel small distances. Nothing like the rest of us, but she's getting there," Kallisto answered Amanda's question, knowing it would not help her hopelessness.

"I'm happy for her," Amanda didn't look at her friend.

"I know this is hard for you. Being around me is different than it was before—but for me, you and I are sisters. Hell, we're stronger than blood. You have been my everything since we were children. I can't let that go. I—no—we need you in our lives. Your mom is going stir-crazy. Nicole has been beating herself up, and Pha—

"Don't you dare finish that sentence. He has nothing to do with this," Amanda gestured between her and Kallisto. "In fact, he has nothing to do with me. So, please, just leave his name out of this." Amanda turned back to the water.

"Fine, but the rest of us need you, Amanda. Not because of what we are but because of who you are to each of us. We love you."

"I love all of you guys, too, but being around you brings a lot of pain, Kalli. Pain I'm not sure I can live with."

"Just come back to Greece with me. We will enjoy YiaYia and the sea. Eat amazing food and laugh—just us."

"That's just it, Kalli. It's never just us anymore. You come with a family I can't bear to be around."

"What if I promise it will be just the two of us for a couple of weeks? Let's find us again. If, after that, you find you can be around Morpheus, Phobetor, and Nicole, we'll have them join us."

Amanda knew Kallisto didn't use *his* name, but when any of the Oneiroi were mentioned, they all were included, whether aloud or not. "Let me speak with my dad. I also want to introduce you to a friend. Can you stay for a night?"

A grin lit up Kallisto's eyes. "Yes. Let me tell my grandmother and Morpheus. I'll be back in just a little bit."

Amanda hopped to her feet and reached out to Kallisto. The gesture was more than just a hand-up—it was an olive branch, showing she was going to at least try.

Chapter XIII

Advice

Phantasos found himself at the mouth of the cave where he and his brothers were created and born, in the Land of Dreams, near the Asphodel Fields. He knew his brothers would not expect him to return to the cave, much less stay there. The cave held memories of their childhood and wars he wished to forget, but it was home.

"Here I will find myself and forget—*her*" Phantasos said aloud to no one.

The mouth was what anyone would imagine a cave to be—dark, wet rocks and cobwebs. The further he trekked, the more unlike a cave it became. Less than a kilometer into the cave, the luminosities of dreamers filled the vast cavern. Dreams lit the forever torches that hung on the walls and from the ceiling. The more intense the dream, the brighter the glow. Nightmares ignited the main hall, making it the brightest cavern in the cave system. Crystal stalactites and stalagmites made the immense rooms scintillate and more brilliant than he remembered, and to his surprise, his father had left several nymphs and daemons to serve—*who? Could Hypnos still come here?* His eyes darted from side to side. He hoped not.

With a thought, Phantasos revamped a few rooms into a place better suited to his liking. In one room, he placed a training facility matching the one at his mansion. Another, he transfigured the ceiling to match his bedchamber on Olympus and conjured an enormous four-poster bed. He knew spelling the space was counterproductive to his goal, but he was only a god. None of the deities were practical when it came to their deepest desires.

"Can we get you anything, master?" A tiny nymph stood in the training room entrance, looking wide-eyed at him. She must be curious why, after thousands of years, he would return to the place he pledged to forget existed.

"No, Thetis. I am good for now. I will call if I need assistance." He did not want witnesses to the destruction he would unleash on the training dummies, sure he would look unhinged.

Once the nymph was out of sight, Phantasos wrapped his hands with tape and unleashed his rage on the room. For the first time, he allowed memories up to thousands of years old to surface. Recollections of war, his mother, Marissa's suicide, and his estranged father started the onslaught. Next came the most painful memories. Amanda—lying on a cold floor after Ares struck her unconscious. Blood and tears flowed like rivers down her face as Phobos held her to his chest with his lion paw wrapped around her neck. The look on her face when she first saw him in his battle form and then witnessed him kill another god. as

With his heart pounding against his ribcage, the abuse of the training room, and his body subsided, he realized his sight was blurry—*tears?* He was shedding tears. That was something the god of fantasy had never done before, not even when he witnessed Marissa's death and the wails of her parents when they found her body.

He wiped his face with a towel and glared at the destruction before him. With a mere thought, he had conjured the room and its structures, and it had not taken much longer than that to destroy it with his bare hands. Falling to his knees, Phantasos allowed himself another thing he had never allowed before—the anguish to consume him. Head bowed and sweat dripping from the tip of his nose, he screamed the name he vowed to one day forget–AMANDA! When had she burrowed under his skin so deep? When had he fallen?

❖————•···•————❖

Amanda returned to camp, where she stretched out on her cot, trying to forget last night, and waited for Kallisto to return. Chaotic thoughts kept her mind so busy that she failed to notice when Mark entered her tent. When she opened her eyes, he was standing over her at the foot of her makeshift bed. "Shit, Mark, you scared me!"

"I'm sorry. I just wanted to talk. You mind if I sit?" he said, pointing to where she lay. Amanda sat up and pointed to a spot beside her.

"What's up?" Amanda noticed his red-rimmed eyes and the look of exhaustion hanging over him. "You look like you've been run over by a semi-truck."

"I've been having strange dreams. Ones that seem more real than any I've ever experienced, and you're in all of them."

"Okay. You thought you needed to talk to me about them?" Amanda could feel the blood rise to her face.

"You know when you have déjá vu, and it's real?"

"I suppose. I don't often have déjá vu." Amanda said.

"Well, I didn't either until the day after the bonfire on the beach. Since that night, it has become all-consuming. I want to ask you a couple of questions, and I need to know the truth. Can you give me the truth?"

"Mark, I think you should see the doctor. I'm sorry, but I need to see my dad before he goes inland. Maybe we can finish this later?" Amanda stood and started to walk past Mark, who continued to sit on her cot.

"Wait." Mark grabbed Amanda's arm.

"Mark, you're hurting me." She looked where his hand wrapped around her bicep. "Please let me go. We'll talk about this later, but it sounds like you are having issues with sleeping, and I'm not a doctor."

"We meant to hook up, and someone knocked me unconscious. I also heard singing and saw—"

"Mark! Let me go." This time, he released her. "You don't look well. Go to the med tent and get something to help you sleep. When you're in a better frame of mind, we'll talk. I need to go," Amanda left her tent and Mark behind and went looking for her dad.

It didn't take long. He was outside his tent, sitting at a table, looking over the footage from their trip. Before she approached him, she stood and watched, thinking about both her parents and how they were taking the news about gods and creatures existing in realms around them so well. Often, she wondered if her dad was putting on a façade. Finding out your wife, daughter, niece, and nephews had the blood of the Greek gods in them must be overwhelming. Just to find out that mystical beings were real was daunting enough, but to be the only true mortal in your house, even if your daughter didn't show abilities, had to be killing him, even if he was good at pretending it didn't. Her heart went out to him. He was so intelligent and kind; through it all, he never treated her differently. *He's my rock.*

"Hey, Dad. Can we talk?"

"Sure. Let me put this away, and we'll take a walk down the beach."

He returned from his tent with two bottles of water. Tossing one to Amanda, he said, "Stay hydrated, kiddo."

Amanda caught the water and immediately drank as they started toward the ocean. Neither spoke until they were away from camp.

"So," Alaric began, "what's going with you? You seem out of sorts."

"Dad, why aren't you freaking out about me and Mom?"

"What do you mean?"

"You just found out not only are gods and creatures real, but you live with two demigods. How are you staying sane?" Amanda picked at the label on her bottle.

"I won't deny the last several months have been difficult, but I'm a scientist. Discovering new and incredible things is what I do. The worst was finding out what you went through. I'm not sure I could have left on this trip without you coming with me. Not that I could do anything if Ares decided to descend upon us. I'll admit, I'm not a fan of the gods hanging about. I don't trust any of them."

"Not even Kallisto?" Amanda asked.

Alaric went quiet for a minute. She assumed he was either trying to figure out how to answer her question or how he actually felt about her best friend since she was Zeus' granddaughter. The only noise was that of waves and seagulls as she patiently waited, continuing to pick at the label of her water bottle.

"Unfortunately, we can't help who we are born to or the blood running through our veins. That being said, I'd be lying if I told you I wasn't concerned. Not about Kallisto, but about the gods she keeps around her."

"The Oneiroi are good, and I'm not around when she visits with her grandfather," Amanda said, defending Kallisto and the gods of dreams. If that was her reaction to her father's comment, she needed to think harder about her own feelings toward the Oneiroi.

"I'm sure the dream gods are as good as they can be. They brought my daughter back to me after all. But, darling, they are still not of this world. Not anymore, anyway."

"I understand what you're saying. I've been running from my friends and family for weeks now. Even Mom. It's hard for me to rectify who they are and who I always thought they were. But there will be a time I have to face the fact that most of my family are of that world."

"And that's why I must allow you to choose your path. Whether I like it or not. Your mother is having a more difficult time with this than I am. You being here with me and rarely speaking with her is destroying her," Alaric had stopped walking and watched the waves as they splashed closer to their feet. "You need to communicate with her. She may have the blood of the gods running through her veins, but she is your mother first and foremost."

"I know, and I'm sorry. I just needed some semblance of normalcy. However, it seems the beasts find me no matter how far away I travel."

"I saw Kallisto at the docks. Did she leave?" Alaric looked from the ocean to Amanda.

"Yes. She's gone back to let everyone know I will be visiting her in Greece and to leave us be. She's letting them know the *only* immortal being I'm ready to spend time with is her. She and I have a lot to discuss," Amanda hung her head in defeat and crossed her arms over her chest.

"Are you sure that's what you want to do?" Her father asked.

"Want? Not so much as I want, but I need to. She's more like a sister than a friend," Amanda admitted. "The irony is that I've always been the one who looked after her. Now, she'll be the one looking after me."

"Amanda, I know your abilities haven't manifested and may never, but know this—there are a lot of reasons to be there for someone. Protection is not always for the strongest to wield. You'll find yourself protecting those you love, regardless of their strength or yours."

"Why am I the black sheep demigod?" She asked as her eyes began to burn.

"You're no black sheep. From what I've learned from your grandmother and great-grandfather, not all demigods are powerful. Some are humans with godly features like yourself. Just learn to be yourself. That clever, witty girl we all know and love. Find her. She's the only one who can help you out of this funk. Come here." Alaric wrapped Amanda in his arms and held her while she cried.

"Thank you, Daddy. I'll either be back here in a few days or see you in Hawaii. Depends on whether I can handle being part of Kalli's new life." They returned to the campsite so Alaric could finish working and Amanda could pack and wait for Kallisto.

Chapter XIV

Satyress

"Let me tell my dad bye," Amanda said to Kallisto. It hadn't taken the goddess long to return to the camp once Amanda finished with her father. Just enough time for her to finish packing and to think and rethink her decision to go to Greece.

"I'll walk with you. I miss Alaric," Kallisto followed behind Amanda.

Outside his tent, Alaric was keeping company with Mark. *Great.* Amanda rolled her eyes. She really hoped to leave without running into her father's righthand man. Unfortunately, the Fates had other plans.

"Hey, Dad. Look who's here," Amanda gestured to Kallisto, who immediately hugged Alaric as if he were her father, too. "Mark, this is my best friend, Kallisto. She's here to escort me back to Greece with her."

"It's good to see you, Kalli," Alaric said, returning the hug. I'm glad you're here to make the trip with Amanda."

"You're leaving?" Mark asked.

"Yes. I'm unsure if I'll return to Hawaii from Greece or come here first."

Mark rubbed his hand through his hair. He seemed out of sorts at the news of her leaving. "I hate that. I was hoping you would be going back out with us?"

"If I have it my way," Kallisto said in mock laughter, "she'll be with me the rest of the summer." Amanda could sense Kallisto wasn't a fan of the young scientist.

"Maybe she'll miss the sharks and decide to return," Mark glared at Kallisto.

"Or she'll love the beaches of Greece even more," Kallisto said with a returned smirk.

"Well, on our way to the...airport," Amanda interrupted whatever the push-and-pull was going on between Kallisto and Mark, "I'll take Kalli to the market to meet Annika." Looking at her watch, she continued. "In fact, we should be meeting her in about twenty minutes, so we need to head out." With a hug to her father and a brief goodbye to the man she almost kissed, Amanda grabbed Kallisto's wrist and tugged her inland.

"What was that all about?" Amanda asked the goddess as they walked up the hill toward the market.

"How well do you know him?" Kallisto asked without replying to Amanda's question.

"Mark?"

"Yes. How well do you know him?" Kallisto asked again.

"He's my dad's righthand guy on this project. I met him a month ago. Why?"

"You said Phantasos met him?" Kallisto asked.

"Well, he knocked him unconscious once and sent him away when the sirens tried to use him to throw me overboard. But that wasn't his fault. Why the strange questions?"

"I'm just surprised Phantasos didn't sense it," Kallisto admitted.

"Sense what?" Amanda stopped walking to look directly at Kallisto.

With a huff, Kallisto looked her straight in the eyes. "He's not completely human, Amanda. I'm unsure what he is, but he's something...other."

"Why would you think that?"

"I can't explain it. I just know," Kallisto looked hesitant.

"Why didn't Phantasos know? Even Poseidon saw him." Amanda's hands began to tremble.

"Those are questions for your grandmother. All I know is that man is *not* mortal."

Amanda's head spun at the strange information her friend was spewing if Kallisto was correct—*Oh shit! I went off with him alone.* "Kalli, what if he wasn't under the siren's trance? What if he *wanted* to throw me overboard to them? What if he had taken me? Or Phantasos hadn't gotten there when he did? I think I'm going to throw up."

"He didn't feel like any being I've ever encountered. Like he's not from any realm I've visited," Kallisto explained.

"Should we go back and demand answers?" Amanda asked, even though her hands shook.

"No. You shouldn't have to deal with this. I'll send Morpheus. Surely he'll know," Kallisto gestured for Amanda to continue walking.

"Okay," Amanda said, taking a deep breath to regain her composure. She then took the lead toward the market until they could see the colorful flags signaling the dazzling marketplace.

"Tell me about Annika. How did you meet her?"

Amanda knew Kallisto was trying to get her mind on other things, so she let her. "We were both shopping for books at the market. We started talking about our favorite book boyfriends and authors. She's wicked smart and tiny—maybe five feet tall—if that. She'll be in the States for the fall semester."

"I'm glad you found someone to hang out with while here—someone without the drama of the Greek Pantheon," Kallisto admitted, but Amanda could see the pain on her face.

"Amanda!" Annika waved.

"There she is," Amanda pointed at the tiny South African beauty at the entrance to the indoor portion of the market, surrounded by every primary color.

"I'm so glad I got to see you before I left. Annika, this is Kallisto, my ride or die. Kalli, meet Annika."

⸎———⸎

When Kallisto's hand touched Annika's to shake, her eyes widened. "You! Amanda, get behind me." Kallisto had only sensed the presence the short, tawny book reader projected once before—on Olympus.

"What the hell are you talking about," Amanda looked confused.

"Maybe we should sit on the benches," Annika pointed to the bench furthest away from the entrance.

Kallisto kept between Amanda and her new friend as her mind reeled at the idea of another immortal in less than half an hour. Apparently, her bestie had not been god and creature-free for almost a month.

"What the fuck is going on," Amanda jerked away from Kallisto. "What's gotten into you?"

"Would you like to tell her, or do you want me to?" Kallisto glared at the young woman before them. Annika looked scared and a little shocked.

"I—I mean her no harm, I swear," Annika begged, stumbling over her words, holding her hands out palms toward Kallisto as if trying to calm a rabid animal.

Kallisto felt her eyes change. She knew they had to be swirling, a new development over the last few months. As her powers matured, she became more godlike. Realm hopping, vanishing and reemerging from thin air, incredible strength, and swirling aqua eyes—to name a few.

"Someone needs to start talking," Amanda said.

Annika hung her head. "I'm a Satyress, sent to watch over you and keep you company while you were here."

"You're a what?" Amanda asked.

"A Satyr. You know—half human, half goat."

"I thought Satyrs were all men," Amanda said as she rubbed hard at her forehead. Kallisto knew Amanda was fighting a headache. How much more could her friend take?

"Don't believe all the human books about mythology. Don't get me wrong, they get a lot right, but they get just as much wrong," Kallisto interjected.

Amanda looked between Kallisto and Annika with tearful eyes. "Why? Why did you lie to me? Why are you here?"

"I never lied. Not once did you ask. Your great-grandfather sent me to watch over you. I'm still me. I'm still your friend," Annika pleaded with Amanda.

"Why did Hermes feel the need to send someone to befriend me, follow me, and betray my trust? I don't need a babysitter. I'm fine."

She's clearly not fine. Kallisto thought.

"This is too much," Amanda said, flailing her arms in disgust. Kallisto wondered again how much more Amanda could take.

"He is concerned for you, especially since an elf is part of your dad's dive party," Annika said under her breath. "Well, damn. Not something I should've said aloud."

"A what?" Kallisto and Amanda said in unison.

"Morpheus," Kallisto said and touched her bracelet. "Now we'll get some answers."

"This can't be," Amanda slowly sat on the bench and shook.

Annika looked at Kallisto and pointed to the bench beside Amanda. "May I?"

Kallisto nodded but kept a close eye on the creature. Beautiful and sweet the Satyr may seem, but she wasn't taking any chances.

"Look, I would have known you were here even if Hermes had not asked me to watch over you. All creatures would have. Our shopping sprees and book talks were all real. I consider you a friend. I hope you will me too."

"Morpheus," Kallisto said in relief.

"Hello, Annika," Morpheus smirked. "I suppose she is the reason for the summons. We should find somewhere less crowded."

⁕▬──▬──▬⁕

Amanda followed along in utter disbelief. Once again, the world spun on its axis, and she felt completely out of control. A female Satyr and an elf—what the hell? *There aren't any elves on Olympus. Are there?*

Finally, the odd group of four found rocks on the beach where they could sit and talk. Amanda thought about the scene they made for the mortals. Four incredibly beautiful people, all walking and talking together. One of the most powerful goddesses ever, a dream god, a half goat half human, and the least rare of them all, a doppelganger. *Sounds a lot like the beginning of a bad joke.* Shaking off her thoughts, she noticed the rocks where they sat. The spot brought back memories of Phantasos, which she definitely didn't need to think about when her mind was already spinning out of control. She immediately shut that thought down by closing her eyes and forcing herself back to the issue at hand. *Satyrs and elves.*

"An elf? There aren't elves on Olympus," Amanda's statement came out more as a repeated monolog to herself. "Are elves really a thing?" Amanda directed this question to Morpheus and Annika.

"Wait. Why are you going on about elves?" Morpheus asked.

"You tell him," Amanda looked sharply at her little friend.

"Hermes asked me to watch over Amanda. He said she didn't want to be around the gods. So, I began by taking strolls down to the beach by the campsite once Amanda arrived. I hadn't noticed the elf until he started radiating that vibrant aura only a Norse creature does. Anyway, I guess he couldn't control it once Amanda was at the camp. But he didn't seem threatening. So, I continued to watch. She wasn't here long before I found the chance to meet her. I figured if we were friends, I could be closer, and she would be safer."

"Do you know the elf's name?" Kallisto asked.

"He goes by Mark. The Norse gods and creatures don't normally come this far south. In fact, the only reason I knew what he was is because I'm rather old, and Hermes has sent me everywhere doing his bidding."

"So, the Norse are here? Why?" Morpheus asked.

Amanda's head was reeling. In less than a year, her world had been turned upside down, and with this conversation, it was being flipped again. *Norse gods? Really? Seriously, what the fuck?*

"Elves live among humans. Always have. Most are scientists or inventors. The Norse gods had their own pantheon; they were allowed more leeway with the mortal world during the Great Casting."

"Great Casting?" Amanda asked.

"When God cast immortals and creatures from the human realm—dividing us," Annika answered her question before continuing with her explanation of elves. "Because of their intellect and the fact they are most similar to humans, God sees elves as helpers to the mortal world—the same reason I have been granted leeway here. I'm really attending university this fall. I never lied. We are still expected to help mortals with our abilities. My ability is my intellect and flying under the radar."

"Why do you speak like a human? Look like a human?" Amanda asked.

"I've been around humans as much, if not more, than the immortals of my Pantheon. I can disguise my looks and I worked hard to learn human dialects and customs. We creatures who are part human work hard to blend with our surroundings, even while on Olympus."

"But," Amanda put her hand on her head and sighed in resignation. "I've been around a creature or two. You are nothing like them."

"Don't put us all into one box, Amanda. We each have our own agenda or that of the god we serve."

"I'm more concerned about the Norse elf," Morpheus interjected.

"Once you hear everything, I believe you will be even more concerned," Kallisto looked at her fiancé. "He's the one who the sirens got to. The one your brother put on his ass."

"Why didn't Phantasos realize he wasn't mortal?" Amanda asked. *Too much.*

"Most gods never meet those from other pantheons. Some of the oldest gods do, but the Oneiroi would have no reason to intermingle with them. In all of history, there has only been one mated couple cross pantheons. They were banished from both," the Satyress explained. "Elves hold great magic. They too can blend with mortals, concealing their signatures much better than even myself."

"Then how did I know there was something different about him? I sensed he was immortal but couldn't put my figure on what he was," Kallisto looked between Morpheus and Annika.

"I don't know. Maybe because you are so powerful; after all, you're the granddaughter of Zeus," Annika answered.

"Well, according to my eldest brother and The Fates Three," Morpheus said, looking at Amanda. She felt herself flinch at the mention of Phantasos and those damn sisters. "You do not possess a god signature. The way immortals have found you up to this point is by the signatures other immortals are leaving behind. But—after hearing all this, I'm not sure that's completely true. What if creatures sense a signature from you? One the gods cannot."

"It's not a signature as what you know. It's different. I can't explain it. Amanda is the only being that's ever felt as she does to me," Annika said.

Great! Amanda thought cynically.

"Maybe we should introduce you to her cousin, Nicole. See if she gives you the same feeling," Kallisto raised a brow at Morpheus to comment on her idea.

"I agree. Would you be interested in meeting Nicole?" Morpheus asked the Satyress.

"I would. I will have to get an audience with Hermes. It may be a week or so before I can leave. Watching Amanda was but one of my duties while here," Annika stood and bowed to Kallisto. If you would excuse me, I will get my business wrapped up and talk with Hermes. Hopefully, I'll see you before long."

Kallisto nodded, with a slight look of shock at the Satyress' reverence, and Annika vanished. "Well, that was weird."

Morpheus wrapped his arms around Kallisto and grinned, "Well, *dea femminile*, you are the granddaughter of the god-king, which makes you a princess."

Chapter XV

Visitor

"You and I are staying in here," Kallisto showed Amanda to the spare room at her grandmother's. "I'll give you a little bit to get settled while I find YiaYia. She's excited to see you."

Finally, given a second alone, Amanda sat on the twin bed that had obviously not been slept in and sighed. *Will my life ever be normal again?*

It seemed that no matter where she went, she would never outrun the immortal world. She pulled her journal from her backpack and began to write. Months of pain poured onto the page. Not as a story, but with bullet points. Words filled with heartache and agony. That was how she thought about her life—in single words and phrases.

- Never alone

- Always watching

- Blood

- Shackles

- Scars

- Abuse

- Tears

- Cold Floor

- Doppelganger

- Hate

- Pain

- Twice – Taken Twice

- Ares

- Phobos

- Carvings

Each word brought back memories, each with agony attached. If she only allowed a word or a phrase, she glossed over the memories, keeping them from eviscerating her.

How could anyone expect her to be a part of this world? All it had brought her was suffering. Just a few months ago, she flew across the U.S. to take her cousin back to Hawaii to help her heal. Now, she was the one who needed treatment and had no way to get it. No matter how hard she worked to escape the world of gods and creatures, they were at every turn. They always followed.

She put her journal away and wrapped her arms around her knees on the bed. Tears had long dried up. She didn't think she would ever be able to cry again. Ironically, Phantasos' leaving broke the final piece that held her together. As much as she hated him, he had buried himself under her skin. *What now?*

University? She smirked. All those words she had just written, and the only thing she could think of doing was college. The next step in a mortal's world after high school, yet she technically was no mortal. Part of what she had been doing in South Africa was mourning the life she thought she would live. Now, pain was the only future she could see. *I'm so fucked.*

"Hey, are you okay?" Kallisto asked.

"I'll be okay. I have no choice," Amanda said, keeping her head atop her knees. She answered without turning to face the goddess. *Goddess. When did I start thinking of her that way?*

Kallisto eased over to the bed across from the one Amanda sat upon. "I know this is hard. But please, I beg you, Amanda, please stop shutting me out."

"That's just it, Kalli. You may empathize with my pain, but you have no idea how I feel. And honestly, I don't want you to."

"Will you tell me?"

"Maybe one day," She never looked at Kallisto, afraid the goddess would see the list of words swirling around in her head.

"YiaYia was supposed to wait on us to make the Baklava. We were gone too long, so she finished it. That leaves us with the rest of the afternoon and evening to fill. Any ideas?"

"A movie or two?" Amanda suggested.

"Sure," Kallisto replied. "How about nail polish and some Grecian decadence in the form of loukoumades and baklava?"

Amanda had always loved Grecian food, especially their desserts. To have homemade loukoumades and baklava by Zenovia's hands—now that sounded wonderful.

"Sounds divine." Amanda licked her lips in exaggeration.

It only took their first movie to start laughing at memories of their times in junior high and high school. All fingers and toes shined with new paint, and Amanda felt whole for the first time in months. It was during the second movie that her best friend burst the happy bubble she had finally found herself.

"I know Phantasos was there when the sirens and Poseidon came. What's going on between you two?"

Amanda's face fell. Kallisto could have asked her about almost anything, but Phantasos and her raptures were off-limits. Instead of answering her well-meaning friend, she stood and gestured toward the stairs.

"It's been a very long day. This morning, I was in South Africa, and my world looked much different. This evening, I'm in Greece with you." Amanda saw regret flash across Kallisto's face. "Look, there are some things I'm not ready to discuss. I'm going to bed. Hopefully, we can wander the city in the morning." Amanda headed for bed and prayed she wouldn't have any nightmares.

✦▬─··─▬✦

Kallisto knew she'd messed up. Pushing Amanda to answer questions so soon was stupid. Leaving her friend to unwind from her day, Kallisto decided to see Morpheus. Within seconds, she was standing in the *Gallery of the gods* where her divine fiancé was taking a payment from some stylish wealthy couple. It felt good to be back in the gallery. Memories of her first time seeing *Ambrose* and the waterfall painting came racing back. So much had taken place since that evening. Wondering between the paintings and sculptures made her miss less harrowing times.

"Thanks again, Ambrose," the well-dressed customer shook Morpheus' hand, and then he and his companion left the two of them alone.

"Good afternoon, Ambrose," Kallisto winked at her dream god. "Or may I call you Morpheus?"

In a flash, the youngest Oneiroi was standing toe to toe with her. Lavender and honeysuckle clung to him like a second skin. He always smelled of Olympus.

"You can call me anything you like. Just kiss me when you do it." Morpheus pulled her against him and begged with his lips and tongue for entrance to hers.

With heavy breaths, Kallisto pulled back just enough to speak. "Now that's a welcome home."

"Not that I'm not happy you are here, but I thought Amanda was with you in Greece?"

"She is. I kinda messed up a little bit. Or at least I hope it was only a little bit."

"Why do you say that?"

"We were laughing and having a great time. Then I asked about your brother. She went to bed after telling me she wasn't ready to discuss him."

"I am sorry. She will come around. Do you know that you taste like baklava?"

Kallisto grinned, and with a wave of her hand, her grandmother's dessert appeared on the desk before them.

"You are getting good at being a god. Did Zenovia make this?"

"She did. Now, since I'm feeding you the best baklava ever, you can do something for me," Kallisto smirked at Morpheus' enthusiasm as he took a bite.

"You want me to talk to my brother about Amanda."

It wasn't a question. He sometimes knew her better than she knew herself.

"I want you to tell him she needs him," Kallisto said.

"Phobetor and I have been looking for him. We want to explain our theory that creatures gravitate toward Amanda, but when Phantasos decides not to be found, he stays hidden."

"We aren't sure about the creatures just yet. Just because Annika was drawn to her does not mean all creatures are."

"I have a hard time believing Mark's presence a coincidence," Morpheus said.

"Let's just see before we tell him all creatures. The fact that she's in love with the ass is enough to warrant finding him."

"Did she tell you that?" Morpheus' eyebrow rose in question.

"She didn't have to. I gotta get back. Let me know when you find Phantasos. I love you," Kallisto laid a chaste kiss on Morpheus' lips and returned to Athens.

❧━━━☙

Sleep was proving impossible. The last few minutes with Phantasos continued to run through her mind, making sleep the last thing her body wanted to do. He finally admitted to feeling something and again allowed those three weird sisters to get in the way.

Tired of tossing and turning, Amanda stood from the bed and made her way around her suitcases to Kallisto's bookshelf. Reading the spines of the paperbacks made her smile. Some things never change. All the books had something to do with mythology. Deciding she had no choice, she picked the only one that could give her answers: *Mythological Creatures and Their Origins.*

Halfway through the chapter on Satyrs, Amanda rubbed her eyes, trying to remove the blurry film that made reading difficult. Fighting, she tried to keep them open since the chapter gave insight into Annika's family. Twice, she shook herself awake to continue reading, but sleep proved too potent.

Fighting once more, she jerked awake. She was standing at the ocean's edge in a long, flowing gown. Periodically, a wave would come up far enough to cover her bare feet with warm seawater. She could smell the salt in the air and hear the waves but nothing else.

"What the hell," Amanda spun around and then pinched herself. She was awake. "How?"

Her legs began to tremble. This wasn't a beach she knew—no birds or laughter from vacationers. Panic set in, and she wrapped her arms around herself. Was she in another realm? Memories of being thrust into captivity assaulted her. Torture, abuse, and fear flashed before her eyes.

"Help! Help me!"

"There is no need to scream. No one can hear you," a deep voice said. Amanda spun toward the sound, still wrapped tight around herself.

"Who's there? Please, just let me go. Don't hurt me," Amanda lowered her quivering form to her knees, ready to beg for her life, and closed her eyes.

"Look at me," a strong male hand tilted her chin.

Gasping hard with sobs wrenching from her chest, Amanda slowly opened her eyes. The being before her was a large, very handsome god with a thin obsidian crown and deep-set green eyes shining in the way only one of the big three could. *Hades?*

"You would be correct," the god's mouth did not move, but she heard him.

I didn't say that out loud. Your mouth didn't move.

"Perceptive child," his lips moved with his words that time.

"It's not polite to read a person's mind," Amanda said strongly, although she felt incredibly weak.

With a slow smirk and a hand to help her to her feet, Hades said, "Maybe so, but sometimes it makes life easier and conversation faster when everyone is on the same page. You now know I can tell when you are lying."

Amanda reluctantly took the god of the dead's hand and rose to her feet. His hand was twice the size of hers and covered in a black leather glove.

"Where are we?" Amanda dared to look around once more as she shook uncontrollably.

"The Elysian Fields. Well, the edge of them. Are they not beautiful?"

"Am I dead?" Amanda's eyes widened, and her heart sped even faster.

"You are not dead, nor do you have anything to fear with me. I did not take you to harm you. I took you to help. Walk with me," Hades said, putting his large, gloved hands behind him. He turned and started walking down the beach, unconcerned that his black leather boots were getting splashed with seawater.

Amanda had seconds to decide—avoid or follow the massive god. She closed her eyes and resigned herself to trail after him.

Chapter XVI

Answers

THE *SKY* DARKENED, BECOMING deep purple and pink, signaling sunset—or at least that would happen if they were in her realm. It was strange to look to the horizon and not see the sun.

How is there a sunset with no sun? She thought.

With a low chuckle, Hades responded, "Do not try to understand the Underworld, child. It is what I make it and no more."

Amanda glared at the god. Again, he'd answered her thoughts. At least he spoke his answer aloud and not in her mind this time.

"You will either learn to deal with it, or you will learn to block us?" Hades outright smiled at her.

"How about you just control yourself on my behalf instead?" Amanda bristled.

"Then stop projecting your thoughts. Not all gods can read your mind as easily. However, many can. You need to learn to block them."

"If you haven't noticed, I don't have a lot of godly abilities. The only *superpower* I was granted was looks. Of which seem to get me in more trouble than help."

"Well, that may be so, or maybe not?"

"Are you always so—"

Hades arched a brow.

"Never mind. Why am I here, Hades?" Amanda was amazed at her ability to stand up to the dark god despite her heart racing.

"I need to give you some information—what I can anyway."

"What do you mean?" Amanda asked.

Hades stopped and turned to her. "There is only so much I am allowed to convey. It will be up to you to heed my warnings."

"Okay," Amanda watched his eyes swirl a mix of black and silver like Phantasos' red when he became agitated.

The dark god began walking again, and she fell in beside him. Hades seemed content not speaking, so Amanda took in the overwhelming, tall, dark, and broody god. He exuded an eerie calm. She couldn't help but wonder how many women threw themselves into the Underworld just to get a chance to be around him. She didn't miss the slight twitch of his mouth once her thought was formed. *Ass.*

The air between them grew thick with unsaid words. He continued looking straight, and she continued to steal glances at his imposing form. *He's more handsome than Poseidon.*

She noticed his mouth turn up in a full grin at that traitorous thought. She rolled her eyes. *Damn it.*

"A thousand years ago, a god did something despicable, and the blame landed upon another. The god who was wronged swore they would never allow another immortal to harm them again, especially the one who harmed them in the first place. Unfortunately, the politics of our world covered up the vile act, and life on Olympus continued without justice. No one ever finding out."

"Who was harmed," Amanda asked.

Hades ignored the question and continued. "Nothing ever stays buried in the realms of the gods. It may take millennia to uncover the truth, but the truth comes out. Often, a war ensues. You see, wars have been started from as small an issue as the beauty of a woman to the overthrowing of a monarch. The one thing they all have in common is the gods' use of mortals. Once the creator of all separated us from the mortal realm, using humans to fight in their squabbles stopped—for the most part. However, some gods can come and go under the guise of helping. Not all of those *helpers* are good or have good intentions."

"As much as this lesson piques my interest, what does it have to do with me?" Amanda asked.

"Whether you accept it or not, you are a part of our world. You may reside in the realm of mortals but never misunderstand that you are not fully mortal. You have grabbed the attention of many gods and creatures with whom you must learn to endure. It is time to accept who you are and embrace the world you belong to. You have more power than you know. Sometimes, the strongest power is the ability to wield others." Hades' eyes glanced from her to the sea, and his head tilted slightly like he was listening to something only he could hear.

"I don't understand," Amanda said as she sat up straight in bed. She was wearing the gown from her *dream*. Her watch glowed red on its stand—2:00 AM.

❖━━━•••━━━❖

It had been a fortnight since Phantasos had last seen anyone other than the keepers of the cavern and Hades. When his ceiling turned black as night, he knew Amanda had been raptured, and an icy dread filled his spine—he immediately called for an audience with Hades. The dark king had promised to protect her.

Residing in the Underworld made his trek to the obsidian castle faster. In no mood to dodge hellhounds, Phantasos spread his wings and flew to the massive doors separating him from Hades. Fortunately, the king decided he would not wait today—unusual since Hades loved for his company to wait with the beasts outside, only opening the doors when completely necessary for his visitors' survival. Either the Underlord enjoyed making his visitors squirm, or it separated the callers whose needs outweighed their whims—separating necessary from unnecessary without any effort. Compulsory needs tended to wait, even when faced with hellhounds. The doors opened as soon as his boots touched the ground before them, and he walked straight in to see the dark god perched on his throne—smiling. Hades' smile was worse than his scowl. If the god was amused, it was always at someone's expense. Since the only beings present were he and the gorgons on either side of the throne, Phantasos was sure this encounter was going to piss him off.

"We had a deal," Phantasos raised his voice as he walked through the doors, tucking his wings behind him instead of vanishing them. He could feel his eyes swirling red and his fangs on display. His battle form rarely made an appearance, and it did not escape him that in the last few months, he wore the look often, and each time, it had something to do with Amanda.

"Yes, we have a deal, so I am a little perplexed as to why you demand an audience and enter my throne room in battle form," Hades' smirk grew, and it pissed Phantasos off more.

"Why is Amanda in another realm? You were supposed to protect her!" Phantasos hissed through his teeth, stopping in front of the dais.

The two gorgons glided forward on the platform, taking a battle stance, daring the Oneiroi to get closer. Even if they did help him rescue Amanda when she was taken by Phobos, they made it clear that any hostility toward their master, no matter the source, would face them and their venom. Low hisses came from them as their scales rippled reading for a fight.

Hades stood and called his vipers back to his side. His smirk grew to a full, teeth-bearing, wicked smile as he walked down the dais to stand before Phantasos. The hissing behind the dark god grew louder; the gorgons did not like their master standing inches before the pissed-off Oneiroi.

With a quiet chuckle, Hades said, "Do not worry, fantasy bringer, your demi was with me."

"That is supposed to make her realm hopping without her friends' knowledge acceptable? What did you want with her?" Women typically fell at Hades' feet. The dark god, alone with Amanda, made his blood boil.

"Not that I need to confess to you, Oneiroi, but I wanted to explain some things to her," Hades' eyes were so black they looked depthless. Phantasos knew he did not like being questioned, but too bad. This was Amanda he raptured, and that *was* his business.

"And you had to take her to another realm to do that?" Phantasos countered.

"As you know, I do not leave the Underworld. So, I brought her here."

"You brought Amanda to the Underworld? Where is she now?" Phantasos felt his nose flare and his eye twitch. He could not believe Amanda was here, in this godforsaken place.

"She is with my grandniece in Greece. What? Did you think I would keep her?" Hades' smirk was back.

"No one ever knows what a god is capable of, especially you," Phantasos relaxed a little, knowing that Amanda was back in her own realm and with the formidable goddess. He had wit nessed Kallisto's transformation into the divinity she was now. Zeus had made her almost as forbidding as himself—almost. He knew she was safe with Kallisto.

"Now, now, Phantasos. Jealousy does not look good on you. She has caught the eye of powerful gods, some of whom have much to lose. Pantheon politics are involved here. She may not understand that, but you should." Hades turned from Phantasos and walked to a cobalt blue orb on the east side of the throne room. He gestured for him to gaze into its depths. "Look, your demi is well and safe."

Phantasos crossed the floor to Hades and the orb. With one look at Amanda laughing as she and Kallisto busied themselves packing for what looked like a day at the beach, his wings vanished, and he could feel his eyes return to normal.

"What did you say to her?" Phantasos asked, not looking up from the orb. Watching her laughing with Kallisto hit him straight in his chest. She was so beautiful.

"You will have to ask her that," Hades smirked.

"Do not test me, old man," Phantasos turned from the orb and glared at the dark god. "Poseidon said you went to see him. It sounds to me like you leave this realm when you wish."

"Only if I must. Now . . . if you want to know what I said to Amanda, you should ask her yourself. My patience is wearing thin, Oneiroi. I will protect her, but so should you. Stop hiding in that cave and do as you should."

"Is this the order I owe you?" Phantasos asked.

Hades bent his head back and laughed. "Oh no, that was just a suggestion. If you do not get your head out of your ass, young god, you will lose what is in your grasp. Once lost, you will never regain."

"You are as bad as The Fates. Stop speaking in fucking riddles and tell me what you said to her," Phantasos could feel his eyes returning to red.

"The Fates are the children of Zeus. Remember that," Hades said right before Phantasos landed on his knees in the cave's bedchamber.

"Ass!" He growled.

As pissed at Hades as he was, he was also thankful the dark god vowed to protect Amanda. Ares would not be a match for the king of the Underworld. Between him and Kallisto being at her side, he was more comfortable than he had been while she was in South Africa.

Masking his signature while in the cave had proved helpful. It permitted him time to gather his thoughts without his brothers bothering him with the constant stream of opinions.

Ares would be coming after him. It had only been three and a half months since Phantasos killed Phobos. If the god of war stuck to tradition, he would mourn for another eight and a half. Phantasos did not believe for one second that he would heed tradition and wait the full year of mourning.

Since the death of Phobos, Phantasos had physically prepared for Ares's return. He was battle-ready. Now, he needed to get into the god's head and figure out his next move. Unfortunately, he would need his brothers' help—if only he could trust them to keep his whereabouts to themselves and not tell their betrothed. He needed time to decide if he would help protect Amanda by other means than staying away from her. Could he watch over her and not be with her? Could he keep himself away from her?

With a flash, he was in Greece, at Phobetor's earthly residence, which was given to him for his days of playing messenger between Zeus and Zenovia. Before lifting his mask, he needed to ensure none of the ladies were there, especially since Amanda was close.

"Hello, brother," Phantasos announced himself to Phobetor.

Chapter XVII

Torture

After two weeks in Greece, Amanda felt a little more like herself. She and Kallisto shopped and sunbathed. They steered clear of *Designed for Olympus* since the proverbial cat was out of the bag. It had come as a shock that the eldest of the Oneiroi owned her favorite Grecian clothing store. No wonder he was always wearing t-shirts with unique sayings and jeans. Shaking her head, she dispelled all thinking of Phantasos. Keeping her thoughts away from that particular god was the only way she could function with some semblance of normalcy.

Kallisto had kept her promise. She hadn't brought any other gods around her except the day they left South Africa, which wasn't her fault. And, of course, the rapturing by Hades, which she had not mentioned to her best friend. Not telling Kallisto was her way of pretending it was all a dream. They discussed her needing the safety of the Oneiroi if nothing else, but Amanda was certain that if anything happened, Kallisto would be goddess enough. Besides, she had thought a lot about what Hades had said. She may not have her own power, but she was more than capable of calling for her friends.

Before Annika came to stay with them, she needed to do the one thing she dreaded the most—have that heart-to-heart with Kallisto. She was afraid opening herself to memories of the worst things that had ever happened to her would take her back to ground zero with her healing. Night terrors, zoning out, spontaneous bouts of vomiting, all she had finally overcome—telling Kallisto would bring up everything she had worked so hard to bury. She heard the shower turn off, so she shook the dread from her mind and plastered a smile across her face.

"What's on the agenda for the day," she asked Kallisto as her friend exited the bathroom.

"Beach fun? Let's go to Kefalonia," Kallisto suggested as she finished dressing for a beach day.

Amanda ran a towel through her wet hair and brushed it out before throwing it in a messy bun. "Ferry or Kalli?"

Kallisto giggled. "Well, it will take over five hours if we go by ferry."

"Kalli transport, it is," Amanda grinned.

※——※——※

Kefalonia was beautiful and quiet—just what Amanda needed to muster the courage to talk with Kallisto. She would have to tell her everything if she wanted her best friend to understand why she needed to stay clear of all immortals. The only problem was that telling her *everything* could cause more damage to her psyche. Those horrific situations had shaped her into the cynical girl she was now, but shaping her and reliving the memories that caused the damage were two different things.

After two hours in the sun, Amanda was finally ready. Or she tried to be. "Okay. I'm going to tell you everything. But I ask that you don't ask any questions during or after I tell you. I ask that you do not look at me with pity or shame; most of all, you NEVER tell anyone. Pinky swear?" She held her pinky out to Kallisto.

Kallisto wrapped her pinky with Amanda's and took a deep breath. "Pinky swear."

"This is the hardest thing I've ever *willingly* done. You have to understand that."

"I understand," Kallisto responded.

⚜⸺⸺⚜

Kallisto readied herself for a horrific tale. She watched as Amanda's hands trembled, and she bit the inside of her cheek. She was about to tell her why she had pulled away from her so drastically—and what those two gods did to her.

"Remember when we were in the coffee shop, and I told you about what I went through with Ares? That's how I remembered it then. It wasn't until my grandmother lifted the cloaking spell that I remembered everything. It hit me like a wave. An all-consuming surge of torture and degradation. He had been tormenting me much longer than I thought. You see, he took me from my bed several times. He played games with my head during each session—a mixture of seduction, pain, and humiliation.

"The first time Ares came to me, I thought he was beautiful. After all, he is a flawless god. His raven black hair and ice-blue eyes on his muscled, tall frame made me squirm. However, that initial thought lasted only seconds. When he noticed my satin camisole and sleep shorts, sparks danced in his eyes, and pure lust transfigured them black. His nostrils flared, and the look he gave scared me. He asked me about you and Morpheus. I remember thinking briefly that maybe I had been wrong about his desire. Then the bastard rounded my bed, leaned in, and sniffed me. When he pulled back, his eyes were filled the black lust I saw earlier and narrowed in anger.

"You know when your brain works faster than the situation playing out before you? When you have mere seconds to run scenarios through your head. Well, I remember wondering what I could have done to piss him off. With one word, I found out why or, rather, who had made him mad. Ares pulled back from smelling me like a dog and uttered the one word that confused me more than his desire did. He spoke Phantasos' name, then vanished in thin air. No explanation given."

"Oh, Amanda," Kallisto began but stopped when she remembered her promise to just listen. She wished she could hold her while she told her story.

◆━━━━◆

Before she began again, she looked away. The rest of her story would take a lot to confess—a lot to permit herself to remember. She swallowed back the bile in her throat, blinked the burn from her eyes, and continued her story.

"The next time he visited, he pulled me from my bed by my hair. One second, I was drifting off to sleep; the next, I was wrenched up in pain. I closed my eyes in agony, and when I opened them, I was no longer in my room. Dark, damp rock walls and the musty smell of mildew surrounded me. By this time, my *fast-processing* brain had stopped managing the situation. It refused to think, and before I realized how much trouble I was in, he had me shackled, spread eagle to the wall, and told me if I didn't cooperate, he would kill my mom—the cold wall bit into my back.

"Dad wasn't home, and I remember thinking, he knows Dad isn't home; that's why he said he'd only kill my mom. Knowing he knew everything about me and my family scared me shitless. He cut my nightshirt open. I refused to look down, but I felt the air on my bare breasts. For weeks after that, I slept in a bra. I thought that if it happened again, I wouldn't be bare-chested. I know, crazy, right?" She wiped a lone tear from her cheek. "Anyway, I cried silently, afraid he would interpret any noise as me not cooperating."

She rubbed her hands down her arms, reminding herself that she was not shackled or freezing. She was warm on a beach in Greece. She leaned her head back, looked to the sky, and tried to gain the strength to carry on. With a deep inhale and exhale, she continued.

"He started at my belly button, and as I shook beneath him, he licked all the way up my body. Going between my breasts as I cried and begged him in whispers to stop. Even though he had threatened my mom, I remember thinking I was a horrible person for *letting* him do that. I know what you're going to say. But self-blame is hard to keep at bay." Several tears were making their way down her face, but she needed to get it out, so she continued her story.

"He persisted up my neck and then licked away my tears. After that, he kissed each eyelid, and the next thing I knew, I was back in my room, on my bed. He had jerked me by the hair of my head, shackled me to a rock wall, and reduced me to a frightened mess—but before he was done, he was gentle." She pressed the heels of her hands into her eyes and took a deep breath.

"It was the third night and the weekend from hell that he took me and chained me to that dungeon wall for hours. The room reeked of death and mildew. He left me alone for the first few hours—it felt like days. My body jolted in fear with every drop of water or scurry of creature. My arms and legs went numb, and I actually began to worry that he wouldn't return. What would happen to me? When he finally came back, he smiled as if he didn't have me shackled in a dungeon against my will. That's when it started. He would release me, give me water, and let me relieve myself in a little room with an open door in front of him every four or five hours. Before binding me back against the wall, he would grab me and ask if I was ready to serve him. I would shake my head, and he would shove me to my knees on the dirt and gravel floor. The last time he unshackled me, he lightly kissed my lips, then each eyelid as he did before. Then I was back in my room. My mind couldn't decide if I was having nightmares or if it was all real. The smells stuck in my nostrils, and the bruising on my knees from repeatedly hitting the dungeon floor made it real. The last time he came to my room was just as I told you before.

"I suppose I felt empowered since I was in my home and not bound against a wall, so I backtalked. That's when he referred to me as a "slutty ass" and threatened you. He then forced his tongue down my throat. Pushing against his chest didn't help—he just growled. I suppose he decided he had taken enough, so he pulled from his onslaught by my hair. The look that crossed his face was terrifying, and before I realized it, he hit me with a closed fist. While I looked up at him from the ground, he told me that I *would* be his and Phantasos was going to die by his hand. I didn't understand his obsession with Phantasos, and while lying on the ground with blood running from my nose, that was the only thing I thought about.

Amanda took a long drink of water, getting up the nerves to continue.

"When he took me from the coffee shop, he asked if I was ready to be his. When I told him to fuck off, he hit me on the jaw. I went down, barely conscious. Then he kicked me a couple of times for good measure. When he pulled me up by my hair, I spat in his face with what little reserved strength I had. That's when he went nuts. He hit me in the face several times. That's all I remember until he returned with you in that house. I heard him speaking to you, but I was in and out of consciousness and didn't know what he said. Everything from then on is a blur, and I only remember bits and pieces, mainly of Hypnos healing me in your living room."

"You don't have to finish this today, Amanda," Kallisto said through the tears that streamed down her face.

She saw Kallisto visibly shaking, and the pain on her friend's face almost made her stop. If she did, she knew she wouldn't ever finish. She needed to hear the worst of it to truly understand.

"If I don't tell you now, I may never. So, if you're up to hearing the rest, I *need* to finish."

Kallisto nodded, and Amanda saw she was white-knuckling the lounger she was sunbathing on.

"When Phobos took me, I fought him—I bit, clawed, spat, and prayed—not again. Once he got me to the basement, he shackled me to a cold metal table. My hands were bound together and fastened above my head to the table. My legs spread apart—each foot chained to a corner. There was no confusion with him. He never had moments of gentleness. Instead, he took physical torture to another level."

Amanda stood from the lounger, walked around for a few minutes, and said, "Give me a minute." She turned from Kallisto, closed her eyes, and let the salt in the breeze clear her mind. *You can get through this.* After a minute, she sat back down and continued her story. She was nauseous, and her insides quivered.

"Once I was completely secure, his smile became more wicked. His lion nose flared, and he, too, said Phantasos' name. Then he asked if I was the Oneiroi's whore. I refused to answer, so he slapped me across the face. Unfortunately, his hand was in the form of a lion's paw, so it hurt like a bitch when my cheek split open. A few seconds later, I smelled copper as the blood ran close to my nose and dripped onto the metal table. Again, part of me wondered what Phantasos had to do with anything. It's crazy to me that I was going through hell and could still contemplate such things.

"The beast tore my clothes partially off and used his sharp claw to scratch marks into my lower abdomen, right above my pubic bone. The stabbing and searing burn had me yelling until my throat was raw. I swear he got off on hearing me scream. His eyes were black with desire, his smile wicked, his tongue rough. When I returned from that hellhole, I discovered the scratches were actually carvings. Letters that formed the words *Phants' whore*.

"The lion not only carved into my flesh—he violated me in that basement. He never raped me exactly, but he used his claw, and if the Oneiroi had not gotten to me in time, I'm sure he would have used more. I bled for over a week. I couldn't leave my bedroom because humiliation, fear, and the need to stay close to the bathroom kept me confined. Hypnos was the only one who knew any of this because he was my healer—now you do.

"I never told my parents. It's not like they could do anything about it anyway. Besides, I know it would rip my dad's heart out. He's human, no match for anyone in this crazy-ass world of gods and creatures. I will never tell him."

Amanda closed her eyes and took a deep breath, then continued. "Phantasos never saw the words carved into me. His gaze was focused on the blood rolling down my face and the half-lion, half-god who held me in his clutches against his chest."

Kallisto shook with anger and could feel lightning as it threatened to spark at her fingertips—a gift from her grandfather. Watching Amanda as she told her story was as severe as hearing it. The far-off look of anguish crushed her heart. She had no idea it was so horrific—none. She mentally told Morpheus to stay away and that she was okay knowing he could feel her distress. *Ares will die.*

"Once Phantasos and Phobetor entered the basement, I could feel their rage. Phantasos' eyes, when he saw the blood leaking down my face, were maddening. He had fangs and fucking wings—I couldn't believe what I was seeing. I know now he thought his battle form was what scared me. It wasn't that. Yes, that was a shock. But, I was scared of what he would do if he knew what all Phobos had done to me. I was relieved when Phantasos killed that bastard, and I breathed a sigh of relief—stupidly thinking it was over. Then Ares showed up and looked at me. I felt him enter my mind. Then I heard him as clearly as if he was standing beside me. According to that prick, I belonged to him, and Phantasos was as good as dead. Again, the only person who knows that is me and now you.

"For the most part, you know everything. To tell you every small detail would take forever, so you got the cliff notes version. I'm not sure if every detail of the basement with Phobos is something I will ever be able to talk about, but you know the worst."

What do you say after a confession of such horror? Kallisto had no idea, but she knew in her soul she needed to confide in someone. The only problem, she promised not to tell.

"Amanda, I had no idea. This rips my heart out. I understand why you don't want to be around immortals. I get it. But this immortal," Kallisto tapped her chest, "loves you and swears on everything holy that she will protect you and your family with all her abilities."

Amanda managed a smile and asked, "Why the hell are you speaking in third person?" They both laughed and hugged for what had to be the better part of ten minutes.

"I promised not to tell anyone, but I think *you* should confide in someone. Your mother, dad, grandmother—someone. Ares needs to die. If you would allow it, I would love to speak with grandfa—"

"No! You promised," Amanda said with wide eyes of panic.

"I know. And I won't say anything if you don't want me to. But—I truly think you need to tell someone. Now, let's get back to YiaYia's. I'm not much of a drinker, but a glass of wine would be nice right now."

Chapter XVIII

Decisions

"Where in Zeus' name have you been?" Phobetor glared at his brother.

"That is of no consequence. I needed my space to think and get my head straight," Phantasos answered his brother's glare with a smirk that he knew would piss him off.

"Well, we had some news, but apparently, you care so little that I will withhold it so you will have no worries," Phobetor countered.

"What news," it was Phantasos' turn to glare with indignation.

"Fine. Amanda may have a signature that only creatures feel and are drawn to."

"What led you to this belief? And, if creatures are lured to her, why did Poseidon seek her out?" Phantasos asked his brother.

"We think he followed the call of the sirens and merpeople. Also, she has a friend who turned out to be a Satyress."

Phantasos arched a brow. "She befriended an immortal creature?"

"Hermes sent her disguised as a human to watch over his great-granddaughter. He has always used Satyrs as spies. Anyway, we can discuss all that later. For now, you need to come back."

Phantasos bit the inside of his cheek as he thought about the theory his brother had presented. "This does not change the fact that I refuse to be the reason, no matter how small, that she is sought or found by a god. Any god."

"If creatures can find Amanda, then gods will follow. She will only be safe if her friends and family watch over her. You know this," Phobetor glared at Phantasos. "I do not understand why you refuse to help."

"I cannot watch her suffer again—ever. The look in her eyes when we found her in that basement. That look torments me day and night—in my dreams. Here I am, a god of dreams who cannot control my own. That has never happened, and I refuse to dive into the reasons," Phantasos made himself at home and poured a lowball two fingers high with amber liquid.

"I learned when I was dealing with Nicole in her dream state that it was not that she was a dream bender that she so easily controlled me—it was because any dreams and nightmares, dealing with her, had me losing control."

"Just spit it out," Phantasos scowled over his tumbler.

"You have a connection to Amanda just as I have to Nicole. Just as Morpheus does to Kallisto."

"You are wrong, brother." Phantasos pointed at Phobetor, knocked back the rest of his whiskey, and poured another two fingers.

"You know. I usually respect the man you are, but this hot and cold act with Amanda needs to end. She is in danger, and you need to figure out whether you will be at her side or floundering in self-pity. If you refuse to be by her side, I recommend you return to your seclusion and forget about her. That means not asking us about her and not discussing her with the god of the Underworld," Phobetor's tone was hard and to the point, making Phantasos' next sardonic comment stop at the tip of his tongue.

Phobetor was right. He needed to decide whether he should physically protect her or work to forget about her. Even if he had placed himself in the servitude of Hades so he would help safeguard the demigod, he needed to decide *his* place.

Phantasos nodded and rubbed his face in defeat. "Give me time to think. I will let you know," he said, leaving without another word from his brother.

Kallisto was sick. Images Amanda's confessions produced sickened her, and revenge was the only thing she could think about. Phobos was dead, so she had to settle by seeking retribution from her uncle, Ares, in the form of his head on a spike. She wondered how she would ever let Amanda out of her sight again. A plan for the immediate future began to form. She knew Amanda was contemplating going to the mainland for college. That had to change. All their family and friends would be close in Hawaii, and whether Amanda wanted to admit it or not, she needed them all—her parents and their small group of gods and demigods.

"I'm going to hop in the shower," Amanda announced, drawing Kallisto out of her planning session.

"Okay. I'll find Yai-Yai."

Leaving her friend to wash up, Kallisto went to find her grandmother and tell her about Annika's upcoming visit. She also needed to discuss leaving sooner than planned. Initially, she would stay in Greece for another three weeks, getting home in time to prepare for school. With Greece a hotspot for all things mythical, she felt Hawaii would be a better choice for Amanda.

During dinner, Amanda could feel the tension radiating off Kallisto. It was even more evident when she barely touched her moussaka, her favorite dish, and refused Zenovia's homemade baklava. Her grandmother cut her eyes to Kalli and asked what was wrong with her appetite.

"I suppose I got overheated today," was her only reply.

"She's upset with what I told her earlier," Amanda stepped in to let Kallisto know they both saw the despair written all over her face and actions.

"I'm just upset. I'll get over it. Since I'm not much company, I'm going upstairs to rest," Kallisto excused herself from the table.

"Well, whatever you said to her, she took it to heart," Zenovia said as she served dessert.

"I told her what happened with Ares and Phobos," Amanda admitted.

Mid-serve, Zenovia stopped and looked at Amanda with sadness. "That couldn't have been easy for either of you."

"No, it wasn't. Fortunately for me, I've had more time to process and realize that if I don't eat, what would be the point of surviving? Kalli hasn't come to that realization yet."

"Just know, Kallisto loves you with all she has. You are closer to her than a sister would be. These last few months have been as bad on her as when her father went missing." Zenovia held up her hand to stop the interruption. "I'm not discounting what you went through. You were tortured, for god's sake. But she is under some crazy notion that she could have stopped your abuse. I know all gods and creatures are far from what you need to be around, but please remember that one goddess loves you more than she loves herself. With her comes a god who would do anything for her, and because Kallisto loves you, he would, in turn, do anything for you. That being said, Thia thinks of you as a daughter, and those brothers of Morpheus care for you, too. Especially Phantasos," Zenovia held her hand up once more to stop interruption. "Not all gods are good. Most are a little good and a lot bad, but those who love you are good to their core and not your enemy. You must remember not all mortals are good, either. They may not be able to vanish to another realm with you, but a human is as capable of evil and torture all the same. Don't block out those who love you, child. Now . . . eat your dessert and think about what I've said." Zenovia placed the remaining baklava in the center of the table and left Amanda to eat in peace.

When Amanda went upstairs, she found a note on her pillow.

I need a little time to process. I'm going to Hawaii to see Morpheus for a couple of hours. Please enjoy some alone time, and I'll be back before you wake up. ~Kalli~

Amanda curled into a chair with a book and thoughts of the last year. It was hard to remember the girl she had been just seven months ago. While contemplating life, she felt someone watching. Moments later, she heard him in her head.

Come meet my horse.

Chapter XIX

Creatures

AMANDA THREW ON A white tank top with blue letters that said, *You Had Me at Ambrosia,* blue jean shorts and sandals. Apparently, the voice had her going to the sea's edge.

It didn't take her long before she was looking around the beach for Poseidon. She knew of his horses from listening to Kallisto's endless knowledge of Greek mythology and couldn't wait to see them. And, if she was being honest, she wanted to speak to the god without Phantasos' interference.

Turn around. The voice in her head commanded.

Amanda's back stiffened at Poseidon's command, but she turned anyway. Atop a most magnificent horse was the stunning god himself sporting a boyish smirk. *Thank the gods he's clothed this time.* The beast he sat astride had to be twice as large as a British Shire with an iridescent coat and a silver mane. *Gorgeous.*

"Wow!" was all Amanda could say. She briefly wondered if he would let her take their picture. This stunning scene would bring a pretty penny to the gallery.

Poseidon's smile revealed how enamored he was with the giant between his thighs. "He is a spectacular creature, is he not?"

"Yes. He is. May I pet him?"

"Of course." Poseidon hopped off the horse's back and beckoned Amanda closer. He lifted her hand and laid it on the stallion's knee since the beast's shoulder was too high for her to touch. The horse lowered his massive nose and sniffed the top of Amanda's head. Tentatively, she raised her hand to pet the beast and was intrigued by its curiosity. The more she petted the horse, the more the horse sniffed her, and when she pulled her hand away, he nudged her to continue.

Poseidon chuckled, "Polemistís likes you."

"I'm sorry, I don't speak Greek."

"His name means warrior. He is over two hundred years old and will live at least another six or seven hundred years."

"He's amazing," Amanda admitted, still stroking the Shire's nose.

"I have many horses, and they are at your disposal," Poseidon said as he moved beside Amanda and petted the stallion.

"Why?" she asked, refusing to look at the mesmerizing giant of a god standing so close to her. He was being nice. Alarmingly so. Not the sarcastic deity he was before. *Is he flirting? Surely not.* Amanda shook the thought from her head.

Poseidon continued to pet the beast. Amanda started to think he wouldn't answer her. After what felt like a couple of long, drawn-out minutes, he finally replied.

"You look like her," Poseidon said, manifesting a brush and starting down the side of his horse. He brushed and spoke to the beast, *"Good boy. How does that feel?"*

She couldn't help but wonder if his double-meaning praises were to see her blush. "Because I look like my grandmother?"

"No. You look like Aphrodite," Poseidon corrected.

Contemplating his words, she vaguely remembered he and Aphrodite had a child together. Yes, the gods got around. Living for thousands of years, they would have to. *Well, isn't this awkward?*

"I suppose you still care for her?" Amanda asked, never looking at the god, just petting the beast's nose.

"Aphrodite is the desire of many men and deities. She is not just beauty—she is the embodiment of love. My time with her was grand, but she is not the one who holds my heart now, even though she once did. When I saw you, memories came flooding back. Any children, grandchildren, or great-grandchildren of Aphrodite should be loved and honored, and it would be an honor to allow you the use of my herd."

Finally, daring to look at the beautiful man beside her, Amanda stood there with her mouth agape and a tear in her eye, not knowing what to think or say. She had come to believe all the Greek gods and goddesses were terrible. After witnessing Kallisto's reaction to the information dump and Zenovia coming down with a reality boost, she felt that maybe, just maybe, her self-exclusion was not such a good idea. If she allowed herself to admit it—she missed Nicole and the rest of her family and friends.

"I'm afraid I'm a little apprehensive about the divine side of my family. After everything—"

"I am aware of what happened with Phobos, and unfortunately, I am also privy to Ares' actions, but you need to understand. Not all gods are bad, and those that are good have bad moments they would rather forget. We live an eternity, and in that time, we make mistakes, some worse than others. Phobos was always unorthodox. He was Ares' favorite and learned from his father's actions. I know he was also the son of Aphrodite, but it was Ares who raised him in his image."

Feeling their conversation was getting too deep, Amanda changed the subject. "So, when should I call on your horses, and what is their range?"

"Range?" Poseidon asked, grinning down at her.

"I won't be in Greece much longer. Can I call for them wherever I am or just on the beaches of Athens?" Amanda shrugged and moved to pet the horse's belly since she could reach it.

Poseidon chuckled, "They are what you would call mythical creatures. If I allow them to cross realms, they have no restrictions on where they can go."

"And why would I need to call on them?"

"They are war horses and will protect you. Plus, they are fun," Poseidon winked.

"How in Hades' name am I to get up there?" Amanda's head was nearly bent backward, looking up at the massive beast's back.

As the question slipped from her mouth, the horse bowed. One knee was on the ground, and the other stretched out in front of him as if he were genuflecting.

Like this.

"Wow. How did he—"

It was not a voice but a thought. Words formed in Amanda's head. Not her thoughts, but—*no, it can't be.*

Why can't it?

"Was that you?" wide-eyed Amanda whirled on Poseidon. He just smirked. "My thoughts—"

"He truly likes you then. When my horses respect someone, they can communicate with them. It is what you would call telepathy—a transfer of thoughts. He knows everything you say, no matter the language you use. Since he is not verbal, he *thinks* into your mind."

"This is crazy," Amanda beams at the creature and his master. "Thank you, Poseidon."

"So, climb up his leg."

"What? Won't that hurt him?"

Poseidon chuckles. "He is strong enough to handle me on his back. You climbing his leg is of no consequence. Now, climb."

Mounting the horse took a minute. She couldn't get over not wanting to cause the beast pain. Once on his back, she shrieked with happiness.

"This is amazing!" She could feel the power beneath her. "Okay, I'm up. Now what?"

"You can either speak your commands or think them. Polemistís will obey and *think* back to you."

With a thought, the horse began a lazy stroll down the beach, his hooves splashing in the water. It was like riding a rocking horse—smooth and effortless. Feeling a little daring, she thought about him walking faster. With a slight jolt, he did just that. The movement of the horse's muscles, the smell of saltwater, and the wind in her hair gave her a sense of freedom she hadn't felt since the god of war decided she was his plaything.

She turned the horse, not wanting to get too far, and saw nothing but the sea, sand, and the three-quarter moon. The sight was beautiful, but Poseidon was no longer there.

"Well, bye to you too," Amanda whispered to herself.

Slowing Polemistís back to a stroll gave Amanda time to think. She unpacked what Zenovia and Poseidon said to her. They were right. Humans were just as capable of evil as gods—not all gods are immoral. But the thought of always being watched over wasn't right with her either. It did not go unnoticed that she'd been all for it when Nicole was being stalked. Now, she understood precisely how her cousin had felt. She knew they would watch her twenty-four-seven if she allowed them back into her orbit. Could she allow such an invasion of her privacy?

The hair on the back of Amanda's neck stood on end when Polemistís stopped dead in his tracks. Someone or something immortal was close. She could feel it. The moment of irony hadn't escaped her. Why could she feel this presence but never Annika's or Mark's? She would unpack that after the feeling of threat was gone. Unlike being watched from an orb, she could sense the being was physically present. No one was close enough for her to see. Or they weren't visible. *What's here with us?* She thought to the beast under her. After all, Polemistís was her only ally present.

There, the horse thought back.

Amanda tried to focus on the surrounding beach. Her only power was beauty, and her sight was only as good as the human she was. She couldn't see much with only a three-quarters moon and slight cloud cover. Panic started to set in when she saw a white cat slinking up the beach toward them.

It's only a cat, she thought.

That is not only a cat, my lady. That is what the Norse call a Mare.

What the fuck is a Mare?

It is a type of witch that comes from the souls of the living. You would call it a demon.

The cat was close enough that Amanda could see its tail twitching. *Why is it here?*

It comes for you, my lady.

"Run!" Amanda said aloud.

Hold on.

Amanda held on for dear life when the horse ran toward the cat, not away from it. *What the hell, Polemistís?*

It was then that she witnessed the fierceness of the giant horse. When the cat saw the massive animal charge toward it, she turned into a beautiful woman. Amanda supposed the creature assumed that would stop the horse from trampling her. She was wrong. Polemistís galloped over the witch, and the scream the mare released was terrifying. Sand flew up around them as the horse stopped and spun around as if he were small and agile. And that's when Amanda watched the witch stand up and disappear. *What the hell?*

The mare has gone, my lady. I will take you home.

As great as the horse was, Amanda needed answers, but the stallion was not the one she needed to ask. Poseidon was gone, Kallisto needed a break, plus she was new to all this too, and Zenovia wasn't from the world of immortals—that left one person.

Polemistís turned and sprinted up the beach toward Zenovia's. *How did you know where I'm staying?*

I am in your head, my—

His transfer of thought stopped, and his pace slowed. The horse huffed just before he came to a halt and tilted his head to the sky. *Griffins.*

"What did you say—think—whatever," Amanda all but yelled over her pounding heart.

Griffins. There are three flying above us. They are protectors—no need to worry.

"Why do we need protection?" Amanda spoke aloud.

That, my lady, is the question. The Shire struck off in a gallop, with Amanda hanging on for dear life. A regular horse would be painful enough to fall from, but the sheer size of Polemistís had her praying she would stay seated.

With great relief, it took little time to get to Zenovia's. The massive beast bowed again, allowing Amanda to slide down his leg effortlessly. *You should stay inside, my lady. I will tell my master what happened.*

Thank you, Polemistís. I hope we meet again.

Polemistís nodded, then let out a neigh that shook the ground around them. He then vanished. *Oh, to be able to vanish.*

Chapter XX

Protection

Instead of returning to the cave, Phantasos went to Olympus to think about what Phobetor had said. *If creatures are the only ones who can feel Amanda's signature, then why did Atropos tell me differently?* He thought.

Phantasos did what calmed him. He walked through his gardens and listened to the many waterfalls. This relaxed his mind and gave him time to think. He had only been back a couple of hours when a young, out-of-breath nymph ran up to him, panting nonsense about mare creatures and griffins, followed by the only word that jolted him to listen—Amanda.

"Breathe and tell me what happened," Phantasos shook the shoulders of the servant.

"Poseidon sent a message to his great-niece, Kallisto, that Amanda may be in trouble. In turn, Morpheus questioned me to see if you were here. He gave me the message and said to come now—everyone, whoever that entails, is meeting in Greece." The little nymph spat everything out in a rush as he wrung his hands with anxiety. He knew names like Poseidon and Kallisto had the guy in a manic state. Those were names of royalty in their world.

With a snap of his fingers, Phantasos donned his weapons and returned to the mortal realm with red eyes swirling.

"I'm fine, seriously. Nothing happened," Amanda said to Kallisto, her cousin, and the two Oneiroi standing before her. Then her back went stiff as chills ran up her spine. Slowly, she turned and saw him. Standing in the doorway to the kitchen, where everyone gathered, was the blonde Oneiroi who made her heart race. The one she thought she would never see again. Everyone went quiet while she and Phantasos stared at one another. She drank him in. Then, her eyes took in his apparent unease.

Phobetor cleared his throat, "We will be in the sitting room."

Her traitorous friends stood and left her alone with swirling red eyes trained on her. She watched as they looked her up and down, searching.

"I'm fine," Amanda whispered.

He took three strides toward her and stopped, still not speaking—still looking her over.

"Seriously, I'm okay," she tried again.

"Not many meet a mare and remain unscathed," Phantasos finally spoke.

"It so happened I was atop one of Poseidon's horses, and it took care of the situation for me."

With widened eyes and brows raised to his hairline, Phantasos asked, "How did you come by one of *his* horses?"

"He gave me use of them. It's a long story, but I'm thankful he did. As for the griffins, I'm not sure why they came. Either someone sent them to protect me, or they themselves sought to do so."

As she spoke, she closed the remaining distance between them. Now, they were standing an arm's length from each other. Phantasos reached up and tucked a wayward strand of blonde hair out of her face. She shivered when his fingertips made contact—then remembered their last encounter. With a blush, she took a step back. It seemed that her body was also a traitor.

"I was summoned and told you may need assistance," Phantasos said.

"Like I just told you and everyone in there," she pointed toward the sitting room. "I'm fine. Well, even I'll admit, when the cat turned into a woman, it made me pause. Luckily, the stallion I was on had no problem trampling the creature."

"I was told that creatures sense your signature, making you a target for all mythical beings. Including those of other pantheons."

"It seems so, but we aren't a hundred percent sure. It's still a theory, albeit one that seems more plausible after tonight," she said just above a whisper.

Phantasos reached for her again, "Amanda, I—"

"Don't," Amanda took another step backward. "The last time I saw you, my emotions were all over the place, and you left because of those damn Fate sisters. I'm sure you will convince yourself, or they will tell you, again, to stay away from the fragile mortal, and I'm not waiting for *another* goodbye because you can't think for yourself where I'm concerned. You can hang out with us while I try to convince the rest of them that I don't need round-the-clock surveillance, or you can go ahead and leave. But understand, no matter what you decide this minute, we will never be in the same state as the last time we saw each other. Is that clear?"

"Perfectly," Phantasos' eyes no longer swirled. They were back to their baby blues. The ones that made it hard for her to look away from. He stepped around her and left the room.

Amanda closed her eyes and took in a deep breath. She had not expected to see the broody Oneiroi for a long time, if ever again. Not that she hadn't thought about him constantly since the last time she saw him on the ship. Her feelings for Phantasos were complicated. She either loathed him, or she wanted to rip his clothes off and finally put an end to her desire—there was no in-between. If he was back for good, or until those three bitches got ahold of him again, she would have to keep her distance. He was the one being who was capable of breaking her in two.

Thirty minutes later, all six were in deep discussion about whether Amanda needed a divine bodyguard twenty-four-seven. Well, five of them were in discussion. Amanda glared at each of them with her arms crossed. She had expressed her refusal, but no one seemed to care what she thought. The arguments were now about the schedule they should keep, which gods they should ask to help, and whether the bodyguard should be physically with her at all times or watch her through an orb or by other means.

"You guys are going to make me scream. I told you I don't need divine interference." Amanda's face felt flushed.

"Oh, but you do," Phantasos was the only one to acknowledge her.

"It isn't up to you. Or them," Amanda waved her hand around to the group.

Kallisto asked, "After everything you told me, do you think I would ever let you take on the immortal world yourself?"

Amanda didn't miss the slight tilt of Phantasos' head at Kallisto's words. *Great.*

"No one knows if gods or creatures are actually after me," she crossed her arms over her chest. She knew she was acting like a petulant child, but two weeks ago, she was running from immortals. Now, they were discussing never leaving her side.

"Just stop right there. You and I both know that's not true. The mere fact a Norse demon went after you tonight proves differently." Kallisto's stern voice eclipsed her defense. "I love you, Amanda, but you're being stubborn. You're like my sister, and I refuse to leave you alone. Either I'm always with you, or we do as we did with Nicole and trade-off. At least until Ares has been taken care of."

"Look, Amanda, I understand better than anyone what you're feeling right now. Put yourself back to when you felt I needed around-the-clock protection. How you felt about me then is how we feel about you now. If something were to happen to you, none of us would forgive ourselves," Nicole pleaded.

"Five minutes ago, I wasn't sure I ever wanted to see an immortal again. Now, a house full of immortals are telling me that I will always have one with me. This is a lot to come to terms with."

"Start coming to terms with it because I will not be letting you out of my sight unless one of these deities in this room is with you," Phantasos' stance of legs shoulder-width apart, and his muscular arms crossed over his well-defined chest showed he had dug in. Whatever she wanted was fine, as long as it was the crew watching her like a hawk. The crew. She had started back, calling their little group the crew, as they referred to themselves before the last abduction. *Great.*

Amanda glared at him. "You are not my keeper."

He let his arms fall from his chest and slowly approached her. His blue eyes began to swirl, and the slight twitch under his left one showed exactly how much he was fighting for control.

Damn, he smells good. Amanda thought, then closed her eyes when she saw the approaching god smirk. *Get out of my head!*

His smirk turned to a wide grin, and he stood toe-to-toe with her.

"That is where you are mistaken, ἄγγελος. I will be your keeper until you no longer need one," Phantasos' smile never faltered.

"You're an ass," Amanda hissed between her teeth, turned, and walked from the room. She could hear him chuckle as she walked upstairs, fuming.

✦━━━━✦

"I believe you will pay for that, brother," Morpheus laughed.

"I am sure I will, but she will not be left alone. Did any of you, besides Kallisto, know that Poseidon was with her just hours ago?" Phantasos asked. They shook their heads in unison. "Did you know Hades took her to the Underworld mere days ago?" Now, four sets of wide eyes stared at him. "That is why I will not leave her alone." He felt possessive on a level he did not quite understand—a stronger urge than ever before.

After thirty more minutes of discussing when each of them would be with Amanda, they started on the possible timeline of Ares' return from the mourning of the gods. It was unanimous—all of them thought he could show any minute. Three months was only a quarter of the mourning period for the gods, but no one thought the god of war would wait much longer before he sought revenge. Definitely not the traditional year of mourning.

"Okay. I'm going to tell each of you this because Amanda won't. Ares threatened her the night Phobos was killed. He can mentally speak to her. Much more was exchanged when he smiled at her that night—not just a creepy grin. He told her that she was his and Phantasos was dead. I promised not to tell anyone everything she told me, but because of the danger, I felt this was important to know," Kallisto hung her head. "I'll tell her I told you that much and why."

A growl came from Phantasos' chest. Everything in the room began to have a red tint to it. "I want to know everything she told you."

"You know I can't do that. If she wants you to know, she will have to be the one to tell you. But understand this; she has damn good reasons not to trust immortals."

Chapter XXI

Athens

A COUPLE OF DAYS later, Amanda decided to speak to Kallisto again. After her friend confessed to telling the crew about Ares' mind fuckery, she ignored her. It had taken a lot out of her to tell Kallisto the stories that kept her awake most nights, so she felt two days of childishly pretending that Kallisto didn't exist was penalty enough. Truth be told, she didn't blame her for discussing that part of her torment with the group, but that, on top of her around-the-clock crew-imposed protection, had raised her petty side, and she was finding it difficult to let it go. Besides, today was the day Annika came to visit, and Phobetor brought Nicole to meet her. Amanda was excited to see her friend again. Even though she lied to her about Hermes and hid that she was a Satyress, she decided to forgive her friend. *No one is perfect.*

"Have you spoken to Nicole or Phobetor?" Amanda asked.

"So, you *can* speak," Kallisto continued to paint her toenails without looking at her.

"Well, I had to get my point across, didn't I?"

"No. I haven't heard from them since everyone was here. Have you heard from Phantasos?" Kallisto cut her eyes toward her, delivering perfect painted strokes to her toes.

Amanda glared at her friend. "You're the goddess watching over me. Why would *I* hear from him?"

Kallisto continued her art, drawing flowers on her big toe with a mischievous grin plastered to her face.

"Funny," Amanda rolled her eyes and grabbed the light blue polish.

When Kallisto sat straight up and glanced at the bedroom door, Amanda knew Annika must have arrived. She capped the polish and jumped to open the door.

The beautiful Annika stood with light-gray curved horns and slightly darker, hooved feet. *Well, damn. She is a Satyress.* Amanda felt the burn of embarrassment flood her face. She knew Annika saw her shock, but damn, she couldn't blame her.

"Hey," Amanda said, giving herself a mental shake before she hugged her friend. "I'm so glad you came."

Annika hugged her back, then held her at arm's length and looked at her from head to toe, much like Phantasos had. The only difference was that he hadn't only been looking for harm—his eyes had been full of heat.

Amanda rolled her eyes. "I'm okay. I'm not sure what you've heard, but I'm in one piece and on lockdown," she said, then turned to glare at Kallisto.

Annika raised one fashionably shaped brow. "Lockdown?"

"Yes. But don't get me started just yet. Come in, and let's catch up. You remember Kallisto," Amanda gestured for her to sit on Kallisto's bed beside them.

"Good to see you again, Kallisto."

"You too," Kallisto returned the sentiment with little enthusiasm.

Annika turned to Amanda, "May I borrow the bathroom? When I realm hop or travel far through a realm, I have to shift to my natural form. So, I would like to freshen up and get ready to see Athens."

"Sure. It's the room across the hall from this one. If you want to wash up, the linens are in the cabinet to the right when you walk in."

Once Annika was out of earshot, Amanda turned on Kallisto. "Why don't you like her?"

"I never said I didn't like her."

"It doesn't take a genius. You were kinda cold toward her just now."

Kallisto released her breath and admitted, "I guess I blame her."

"What? Why?" Amanda's forehead wrinkled in confusion.

"While I was walking around like a zombie worried about you and our friendship, you were with her. I know it's silly, but I can't seem to help it. I'll get over it," Kallisto hung her head in shame.

"Kalli, even when I couldn't be around you, no one could ever take your place." Amanda reached over and hugged her best friend, and for the first time in months, she felt like Kalli was still the girl she had always been and not the goddess she'd become.

Twenty minutes later, the three girls were on their way to D.F.O.'s (Designed for Olympus) or better known as the best place in Athens for young adults to shop—*even if its owner was an ass.*

One step into the beautiful clothing store, and she felt him. It was not like he was watching her, but she could feel his presence—seconds later, her feeling proved correct. There, just on the other side of the wall of the graphic tees, stood Phantasos talking and laughing with a gorgeous woman. Kallisto's head snapped around to see her. Whatever she saw made her pull her to the side and start talking. Unfortunately, Amanda had no clue what she said. All she felt and heard was the blood pumping through her veins. Her skin felt feverish, and her upper lip began twitching.

"Amanda!" Kallisto gave her a little shake. "Snap out of it. Ignore him."

"I'm good. I didn't expect him to be here, and I definitely didn't expect him to be openly flirting with the help," Amanda's fists were clenched at her sides as she desperately tried to calm her *anger—jealousy? What in Hades' name is my problem?*

"Is that—?" Annika started to ask.

"The eldest Oneiroi douchebag—Why yes, it is," Amanda answered Annika's perceived question. She then turned and walked back the way she'd entered.

◆—◆—◆

The chill of her presence ran up his spine like a jolt of lightning. Phantasos knew she was close.

"Excuse me," he said to the long-legged brunette he had been discussing the new inventory with.

To his surprise, he found Kallisto and a Satyress in human form, but no Amanda.

"Where is she?" That was all he said to them. Kallisto pointed to the side door where Amanda had fled.

"If I were you, I would leave her alone for a few minutes," she warned.

Phantasos turned around and responded, "You should be with her. If you are not going out there to find her, I will." Phantasos flung the door open and started his search. She was not far; he could feel her. He closed his eyes and concentrated. *There you are.*

Self-preservation had Phantasos hanging back as he watched the demigoddess. She paced in front of the fountain a block down from D.F.O., fidgeting with her nails. Anyone else would think her mental retreat was due to nervousness, but Phantasos could tell she was not so much nervous as she was pissed. The rolling of her eyes every five steps or so gave her irritation away, and for some reason, he was sure it was geared toward him. *Great.*

He loved verbally sparing with Amanda, but not when she was that worked up. Before he could come up with a reason to be watching her, she stopped and looked straight at him. Impressive, since he was a good twenty meters from her. He smirked, and she glared. *Maybe this will be fun.*

About halfway to her, Phantasos realized he had started walking toward the unhappy demi. It did not seem that he could help himself. He heard mortals refer to the opposite sex as—going to be the death of them. He knew she would be—but before that happened, he would do what his body and mind had been fighting against. *Mine.*

The more he closed the distance, the more beautiful her scowl became. *Gods, I must be going mad.* With two meters left, he pushed his hands into his jean's pockets, not trusting what he would do once he got to her. His nervous signs finally showed, and he caught himself biting his bottom lip. One meter separation—three feet. Now toe-to-toe. They stood still, looking at each other—neither spoke. He knew it was not just him thinking about the last time they were alone; her face was flushed, and she looked back and forth from his lips to his eyes. *Yes. This will be fun.* Phantasos opened his mind to read hers.

Amanda knew the second he tried reading her. He was biting his lip, then with a thought, his cocky smirk was back. Finally, a slight tilt of his head and the crease between his eyes—aggravation. Yep. He hit the block. She grinned. Then she pushed back to his mind and returned his cocky smirk with one of her own. *Not so easy anymore.* She'd learned a lot from speaking with Poseidon's monstrous horse.

It was then, while shoppers, tourists, businessmen, and women busied themselves all around them, that it happened. In the middle of the week in Athens, Greece, Amanda saw the domineering look that crossed the eldest Oneiroi's face seconds before she found her body pressed flush against his, one hand fisted in her hair, the other against her lower back, and his lips, tongue, and teeth devouring hers.

It was at that moment her arms wrapped around his neck, and she gave as good as she got. *You know I still hate you?* She pushed her thoughts toward him as they continued their PDA.

Back at you, beautiful. She felt his smile against her lips.

We're in public. Amanda thought, unable to speak aloud.

Mortals cannot see us. I made sure of it.

Talented.

This is nothing. He released her mouth but continued to hold tight and winked.

CHAPTER XXII

MEMORIES

IT TOOK SOME CONVINCING to get Phantasos back to Zenovia's, but Amanda was nothing if not persuasive. Her mind was reeling from what had just happened in the middle of the city of Athens. He claimed her in front of the people busying themselves around them and any gods or creatures who may have been watching. Questions and concerns assailed her mind. Oh, to be the carefree girl she once was.

Kallisto and Annika were still shopping, and Zenovia was out, which gave them time to discuss what had just happened.

"Have a seat, and I'll fix you a drink," Amanda pointed to the kitchen stools that lined one side of the island. She needed a little space to think. Since the epic mind-blowing kiss, Phantasos had not stopped touching her. He either held her hand, had his hand on her lower back, or his mouth on hers since they had stopped several times for *breaks* on their walk back to Kallisto's grandmother's.

"You seem nervous," Phantasos said.

"A lot has happened in a short amount of time—And that's just today," Amanda said, setting a glass of Agora in front of him and taking the stool next to him. "I'm just concerned about who or what may have seen us."

Phantasos lifted a brow as he took a drink. "Everyone already knows."

"What do you mean?"

"The reason the Fates have continued their warnings for me to keep my distance from you, the reason Ares really hates me, and the reason my presence in your life is dangerous is all because we are meant to be. It is rare for immortals, but when it happens, it is intense."

"What the hell are you going on about?" Amanda scrunched her forehead.

"Some call it mates, some call it imprinted, and others refer to the phenomena as marked. We do not have a name for it since it is so rare. It is hard to explain, but any deity or creature you encounter would know you belong to me. Not with me, to me. There is a difference," he raised his hand, stopping her from interjecting that she belonged to no one. She tightened her lips, effectively allowing him to finish his thought. "But do not worry. I have to claim you for us to be bound. That is when it becomes absolute."

Amanda gave a forced chuckle, "You have to be kidding me. Right? I mean, that's some insane storybook shit."

"No. I am not kidding. And that makes us," he gestured between them, "not good together. If I were to mark you and then die, you would become a shell of yourself. Knowing Ares and I will be fighting soon, I refuse to do that to you. I refuse to be the cause of your pain. The reason the light leaves your eyes."

This conversation was both strange and pissing her off. How dare he use words like belong, as if she were a thing. "Mark me? And may I ask how you would do that?" She asked and was rewarded greatly when Phantasos' face went scarlet. She had no idea that gods could blush until that moment.

"I would take you," he said with a considerably deeper pitch.

"And by that, you mean?" She was enjoying his discomfort.

"We would fuck."

She had to give it to him. When he finally decided how to respond, he straightened his spine and smirked. Now, it was her with a flushed face. Once she shook off his talk of them fucking, her mind started spiraling.

"Back up. Why would those three bitches warn you away from me since last year if we were *meant* to be?" Amanda mimed air quotes.

"Because they knew you were of godly descent, yet they warned me away because you felt mortal—no god or demigod signatures. You would not survive in our world for long. Plus, they, as one, can forecast the future. I suppose they see a not-so-glamorous outcome between Ares and me."

"I still don't understand," Amanda finished her Agora. She loved the citrus and honey mixed with soda water. "When did you suspect we were . . . *mated . . . fated*?" Amanda drummed her fingers on the table. "And you mean they see the outcome of you and Ares, and you die?" She felt sick.

"I had my suspicions when I reacted to Ares taking you like I did. What I felt at that moment was pure, lethal rage. I was so mad and shaking that I could not summon my battle form. That had never happened. As you have witnessed, that form has a mind of its own when I am around you now. I normally had to will it out of me. I have not had full control over my basic instincts since I met you. And the battle outcome is a theory. The Fates would never tell me. Besides, predicting the future is not set in stone, even for the bitch sisters. Free will can change the future depending on a person's actions or reactions. Even though they see the future, it can and often does change. My bet is they are being cautious."

"Why were you such a prick afterward, then?" Amanda asked, unclenching her fists and relaxing. She had not noticed how nervous the discussion of Ares winning their impending clash had caused until the weight lifted. *It's not set in stone.*

"The warnings."

"So, the sisters' warnings made you be a dick to me?" Amanda scoffed. "Yeah, right."

"My last relationship ended in tragedy. Not only in the death of the mortal woman, but our Pantheon lost their dream god of fantasy."

Amanda could tell by the set of his eyes and the sudden tension in his shoulders that speaking of Marissa's death was not something he wanted to do, yet here he was trying to explain.

"Marissa, correct?"

"Yes."

"Will you tell me about her? Please?" Amanda placed her hand on top of his.

"If I do, can we not speak of her again?" He asked.

*　＊━━━━━━＊*

With a deep inhale of resignation, Phantasos nodded. "I was helping her father through some tough times. He was a writer who drank heavily. So much, he had not written in over a year. With only the odd jobs she helped with, their main source of income dwindled. So, his wife called upon me to help with his dreams, hoping subconsciously he would wake and no longer want to drown in the bottle but instead, drown himself in the pages of his work. I went to him and created fantastical images. Plenty enough to ignite his imagination for writing. It took weeks of visiting the author. One night, his daughter woke him from a dream I had manifested. She heard him yell out with the pleasure of seeing mythical creatures. Apparently, he had fallen asleep while sitting at his writing desk. I had been in his dreams so often by that time I no longer watched where he lay, I just entered. Her voice caused him to place her in the dream I had conjured. When I saw her, I went weak. At that point, I had never seen anyone as beautiful. She mesmerized me." Phantasos raised his glass to drink and to see how his story affected Amanda since she had tightened the hand that sat on his.

"No one had ever sparked that type of interest in me. I had slept with many goddesses, nymphs, and daemons, but never had I been intrigued by a human. At first, I felt she was unequal, and I had to be mistaken in my reaction to her. Then I saw her again a couple of weeks later—the same type of situation. Her father was writing all the time, late into the night, causing him to fall asleep where he sat. This time, I pulled from his dream and watched her on her plane. She helped him to bed beside her mother and kissed him lightly on the forehead. I was enamored of her love for her father. Being a god, I was never that close to either of my parents. I started going into only his dreams instead of seeking out my other dreamers—to watch her. Finally, one night, after seeing her crying over some prick mortal who had chosen another girl over her, I went into her dreams to help with her pain. I painted illusions of magical creatures she found fantastic. I will spare you the details, but for months after that first time going into her dream state, I only went into her father's imagination, keeping his mind on his fantasies so he would finish his novel and then straight to Marissa's dreams. After over a year, I stopped going into her father's dreams since he had finished his book and was so excited that he started the second one without interference. Now, it was just Marissa and me. I began taking her to other realms. Showing off my world and the world I wanted her to be a part of. My father realized there were issues and warned me. I did not care. All I wanted was her. The next thing I knew, I was taking her to Olympus. She had started having problems with memory and fatigue. Once I started taking her to my Pantheon, the talking out of her head and strange behavior worsened. I often had to tell her who I was and what I was doing with her. She had moments of clarity but always thought I was a dream since she could not remember my face. In one of those moments, she killed herself on the Mount. Her last words were, *this is all a dream. See . . .* then stabbed herself in the heart, right in front of me. I grabbed her as she fell to the floor of my bedchamber. Blood was all over her chest, me, and the floor. It was so thick and sticky I could not sling it off my hands, so I screamed for my father, Hypnos. He came and was furious. For me, he sealed her wound and spelled it not to show, but death he had no control over. I changed her into a dressing gown since she was wearing a peplos, then took her to her bed in the mortal realm, where I laid her for her parents to find. Her mother would not stop screaming, and her father took the bottle back like an old lover. I watched them from an orb day and night. For every drink he took, I took three. Every scream her mother made, I sliced into my flesh wherever was convenient. After a month, her mother killed herself, ironically, the same way her daughter had. Her father drank himself to death. It took eighteen months for that to happen. I never returned to my Oneiroi duties, which caused issues in all realms. Hypnos refused to look at me. I returned to the dream world over a hundred years later when Morpheus needed my help. That is when I met you."

Most mortals think gods are beyond real emotional pain, but the truth is that gods are so in tune with pain that they often wage wars and destroy worlds. When Phantasos looked down, he noticed the memories shook him. His hands were shaking. Slowly, he looked back to Amanda, who also watched his trembling hands. When she looked from his hands to him, he saw the tears that clung to her cheeks and chin. He knew touching her would collide the emotions from his past with the ones from his present, but he could not resist. With his thumbs, he wiped her tears and pressed a chaste kiss on her brow line.

"Do not cry for me or her. Her death took not only her but her parents—and a large part of who I was. Now, Hades takes care of them. They are together and do not remember the details of their demise. A century later, it is still raw to me. My healing finally began the day I saw you. So, please, my ἀγγελος, do not cry."

✦⸺·⋯·⸺✦

The night ended with the return of all the home's current occupants and quizzical looks from one goddess and a Satyress, which Amanda pointedly ignored. She had no clue where her relationship with Phantasos would lead. He basically told her nothing, refusing to place her in any more danger than she already was. Honestly, she didn't know if she wanted anything more than this day and evening with him. For the most part, he had been an ass, one who saved her life many times, but still an ass. Today was the first vulnerability he had shown her. What was one day compared to months of bickering between them? True, she was more than physically attracted to the man; after all, he was a god. *No. That's not it.* She was surrounded by Greek divinity, and he was the only one who affected her on that level. *Stop lying to yourself, Amanda,* she thought as she removed what little makeup she'd donned that morning as she got ready for bed.

Afterward, she moisturized, slowly brushed her teeth, and basically held up in the bathroom as long as possible. Unfortunately, it was time for Amanda to return to her friends and their interrogations. *Ugh.* The look on Kallisto's face when she and Annika entered the house from their shopping excursion was priceless. They walked in to witness Phantasos sitting beside Amanda on stools in the small kitchen. Both laughed at a story the god was telling about him and his brothers when they were young and impulsive. Amanda was sure the scene Kallisto saw indicated her and Phantasos' newfound interest in each other, but Amanda refused to admit that to anyone, including herself. So, leaving the bathroom caused a touch of anxiety to swarm in her stomach. Hand on the doorknob, Amanda stood straight, took a deep breath, and slipped on the look of nonchalance.

Well, shit. So much for indifference. Amanda walked into the shared bedroom with both women standing, Kallisto with her arms crossed over her chest and Annika with her hands on her hips, still wearing the look of a human. Kallisto actually tapped her foot.

"Well?" Kallisto asked.

"Well, what?" Amanda busied herself with turning back the cover of her bed.

Both goddess and creature rolled their eyes in unison. "What was going on between you and Phantasos this afternoon?" Kallisto answered, still tapping her foot.

"Nothing, really," Amanda continued to busy herself, trying to decide what book to read.

"Nothing, really? Are you serious, Amanda? I'm not stupid. Annika, tell her. Tell her what we saw."

"We saw you glowing with laughter at something he said. Even I know you don't do that," Annika relayed the image Amanda knew they saw.

So much for nonchalance.

"Why do you speak using contractions and the gods don't?" Amanda decided to ignore their questions and ask one she had wondered about.

"What?" Annika's forehead wrinkled.

Yep, Amanda had thrown Annika off-kilter. *Perfect. Now, control this conversation.* "I've just noticed that the gods' speech is proper, at least most of the time. They even refuse to use contractions, which is just strange. But you don't. You speak perfect new-age British posh.

"New-age British posh? Is that something you came up with on the spot?" Annika giggled.

"Enough. Stop deflecting, Amanda. What's going on between you and Phantasos?" Kallisto brought the conversation back to its beginning theme.

Amand rolled her eyes at both women, grabbed a copy of *Emma* by Jane Austen, and hopped on her bed. She caught herself in a daze of memory, biting the inside of her cheek when Kallisto cleared her throat, telling her to get on with it.

"We have mutually decided to put our dislike for each other aside for the good of our friends," Amanda flipped through the book instead of looking at her friends who still stood, arms crossed, glaring. *Shit. Can they tell we kissed?*

"Uh-huh. Well, I'll believe that when I see it. Plus, not for one second do we," Kallisto pointed between her and Annika, "believe that's it. You two were animated and, dare I say, happy when we walked in. You two have NEVER been animated with each other, let alone happy in each other's presence."

"Well, that's all it is. Now, I'm tired, and we have a lot to do over the next couple of days, so I'm going to read until I cannot hold my eyes open and then get a good night's sleep," Amanda said, as she buried herself deeper into the covers and flipped on the reading light.

Chapter XXIII

Wolves

Annika slept on an air mattress between Amanda and Kallisto's beds. This spot on the floor proved convenient when Amanda bumped her mattress as she left the room at—Annika looked at her watch—three thirty in the morning. *Where in Hades' name is she going?*

Annika flung back her cover and donned her human form before she followed after her friend. It was when Amanda turned her face toward her and looked straight through her with lifeless eyes that Annika's blood ran cold.

"Amanda. Where are you going?" Annika said, just above a whisper. No answer. Amanda turned back to the door and fiddled with its locks.

"Well, damn," Annika swore as she flashed back to the bedroom and shook Kallisto from her sleep. "Amanda is in an unresponsive state, working the front door locks. Come on."

Moments later, Annika and Kallisto stood outside the open front door, and Amanda was nowhere in sight.

"Damn. How could she have gotten away so fast?" Annika's voice shook.

"Morpheus!" Kallisto raised her voice and tapped her bracelet. Seconds later, the Oneiroi to the gods appeared before them.

"Yes?"

Annika told Morpheus what had happened, and in seconds, all three Oneiroi and one gorgeous demi, who Annika guessed to be Nicole, stood before them.

Phantasos' eyes swirled red, and his hands pumped in and out of fists at the sides. "Split up. I tried reaching her through telepathy and got nothing. She is blocking me."

"Not just you," Annika said. "Kallisto and I can't get her either. If she's on her own, she can't get far." Everyone's faces fell with a tinge of fear. The word *if* hung in the air with trepidation. This scenario was way too familiar when it came to Amanda.

"Give me a minute to search," Morpheus said, then turned to mist and rose high above the homes. Corporeal again, he delivered the news: "She's already at the Temple of Zeus."

❖━━━━━❖

Without waiting, Phantasos flashed to the temple. There Amanda stood unmoving with a giant white wolf stalking toward her. He placed himself between her and the snarling beast. Seconds later, the creature turned from a giant wolf into a wolf cub whose growls turned to whimpers.

He turned around to see that Amanda had collapsed to the ground, gasping for air. "Amanda," Phantasos ran to her as the others appeared around them.

"What happened? How did I get here?" Amanda sobbed. "Why am I crying?" She looked up at him with the same fear he had seen one too many times. Her body trembled. His heart clenched.

"Shhh," Phantasos crooned, pulling her into his chest while stroking her hair.

Phobetor walked over to the pup and picked him up by his scruff. "Was this a full-grown mut just seconds ago?" Phobetor asked his brother, who was trying to comfort the crying demi.

"Yes. It is one of Ares' wolves." He stated for Kallisto and Nicole. "He has eight of them at his beck and call. He sends them out to gather information and kill," Phantasos said as he helped Amanda stand.

It was when she fully stood before him, and his hands were helping her balance, that he noticed she was in nothing but a black lace camisole and matching panties. His eyes grew wide, and the thought of his brothers seeing her like that had him flashing shorts and a D.F.O. t-shirt on her that said, *Eyes up here!* With an arrow pointing up.

"Wait. What are you saying?" The spot between her brows wrinkled in confusion.

Answering Amanda and the rest of the crew, Phantasos explained what happened in the seconds they appeared at the temple with him. "When I got here, that pup," Phantasos pointed at the white fuzzball, "one of Ares' snarling giant white wolves was stalking toward you, and you just stood there, in front of the mongrel, unflinching—motionless—catatonic, but with your eyes open."

"He sent a giant wolf after me?" Amanda's voice was soft and weak, her eyes wide and wild with fear.

Phantasos wanted nothing more than to take her to the cave and hide her for eternity. *Damn*, he ran his hand through to the top of his hair.

"They know," Nicole said.

"They know what?" Kallisto asked.

"They know creatures can find her. I bet he sent the wolf to find out where she is," Nicole continued.

"Athens is too close to home base for all things Greek Pantheon. We need to get her home," Kallisto said.

"Let's get back to the house," Nicole said. She took Phobetor's arm, and Phantasos latched his around Amanda's waist. The group and the pup flashed back to Zenovia's, where she stood in her kitchen, waiting for her house guests to return.

"What happened?" Zenovia's voice shook as she looked Amanda up and down. Then, she scanned her eyes over her granddaughter and everyone else.

"Ares sent one of his white wolves after Amanda," Kallisto answered her grandmother.

"I'm going to lie down," Amanda said as she pivoted around the crew.

"We really need to discuss what happened, Amanda. How did you end up at Zeus' temple so quickly?" Phantasos asked.

✦───··──✦

Amanda turned back to face her friends. All seven faces, including Zenovia's, looked scared—for her. Those were the faces she hadn't wanted to see. The same faces everyone had each time she was saved from the clutches of evil, and for weeks after. *Why me?* It was the mantra that continued to scroll through her mind.

"I have no idea," Amanda's eyes began to burn from the pressure she exerted as she tried to keep from crying. "All I know is that he sent a feral dog after me. Would that wolf have killed me if Phantasos hadn't gotten there in time?"

"Those creatures," Morpheus points to the wolf cub, "have many abilities and uses. One of which is that Ares can see through their eyes. If he was unsure where you were before, he knows now."

"He's the god of War. I never suspected he couldn't find me. I just hoped it would be longer than three months. There's nothing I can do. One day, he'll come for me. Now, I'm tired, and since my sleep was so rudely interrupted, I'm going to bed. We can discuss this once the sun is up and I've had at least one cup of coffee." Amanda turned and left the room without being called back.

Amanda pushed open the bedroom door to find Annika had beat her there. She knew the Satyress was protecting her, but what she really wanted was to be alone for a few minutes. Knowing Ares was behind her, sleepwalking into the city of Athens to meet up with his dog, she had her mind and flight instincts on overdrive.

"I'm glad you're okay, Amanda. You gave me a scare," Annika said.

"Me too," Amanda admitted. She looked down at her t-shirt and smiled. Apparently, Phantasos' sense of humor hadn't been cracked. She changed into PJs that were a little more appropriate for a middle-of-the-night walkabout—just in case. Come to think of it, she couldn't find the ones she was wearing. *Note to self: ask Phantasos where her nightclothes went.*

"Will you be okay up here by yourself?"

"Yeah. I need some time to process. Don't worry about me." Before tucking herself into bed, she looked out the window. At first look, nothing was amiss. Then she saw the shadow of a large dog, or was it a wolf, standing eerily still across the alley in the shadow of the neighbor's house?

Kallisto was seething and ranting about her being taken while in her Yia-Yia's home. She knew Amanda wouldn't want her to console her, so she discreetly asked Annika to watch over her.

"This will not happen again. I agree with Kallisto—Greece is too fucking dangerous," Phantasos paced like a cornered tiger. His eyes swirled crimson, and by the slight change in his speech, Kallisto knew his fangs had joined in the battle. Every few steps, she could swear he shimmered. Morpheus had once conveyed the strength it took to control their battle forms while interrogating him after the night Phobos took Amanda. He had told her that Phantasos was the best at control. Nothing seemed ever to shake him—until he found out about her abduction. It seemed the combination of donning his battle form that evening and seeing Amanda's tortured form in Phobos' claws sent him back thousands of years. Since then, Morpheus said his brother was having difficulty maintaining control. *Maybe we should go outside just in case his wings decide to show themselves.* Kallisto relayed to Morpheus through telepathy. After all, her grandmother's home barely accommodated the large Oneiroi as it was.

"Are you good, brother?" Morpheus asked Phantasos.

Phantasos stopped his patrolling of the kitchen and looked at his brother. "No. I am not good, Morpheus. He sent his mutt after her. Not only that—who woke her and put her in that unresponsive state? He would have had to know her location, not send a white wolf to locate her." With invigored anger, Phantasos started pacing again.

"I'm going back to bed. It sounds like you will be up for some time. Please make yourselves at home," Zenovia said, following Amanda's example.

"Could the state you found her in have been Hera's doing?" Phobetor voiced what everyone else was thinking now that Zenovia was no longer in the room.

"Unless he has another sneaky bitch in his arsenal, I'm sure it was her. I would speak to my grandfather about it, but anything to do with Ares right now is not a welcome topic between me and him," Kallisto said, pulling out chairs for herself, Nicole, and Annika, who had just returned downstairs. "Let's decide our next steps."

"Shouldn't we wait for Amanda to do that?" Annika asked.

"No matter what we come up with, she will need convincing. So, better we work things out now since time is of the utmost importance," Nicole answered Annika as she took a seat at the table. "By the way, I'm Nicole. Amanda's first cousin, the dream bender."

"I thought so. Nice to meet you." Annika bowed slightly.

"I knew that prick wouldn't wait the one year of mourning," Phobetor shook his head.

"Apparently, his mother doesn't subscribe to the practice either," Nicole said under her breath.

Kallisto waved her hands, gesturing for the Oneiroi to have a seat as extra chairs appeared. *I'm getting good at this.* She thought to herself. "Take a load off, guys. We may be here a while."

She watched as Phantasos fought his protector's instincts, calming himself enough to retract his fangs and turn his eyes back to baby blue. However, they continued swirling, showing his agitation was ever-present.

"She will need full-on twenty-four hours a day shadowing. When she sleeps, someone watches. When she bathes, someone watches. When she—"

"We get the picture, Phantasos. You know she's going to flip her shit when we tell her, right?" Nicole said, stopping him from listing all the embarrassing things Amanda would have to endure. "This is different than us just watching after her."

Phantasos lost the battle with his eyes. "It is no longer okay for gods to only be in the same room as she sleeps. Someone will always be awake watching over her. In fact, at night, it will be an Oneiroi so they can be with her in her dreams as well. During the day, there will be the crew members who are around her and one watching over her. Double protection at all times. And—I do not care what she thinks. This is her life we are discussing."

"Oh, I get it. But she won't," Nicole looked at her fingernails.

"On another subject," Kallisto spoke directly to Annika. "Do you feel Nicole's signature? How is it different than Amanda's—whatever it is?"

"Nicole feels like a powerful demigod. Amanda feels—pure. I can't describe it. She doesn't feel like a god at all, but she feels important," Annika answered.

Chapter XXIV

Dream

"What are you doing here?" Amanda asked the Oneiroi, who had just appeared by her side. They stood on a gorgeous Punalu'u Black Sand beach on the Big Island of Hawaii. She loved visiting this particular beach with her father. At least once a year, he would take her snorkeling with the sea turtles. She was always amazed at how the ocean calmed as soon as they stepped in.

"Protection," he replied.

"Who's going to protect me from you?" Amanda asked, her lips twitching as she continued to look at the waves. She wasn't wearing shoes, so she dug her toes in the warm black sand.

"No one," Phantasos smirked.

"You know, I can't tell if this is real or not. Am I dreaming?"

"Why can it not be both?"

"Because if it's a dream, I don't have to worry if I do this—It won't count," Amanda said, closing the minimal distance. She wrapped her arms around Phantasos' neck and kissed him. *It sure feels real.* She felt his lips turn up in a mischievous grin.

Phantasos wrapped his right hand in her hair, tightening his fist just enough to make her gasp, allowing him to deepen their kiss. She smelled like the sea and jasmine. His mind took off with memories of her. The first time they met in the gallery, the impromptu errand Morpheus sent them on so he could have more time with Kallisto, standing above him on the staircase in *that* dress, when he pulled her into the bathroom in Tennessee, finding her beaten on the floor, Phobos licking the tears and blood from her neck and face— *What the hell am I doing?*

"What's wrong?" Amanda asked.

Phantasos sprung free from her like she was on fire and he had gotten burned. His heart raced, and his eyes were fucking swirling again. He could feel them. Closing his eyes to concentrate on calming his libido, he answered, "You have been through too much for me to manhandle you like that. Plus, if I let myself . . ." He ran his hands through his hair and looked to the heavens. "I should not have shown myself. I am supposed to be keeping you safe, and here I am groping you."

"Let me be the judge of what I'm capable of handling and what I'm not. You do know I'm an adult with a mind of my own?" Amanda asked with her hands on her hips, looking like she had just been thoroughly kissed with tasseled hair and slightly swollen lips.

Damn. What in Hades' name is wrong with me?

Ignoring her question and exquisite stance—legs slightly parted, arms crossed over her chest, pushing her—Phantasos shook his head free of everything his body asked him to do and looked around where they were.

"Tell me about this place. I like it," he said as he walked toward the water, leaving her to follow.

"My dad did a study on sea turtles when I was about seven years old. Of course, this was where he often came; sometimes he would bring me when he did. I fell in love with this beach. The black sand and the sea turtles made it magical. I went through a phase where everything revolved around sea turtles. We still come here at least once a year. The amazing thing was that no matter how choppy the water was, it always calmed down when we stepped into it. Very few people snorkeled here because of the rocks and rough waves, but we never had a problem," Amanda stood beside Phantasos, both looking toward the open ocean.

He could feel the heat radiating off her. Knowing she was a demi and it was not him specifically luring the gods to her made it harder for him to stay away. His resolve was waning. How much longer could he keep himself from what he wanted? Phantasos closed the inches between their hands and entwined his fingers with hers. The jolt of electricity that went through him must have been the same for her since she flinched and looked at their hands just as he did.

In a hushed voice, Amanda looked back to the sea and asked the question that haunted him. "Will Ares kill us?"

"He will have to get through me to you. If I fall, you call for Hades," Phantasos answered, not looking at her, his eyes trained on the rocks before them. If he looked at her, he might have decided to hunt Ares down before she woke.

"You guys decided to watch over me like we did with Nicole, didn't you?" Amanda asked as she continued observing the waves breaking over the rocks. "Never leaving me alone. Ever."

"We did."

"I figured. Have y'all decided who gets what shift?"

"We are waiting for you to wake before we put the final touches on our plan," Phantasos answered, tightening his hand around hers.

"Can you please take my nights? I don't want anyone else in my dreams."

"I will do whatever you want, my ἄγγελος," Phantasos turned to look at Amanda. "I am not sure I can let anyone else watch over you as you sleep."

Standing on the black sandy beach, a world away from where Amanda's body lay on a twin bed in Greece, Phantasos knew he would conquer the world if it meant she stayed safe.

✦━━━━✦

Amanda followed her nose to the kitchen for some ambrosia, a.k.a. coffee she could smell from their bedroom. When she woke, she was the only one left in the room. Her first thought was of the dream—the kiss that ended way too quickly. Knowing the Oneiroi as she did, she and Phantasos had shared everything her imagination conjured. Apparently, she'd needed comfort and fabricated one of her favorite places her father had taken her for years. Sharing that part of her with the eldest Oneiroi seemed more intimate than the kiss. She touched her lips as she descended the staircase.

Just as she thought, everyone, including Zenovia and Thia, Kallisto's mother, waited for her. "Wow, I wasn't expecting an audience this morning. If I had known, I would've dressed more appropriately," she looked down at the t-shirt and panties she wore.

The shirt was the one Phantasos had conjured at the temple. Before her eyes, her clothes turned to shorts and a new T-shirt that said, *Yep. Taken. So Don't Ask.* Biting her lip, trying not to smirk, she and everyone else looked from her shirt to Phantasos, who sipped his coffee nonchalantly. She was fairly sure this wasn't a shirt he sold at D.F.O., even though it bore the symbol on its sleeve.

"Well, now that's settled, let's discuss the issue at hand," Thia gestured to an empty seat at the table for Amanda to sit in.

"I have a feeling I know what's going on here. So, removing the elephant from the room—you," Amanda looked at each person, "are going to watch over me every minute of every day no matter what I say or do to try and stop you." Amanda thanked Zenovia for the cup of java she placed before her. She noticed Phantasos' attempt at not grinning. "Remember, I was one of the leaders in Nicole's surveillance. It doesn't take a rocket scientist to figure out why all of you are standing in this tiny kitchen waiting for me to wake up."

"You seem rather calm, considering," Kallisto's forehead pinched. "Go ahead, let's hear why you refuse us guarding your every move."

"Last night scared the fuck out of me. Sorry, Zenovia, Thia," Amanda winced, momentarily forgetting her manners in front of them and allowing her *Amanda tongue* to speak freely.

"Don't censor because of us, dear," Zenovia said.

Looking sheepish, Amanda continued. "I don't want to go through what I went through before." Amanda heard her voice crack. "Most of all, I don't want all of you put into a situation where you have to rescue me again. So, if heading off any potential problems gives us the upper hand, I'm all for it."

"Is anyone else as stunned as I am?" Nicole's eyes were wide. "In a million years, I never expected you to give in, let alone so easily. Are you sick?" Her cousin pressed the back of her hand to her forehead.

Amanda laughed, "No. Just tired and anxious. Let's say this past year has changed the way I process information. Now, let's discuss logistics. Who am I dealing with, and when?"

Over the next hour and a half, they discussed security detail. Everyone agreed that it would be easier to protect her in Hawaii.

They also agreed that she would enroll, along with Kallisto, at the University of Hawaii, Maui campus. Her father would be proud. Next came the question of who watched her and when. Again, everyone stared at Phantasos when he said he would take most of the details, including all nights and the days Amanda was in school. Amanda just listened, remembering the feel of his hand entwined with hers on the beach. She refused to look at him to keep herself from blushing, but she felt everyone looking back and forth between them. She felt their questions, knowing an afternoon of integration from her roomies would follow the meeting.

"When will we leave for Hawaii?" Amanda looked to Thia for her answer.

"Tomorrow. That will give you time to pack and whatever else you may need to do. I'm heading back now to let your father know to expect the return of teens and gods." Thia kissed her daughter on the cheek and hugged her mother before vanishing.

"Not sure I'll ever get used to that," Nicole said.

⁂

"Spill," Kallisto demanded.

Amanda knew this was coming, but she couldn't help but play dumb. "What?"

"You very well know what. What was that all about down there? You gave in way too easily. Especially when Phantasos said he would take nights and days when you were in school. I mean, I expected that from him since he's so demanding. But you didn't put up any fight. None. What's going on between you two? And none of the bullshit you gave us last night."

"I honestly don't know. We kissed—a few times. Not like we haven't before. It's like we can't stand each other, but can't stand to not be around each other. Well, we used to not stand each other. Something's different. However, he said we will never be a *thing* because of the politics of the gods."

Kallisto stood with her arms folded. "And?"

"That's it," Amanda said as she pulled her cover-up over her bathing suit. The three girls were heading to the beach for their last day in ancient paradise. Today, Kallisto and Annika were her *security detail*. She wasn't sure who was watching via orb.

"We're not buying it," Kallisto spoke for both her and Annika.

Thirty minutes later, the women were setting up their tanning spots when a handsome man stepped between Amanda and the sun's rays. Looking up into the eyes of Hermes, Amanda gasped.

"Damn it, you scared me," Amanda hopped to her feet. "Why are you here? As you see, your spy is with me." She points to Annika, who rose to stand beside her. She felt a little bad about her spy comment when Annika flinched.

"I came to find out what happened last night." Hermes looked slightly out of place in his white button-down shirt and black suit pants. Thank goodness he left his jacket and tie wherever he came from.

"You could've asked any of the gods present, why are you here, in that?" Amanda gestured to his clothes.

"I do not plan on being here long. Now, what happened?"

With a brief rundown given by all three ladies, Hermes listened and only stiffened when he heard the wolf was stalking toward his great-granddaughter when Phantasos appeared.

"Sounds like Hera's doing. She could have sent one of Ares' wolves as easily as he could since she is the one who gave them to him," Hermes' eyes darted around in thought as he nodded. "Ares cannot render you unresponsive to the Oneiroi. That has to be Hera or Zeus. Annika, stay with her," then he was gone.

Amanda looked at Annika, "Your boss is one strange being."

"He's straight to the point. But never forget. His blood runs through your veins."

"Don't remind me."

CHAPTER XXV

SCARS

WHAT WAS SHE THINKING asking Phantasos to watch over her at night? It was easier when Kallisto looked after her. She didn't have to conceal her body when changing or showering. Kalli already knew of her scars. Trying to wash your body and cover it at the same time was almost impossible. She had to decide which parts she was okay with showing. So far, her ass was the only thing she allowed. *Ugh.* The thought made her squirm.

They had been back from Greece all of three days, and hiding her scars was not something she considered when she opened her big mouth and asked Phantasos to be around in her most intimate moments.

Closing her eyes, she prepared for another shower in front of the eldest Oneiroi. Surely, he was being a gentleman.

Five minutes into her shower, she felt the air shift. Unfortunately, she was in the middle of rinsing the shampoo from her hair, unable to open her eyes. Panic set in when she realized she had been using both hands instead of one. *Damn it!*

"Who did that to you?"

Amanda stiffened at his words. She knew it. He'd seen the scars. *I guess he's not such a gentleman after all.* "Do you mind? I'm in the shower, naked, if you haven't noticed."

"Oh, believe me. I have noticed. I also noticed the odd way you cover yourself. So, as any intelligent being would guess, you are hiding something."

"I'm hiding my private girl parts from you." Amanda stepped from the shower, covering the flesh over her pubic bone and her breasts. It was at that moment that she realized she didn't care that he saw her nude. She cared only that he saw the scars. She'd have to think more about that later. Now, she needed to figure out what she would say to the deity blocking her bathroom door with his arms crossed. She turned her back and wrapped a towel around herself.

The look on his face was very close to the one he bore when she was in Phobos' clutches. His eyes were crimson, and she bet he would have fangs if she could see inside his mouth. He looked ready to kill—again.

"Amanda, you seem to think I give a shit about your girl parts at this moment. I want to know who put those scars on you. Now!"

"Move, Phantasos. Let me dress while I think of a good lie to tell you," Amanda pushed the god away from the door so she could go to her dresser and get clothes. Then she marched to her closet, dressed, and geared up to tell her story to another deity. *Fuck, Fuck, Fuck.* She thought as she pulled the hair that framed her face.

❖━━━━━━❖

Phantasos felt like a caged animal. He wanted to kill whoever did that to her. Unfortunately, he guessed he had already killed the one responsible. Had he known, Phobos' death would have been slower. *How long does it take to don clothes?* Standing in front of her closet door, which Amanda had closed, Phantasos threatened. "If you are not out here in one minute, you will be explaining those scars to me in your closet."

"Fine," she said as the door creaked open. "Have a seat. This is not a story I want to go into detail about. I will only tell you who and not the story. After this, don't ask me again."

Phantasos nodded and took a seat on the edge of her bed. With his elbows on his knees and his face in his hands, he geared up to hear what she had to say.

"Phobos asked me if I was your whore. Then he proceeded to carve it into my flesh. He's dead. You killed him, and that's all that matters now."

"Who knows about this?" Phantasos asked, his face still in his hands.

"For a long time, only your father. I made him promise never to tell anyone. Especially you. Reluctantly, he agreed but thought I should tell someone. It wasn't until we were in Greece that I confided in Kallisto. They are the only two who know. Now you."

Both sat in silence. It was taking all his willpower not to destroy everything in his path or go to his father and confront him for not letting him know what happened to her.

"What else?" his large hands still covered his face.

"I told you not to ask. Some things are not meant to be shared with others. This is my burden to bear," Amanda said. He could hear the sadness in her voice and knew she was hiding a lot more.

When he finally looked up from his hands, he wiped a traitorous tear from his face. "I know there is more. One day, maybe you will trust me enough to confide in me. That bastard scarred you because of me—because of our bond. I am so fucking sorry, Amanda. He stood and pulled her up to meet him, then engulfed her in a hug, hoping she could feel his concern and pain. Her body began to shake, so he held her tighter.

Once she finally succumbed to sleep, Phantasos sat beside her bed. She looked so peaceful. He knew without doubt Phobetor had intervened at some point and allowed her to sleep without nightmares. He made a mental note to thank his brother. But his father. He would be visiting soon, whether his father was welcoming or not.

He had not set out to watch her shower but noticed odd behavior and knew she was hiding something. He hoped it was a less-than-glamorous tattoo or an odd birthmark. Instead, he found a pink jagged scar stating she was his whore. The blood drained from his face at that moment, and he lost all common sense. The next thing he knew, he was pulling back her shower curtain and demanding who had hurt her.

I should have gotten to her faster that night. He mentally berated himself.

⋄⊳——⊷——⊲⋄

"It's been two weeks since I told Phantasos, and I've yet to lay eyes on him," Amanda answered, what had to be the hundredth time Kallisto questioned her about the fantasy maker. Even she could admit she was irritated, especially after telling the last customer that Greek gods were mostly assholes and receiving a reprimand from John, the gallery's manager.

Kallisto held up both hands, palms out. "Okay, okay. Why is he staying invisible?"

"I assume because those three weird sisters haven't given him the okay to do whatever they think he wants. Anyway, I refuse to let him know it bothers me. Especially after seeing him wipe a tear from his own face. I mean, what the hell?" It was Kallisto and Morpheus' turn to play bodyguards.

"Does Kai know you're back?" Kallisto asked, thankfully changing the subject.

"I told him yesterday. He's at his dad's on the Big Island. He plans on coming over when he gets back."

"What are you going to do?" Kallisto asked as she dusted the frames, and Amanda took care of the sculptures.

"What do you mean? Nothing's changed, really. Unless he's started dating someone seriously. Mark ended up being an elf, which still freaks me out," Amanda said as she dusted a miniature replica of Hades' Cerberus made from Onyx. Fingerprints on sculptures made from Onyx were almost impossible to dispel.

"You know very well I'm not talking about Mark," Kallisto said, stopping her dusting and looking at Amanda.

"He told me that I was *his*, but nothing could ever happen between us," Amanda had given up. There, she told her bestie what she wanted to know.

"He what?"

"You heard me." Amanda put the Cerberus down and walked to the back of the gallery, thankful Morpheus was running errands and John was in the back helping unload a truck.

"He actually said that?"

"Yep. Evidently, we're meant to be together but can't be," she rolled her eyes. "He kissed me several times. We began to get along, but nothing since I admitted to him that Phobos scarred me. So, if Kai wants to go out with me, I don't see why not." Amanda grabbed her water from under the counter and took a long sip. She had been constantly thirsty lately.

"You know gods work differently than men, right?" Kallisto asked.

"Yes. They are a lot more arrogant and flightier," Amanda said, grabbing her clothes and walking to the next sculpture, sarcastic and frustrated.

"If he thinks you belong to him, he won't take you dating very well. Maybe you should be concerned for Kai's life." Just then, the door chimed, and Amanda was saved by a baby-faced man in a Henley top and faded jeans. His tortoiseshell glasses and Rolex rounded out his look—rich.

Amanda made it about ten feet from the customer when Kallisto flashed before her. "Why are you here?"

"What's going on?" Amanda's wide eyes looked the man over once more.

Without looking at the man, Kallisto answered her. "He's not a human man. He's another Satyr. And I repeat," Again, Kallisto addressed the man. "Why are you here?"

"I was sent to keep an eye on you, Amanda. Hermes sent me. You may ask Annika about me. She is my half-sister."

"Until your story pans out, you are not allowed here—Annika's at the library. Come back with her, and you will be allowed. Not until then," Kallisto's eyes darkened and swirled.

What the hell? When did her eyes start doing that? Amanda wondered.

"I understand. I will be back with my little sister. In the meantime, I will let Hermes know you are being taken care of," the well-dressed Satyr left.

"How did you know?" Amanda asked.

"Know what? That he wasn't human?"

"Yes. How can you tell?" Amanda felt nothing off kelter from the cherub-faced man.

"His signature was different. It was not near as strong as a god's, but strong enough to be a creature. I knew he was a Satyr because it felt like Annika's and Satyr's signatures have a specific register."

"What good is being a demi if I can't feel the difference between a cute, rich human man and a mythological creature?" Amanda huffed.

"That's what you have me for," Kallisto smiled.

For the next hour, they listened to music and busied themselves cleaning the gallery.

"Annika texted. The man is her half-brother. She's not happy that neither he nor Hermes let her know he would be showing up. My great-granddad must be checking to see if my security's secure," Amanda rolled her eyes as she read Annika's message.

It wasn't five minutes later when Annika and her brother walked into the room through the back door. John had given Annika a part-time job with them. The Gallery of the gods literally supported gods and creatures.

"Everyone, this is my brother, Thando. Thando, this is Morpheus, Kallisto, Amanda, and my boss, John.

"Nice to finally meet you," Thando said to Morpheus, then hugged the Oneiroi. Morpheus' eyes almost popped from his head. He wasn't a hugger unless they came from Kallisto or her mother. Kalli giggled at Morpheus' stiffened posture.

Restraining from laughing, Amanda interrupted the Satyr's enthusiasm. "So, how long have you been spying for Hermes, Thando?"

Thando moved from Morpheus to Kallisto and hugged her just as tightly before answering. "Spying is usually my sister's thing. Hermes asked if I would do him this favor. I had to accept the job since it allowed me to meet Morpheus and Kallisto in person."

"He won't be around long," Annika interrupted her brother's *fan-girling*.

"Now, now, sister. I do not see why I cannot stay for a while. After all, surely more eyes are better."

Amanda cleared her throat. "As much as I appreciate the sentiment, Thando. I'm a very private person. It takes a lot for me to allow my best friends to stalk me twenty-four-seven. I'm not comfortable with beings I just met watching me do all the things a human has to do on a daily basis. Sorry. Just saying."

"That is fine. I understand. So, tell me. Where are the other Oneiroi?" Thando's fandom knew no bounds.

Everyone got to know Annika a little better as they watched her interact with her brother. Satyr's siblings seemed much like human ones; they irritated each other but loved each other just the same.

After closing, Amanda went home for some much-needed sleep. Hopefully, tonight, she could turn her mind off and not lie in bed thinking about the god watching over her.

Amanda had to travel everywhere with either Kallisto or Morpheus. She supposed once classes began, she would ride with Phantasos to school unless Kallisto had courses at the same time. Unfortunately, Kallisto's major was ancient civilizations, and hers was marine biology; besides their literature class, their schedules were vastly different and on different sides of the campus.

Classes began in two weeks. *Ugh.* That meant more time with Phantasos watching. She didn't understand his keeping in the shadows, not since their conversations in Greece. Not since he kissed and — *forget it, Amanda. He's not for you.* That's all she seemed to do lately. Reprimand herself for wondering about Mr. Fantasy.

Waking only twenty minutes ago meant Phantasos was still watching over her. She could feel him, but he had not spoken with her since he learned of her scars. Nothing seemed to rattle him. She'd worn her skimpiest nightwear, read explicit books, played coy, and seductress—nothing. Not one word. *And I'm thinking about him again.*

Her mother called, letting her know Kallisto was at the door. It said a lot when her friend coming through the front door felt odd. Since Kalli had learned of her abilities, she just popped in whenever she liked.

"Coming, Mom."

✦⊢———⊣✦

What was he thinking when he decided to take the fucking night shift? He had endured Amanda wearing too little for his imagination to wearing nothing while rubbing soap all over herself and moaning in her sleep only to look into her explicit dreams he had no business seeing. Phantasos had decided the way he would die would be by overstimulation. He was never meant to be celibate, but thinking of anyone else in that manner felt wrong. He was positive he would be unable to keep from her much longer. It was easier when they feigned hating each other. Well, he pretended. He was fairly sure she hated him or did in the beginning. After the last two weeks, she may hate him again. After all, he was *ignoring* her—treating her like a job. She did not understand that he saw and heard her—all of her—all the time.

Needing to focus on something more practical, Phantasos flashed to the cave, where he vented his frustrations on the practice dummies until exhaustion set in, and he had no choice but to nap.

Three hours and five stores later, Kallisto and Amanda were laden with bags and boxes. It had been months since they'd shopped together, and she had missed it. It was moments like this that she felt so thankful Amanda had forgiven her.

"Let's get an iced coffee," she suggested as they passed Cold Brew.

"That sounds good. I'm tired and so thirsty," Amanda said, following her into the air-conditioned room, where the smell of coffee and hints of chocolate enveloped them.

"I love the smell of this place. Coffee and chocolate, there are no better scents," Kallisto said right before her back went ramrod stiff. Looking around, she searched for the creature.

"What's wrong?" Amanda whispered.

"There's a nymph, no two, close by. I don't think they're in here. I believe they are just outside."

"They can kiss my ass. I want coffee," Amanda snapped.

Kallisto touched her bracelet. Seconds later, Morpheus walked into the coffee shop. "You two, okay?" he asked.

"I feel two nymphs close by. Just outside here," Kalli said.

"I feel them, too. Give me a few minutes, and I will question them. Do not leave this shop until I tell you everything is clear," Morpheus said, turning and walking out.

"Why do you think they're here?" Amanda asked.

"Either on Hermes' orders or to keep an eye on you for other reasons."

Morpheus returned alone, and Kallisto realized she could no longer feel the signatures. "What happened," she asked.

"They felt *the pull* of Amanda and followed it. According to the nymphs, anyway," Morpheus said. "I will look into their minds once they sleep and find out why they were really here. Until then, I think it is best if you two return to your house since Thia will be there."

"Fine," Amanda spoke up. "We can go to Kalli's."

"You take Amanda. I will send your car over tonight. No need in driving when nymphs are in this realm looking for the pull on their senses," Morpheus said.

"I'm getting my coffee first," Amanda raised her brows.

"I will wait with you," Morpheus said.

Once the girls had their coffees, Kallisto locked elbows with Amanda once they were in the clear and took them to her house.

"I'm not sure I'll ever get the hang of being in one place one minute and seconds later in an entirely different one," Amanda said as she smoothed her shirt down. "This is getting out of hand. Since my grandmother lifted the veil over us, I have met more creatures than I thought was possible. And even stranger than that, not all are from the Greek Pantheon. I suppose any possibility I ever had of being normal again is truly gone."

Kallisto's heart hurt for her friend. None of them asked for all this craziness, but it was definitely here to stay. "I understand. I never asked to be a goddess. Well, maybe I wished for it, but nothing prepared me for what we're experiencing now. This thing with Ares is crazy. Unfortunately, he happens to have a crazy ass mother and a vengeful father, who so happens to be my grandfather. The gods don't beat by the same drums we do."

Amanda gave a forced smile, "You're a goddess."

"Yes, but I wasn't born into their world. I may have their blood and power, but my heart and soul are all human."

Kallisto spent the next several hours trying her best to lift Amanda's spirits. She ordered them pizza, brought down nail polish and charcoal masks, and put on a movie with Chris Hemsworth. Halfway through the movie, she received a message from Morpheus stating that the crew will gather at her house shortly.

"Shit, shit, shit," Kallisto earnestly began cleaning up the coffee table and pulling the dry mask from her face.

"What's going on?" Amanda asked.

"I just received a message," Kallisto tapped the side of her head. "The rest of the crew will be here any minute to discuss the nymphs today."

Amanda's eyes widened as much as they could with the black mask on her face. Before she could remove the charcoal, Nicole and Phobetor appeared in front of her.

"What in Hades' name do you have on your face?" Phobetor asked.

"It's a charcoal mask," Nicole answered for Amanda, who pulled at the edges, trying to work the mask off. "They clear out your pores."

Seconds later, Annika, her brother Thando, Morpheus, and Phantasos appeared beside Phobetor. Kallisto felt for Amanda, especially since she only had half her mask off, and he was there.

✦⟞⟝✦

Of all things holy, why me? Amanda thought as she looked at the group before her. A charcoal mask covered her face from the bridge of her nose to her hairline, and her hair was balled on top of her head. She wore fuzzy socks, pink night shorts, a white tank top, and no bra. *Yep. Kill me now.*

"Thanks, guys, for the heads up. I'll be back in five." She ran from the room and upstairs before she had time to register the amusement on their faces—or on *his* face.

She felt the shift in the air behind her as she peeled the rest of the mask from her face. Still, in her braless state, she refused to turn around. "What do you want?"

"To apologize," his deep voice sent shivers up her spine.

"For what?" She almost had all the charcoal off her face. Evidently, when in a hurry, the mask goes into some refusal mode, and what should have taken a minute took five to remove—four minutes more than she had.

"For not talking to you. When I saw you downstairs, it hit me what a bastard I have been," Phantasos admitted. "Our friendship came a long way over the summer, and here I am, putting it back to where I hated it being."

"Friendship," Amanda said under her breath without turning around. The mask was gone, but she still refused to look at him. After all, her tank top spoke volumes. She in no way wanted him to see her attraction to him—especially after he used the word *friend. Ugh. I'm such an idiot.* "Rest assured, *friend.* Our friendship is fine. Now, please leave so I can change into something more appropriate for a *friend* invasion." She was well aware of her sarcastic tone but didn't care. He'd hurt her—again.

"Look at me, Amanda," Phantasos' tone was stern.

"I'm not decent. Please leave."

"I have seen you in far less. In fact, I have seen you bathe, dress, and—"

Amanda interrupted him. The thought of how she'd dressed in little nothing and bent and twisted in hopes he would cave to her seduction was more embarrassing now that he'd used that word—*friends.* "Stop," she spun around with her arms crossed, shielding *them* from view. "What do you want, Phantasos? I told you our friendship is good."

"For Hades' sake, Amanda," he ran his hand through his hair. "I do not want to be friends."

"So, you don't want our friendship to be good. Well, I guess we can just—"

Before she could finish her rambling, Phantasos moved faster than she could register what was happening and, in that same movement, had her pinned to his chest and his lips on hers. Once reality hit, she closed her eyes and opened to him. Their kiss lasted longer than any before. It felt like a beginning and an ending all in one.

He pulled his lips from hers and pressed his forehead to hers. "Unless Ares is stopped, we cannot be more than friends. It is not what I want. It is what is best." With a kiss to the tip of her nose, Phantasos left the bedroom, by the door this time.

Staring at Kallisto's bedroom door, Amanda allowed the pent-up tears to fall. *Friends.*

Chapter XXVI

Library

The following two weeks went by in a flash of work and preparation for college. Established in their impromptu meeting two weeks prior was that creatures were going to pop up. The nymphs had told the truth. They followed a unique signature that led them to her. *Great* was the only thought she could muster that night after yet another strange being had snooped around. Unfortunately, the brief notion was followed by the object of most of her thoughts. Her mind stayed glued to the Greek god with gorgeous blonde waves, full lips, and sky-blue eyes—the one who decided to friend-zone her—*again.*

The next morning, with mirrored thoughts from the night before and a deep breath, Amanda chastised herself. She'd promised to stop dwelling on the eldest Oneiroi and start living for herself. That meant walking into the ornate gothic-styled building before her—English Lit.—*College English Lit.—this is it.*

"Ready?" Kallisto stood with her.

She knew her bestie was as nervous as she was.

"Nope. You?" Amanda continued to stare at the beautiful architecture instead of facing Kallisto, her heart racing. Irony wasn't lost on her. She had endured so much over the last year, and entering college for her first class had made her palms sweaty and her head feeling strange—*nerves.*

"Not in the slightest. I can't believe this is happening. We. Are. In. College," Kallisto said, emphasizing each word, making Amanda's brow join in with her palms.

"Here goes nothing," Amanda said as she stepped toward her future beside her best friend and one of the most powerful goddesses of the Greek Pantheon. Life sure had changed, *and not all for the better.*

⁕⸺▪⸺⁕

Phantasos gripped the railing of the top-level banister in the college library, invisible to readers and those kissing in the stacks behind him. He was sure he would go completely mad if one more human asshat, a word he learned from Amanda, looked at her with lust one more time. He could smell their desire for her and Kallisto and was sure the pricks would die if Morpheus stood in his shoes. Luckily for mankind, Kallisto just left for another class, leaving Amanda with her new friends. The rail creaked under the pressure of his tightening grip. This was his fourth experience with jealousy, and each one was due to the demigod on the first floor who now sat with two girls and three, *fucking three,* boys. He refused to think of them as men. All three of them were interested in Amanda. *Nope, not happening.* He had seen enough for one day.

Materializing, wearing a gray Armani Suit jacket over his white D.F.O. T-shirt stating, in bold black script—*Fantasy Made Real,* he walked down the staircase, keeping his eyes trained on the group. He did not give a shit if someone saw him emerging out of thin air. Humans were interesting beings. They *saw* what they could comprehend. If they saw what they could not comprehend, they shook it off. It was rare when they would convince themselves that they had misread the situation.

Those who did not shake it off and told the tale were usually considered *not all there* by the rest of humanity.

Right before he stepped off the stairs, Amanda looked up and stopped talking to stare open-mouthed at him. The shock on her face was priceless. He tilted his head, acknowledging that he saw her, too. Everyone seated with her turned to see what had caught her attention. When the mouths of the other ladies fell open and the boys' eyes narrowed, he could do nothing but smirk as he sauntered to their table.

"Uh, Pha, I mean Christos. What are you doing here?" Amanda stammered, face flushed.

He had to give it to her, she thought fast on her feet. Calling him by his given name would definitely raise eyebrows. She thankfully remembered his alias from months ago.

Good catch, ἄγγελος. He pushed his thought into her mind.

The girls at the table looked at her with curiosity written across their faces. The boys continued assessing their competition. Not that he would ever compete with them. They could not play in his league.

"I came to see how your first day was going. And to take you home," Phantasos saw the girls biting their lips and their eyes perusing his body in his periphery, but he never looked away from Amanda's bright blue eyes.

"Hello," the redhead at the table held her hand out to him. "My name is Shannon."

Phantasos reluctantly moved his eyes from Amanda to the flushed redhead and turned his smile up a couple of watts. "Hello, Shannon. He took her hand and kissed her knuckles. "I am Christos."

Not being outdone, the brunette elbowed her friend and introduced herself. After their introductions, he looked back at Amanda, whose eyes were narrowed. *Jealousy.* His grin grew—an eye for an eye and all.

"Is your accent Italian or Greek?" Shannon asked.

"I am from Greece," Phantasos answered, still looking at Amanda. "If you ladies do not mind, I will ask to take Amanda off your hands." He never addressed the males at the table and continued to look at only Amanda.

Amanda gathered her things with a half-hearted smile, let the group know she would see them on Wednesday, and followed him out the library's front door.

"What the hell was that?" Amanda shrieked at Phantasos as soon as they were alone.

"I have no idea what you mean?" he smirked, one hand in his suit pants and one on her lower back, guiding her to his motorcycle.

"Wait. You want me to ride that," Amanda pointed at the red Ducati Diavel V4.

"Yes. Is that a problem?" Phantasos was pleased her questioning was now all about his bike. He wanted to discuss his jealousy as much as he wanted to see her with those asshats.

"Well, I've only ridden a bike a couple of times. It looks fast. And you're in a suit, for Zeus' sake."

"It is fast. And, once we are on the bike, my clothes will be sufficient," Phantasos loved the slight anxiety playing across her face. She looked excited and a little scared. "Here," he handed her a helmet.

"Aren't you going to wear one?" Amanda removed the hair tie from her wrist, and put her hair in a low ponytail, then pulled on the helmet.

Phantasos smirked, "I am a god. There is no need." He slung a leg over the bike and gestured for her to get on behind him. Now, hold on my ἀγγελος."

Amanda gave him one last anxious look and mounted the back of the bike. He felt her jump when his suit turned to jeans. He kept his t-shirt on, though. *She needs a reminder.*

Phantasos was damn sure this was a bad idea, but he did not give a fuck. After watching human boys and men fawn over her all day, he no longer cared. Being on the bike with her reminded him of the man he was before Marissa's death—carefree and reckless.

When he went around curves, her legs and arms tightened around him. So, he took the curviest roads at dangerous speeds. When Amanda giggled, his heart surged. *Nope, not good.* Being this close to her was making him lose his mind.

⁕━━━⁕

This was the most fun she'd had in so long. The warm body she was pressed to at speeds she could barely comprehend made her feel alive. *Damn, he smells good.* She could live without the curves, though. She feared their knees would hit the road each time they rounded a bend. Her hands and legs squeezed, readying for impact. This seemed to encourage him to drive faster. *Where are we going?* The mental discussion made riding a bike even better. *Intimate.*

Deciding to take matters into her own hands, Amanda allowed them to roam when on straightaways. She'd just thought the tightening of her legs made him drive faster. When she ran her fingertips over his hard-defined abs and then placed them flat on his thighs as far as she could reach and slowly moved toward them, he revved the bike, and the front wheel came off the ground. At that moment, she'd never clung to another being as tight as she did Phantasos. Her mouth hurt from smiling so wide. Returning her arms around his waist, she buried her face in his back and giggled. She could, without doubt, get used to this.

They rode for almost an hour. Pulling her face from his back, she saw they were getting close to her house. What's next? Would he come in? Her dad was still in South Africa, and her mom wouldn't be home for several hours. Her hands began to sweat, and she felt her heartbeat pick up. How long had it been since a man made her sweat with nervous energy? Oh yes. It was the night the man she was clinging to took her to the art gala.

Zoned out in memories of that night, Amanda was jarred back to the present when the bike slowed to the front of her residence. It stopped, and Phantasos didn't move. Not wanting the moment to be any more uncomfortable, Amanda removed herself from around the deity and handed him his helmet.

"Thanks for the ride," she felt the blush heat her face and neck. He raised his chin in recognition of her thanks and fucking drove off. *Seriously?* Amanda stood there, hair a mess, dumbfounded.

"Fine. I'm done playing his games and waiting—Done!" Amanda swore loudly.

Checking her phone to see if Kallisto had called, she noticed Kai had texted again. He had returned from vacation a few days ago and texted, but she had yet to answer. Not wanting to admit it, to even herself, she was waiting to see if Phantasos would pull his head out of his ass. Obviously, that was a no. So, she texted her ex back. Kai was always up for a good time.

Twenty minutes later, she was in the passenger seat of his jeep. In the backseat was Kai's best friend, Mike, and a new girl. She couldn't help but wonder what happened between him and Shea. She liked Shea. Oh, well. They were all young. She grinned inwardly. She was technically young, but after the last eleven months, she felt much older than her eighteen years.

Kai was so laid back. He never asked why she had waited to text him back. Instead, he asked if she wanted to go to a beach party. When she'd answered the door, he smiled without a care. His wavy black hair had grown over the summer and was now to his shoulders, and she could have sworn he'd gotten taller. Those damn brown eyes told her he was a lot more into her than she was him, but she'd never tell him that. He was very handsome, although he was no Greek god. *Stop it, Amanda.* She inwardly scolded herself. Here, she sat beside a great guy her own age. Still, she had to admit to herself they were in different places. He was young and without worries. Technically, she was young, but her life was riddled with burdens and uncertainties.

Damn it. She'd forgotten. Phantasos may have left on his motorcycle, but he was not gone. She felt his presence. After the stunt he pulled, taking her from her friends at the library, giving her a great hour on the back of his bike, then leaving her with a chin tilt, he had better stay invisible. *I hope he enjoys being a voyeur.* Not that she'd be having sex with Kai. She'd lied to Phantasos. She hadn't slept with Kai. But his arrogance at the library and that damn chin tilt had pissed her off. A grin spread across her face.

Kai jumped out of the Jeep and ran around, pulling Amanda into their second hug since he had met her on her porch. Then he and Mike grabbed the cooler out of the back of the Jeep. The four made their way to the large stack of wood under construction for the evening's festivities. Amanda jumped in and helped everyone set up the area around the fledgling bonfire. The fire would get huge, so she ensured their seats were back far enough to avoid getting too hot. Beach parties were about hanging out with friends and making out once a sufficient number of beverages were consumed. The friends part would be a stretch since Mike's new girlfriend wasn't nearly as nice as

Shea had been. Amanda needed the scoop. Feeling a little bad about comparing the girls, she tried to find common interests with her. Her name was Leilani. She was beautiful with no hobbies and had the perpetual look of someone who thought everyone was beneath her. They would have to count on the guys to alleviate awkwardness.

"What's up with Mike's new girl? She's not very nice," Amanda asked Kai as she leaned back against him. They sat on a blanket, his back against driftwood, hers against his chest. His legs cradled her, and she had to admit that the closeness felt good.

"She's mad because I won't go out with her best friend,"

Kai said. "She's been after me since she and Mike started dating."

"Why didn't you go out with her?" Amanda asked.

"I was waiting for you to return."

A wave of guilt hit her stomach. She didn't feel for Kai as he did her. Her traitorous mind was always on a blue-eyed Greek god.

"What happened between Mike and Shea? I really liked her," Amanda said, changing her thoughts back to Mike and his new woman.

"Shea wanted to date other people, so she broke up with him right after school got out for the summer. He moped for a month, then another one of our friends set him up with Leilani."

"That sucks," Amanda said as she watched the flames jump around. A sudden flash of déjá vu hit her. It seemed like yesterday she was sitting on a South African beach with her father, flirting with Mark beside a bonfire. *What am I doing?*

Just as she wondered what the hell she was doing, Kai leaned down and kissed her. *Well, damn.* She'd forgotten how good his kisses were. Neck bent back to meet his lips; she pulled at the back of his long hair. Needing the connection, she decided to think about calling it quits with Kai another day—tonight, she'd enjoy him and the ambiance.

Chapter XXVII

Bath

Losing herself in the warmth of Kai's body and lips, Amanda almost forgot about her Greek problem. That was until someone tightly grabbed her arm and jerked her to her feet, away from Kai's hold.

"What the hell, man? What's your problem?" Kai quickly stood before her Greek problem, who was holding onto her arm like a vice.

"If you want your teeth in your head, sit back down. Amanda is coming with me," Phantasos snarled, glaring at Kai.

"Let me go," Amanda tried to jerk her arm free of the god to no avail. Phantasos slowly turned to look at her with red eyes. She hoped to God above that Kai could not make out his eye color in the dark. Not pleased with the situation, she knew if she made a scene, Phantasos would do something stupid, and the least of her worries would be Kai seeing the god's eyes.

"You heard her. Let her go," Kai glared at the deity, not knowing he was the closest he'd ever been to death.

"It's okay, Kai. I'll call you when I get home," Amanda knew she had to get Phantasos off the beach away from the teenage boy. Plus, he held her arm tight, so she needed him to calm down.

"Who is this jerk," Kai asked.

"He's fam—" Phantasos cut off Amanda's words.

"She is mine. Never touch her again." With that, Phantasos rushed her from the party and held on to her arm until the bonfire was a distant flicker.

"What the hell are you doing?" Amanda yelled at the god. She was sure her arm would be bruised tomorrow—his high-handedness had gone too far.

"I will not watch you make out with that human boy. Is he the one you were fucking before you went to Africa?" Phantasos continued at a brisk walk, now pulling Amanda along since she was no longer trying to keep him from killing Kai.

"Let me go, Phantasos!" She wasn't about to answer his question.

In one swift move, he let her arm go and then grabbed her by the throat. His eyes swirled red, his fangs shone in the moonlight, and he looked absolutely murderous.

Fear gripped her, and what she felt was a furred claw squeezing her throat. She felt lines of moisture roll down her cheeks, and her heart was racing.

"You will not warm any man's bed—mortal or immortal. Do you understand me?" After his words, his red eyes widened. He loosened his grip and then removed the tears that rolled over her jaw.

"You don't control me," Amanda barely got the words out.

"Amanda, listen to me closely. I am yours, and you are *mine*. I will never allow another being to harm you or be in your bed," then he was all lips, teeth, and tongue as he devoured her, one hand moved to her hip and the other in her hair. "I am so sorry I scared you. Forgive me ἄγγελος?"

She vaguely felt a shift in the air. When he released her from his possessive onslaught, both panting, she looked around at a place she'd never seen before. The furnishings were beautiful, even if they were in a—*cave*? *What the heck?* She jumped when her gaze landed on two wide-eyed nymphs watching them.

"Uh, Phantasos. Who are they?" She could feel the flush on her face. They had been making out in front of them. "Are we in a cave?"

"They are the house nymphs. This is Thetis. She's in charge." He rubbed one hand down his face and took a deep breath. "We are in the cave my brothers and I were born in and lived in for hundreds of years. This is where I went after I killed Phobos." Phantasos grabbed her hand, intertwined their fingers, and turned to Thetis and the other nymph, still watching their exchange. "Prepare us a bath, and then you may take leave to your quarters."

Amanda watched as he ordered his staff, and then it dawned on her that he had asked them to prepare one bath—for both of them. *Did I hear him right?*

❖━━━❖

What was he thinking? Bringing her to the Underworld, even if they were in the Asphodel Fields. This could be either very bad or the best decision he had ever made. He was sure Hades felt her presence as soon as he flashed them to the cave, and he would deal with the king of the Underworld later. At that moment, a lethal mixture of anger, desire, and the need to possess burned through his veins. The Fates had warned him time and time again. He supposed he should continue to heed their warnings, but he had stopped Amanda from being with two different men in a month's time. Plus, he had just scared her. He knew when he grabbed her throat and saw the look in her eyes, she was remembering the same thing he thought of—Phobos' hold on her. Knowing she was meant for him had slowly eaten away at his ability to keep away from her—*warnings be damned.*

Once the nymphs left the room, Phantasos turned to Amanda. He could feel his eyes swirling and knew they were crimson. Fortunately, his fangs had retreated.

"Amanda, I cannot keep doing this. All immortals fight their innate instincts to make decisions. We do not always win the battle inside of us. As a mortal man would say, the instinct to ravish you has me by the balls."

Her sheepish smile at his humanism made him relax a little. She was the most perfect creature he had ever seen, and her ability to piss him off made him just as hard as when she allowed him to touch her.

"Don't you think that I would become a shell of myself if you were to die, even if you never claimed me?" Amanda asked.

Memories of the husk he had become after Marissa died came to him. She was not bonded to him, but her death had rocked his world and that of his Pantheon. He supposed just having a bond would cause Amanda to retreat into herself. He had not thought of it that way. But if a bond made that pain worse—

Looking deep into her eyes, Phantasos thought of the worst-case scenario: he died, and Amanda lived without him; she died, and he burned down the mortal realm. At that moment, he could no longer find a plausible reason to hold back his desire. He was sure, no matter the outcome, if either of them were to succumb to death, the other would be distraught, no matter if he had claimed her.

He reached out and tucked a wayward strand of hair from her face to behind her ear, then cupped her cheek. "What do you think?"

"I know I'd be shattered," Amanda pressed her cheek against his palm.

Phantasos picked her up bridal style and took her to the bathing chamber.

He sat her down by a large pool of water. Steam rose from its surface and warmed the ambiance of the otherwise cold stone around them. Without looking away from her eyes, he grabbed the hem of her bathing suit cover-up and pulled it over her head. With an audible breath, he looked at all her smooth, sun-kissed skin covered by what humans considered a bathing suit. He found the term interesting. The only bathing suit he was accustomed to was bare skin. Rectifying the situation, he pulled on the ties at her back.

"Fuck," Phantasos growled. "I have seen you bathe but never stood this close, and I always looked away after a few seconds," he winked, then thought of the time he witnessed her scars. That moment was much different.

⊹▸————▪▪————◂⊹

Did he just wink? Holy hell. The literal fire in his eyes made her nervous and caused burning in her core, not to mention she was topless, standing inches from him. Weirdly, that didn't bother her at all. Instead, she was about to self-combust. With one finger, Phantasos began at her temple and slowly dragged it down her face, over her neck, and then around a nipple. The line he traced burned like a fire, marking her. She was sure every bit of skin left in that finger's wake was red and raw. Everything went dark when she closed her eyes and allowed the feelings to dominate her thoughts.

When he lifted his finger from her breast, she opened her eyes and looked at him. Biting his lower lip, he was staring at her bathing suit bottoms. He must have sensed her gaze because his eyes flicked to hers.

May I? Came his voice—in her head.

Shit, she'd forgotten he could do that. She nodded.

Phantasos' eyes flared even darker, black with a crimson ring. He hooked his fingers into her suit bottoms and achingly, slowly pulled them down her legs. The feel of his fingers sliding down her legs and his flared nostrils had to be the most erotic thing she had ever experienced, which included some very sexy scenes in the books she often read. He waited until she stepped completely out of her bottoms, then, while on his knees, kissed the scars carved across her pubic bone.

You are so beautiful, my ἄγγελος. Phantasos' spoke into her mind before standing to his full height.

In one swoop, he had her cradled bridal style again and carried her down the stairs into the heated water. She felt his clothes vanish before they were completely submerged. *That wasn't fair;* she spoke telepathically. *I didn't get to see you naked.* His chest rattled against her ear when he chuckled.

There will be time for that, my ἄγγελος.

The intimacy of telepathy wasn't lost on her. She wondered what sex would be like if you could be in the mind of your partner.

Wanna find out?

Are you listening to my thoughts? Amanda's full body flush had nothing to do with the warm water making its way over her breasts.

I cannot keep from it when we are in this state, and you are projecting them at me.

"Well, shit," Amanda said aloud, and Phantasos laughed.

Once fully submerged, his mouth was on hers again. Their bodies were now flush against one another, and she could feel his arousal against her stomach. If she was on her knees, the water came just under her chin. *Would it be inappropriate if I pushed away and looked?* She thought.

He grinned, not moving from her lips.

Damn it. I keep forgetting.

This time, he chuckled against her lips, and she could feel a slight redness in her face. His hands roamed her arms, shoulders, and back, leaving goosebumps in their wake.

Her hands equally explored his muscular frame. *Yep, built like a god.*

With a quick spin he had her back to his chest. Holding her by the neck, more gently this time, he whispered into her ear, "I am going to devour you whole tonight, my ἄγγελος."

Full body shudders. *Can people actually die from anticipation?*

The journey makes the destination a lot sweeter; his voice in her mind was like a caress.

CHAPTER XXVIII

LOVE

HAVING AMANDA AGAINST HIM, in his bath, naked—was
the best kind of torture. Her skin was soft and smelled like
the ocean, jasmine, and her. Reaching around her, he cupped
her full breasts and plucked lightly at her taut nipples. The
moans that came from her made his need grow harder. He
felt his fangs push through again. Ironically, with all the
beings he had been with over the millennia, no one had ever
brought on his battle form. Not even Marissa. It seemed his
need for her sexually was synonymous with his need to protect her. Without having to investigate that phenomenon, he
was certain that made him a lethal weapon when it came to
her.

Phantasos pulled her to the side of the pool, where a seat
was built for two with a rounded edge for his back. He
stretched out and laid her against his chest. Manifesting a
loofa and soap, he gently washed her chest and arms.

"Penny, for your thoughts," Amanda said.

"Sorry, but I do not understand," he admitted, still content watching the goose flesh on her arms as he lightly washed
her body and trailed soft kisses down her neck. *Ambrosia.*

"It means I'll give you a penny—American change worth
the smallest amount possible if you tell me what you're
thinking."

"I am not sure my thoughts are worth only a penny. How about I show you—later?" He smiled against her head and laid a soft kiss on it.

"But I want to know what you're thinking right now," She was adorable when she pouted.

"I was thinking about how you bring out the best and possibly the worst in me."

"Worst?" Amanda turned her upper body to look at him.

"I fight and lose the battle not to change form when you are around. I have never had that happen before. It seems my battle form is more emotionally driven than I ever knew. It manifests when I am angry at you, jealous of men around you, or aroused by you. I was the embodiment of self-control until—*you*."

"You didn't bare your fangs or glare with red swirling eyes while with Marissa?" she leaned against his chest and looked to the ceiling.

"No. Only you."

The last twenty-four hours had given her whiplash. That afternoon, she was riding on the back of Phantasos' bike, thrilled and excited to travel so fast while wrapped around him. Then, the indifference he showed her when he dropped her off at her house had her fuming. Next, she'd made up her mind to let him go. And now to this—naked—wrapped in his equally naked body, lying in a warm, balancing on the edge of a hot, pool of water in a *cave*.

She studied the cave as she enjoyed his ministrations. Stalactites hung from the vast ceiling in all shapes and sizes. The room they were in was huge. She could only imagine the size of the rest of the cavern. Every once in a while, the jagged walls would emit a sparkle. Not having any geology knowledge, she had no clue what rock or sediment would cause the effect. The color of the ceiling and walls had a lot more black in them than any of the caves she'd explored when visiting her grandmother. Plus, knowing Phantasos, she was no longer in her realm. *He did say he was born here.*

"Phantasos?" She caught his attention as she was losing hers. *Damn.* He was squeezing warm water from the loofa over her bare breasts.

"Yes, my ἄγγελος," his voice was deeper than usual, and his accent more pronounced. That voice alone could send her over the edge.

"I know we are in the cave you were born in, but where are we? Olympus?"

She felt him tense. "No. We are in the Asphodel Fields. Hades' realm—the Underworld."

That was not what she was expecting him to say.

"We're in the Underworld. Right now?" Amanda asked again. Maybe he hadn't understood her question.

"Yes. But on the good side," he continued caressing her.

"Should that concern me?" she closed her eyes.

"No. I will deal with Hades if he has an issue with it. He brought you here; I suppose I can, too. Now, what do you think about me showing you my bedchamber?" Phantasos smiled with hooded eyes.

Blinking rapidly, Amanda processed his question. Her heart picked up pace, and with a sultry voice she didn't recognize, she replied, "Yes."

As soon as the word left her mouth, he stood with her, once again cradled in his arms. This was becoming the norm. In a blink, she went from seeing the pool to seeing a substantial ivory engraved bed surrounded by black and gray jagged rock walls. The bed against the obsidian room was magnificent, warming the space. The ceiling was even higher than the two rooms she had already seen. *Stunning.*

"Wow," her eyes tried to take in the enormity of what she was seeing. "Oh, shit!" Was all she could muster in midflight as she flew through the air and landed in the middle of the gigantic bed.

With a chuckle, he landed above her, cradled between her thighs, holding his large frame up with his forearms.

"We're getting your bed wet," Amanda squeaked.

"I hope so," *he fucking winked—again. Who is this man?* Then, she realized he had heard every word when his light-hearted smile turned mischievous.

About to be a fantasy come true. Do you want this in a dream state or here—awake on all accounts?

"If I say dream state, does that mean it's not real?" Amanda asked aloud.

"Not in the one I would conjure. It would be as real as we are now. It would be more like realm hopping. Remember, I am the fantasy wielder."

"I see. I prefer to stay here—if that's okay with you," Amanda felt her skin heating under his stare. She knew he was the only fantasy she could take at that moment.

"It matters not where we are. I need to be here," he put his hand between them and gripped her sex. "Fuck," he closed his eyes and smiled. "Wet—Warm—

"Phantasos," Amanda squeezed her eyes shut, trying to forget about the pleasure between her legs and his gratifying weight on her chest. She needed to tell him something.

Yes? Speaking into her mind and kissing her neck did not lend to control of thought.

"I wanted to tell you that I lied to you," she finally got out.

"About?" he stopped moving, the now two fingers making her pant uncontrollably.

"I was never with Kai. In fact, I've only done this twice ever. And that was with my tenth-grade boyfriend, who proved to be a dick. It's been a couple of years since I allowed anyone to—"

Phantasos placed his index finger over her lips. His smirk showed complete elation. "Let me be your last."

Damn that voice.

His fingers began to pick their provocative rhythm back up, causing her eyes to roll back. Then he kissed her hard, moving his lips down her body. Every few inches, he would bite her flesh, not too hard, but it stung just enough that when he swirled his tongue to dispel the discomfort, she let out sounds that would be embarrassing if she had room in her mind to care.

Removing his fingers to a moan of protest, he looked into her eyes and sucked her arousal from them. *Fuck.* Phantasos then kissed all the way to her right foot, placing one gentle kiss in its arch, then another in the arch of her left foot. Continuing his way back up her left leg, he stayed true to using his lips, teeth, and tongue—*That tongue!*

Phantasos chuckled against her skin, the vibration running ahead of him—straight to her core. Finally, he reached her apex, where his fingers found her wet, and his tongue began to dance across her bundle of nerves. *Phantasos!* She exploded with pleasure after seconds. His body stiffened, and he, too, shook against her thighs. *That was embarrassing.* She told him, mind-to-mind. *I bet you're all proud of yourself. You barely touched me.*

I am just getting started. That was one.

Are you counting my orgasms?

Our orgasms.

What?

He flicked his eyes up from between her thighs and grinned. *Just wait, my ἄγγελος. You will see.*

Never mind, that was the most erotic thing she'd ever seen.

Caressing her body with his mouth, torturing every inch of her as he slowly climbed back up her body, coming face to face and staring into her eyes. She could swear he could see through her.

"Look at me, Amanda. I want to see your eyes when I enter you and make you mine."

"Condom?" she asked.

He shook his head. "No need. I am a god, remember? I can sense you are not; what is the word humans use?"

"Ovulating?"

"Yes," Phantasos smiled. "Trust me."

"Okay," she knew he would never allow any pain to come to her. Her mind reeled. He knew who was after them, and pregnancy would not be a good idea. Plus, he may be a god, but she was still young in human years. Bare. He was about to take her bare.

Her reflection appeared in his eyes. She looked wanting and sexy. This is how he was seeing her. At that moment, her heart stopped racing, and pure lust gripped her. He rubbed her sex with the head of his. Spreading wetness all over them both. He stopped at her entrance and slowly pushed in, giving her time to expand.

What the hell! An immediate pleasure she could not fathom skated through her body. She felt everything. *Holy fuck, Phantasos.*

Yes?

I might have a heart attack. It's too much. She was not experiencing one-sided carnal pleasure, which she was sure would be amazing. No, she felt her pleasure—and his. She could feel everything he was feeling. *Are you feeling what I'm feeling?*

She felt his smile against her lips as he plundered her mouth, covering both of their moans.

This is what it is like to be fated and taken. That is what I meant by our orgasms. I felt yours earlier; you will feel mine, too.

I may not survive this. Oh, god. She felt her own tightness and heat. What it was like for the man and, of course, her own pleasure—every hair follicle on her body, and his, stood on end. Every inch of him gliding in and out shot so much bliss through her body that she was not sure she would live. Thank goodness she had the blood of the gods running through her veins. That may be all that kept her conscious.

He pulled from her body and moved behind her, laying them on their side and re-entering her heat. His arms wrapped around her, and she felt his entire body against hers.

"I love you, Amanda."

"I love you, Phantasos," and that's when his orgasm took them from unimaginable bliss to a pleasure she could not handle. Darkness.

Blinking her eyes open, Amanda felt like all her limbs were weighted, and tingles ran up and down the length of her body.

"Did I lose consciousness?" Amanda slowly sat in the enormous bed and watched the Greek deity saunter toward her with a wet cloth.

With a smile, Phantasos nodded and then ordered, "Lie back."

She looked from him to his possession with curiosity. He then did something that almost made her black out again.

Phantasos took the warm cloth and began to clean her from where he had made her his. Before he looked back at her face, she closed her gaping mouth. Was this the god who had her on a rollercoaster for almost a year?

With a flash of his other hand, the cloth was gone. She couldn't help but wonder where he'd sent it to. Walking to his wardrobe, he removed loungewear for them both. This made her curious.

"Why do you use your powers to dress sometimes, but others you don't. I mean—why not always just, poof?" She mimed the poof.

"Just proof?" Phantasos mimicked with a wink.

"Yes, just poof," she could feel her smile match his.

"I do not have an answer. Sometimes the moment calls for it, and sometimes it does not," he lifted the cover and moved in beside her. "Come here," he opened his arms for her to enter.

"I passed out. Now, that's embarrassing," Amanda was glad her back was to his chest because she could feel the flush rising.

"From what I have heard, fated sex often leads to unconsciousness. You were not out long. About thirty seconds was all."

A half a minute for him to witness her in a postcoital blackout—*Great!*

"You were and are gorgeous after orgasm. Stop concerning yourself," he whispered against the top of her head.

Amanda felt another wave of embarrassment. She wanted to be as desirable to him as he was to her. Knowing he had millennia on her made her more self-conscious than she would be with a man who not only looked her age but was her age. Would she ever stop feeling awkward around him?

"Will you tell me about this cavern?" she asked.

"Later. Right now, we should discuss what just happened between us," Phantasos tightened his arms around her.

"Uh. Okay, I guess." The last thing Amanda wanted to do was verbalize what just went down between them. It was one thing to be lost in the moment of sexual tension and bliss—another to discuss it once you were sated and spooning.

"I claimed you. All immortal beings will sense the change in us both. They will know."

"So, my mother, grandmother, and our friends will know we just had sex?" Amanda was mortified. "That's—" she had no words to describe how messed up that was.

His hold tightened again. "Yes."

"Yes—just yes? That's all you have to say?"

"There is nothing else to say. It is part of our signature now," Phantasos said.

"Well—" Amanda's mind raced. "Maybe since they can't feel a signature from me, they won't know." She clung to hope.

"They will feel it from my signature. Besides, how do we know that is completely so? The gods could tell we belonged together before your concealment was lifted."

"How?" Amanda asked, hoping he was wrong.

"First, I will be more of a shadow than ever. You are more than eternally stuck with me. Second, everyone already knew how we felt. According to our friends and my brothers, we are the only ones who needed to be convinced."

"Having my family know is going to be difficult. My mom shares everything with my dad," she groaned, covering her face with her hand. "My dad knowing is mortifying."

"Your parents will learn that the life of an immortal is quite different from that of a mortal. Lifespans are just the beginning; as I mentioned earlier, we are controlled by our basic instincts and constantly work to regulate our actions. Humans have made it an art not to listen to their intuitions. In many cases, that gets them killed."

"What do you mean?" Amanda asked.

"Warriors and protectors use their senses to fight and protect. That was why immortals were made. We fight to avoid being savage. Humans were made to be protected by immortals. This allowed them to push their instincts to the back of their minds. Often, those instincts take over, though. Especially when it comes to mortal mothers and the military. But for the average mortal, they have smothered a lot of their natural intuitions. If humans allowed their senses to guide them, many would stay away from danger. Instead, they run straight into it. That is also why I can appear out of thin air, unnoticed, in the middle of a college library."

"Interesting," Amanda rolled to her back so she could see Phantasos' face. "My parents have no idea that I wasn't a virgin."

His body tensed briefly, then he relaxed and said, "Good. I am glad they will think it has only been me."

Slowly, Phantasos' hand caressed her stomach and rubbed circles over her heated skin. After several more hours of bliss, she woke from another blacked-out state, completely sated.

Chapter XXIX

Classroom

THE NEXT THREE WEEKS were a mixture of amazing and mortifying, just as she had expected. Her father was not happy to learn his little girl was *fated* to an Oneiroi. She actually thanked God that Phantasos was immortal. She was sure if her dad could have wounded him, he would have. According to her dad, no matter her age, she would always be his little girl, and no one, not even a Greek god, was good enough.

Phantasos had not been wrong. When he was on duty to watch over her, he was visible. Often, they realm-hopped or went to amazing places on Earth. Life was great. There had only been a couple of creatures pop up. She could only think that when he claimed her, her new signature that only the creatures could sense became different enough to keep the masses away. After all, no one wanted to be on the wrong side of any of the Oneiroi. Or could it be the presence of her Oneiroi? *Her Oneiroi.* Of course, everything they came up with was just a possibility. None of them knew if her signature or lack thereof had anything to do with the creatures.

It was the beginning of October, and she and Kallisto had settled into life as college students. Lit class was by far her favorite. It had taken a lot of convincing for Phantasos not to follow her into the classroom. She wanted, no, she needed that time without him—time to be around Kallisto and celebrated stories written by brilliant authors. After the first couple weeks, he became more comfortable leaving her alone with Kallisto, as they enjoyed literature class without him hovering.

It was their second test in the class, and this one was all about Jane Austin's mark on romance. After finishing their examination, they were to leave quietly to allow the rest of the students time to finish. It hadn't been a shock when, out of the corner of Amanda's eye, she saw Kalli turn her test in and return to grab her backpack. Both of them were avid readers, but Kallisto loved the classics where she was more of a rom-com girly, and when she really needed an escape, she loved to dive deep into high fantasy. The classics were great, but not her go-to. So, she wasn't surprised when her bestie finished her test before anyone else, effectively leaving her alone for the first time in weeks.

Twenty minutes later, Amanda finished her exam. As soon as her paper landed in the tray, she felt it or, better yet, some-one. And this time, she was positive it wasn't Phantasos or another of her friends. Someone in the room was watching her. Slowly, she turned from the tray and frantically scanned the room for—There, in the back, sat— "No." *...Please, no. It can't be. I'm seeing things.*

"Miss?" the professor's aide asked, waking her from her stunned, unmoving silence. "Are you okay?" Or that's what she thought he asked.

She squeezed her eyes shut. When she reopened them, she saw a girl hunched over her test, writing quickly where she thought she had seen a nightmare. Ignoring the concerned aide, Amanda grabbed her things and hurried to the door.

Taking one step into the bright sun, she finally let the air out of her lungs.

"Amanda, over here," Kallisto called to her.

She stood just feet from her best friend, but it felt like miles. How was she going to explain what just happened?

"What's wrong?" the ever-astute Kallisto asked.

"I'm calling Phantasos. I'm not feeling so well," Amanda answered. "He'll take me home."

"You were feeling fine before the exam. What's wrong?"

"Can we discuss this later? I really want to go home."

"Sure. I'll come by after my classes."

Amanda called for Phantasos using nothing but a thought. Their connection was getting stronger, much like Morpheus and Kallisto's had. She was also better at blocking him. It only took him one look at her to start questioning her just like Kallisto had.

"What is wrong? You look green." Phantasos placed his hand over Amanda's and nodded to Kallisto, conveying he would take it from there.

"I'm not feeling well. Can you take me home so Kalli can finish with her classes?"

"Of course. Wanna ride the bike or just—"

"The fast way would be great," Amanda looked past him and searched the campus buildings for those ice-blue eyes and jet-black hair pulled into a topknot—the crooked smirk of evil perfection. She continued to hold her block in place. If Phantasos knew what she thought she saw, he would go ballistic.

"As you wish." Amanda saw concern in his eyes.

A second later, they were in her bedroom, where she excused herself and continued straight to the bathroom. Gripping the bathroom vanity, she worked to calm her racing heart and racked her brain to understand what she had just seen. *I thought I saw.* She corrected herself mentally. Why would she, all of a sudden, after months, see him out of the blue if he weren't actually there? Honestly, she hadn't thought about Ares in weeks. Not since she and Phantasos had become more. Her brain didn't have the capacity to think of much more.

⟡⸻⸻⟡

Phantasos had no idea what had spooked Amanda, but she looked scared when he answered her call. The summons itself was startling. Never had she *thought* his name, and he physically felt her need. The fear he felt through that mental call, plus the intensity of the pull, had his senses on high alert. Something was up, and he was determined to find out. He was a little annoyed that she was blocking her thoughts.

It took her forever to come out of the bathroom. He was taken aback by her tear-streaked face and red-rimmed eyes when she did. No longer annoyed.

"What happened?" he crossed the room and wrapped her in his arms. It pained him to see her so upset. Where he had always felt that way. Since their bonding, that was the only thing he cared about—Amanda's physical, mental, and emotional well-being. He could feel her heart racing, pounding through their clothes. This had him bracing for the worst. Whatever had his ἄγγελος so distraught had better prepare to face his wrath.

"I think I'm going crazy," her words came out muffled with her face buried in his shirt.

"Tell me what happened."

Amanda pulled her face out of his chest and told him her story. "After my exam, when I was turning my test in at the front of the room, I felt someone watching me. The feeling I used to get when—" Amanda stopped talking and looked into his eyes.

"Go on," he pushed for more, almost positive he knew what she was about to say. Waiting half a second for her to say—

"The feeling I always got when Ares was around. When I turned to face the desks and those who were still taking the test, I saw . . . I mean, I thought I saw him sitting at one of the desks in the very back. He gave me the same wide grin he always did before he punished me. I panicked and closed my eyes tight, and when I reopened them, the seat had one of my classmates finishing her test."

Phantasos was unsure what to say or think. Had she seen him? It was definitely possible. Ares has the ability to make you see things. It is possible he was either physically there or controlling her visions. Either way, he may be done with his mourning isolation.

"Did I ever tell you the story Hades told me when I was in Africa?" Amanda asked.

"No."

"He told me of an immortal who was wronged by a vile act from another god. The act was blamed on a third being. The one harmed swore never to allow anything like that to happen again. Apparently, this story has something to do with me needing to be careful."

"He never said the name of any of the deities, or what happened that was so foul?" Phantasos asked.

"He didn't. When I asked him questions, I found myself back in my bed. I wonder if the vile being was Ares," Amanda contemplated aloud.

"It could be, but it could be anyone," he answered. "I want to take you back to the cave for a while."

"No. I refuse to run. No matter what, everything will come to a head. If not now, in time. As Hades said, nothing ever stays buried."

"Would you like to speak with Hades again?"

"You can do that?"

"Yes. He will not like it, but he will get past it," His smirk made her laugh.

❖———◦———❖

After splashing cold water on her face and donning jeans instead of shorts, Amanda held tight to Phantasos as he removed a coin from his pants pocket and rubbed it between his thumb and index finger. One second, she stood in her bedroom; the next, she was outside black-carved doors, standing twice as tall as Phantasos, surrounded by heat and howls. She tightened her grip on the Oneiroi.

"What the hell is making those horrible wailing sounds? It sounds like women screaming."

"Hellhounds. Hades' favorite has three heads and one body. Its drool makes puddles that can cover the toes of my boots," Phantasos told her about the Cerberus at the gate as they waited. Hades knew they were there. He always did. He just wondered how long he would make them wait.

It was not long before red eyes blink in the distance. "Are those the hellhounds?" Amanda's swallow was audible. "I don't wanna die down here."

Before Phantasos could comment, the doors creaked inward, allowing entrance. As soon as they stepped into the dark throne room, the doors slammed shut, and all that could be heard was the hissing of snakes and their shallow breaths.

"Gorgons," Phantasos whispered.

"Madusa?"

"She is dead. The ones on either side of Hades are her sisters. Stay close to me," the Oneiroi said, walking toward the dais where Hades sat on his black throne, flanked by the hissing Gorgons, waiting.

Amanda kept pace with every step Phantasos took, staying by his side when all she wanted to do was bolt. The closer she got to the god of the Underworld, the more she recalled his striking features. The thin obsidian crown wrapped around his head was in stark contrast to his paler skin. He was shirtless, *Damn.*

Noticing Phantasos eyes cut her direction, she knew he heard her thoughts. Further confirmation of his knowledge was the very faint growl from his throat as he grabbed her hand, lacing their fingers midway down the center of the room. She must be crazy because his reaction caused her amusement. Who in their right mind forgot, even for a split second, that they were about to face the god of the Underworld while he sat on his throne? Mentally correcting herself, she again focused on the king before her instead of the fantasy beside her.

Those *striking* features on the throne were set in a grim, straight line. Hades wasn't happy about their intrusion.

Once ten feet from the platform housing the dark god, they stopped. Amanda gave Hades a halfhearted smile. His only movement came from his eyes. They jumped to their clasped hands.

"We need an audience with you," Phantasos announced, seemingly unconcerned with the stern look projected at him.

"I see. Why?" Hades' voice was deeper than she remembered. She could feel the three words vibrate in her chest.

Amanda tightened her hand, silently telling Phantasos to let her talk to the king.

"I believe Ares showed himself to me today. I have also been thinking about what you told me on the beach. I think the vile one in your recollection was the god of war. Am I wrong?"

Hades cocked his head. If she didn't know better, the corner of his lips twitched. "What makes you think that?"

"He's the one after Phantasos and me," Amanda glanced at their entwined fingers, showing the king they were unified. "If the story you told has any bearing on me, it must have something to do with your nephew."

Hades stood and ordered his Gorgons to stay on the dais. Their hisses grew louder. He then walked down the steps and stood directly in front of her.

"I see you have been claimed since we last spoke," Hades addressed her.

"Because our hands are clasped, or can you feel that from me—or just from him," She gestured toward Phantasos.

Again, Hades smirked. "Astute," the king complimented her. "Follow me. Both of you."

Phantasos never let her hand go. She was a little shocked by the blatant claim and his silence. He had understood her need to address the dark god.

The action of stopping made her jolt back to the moment, and the on-slot of her senses made her shudder. Moans of the condemned floated down the hall, and her skin rose in goose-bumps. Her mind had wandered while walking behind Hades and beside Phantasos for what had to have been ten minutes or more. She found herself by a cell, one off by itself. No moans came from the cell before them. No sounds at all.

CHAPTER XXX

PRIAPUS

INSIDE SAT A DIRTY bearded nymph with legs no bigger than Phantasos' forearms. "Who is this?"

"Ask him," Hades suggested.

Amanda spoke up, and he tightened his hand, letting her know he was there for her. His protective stance said everything the prisoner needed to know. *Do not fuck with her.*

"Uh, hi. What's your name?" Amanda sounded like she was speaking to a toddler.

The nymph looked up from staring at the floor, his eyes widening when they landed on hers. Phantasos had a bad feeling. His instincts were to grab Amanda and throw her over his shoulder, then vanish to a place where no more sadness or evil could ever touch her again.

With a scratchy and barely audible voice, the prisoner spoke, "Angelia?"

"No. That's my grandmother. I'm her doppelganger, Amanda. Do you know her?"

The prisoner's face popped toward Hades, who stood behind them with his back against the wall and arms over his broad chest. When Hades nodded his approval, for what Phantasos had no idea, the prisoner looked at Amanda again.

"You brought the eldest Oneiroi with you, why?"

"We are fated. Where I go, he goes. Can I ask your name?"

"Priapus," his voice was scratchy.

Phantasos squeezed Amanda's hand, telling her he wanted a turn. "I remember you. You are the one—" Phantasos spun on Hades. "Why the fuck would you bring her here to see this God-forsaken creature? He raped her grandmother for Zeus' sake." Phantasos' voice echoed loudly off the black walls, making the prison seem larger.

"Ask him if he did it." Hades was calm, unflinching under the Oneiroi's red eyes.

✦———✦

"He did what to my grandmother?" Amanda covered her mouth. *This cannot be true. I'm goin' be sick.*

"I never touched Angelia. We were only friends. My mother worked for her mother. She and I grew up together. It was not me," the prisoner's voice still scratchy but more earnest and determined.

Amanda felt the room spin. Someone, if not this prisoner, raped her grandmother. Her eyes began to burn. She was about to lose it.

"Then who was it?" She heard Phantasos growl out the words she wished she could ask, but with the room spinning, she was incapable.

"I have been tortured for almost a thousand years, and in that time, Zeus never asked me if I did it. He just continued to make me suffer for another's crime. A disgusting crime at that."

"Well, I am asking. Who did it?" Phantasos looked ready to cross the bars and kill the prisoner.

"If I tell you and he finds out, I will have suffered for almost a millennia for a crime I did not commit by the god who did or the king who thinks I did."

"Your choice is to die by Zeus' hand or mine." The Oneiroi stood so still waiting for the nymph's answer that Amanda was sure he wasn't breathing.

"If I tell you, you have to promise to kill me. I do not want to die at the hands of my torturer. I especially do not want to die by his son's bloodstained hands."

Amanda watched Phantasos contemplate the situation. She saw him look the prisoner up and down. He had to be looking at the horrible state the nymph was in. A thousand years of torture should have killed the nymph, but it looked like Zeus was purposely keeping the prisoner alive.

"If you are innocent, why do you ask that I kill you?" Phantasos asked.

"Once I tell you everything, I am dead. Plus, I am tired. I know I will go on to the Elysian Fields. I tried to help her."

"Fine," Phantasos looked at Hades, who again nodded. "I will do as you ask. Who raped Amanda's grandmother?"

◆━━━◆━━━◆

Priapus

"Like I said, Angelia and I were friends. Best friends, if I am truthful. She was as beautiful on the inside as she was on the outside, but she was like a sister to me. I loved a nymph who worked in Aphrodite's mansion. From what I understand, she went missing when I was imprisoned. I suppose there were to be no loose ends," he felt a lump in his throat. He had not thought of his love in ages—shame washed over him.

Shaking off that memory, Priapus continued his story. "Angelia's beauty was as potent as her mother's, if not more so. Ares had always wanted Aphrodite. They had been lovers before she and Hermes wed. If my memory serves, they shared two sons, but she would never marry him. In fact, she stopped going to his bed several millennia before she and Hermes married. The brothers hated one another because of Aphrodite's past with Ares, so they stayed away from each other."

"When Ares saw Angelia, she became his new obsession. He would turn up wherever she was and make her uncomfortable. He would whisper things in her ear and touch her anywhere he could without being too inappropriate. Once, she told me that he said she would be in his bed one day—soon. She was afraid and repulsed by the god and, due to his station, unable to tell anyone."

"In his sick and twisted mind, he loved Aphrodite, but she loved his half-brother, Hermes. So, he decided he would take their daughter if he could not have her. The only problem was she was half of the god he despised." Priapus stopped his story and closed his eyes. One tear ran down his cheek.

"This went on from when she was sixteen until—" he paused for another moment, rubbing his hands down his face, removing the tear. "We thought Ares' obsession would stop once he and Aphrodite married. After all, the fucker had who he wanted. But, no, he continued his torment when her mother was not around." Anger grew in his tone.

"I will never forget the look on Angelia's face and the tears running down her battered cheeks. I found her in her bathing chamber, curled in water so hot her skin was bright red and had started bubbling in places. I scrambled to get her out of the bath. She was limp, almost unconscious. She had magicked the water to boiling. I sustained burns getting her out. She was naked, covered in bruises and burns, and barely hanging on." Priapus choked on the memory. His one tear became two.

"When I asked her what happened, she looked into my eyes with so much pain and said—"He finally got me.""

"When I saw the blood running down her thighs, I figured it out and then vomited on the side of the bath. I am not sure what all he did to her, but it was barbaric. I wrapped her in a towel and carried her to her bedchamber. After making her as comfortable as I could, with salves, I put her between the cool sheets on her bed and held her until she finally fell asleep. I was so drained I fell asleep, too."

Needing to move around, he paced behind the bars. He had not allowed himself to think of that day in hundreds of years. It was still raw. Not because he was imprisoned but because of the pain his best friend had endured.

"I was woken by two guards when they pulled me by the hair of my head from her bed. The next thing I knew, I stood before Zeus, Hera, and Ares. One of the guards told a lavish story about hearing me yelling at Angelia and her begging me to stop. Zeus went rigid and red-faced. Ares smirked, and Hera stood immobile—emotionless. Zeus locked me in here and now, but he only comes by once every few weeks. In the beginning, he came multiple times a day. Over time, the abuse slowly became spread out. The longest time between beatings was three months. You would think that a blessing, but he made up for it when he finally showed."

"I swear to you on my last breath, all I have told is the truth. Hades knows. Now, fantasy maker, you must hold up your end of the deal."

✦■——··——■✦

Hearing Priapus's story made Amanda's stomach tighten with pain. She swayed on her feet and saw yellow spots of light everywhere. It took everything she had not to succumb to the yellow stars and hear everything he had to say. Her own story could have been much worse.

Once his story was finished, she woke cradled in Phantasos' arms on her bed. At first, she assumed she had fainted, but once woken enough to search her memory, she remembered Phantasos questioning Hades as he rubbed his flattened palm down her face, placing her in a deep sleep.

"He raped my grandmother, Phantasos. He's a monster. Why's he allowed to live?"

"Ares has always been a wild card. He fights like a beast winning wars for his father, but he has always treated women with disdain. All but Aphrodite. He practically worships the ground she walks on."

"Why does Zeus allow this? She's Aphrodite's daughter."

"I do not believe Zeus thinks the rumors surrounding his son are true. He only punished him by allowing me to render justice after he took you and Kallisto. Aphrodite sees Ares only as he treats her. Which is like a queen."

Amanda thought about Phantasos' words and remembered his vow. "Did you kill the nymph? Like he wanted?"

Phantasos turned his eyes from hers when he answered, "Yes. I used the Atlantean dagger Thia gave me. I had given it back after Phobos, but when she saw me last, she told me that your protection meant death to any god or creature who sought to harm you." Phantasos' words were almost a whisper. By his demeanor, she could tell the death of the nymph was not something he wanted to do or discuss.

"I need to go see my grandmother. The reason she left Olympus and never looked back, the reason she shielded all of us—it makes sense now. Will you take me to her?"

"Of course," Phantasos said, nodding.

"I should first tell Nicole, Mom, and Kellie what we learned. They may want to go with us."

"We should sleep first."

Chapter XXXI

Parents

Phantasos had taken Amanda back to the cave after learning of Angelia's abuse. She wondered if her stomach would ever be the same. Unable to eat, Phantasos had insisted she at least kept water down before she told her family the story.

Good to his word, he gathered her family in her Mom's living room. At first, he refused to leave her, but after a small argument, he agreed to stay upstairs while she told her parents, aunt, and cousin what her grandmother went through at the hands of Ares. It took a lot out of her to tell the story Priapus told, and seeing the pain and disgust on their faces caused her nausea to return.

Each of her family members took time to come to terms with what they heard, letting the truth set in after she delivered the horrible tale. Next, they discussed whether they should tell Angelia they knew about her horrible past. The pros were to show her they loved her and stood firm by her side—and they understood and forgave her for suppressing their signatures. The cons were opening up the horrific wounds Angelia endured and taking the first steps in verbally declaring how evil Ares was to the Greek Pantheon.

Having an heir of the Pantheon's royalty be the victim of his torment would implode Olympus' current facade of peace, even though it occurred a thousand years ago. Zeus would have no recourse but to acknowledge his son's dark side.

After several hours of debating, a unanimous decision was made to let her grandmother know that they not only knew of her past with the god of war but were willing to fight the bastard on her behalf—*and mine.*

✦———■———✦

"Amanda," Phantasos tapped her shoulder, interrupting her conversation with her mother. "Can we talk for a minute? I'm sorry, Kathryn. I will return her after a quick discussion."

"No worries. I was about to check on Kellie anyway," Amanda's mother left them, staring into each other's eyes.

Amanda crossed her arms over her chest. A stance he had come to know as her *don't fuck with me pose.*

"What's up?" She asked.

Damn, he loved seeing her gear up to argue. There was nothing like Amanda's smart mouth when angered. He knew what she saw. His scrunched forehead, followed by a mischievous grin. He could not help it. Was she wondering if he was about to whisk her away to a faraway realm, locking her up until his pantheon was set to rights? She would not be far off base. He had thought about it. But instead, he needed to let her know the Oneiroi would return in a few hours. They had things to discuss. Phobetor knew of the situation since he was with Nicole when the hammer dropped. Morpheus needed to be caught up, and they each needed to figure out their next steps.

"We are going to get Morpheus," he gestured toward his middle brother. "We have a lot to discuss. I will send Kallisto here. Between her and Nicole, you will be safe. All you have to do is summon me."

Tucking her hair behind her ear, he looked deep into her eyes, searching for fear. What he saw was determination. Amanda had hit that spot deep inside herself. The one that was done taking shit, the one that was ready to protect those she loved, so they would never endure what her grandmother had survived. He kissed her forehead and then left her standing in her parents' living room.

"Looks like you updated it, at least," Morpheus stood in the main room of the cave, arms spread out, spinning in a circle. "I never thought I would come back here."

"Olympus is not safe. This was the only place I could think of where Ares, hell, even Zeus would think twice before they just popped in. Want a drink?" Phantasos asked as he crossed the room to the bar. He needed one to calm his nerves. This was the first time he was far from Amanda since they were fully bonded, and he hated every second of it.

"Two fingers, please," Phobetor answered. "I knew Ares was horrible, but what he did to Angela and Amanda was revolting."

"We have several strong gods in the immediate royal line who will stand on our side. However, we need another king. Hades will either side with us or sit back and watch, but I am certain he will not fight against us. I have no idea where Poseidon's loyalties lie, though," Phantasos said as he poured drinks.

"You have seen the king of the seas since either of us have. From what Kallisto said about him lending Amanda the use of his horses, he took a liking to her," Morpheus said, taking his tumbler of whiskey mixed with Ambrosia.

"His interest in her had better stay platonic," Phantasos glared at the youngest Oneiroi and handed the other tumbler to Phobetor without looking at him. He wanted Morpheus to see his words referencing Amanda with any man, god, or other should be delivered with more care. *Damn. I need to get a hold of myself.*

"Sorry, brother," Morpheus gave him a half-smirk. "I forgot you are in estrus after over a century of—"

Phantasos balled his hand into a fist and took two steps toward his youngest sibling.

"That is enough, brother," Phobetor clapped Morpheus on his shoulder.

At least one of the idiots got it. Amanda had gone from being a distraction to an obsession in one long, intense night—every night since their first together made his mania grow.

"We need to know what strength Ares will bring to his day of vengeance. I thought we should split up and find out who we need to be wary of." Phantasos worked to ignore Amanda's pull on him. Even though he had just left her, his need to protect her was stronger than any instinct he had ever experienced. He began to pace. *Maybe coming to the cave was a bad idea.*

"You have a decent relationship with the weird sisters," Phobetor said to Morpheus. "You should meet with them. I will take Poseidon since he and our big brother here have been in contact recently, and I can feel the resentment coming off Phantasos in waves."

Phobetor laughed when he saluted him with his middle finger. "If he were to look at Nicole like he looked at Amanda, you would not be so fast in volunteering to see him either," Phantasos knocked back the remainder of his amber liquid and continued, "I will meet with Hades—again. Alone this time."

⊹⊷——⊶⊹

Amanda paced the front of her bed where Nicole and Kallisto sat, switching between biting her nails and rubbing her wrists where the cold manacles had once been. She could not shake the vision in her classroom. It was the first time since the night Phobos had taken her that she had seen Ares' face, even if it had been a vision and not reality. What sucked about memories, or the ones she had at least, was they came with smells and voices. Lavender and his masculine scent would have been alluring if it didn't turn her stomach after weeks of torment. When she closed her eyes, she swore she heard his low chuckle—the one he got whenever he noticed her wince.

"Amanda, you need anything? To talk about—" Nicole began but was cut off.

She could hear the concern in her cousin's voice. Should she lie and tell them she was good? Only a couple of months ago, she had sworn off the divine—including the two who stood in the room with her.

"Kalli, do you think you could find Annika? I haven't seen her in a while," Amanda ignored the elephant in the room. Nicole's scowl wasn't lost on her.

"Sure. Give me five," Kallisto vanished.

"I guess you told me," Nicole said, raising a brow, waiting for her to dodge the subject again.

"I'm not sure I want to discuss him.

"Oh, I get it, cousin. But we need a plan. This bullshit cannot continue. Whether any of us want it or not, Ares," Amanda felt herself flinch when Nicole said his name, "will fight Phantasos and come for you. He's obsessed like he was with our grandmother. I can't bear to think of him harming you again, especially not like he did her."

Amanda fell to her knees. "How much can a mortal take?"

"You're not mortal," Nicole kneeled in front of her. "And you're stronger than any of us. You've just forgotten who Amanda really is."

She knew her cousin meant well. Unfortunately, she didn't fully understand that, unlike her, she was without powers or even a god's signature. Between her looks and some weird ability to enthrall creatures—a true Snow White she was. Hell, her abilities fell short even compared to the nymphs she'd met.

"Oh, sweetie," Kallisto said when she returned to the bedroom. She, too, kneeled to the floor with them, and they all held on to each other. "It will be okay. Those men of ours will do everything they can to protect you."

Sniffling because apparently all she could do lately was leak, Amanda responded, "I know they'll try."

"Annika will be here later. She had something she was doing for Hermes."

"Okay. I'm going to bed," Amanda gave a halfhearted smile.

Turning over in bed, Amanda looked where her phone was on a base lit up with the time. It was three thirty in the morning with no sleep in sight. Her mind replayed her days with Ares, the horribleness of Priapus' story, and how much she wished she could leave it all behind. She missed knowing herself. Succumbing to a night of no sleep, not even restless sleep, Amanda eased herself from her bed and headed downstairs to the kitchen. As she rounded the corner, she saw the kitchen light on and heard whispered voices. Concentrating on the cadence of the whispers, she figured out her parents could not sleep either.

"She doesn't hate you, Kathryn. She's confused, and the realization that her entire world was a lie for her first eighteen years of life will take time to overcome. She loves you, but you, your sister, and her cousins—not to mention her best friend—represent pain. Give her time," her dad took up for her. Damn, she loved that man.

It took Amanda a few more minutes to realize her mother was crying. That was definitely not what she had wanted, but she couldn't help how she felt. Now, not only did her mom's side of the family and her best friend represent the Greek deities, but also the man she was trying hard not to think about.

"I'm trying, Alaric, but seeing her flinch when I go to hug her is more than I can take," her mother's voice was filled with emotion—she could hear the sadness and a little anger.

"When was the last time you tried to hug her?" he asked.

"When boarding the plane to South Africa," Kathryn sounded regretful.

"Maybe you should try again. She's come a long way since June," Alaric said.

"I will. I just don't want to push her. But keeping her at arm's length is killing me."

Amanda rounded the corner and entered her father's office when she realized they were leaving the kitchen. She didn't want them to know she was listening to their private conversation. It made her feel like shit that her mother didn't want to get too close to her for fear of seeing her flinch.

Once behind their bedroom door, Amanda walked from her father's office to the kitchen, where Annika waited for her. She sat at the breakfast table, her beautiful curls framing her face and her ram-like horns on full display.

"When did you get here?" Amanda asked.

"Right before your parents decided to leave the kitchen. I remained out of view while they finished their conversation. I almost flashed to the office but thought better of it. I didn't want to startle you. I heard your parents talking. Do you want to talk about it?"

Amanda shook her head. "I'm so glad you're here. I was doing much better after Phantasos and I figured out our relationship. Then I went and had a small nervous breakdown."

"What do you mean?" Annika looked confused. Evidently, no one had told her.

"Would you like something to drink?" She asked the Satyress. "This will take a few minutes."

"Water, please," Annika answered.

While pouring their waters, Amanda told her friend the story of turning in her test and seeing Ares, then the story of what happened to her grandmother, pinky-swearing her to secrecy since Angelia's father was Annika's boss.

"Now, I'm back to how I felt after the abduction. I'm not sure I want to be around this life. Not that I have a choice. Can you tell me what I feel like to you?" Amanda could feel her face flush. *What a strange question to ask.*

"Okay. Why?" Annika's eyes narrowed.

In a moment of word vomit, Amanda explained her thinking. "If I can figure out what I feel like to creatures, maybe I can ask my grandmother to place a more specific concealment on me. Then, in the dead of night, I can escape this crazy world I've been forced into. Put all this behind me," Amanda hung her head.

"That would mean leaving your family, Kallisto, and Phantasos," Annika's voice sounded sad but understanding.

"I know. Seeing, or thinking I saw, Ares again, then learning what he did to my grandmother. It's done something to me. There's a fear beyond what I felt before. Ares' obsession has been a known fact since last year. Now that Phantasos has claimed me I have a feeling Ares will abuse me like he did grandmother. If he does that, Phantasos will go mad. My family will go after him and die. It's best if I disappear. So. Will you tell me what my signature, or whatever you call it feels like to you?"

"Before I answer that . . . do you think Angelia will conceal you from your friends? From her daughter?"

"Yes. Once I tell her my fears—there's much more at stake here than the life of one demigod wannabe. She will help me disappear. Just like she did."

"Fine. The pull is otherworldly. You don't feel like a Greek god or any creature I've been around. It's a pull beyond any I have felt in the six millennia I have been alive—It's iridescent and ethereal. Not sure she can mask that, but I understand if you want and need her to." Annika took her hand, "You are a strong woman, Amanda. I will always be here for you, not because Hermes makes me, but because I'll always consider you a friend."

"Wanna go sit on the beach with me?" Amanda squeezed Annika's hand, released it, and walked to the back door, where her flip-flops sat. "I need some fresh air."

Chapter XXXII

Fates

THE FULL MOON CAST a warm glow over the beach, and its reflection in the still ocean made the world feel endless. It was hard to believe there were more realms beyond what was in front of her. She and Annika sat where the waves rolled over Amanda's feet and Annika's hooves. It was warm and reminded her of South Africa. They sat in long silence, both in their own heads.

"Did I ever tell you about the sirens' songs?" Amanda asked her friend without looking away from the retreating water.

"No. Was it beautiful? I've heard that it is," Annika tossed a small shell into the water.

"It was mesmerizing and eerie. Beautiful wouldn't be a word I would use to describe it." Amanda looked at her friend and finally resigned herself to lay it all out there. "The reason I ask is because they use songs to snare unsuspecting humans. I've realized that all immortals and creatures use something to lure humans. Example . . . Aphrodite uses her sensuality. Ares uses his strength and cunning. Even Kallisto uses her sweet charm. How can mortals withstand such powers? We have no option. I think that's what freaks me out the most. No matter what, I'm drawn to the gods. They all hold something over me. And I'm not in control."

"Amanda," Annika's eyes roamed the sand as if trying to find a way to deliver her message. "I know you don't believe this, but you are not mortal. Not completely, anyway. Your mother's side of the family belongs to the royal line of the Greek Pantheon. You are not fully human, whether your powers have completely manifested or not. You have strength in you that you have yet to tap. Try not to shy away from it and, instead, embrace it. Now, if we don't get back to the house, there will be a hunt out for you, and my boss will kick my ass for the scare. Not to mention what your bonded would do. Don't think I didn't notice. You're fully bonded now." Annika smiled.

Amanda smirked, then changed the subject. "Will you ever tell me how you ended up working for my great-grandfather?"

"Maybe someday. We've been out here for over an hour. We really need to get back before the cavalry is deployed."

Amanda smiled at her friend, and they both stood to head back. That's when she saw him. "Annika," Amanda grabbed the Satyrs' shoulder. "Do you see him?" Amanda pointed to the dark figure standing on lava rocks about ten meters up the beach.

"See who?" Annika asked, looking from where she pointed back to her.

"It's him. Ares. His arms are crossed over his chest. You don't see him?" Amanda could hear the panic in her own voice.

"I don't, but that doesn't mean he's not there. Give me your hand." Once Amanda's hand entered Annika's outstretched one, they found themselves in her bedroom.

"Kallisto, wake up," Amanda shook the goddess awake and told her what she'd just seen.

"Are you sure you—" Kallisto's eyes widened from slits to saucers.

"He's back," Amanda shook. "No doubt in my mind."

"I ask for an audience with the sisters," Morpheus answered the centaur guarding the gates to The Fates mansion.

"Are they expecting you?" The centaur towered over him with his arms crossed.

"Since they collectively see all, I suppose they are," he tried hard not to roll his eyes.

"We will see if they want to grant your wish for a meeting. Clanis, go see if the sisters have time to see the youngest Oneiroi," the older guard ordered a much younger stallion.

It only took the centaur a couple of minutes until he was running back down the hill to inform him that the triplets were ready to see him.

When Morpheus walked into the tension-filled throne room of the Moirai, he glanced at each sister, curious as to what had made them so uptight. They always met their guests with poise and were always in sync, acting like a unit, but as he approached the dais, he could feel a deep-seated irritation radiating off Clotho, who was always smiling. Well, not always; she looked arduous, trying to smile while the corners of her lips stayed turned down. Lachesis did not look much better but could keep her irritation off her face.

"Moirai, good afternoon," Morpheus bowed slightly at his waist.

"You are here to ask if we will stand against our half-brother and our Father," Atropos announced without asking any questions or riddles, and it did not go unnoticed when her sisters shot what could only be described as dirty looks in the middle sisters' direction.

Interesting, he thought.

He blinked a couple of times, grounding himself. He had expected the dance they usually did. With a grin, he answered, "Yes."

"We told you no deaths. Your brother has gone against all of our warnings," Atropos continued.

The hair on the back of his neck stood on end. Atropos had visited Phantasos in his home, warning him against Amanda. *What is she up to?*

"Well, ladies. Since you know why I am here, I suppose you will spare me the riddles and tell me which side you will stand with."

Atropos laughed. "Tell us, Morpheus, which side will you fight with?"

He just stood there, blinking.

"What our sister is trying to ask is, would you be able to fight against your family?" Lachesis asked.

"No. Is that your answer? Will you stand with your father and half-brother?" He looked between the three sisters, but his gaze landed on Atropos since she was the one who would cut the strings.

Morpheus' eyes began to swirl. They knew. They knew about Angelia, about Phobos, about Amanda. "You ladies knew. You knew every time we asked for an audience. You knew what Ares did to Angelia. You knew what he did to Amanda and what Phobos did to Nicole and Amanda. If you stand against us, then not only have you given permission for your brother," he deliberately left off the half, "to harm goddesses, but you have also given him the okay to harm mortals. There is a higher power than you. An entire realm of them. If you anger The Almighty by harming mortals, he will step in with his army." He noticed Clotho and Lachesis flinch.

"The Moirai will not fight. We will not stand against either side," Lachesis answered Morpheus' question.

"If you cut any of the Oneiroi or our friends' strings, you will have taken sides. Leave us be. Let us fight this battle."

"That we cannot promise, Oneiroi," Atropos answered.

"I am not asking, ladies. If you know all. You know the balance of power for this Pantheon is hanging by a thread," he grinned at Atropos. She glared back.

"Do not threaten us, Morpheus," Atropos snarled. He had never seen her like this.

"Then stay out of the battle. Thank you for giving me an audience." Morpheus spun on his heel and left the sister's mansion, clenching his fists.

It seems the Moirai are divided. Morpheus thought. He had never witnessed such.

⟡————⟡

Standing on the cliffs of Milos, Greece, overlooking the Aegean Sea in the moonlight, Phobetor waited. He had sent word that he needed an audience with Poseidon. Of all the kings, he was the hardest to seek out. Hopefully, he would show.

It was rare for Phobetor to have time to think, but since he found himself waiting, his mind began to wander over the last century. From his fall from grace with torturous nightmares to his days ferrying messages between Zeus and Zanovia and now to the love he had finally found, his life had improved greatly. It was unfortunate that after all his millennia, he had just now found love and was about to engage in a political battle of epic proportions. *Could life be so cruel?*

Deep in thought, Phobetor failed to notice when a school of merpeople heads surfaced just below the cliff he was on. Not until the tips of a trident began to emerge from the still water did he notice the action below him. *He did show.*

"Come closer, Oneiroi," the booming voice of Poseidon radiated across the water and up the cliff where Phobetor waited.

"I will meet you on the sand. Not in the water," Phobetor answered the giant god. He was not stupid. On land, they were close to being evenly matched—in the water, he had no leverage if things became critical.

Poseidon chuckled, "As you wish, Fear Maker."

Both gods flashed to the sand while the merpeople watched from the water, now visible from their waists up. He could not help but admire their unique appearance. Each held the beauty of an immortal with a bluish tint to their skin. With hair of various colors and well-defined abs, the sea creatures were in a league of their own. If the king of the sea had an army of these creatures, his brothers should watch their backs.

"You asked for an audience. Since it has been more years than I would like to think about since we last spoke, I assume the reason has something to do with the doppelganger," Poseidon raised a brow.

"You would be close to correct. However, I was sent to find out which side of the upcoming battle you will support."

"You know no love is lost between Zeus and me, but the Pantheon must stand. I suppose it depends on how far this *battle*, you are calling it, will last," Poseidon answered without hesitation.

"It should be a fight only between Ares and Phantasos so long as Zeus, Hera, and their minions stay out of it—it will end with no further conflict. I need to know, if your brother steps in, which side will you assist?" Phobetor crossed his arms over his broad chest, taking a stance. No god, not even Poseidon would cross him unless absolutely necessary.

"The only way I will intervene will be if Ares harms the doppelganger."

"Why?" He was not expecting that answer.

"I promised Hades," Poseidon answered with a shrug.

"You see, that, too, is an interesting stance you make. What is so important about Amanda that you and Hades would cross your Pantheon?"

Poseidon grinned, all teeth and bright eyes, "We all must draw a line in the sand somewhere, Oneiroi." Then he vanished.

Standing alone on the beach, Phobetor thought about what Poseidon had alluded to. Why Amanda? Why does a demi with no powers and no political pull have that much persuasion over two of the most powerful gods of their Pantheon? *Things are not adding up.*

Chapter XXXIII

Angelia

Once outside the gates of the Moirai mansion, Morpheus felt Kallisto's pull. She was upset.

It took him less than a second to materialize in Amanda's bedroom, where his fiancé stood wide-eyed with mussed hair. She had just woken up and was still in her sleepwear. The other two in the room were fully dressed. All bore the look of panic.

"What happened?" he asked.

"I saw him again," Amanda said, then detailed what just happened.

⋆ ⸺ ⸺ ⋆

"Hades. Open up," Phantasos pounded on the large black doors of the throne room. Thankful the coin still worked, and he was able to bypass the ferryman and the Cerberus. Now, he just waited on Hades to grant him access.

With a loud creek, the doors slowly opened. On the dais stood the god of the Underworld and his minions. He looked pissed. Great, Hades was not the only one upset. Determined to find answers, Phantasos closed the distance quickly.

"What has you beating on my doors without invitation, dreamer?" Hades wore his thin obsidian crown and no shirt.

Had he been asleep? Does he wear the crown to bed?

"I am sure I know the answer to the question I was sent to ask. However, I will ask it anyway. I also have questions of my own."

"My wife waits on me. Ask your questions quickly before I lose my patience."

"I was sent to ask which side you will stand with if this fight becomes a battle?"

Hades' brows raise. "You know the answer. What else?"

"Why?"

"Why what?"

"Why do you care what happens to Amanda?"

"You asked me to protect her," Hades half smirked. One that said more than what he verbalized. There was more to it.

"Yes. But you have gone above and beyond. Why?"

"There are many reasons. You asked me to and, in return, became indebted to me. Plus, I have never condoned the ill-treatment of females. And if you must know, my wife and Angelia were once close friends."

Phantasos nodded and thought about what the deity before him said. "If I win this fight, what will happen to me? If I lose, I die, but if I win, then what?"

"If you kill Ares, you are as good as dead, but so is Ares."

Phantasos felt himself flinch. Damned if he does, damned he does not. Sounds about right. "So, I just take him with me. Death to us both," Phantasos said under his breath.

"There is always a way. It just happens that most of the time, instinct takes over and chooses our path. Stay in control at all times; perhaps you may find a way to avenge your doppelganger and keep her—without losing your life. My wife awaits my return. Leave," Hades and his stern look vanished, leaving Phantasos alone with the gorgons: *damn gods and their riddles.*

Amanda stood at her bedroom window, waiting and thinking. She could hear the murmurs of everyone else behind her, seated either on her bed or the only two chairs. Phobetor and Nicole had joined their party. The only one missing was Phantasos. Amanda could see the Satyress' reflection in the glass. The world she now knew still amazed her. Behind her were gods, goddesses, and a Satyress. Never in her wildest imagination would she have guessed how incredibly beautiful inside and out a half-human half-goat could be. What made her new friend work for Hermes? Was he good to her, or did he hold something over her?

Amanda put her forehead on the glass. She felt like she was way in over her head, and her plea to her grandmother to disappear had to work. She knew the people in the reflection of her window would be upset, sad, and possibly pissed, but she needed to think about her own sanity. She lived in a world where she was virtually helpless. All those in the reflection were not.

While in the middle of her inner debate, she heard *his* voice. Phantasos was back. She spun around, locking eyes with him. He asked everyone to give them a few minutes without turning from her gaze. Before Amanda could register they were alone, she was standing in the middle of her bedroom and he was kissing her.

He engulfed all of her senses, making her legs tremble. How would she be able to walk away from this? It was times like that moment that made her waiver.

Amanda reluctantly pulled back from their searing kiss. "He's back." With that bomb, she gave him the cliff notes of what she saw on the beach. They had suspected Ares was back, but she was positive after the night she had.

"Fuck!" Phantasos cursed, then released her and rubbed his hands down his face. He then looked straight into her eyes and told her she would be okay.

What she saw in his eyes cut her deep. He was crooning that she would be safe, unknowing she was about to break him in two with her disappearance.

⊹⊹———⊹⊹———⊹⊹

Once again, everyone gathered in Kathryn and Alaric's living room. Phantasos held Amanda around the waist, this time with a possessive smirk. Annika, her Aunt Kellie, her mother, and her dad were added to their motley crew. It was time to lay out everything they had discovered. The only thing that would not be discussed was Amanda's plans to have her grandmother help her disappear. The hard part was keeping her thoughts under control. If Phantasos found out, she was sure he would stop her.

"We are going to ask Angelia to come here without your father," Morpheus spoke directly to her mother, Kathryn, and Aunt Kellie.

"We thought telling her what we know would be much better if said privately. We doubt she told Grandfather of her attack," Nicole explained their decision.

"Should we call for Angelia before we tell what we learned from Hades, the Fates, and Poseidon?" Phobetor asked.

"I think so," Kathryn spoke up. "After what you told us and how you found out, she should know everything we do. She can decide if she wants Hermes and Aphrodite to know."

Amanda noticed the possessive hold her dad had on her mother's hand. He was in the same boat she was in. They were the only two in the room without abilities. A little bit of guilt rose in Amanda's chest. Why had she not spoken to her father about that? Did he feel as helpless as she did? She made a mental note to talk to him after they met with her grandmother. Maybe he would want to go away with her. No, he was much stronger than she was. She was sure he would stand by her mother's side. After all, he wasn't targeted by the god of war like she was.

"Agreed," the women said in unison.

Ten minutes later, Angelia stood in the middle of the room with a look of concern on her face. "Has he returned?"

"Yes," she answered her grandmother. "But that's not why we asked you here."

Angelia looked over the room. Her brow wrinkled. "Okay. Explain."

"Please have a seat," Phantasos manifested another chair. Angelia sat, and Amanda couldn't help but notice the slight tremble in her grandmother's hands.

"There are a few things we need to discuss. First, know that Poseidon and Hades seem to have a vested interest in our current situation. Poseidon has loaned me his horses when needed, and Hades introduced us to Priapus."

Angelia's eyes jerked to Amanda's. A look of horror crossed her features. "What did you say?"

"Hades had told me a story over the summer but never told me names. When Ares started popping up again, he decided to take Phantasos and me to Priapus' cell and have him tell his story—your story—or what he knew of it. We better understand why the bastard is after me, and we know why you concealed our abilities. Their abilities." Amanda pointed to Nicole, her mother, and her Aunt Kellie. "I'm speaking for all of us. We are so thankful you kept us safe—we love you. Also, we're sorry for being such assholes about all of it."

Angelia's shoulders began to shake, and tears followed, streaming down her face. It didn't take a genius to know she was thinking about all the pain she endured. The men looked uneasy, and all four, including her dad, decided to visit the kitchen for drinks and snacks.

After over an hour of tears, hugs, and apologies, Amanda called for the men. They needed to form a plan or as much of one as possible.

Each god entered, her dad in tow, and he looked murderous. She looked from her dad to Phantasos, questioning what was going on.

⁘—⁌—⁘

"We discussed what we each learned today. Before we tell you what we came up with, we want you ladies to hear what Hades, Poseidon, and the weird sisters had to say about the upcoming conflict," Phantasos began as he looped one arm around Amanda's waist. He felt her tense when the Moirai were mentioned. She detested them as much as he did for their meddling ways.

Phobetor stepped forward. "I spoke with Poseidon. He will only intervene if Amanda is harmed. He stated that the Pantheon needed to stay strong."

"Not that I have an issue with him keeping my daughter safe, but why does he care? She's nothing to him," Kathryn asked.

"He says it's because he promised Hades."

"Why does Hades care?" Kathryn asked.

"Because I asked him to. In return, I owe him a debt," he saw their confused looks. Only he and his brothers knew they each owed Hades a debt. This made Hades a very powerful god, with the Oneiroi in his back pocket.

"What did Hades say?" Nicole asked.

"Hades will also help if Amanda is harmed. As we all know, no love is lost between him and Zeus. He cannot stand his nephew for what he has done."

Angelia hung her head. This has to be so difficult for Amanda and her grandmother.

"What about The Fates Three," Angelia asked, still staring at the floor.

A menacing sound from Alaric made the room look from Angelia to him. His eyes blazed. If he were a god, Phantasos knew his eyes would be swirling. In the kitchen, when Morpheus told of his brief interaction with the Moirai, Alaric snarled and asked not once but twice for confirmation that Atropos had an issue with Amanda. Why, no one knew. He supposed having another god, one from Zeus' loins, angered by his daughter, made him even more concerned.

"They are divided for the first time that we have ever seen. They say they will not intervene. However, Atropos may still cut our strings. Something has her rattled, and her sisters are not happy with her. It is definitely a first," Morpheus said.

"At best, the most powerful of the Pantheon has agreed to stand down and allow Phantasos to fight Ares without intervention. It depends on whether Ares brings his parents to the fight. If they get involved—God help us all," Morpheus said.

Chapter XXXIV

Letter

Three weeks flew by—no more sightings of Ares. However, no less than three creatures a day seemed to pop up out of nowhere. Amanda went to her classes under the watchful eye of Phantasos every day. Each night she spent in his arms. She had decided to wait a bit before asking her grandmother to hide her. Having Phantasos for just a little while longer. The only problem was the guilt. She felt it build the longer she waited. If she were truly gone, that would eliminate a big problem. Phantasos could concentrate on kicking Ares' ass and nothing more.

"I love you," Amanda said, turning her face to Phantasos, whose chin was propped on her shoulder. She sat between his legs, his arms cradling her. They sat on a large blanket covering the black sand, watching the waves and waiting for shooting stars. She soaked it all up, hoping these few special moments would pacify her for as long as she had. She committed each look, kiss, and laugh to memory.

"And I, you," he responded. Then he hopped up and threw her over his shoulder. She kicked and laughed as he submerged them deep in the water.

That was her last night with him. She orchestrated a situation where Phantasos could take a breather from watching over her while she went shopping with her grandmother. Thinking back on the night before made her heart ache. She could only hope that one day it would become a comforting memory.

"So, what's up, honey," Angelia asked her as they sat down to eat lunch. Amanda had not been lying. She *was* shopping with her grandmother. "We never shop. What's going on?"

"I want you to place a concealment over me. I've asked Annika what my signature feels like to creatures so you know the difference in the spell you must conjure. I want—no—I *need* to vanish." There it was. Everything was laid out in a rush. No going back.

"You would leave your family and friends? Phantasos?" her grandmother asked, looking from eye to eye, assessing whether she had thought it out.

"I'm not like them. If I stay, I'm putting everyone at risk. Ares won't give up. The only other mortal in my family is Dad, and I've already discussed this with him. He promised not to tell Mom. I asked him to go with me. He understood why I wanted to leave and agreed but said he would stay with her; then he set me up with an apartment and an account with some money until I got on my feet. He also spoke with the dean and got my classes online for the rest of this semester. I'll only return if Ares is gone—maybe not even then. If Phantasos manages to beat Ares—if he kills him—Zeus and Hera will go crazy. It's a lot easier to destroy what a god loves, especially if that love happens to be a mortal or, in my case, mostly mortal. No matter what, I'm a liability to my friends and family. I'm a pawn in a game I don't want to play anymore," Amanda watched her fingers entwine as she spoke, trying desperately not to cry, but the burn behind her eyes wasn't subsiding.

She felt her grandmother looking at her for what felt like forever. "What did Annika say your signature felt like?"

"She said it's iridescent and ethereal—otherworldly. Nothing she's ever experienced. Can you conceal something like that?" Amanda heard the hope in her own voice.

"I believe I can. Just understand that this is uncharted territory. I'm unsure how long it will last, if I can reverse it, or if it will even work."

"I understand. Can you do it today?" Amanda asked.

"I can do it now if you wish," her grandmother said sadly. She took hold of her hand and squeezed lightly. Understand, once I do this, it will be up to you if you ever see your loved ones again. If it works, they will not be able to find you."

"I understand," she swallowed any doubt and straightened her spine. She wasn't just doing it to stay safe and away from immortals; she was protecting her family and friends from being their weakest link. "I'm ready."

"Do you not want to say goodbye?" Angelia asked.

"I made sure my last interactions with each person were positive, and I told each one how much I love them. Give me at least twelve hours, and then you can tell them what I asked of you."

"Okay. Let's walk out to the beach. Away from everyone," her grandmother said as she stood from their table and led them to the park.

Angelia took her hands and whispered ancient Greek words Amanda didn't understand. The more she chanted, the stranger Amanda felt. Once all the words were said, Amanda felt an invisible veil cover her, then nothing. Normal.

"My cell phone is in my purse. There are letters to each person in there as well. Once the twelve hours are up, please hand them out. I know I am about to break my mother's heart, not to mention my friends, but can you please let Phantasos know that I meant every word? I will love him forever or until my last breath."

"I will. I love you, Amanda. I am so very sorry you are dealing with this. If I could go back, I would have told your mother and Kellie. At least then, everyone would have been prepared."

"Don't. What's done is done. I understand. I'm sorry we judged your decisions. Ares needs to pay for what he did. All I know is that I can't be the pawn in this game. I love you. Can you do me another favor and take me to the mainland?"

"Yes. Where do you want to go?"

"Los Angeles. There, I can disappear." She didn't want her grandmother to know exactly where she would be. Only her dad knew that. Once in LA, she would catch a ride to Anaheim, where her new life awaited.

"Done."

❖━━━━❖

"What the fuck did you just say?" Phantasos shook with anger. Every cell in his body felt like it was on fire. *Amanda left. Her grandmother concealed her. She's no longer on the islands.* He was sure he would explode. This cannot be happening. "She is gone?" his voice cracked before he hit his knees, and an animalistic wail came from deep in his chest.

"I'm so sorry. She left these letters—one for each of you. Please understand. She's not like any of us. She doesn't have power and will always be the one needing protection. She will always be the pawn, the one who will suffer. She's protecting herself and each of you," Angelia held out the letters and Amanda's cell phone.

Phantasos removed his palms from his eyes. Still on his knees, his spine straightened, and his wings burst from his back.

When he looked up, he knew his face was frightening from the flinches and everyone's retreating steps. "Where did you take her?" Phantasos' wails turned into a menacing whisper. His eyes swirled crimson, his fangs were fully displayed, and the air around him shimmered. He was seconds from losing all control.

"I can't tell you that," Angelia sounded contrite but stood her ground for her granddaughter. Any other time, he would applaud her, but not now, not when Amanda was alone. Not when Ares was looking for her.

Before he registered what he was doing, he had Angelia by her neck, dangling off the floor. His wings stretched wide, and his fangs dripped with venom as anger took over. Everything went red, and muffled screams echoed around him.

✦━━━━━━✦

"Morpheus, grab his other hand," Phobetor yelled for help.

It took all Phobetor had to pry his brother's fingers off Angelia's neck. "Why did you not stop him?" he asked her once Morpheus had Phantasos on the other side of the living room. Once again, they were in Kathryn's house. This time, everyone but Amanda was present.

"He's in pain, and I'm immortal," was Angelia's only explanation.

"This is fucked up," Phobetor shook his head and walked across the room to help Morpheus calm Phantasos down.

It took the better part of an hour to get the eldest Oneiroi to a point where he could see reason. His wings vanished, but his swirling eyes and fangs remained. He took up his usual pacing of the room.

"We will find her, but this may be better for her until Ares is no longer a problem," Phobetor said.

Without looking at him, Phantasos responded, "I know." He stood still and then walked out the front door.

❖━━━━━━❖

"I can't believe she left without saying goodbye to me," Kallisto cried into Morpheus' chest.

"Have you read your letter?" he asked.

"No. I will, but I can't bring myself to do it right now. This is too raw."

Kallisto curled up on her bed and sobbed. Night turned to morning, and her heart felt like it was bleeding. It hurt when Amanda left for South Africa, but she at least had hope. This time, it felt like all hope was lost. She had only gotten a couple of hours of sleep. Morpheus had offered to help her, but she declined. She needed to think. To process what Amanda was thinking.

Memories of their ten-year-old selves played through her mind. Amanda's smart mouth and protective nature called to Kallisto's more stoic disposition. There was never a time they didn't have each other's backs, and Amanda was always the one calling the shots with her big personality.

On her nightstand sat *the* letter. The damn thing taunted her. That envelope held Amanda's last words—*she always got the last word.* Kallisto grinned at the thought. Once opened, she would read the end of their chapter—the end of a friendship that was more like sisters. Resigned, she leaned over and picked up the envelope that held what felt like a bomb, ready to blast her world apart. She could have sworn it weighed ten pounds if she didn't know better. Closing her eyes, she gathered the strength to open the mocking letter.

Through tears, she read Amanda's neat scroll.

Kalli,

I know this comes as a surprise, but please know I had to. I'm not only protecting myself, but I'm protecting everyone I love. Yes, most of you are immortal, but I can't be everyone's weakest link. You have the right to live a life full of love and one where you don't have to take turns watching over the powerless demi in the group.

Anyway, leaving you will be the hardest. You have been my world since we were ten years old. Remember the day we met? Damn, we've had some good times.

Remember those times. There are so many to choose from. Please keep an eye on my parents. Dad knew I would be leaving, but Mom had no clue. I know she will be as hurt as you are, but this decision was not taken lightly.

I have no doubt Phantasos will hate me for this. Maybe someday all of you will forgive me. Just know I will be okay.

Take care of yourself. Know that I love you, and there will never be a day that passes without you being in my thoughts.

With All My Heart,

Amanda

Kallisto dropped the letter on the bed and buried her face in a pillow. Pain ripped at her insides. Losing someone caused physical pain. She now had first-hand knowledge of what it was like to have a broken heart.

Chapter XXXV

Why?

Pacing his bedchamber, Phantasos was consumed with thoughts of where Amanda would have gone and how to get her back. Every step felt like his heart would rip from his chest. Every breath was hard to perform. Living hurt. It had been two days since he discovered she had help disappearing. He understood her desire to keep everyone safe, including herself, but she failed to grasp that Ares would not be deterred. She had no concept of an immortal's timeline. What felt like an eternity to a human was a mere blink to a god. Ares might be eager to have her and end him, but on a human's timeline, that could be years, possibly centuries.

As he continued his mental perusal with laps around his bed, the only thing coming to mind was the odd behavior of the weird sisters, particularly Atropos. He believed she was worried about him and the problems that having a demi with no signature could pose until Morpheus told him about his visit to the Moirai mansion. It seems there is a lot more going on than any of them had considered. His brother said the sisters were divided. He needed to know why.

It took only minutes to gather his brothers by telling them he needed their help. With a bit of coaxing, all three waited at The Fates' gates. Again, they waited for the centaur Clanis to return to see if they were granted an audience.

"What is taking so long?" Phantasos patrolled. His Oneiroi battle form had been present in varying degrees since he found out Amanda had fled. By the red tinge closing in, coating everything in crimson, he knew his eyes had changed—and having to wait fueled his anger. His gums were aching, and he was moments from showing fangs.

"Try to stay calm," Phobetor suggested.

Phantasos returned his suggestion with a wave of his middle finger.

His brother laughed, "Good to see you are still you, brother."

"Here comes the centaur," Morpheus pointed to where the beast galloped down the steep hill.

"About damn time," Phantasos said.

"The sisters said they will see you. Follow me, please," Clanis said, turning to lead the Oneiroi up the hill to the mansion.

Once inside the imposing mansion, they again waited. He knew the sisters were fucking with them. They had never had to wait before, which concerned all three brothers.

"This does not feel right," Phantasos said as he passed his brothers, pacing while running his hands through his hair. He had gone from irritated to pissed, and nothing in his arsenal was helping him calm. Not only was he sporting swirling red eyes, but now he had fangs, and his back tingled as he desperately tried to keep his wings from forming. The Moirai would take it as a sign of aggression if he entered their throne room in full battle form. He supposed that would not be far off the mark. Having to wait tested his patience, and after losing Amanda, he had very little left.

"Agreed," Morpheus said.

"I agree, too. They know why we are here. The question is, why make us wait?" Phobetor took up pacing in the opposite direction of Phantasos.

After all three brothers had begun to pace the foyer, the doors to the throne room opened, and Clotho's voice beckoned them in.

Before any of the sisters could greet their guests, Phantasos held out a hand, palm out, and said, "We have waited long enough. Let us cut the regular banter and question evasion. Tell us the truth as to why you do not want Amanda and me together."

The sisters looked between each other and back at them. He could tell they were not expecting him to be quite so blunt right off the cuff. Clearing her throat, Lachesis waved her hand, and three chairs manifested behind each of them.

"Have a seat, Oneiroi," the eldest Fate motioned them to the chairs.

"No thanks," Phantasos said.

"You can either have a seat and calm yourselves, or you may leave, but you will not stand there in your battle form and demand anything," Lachesis leveled her eyes at Phantasos.

Being the only one on the verge of full battle armor and not far from battle rage, he knew she was trying to help him calm down. Unfortunately, if it were that easy, he would have made himself calm down before he had Angelia by the throat the day she helped *her* leave.

"Fine," Morpheus was the first to concede and sat. Phobetor let out a deep breath and followed the youngest Oneiroi's example. They waited for him to give in. After a long stare-off with the sisters, he finally took the last chair.

"Now that you have us on our asses, tell me what I want to know," his words came out stern, followed by a feral growl.

"Please excuse our brother. He is having a challenging time keeping himself from destroying everything or anyone who may pose harm to Amanda." It was his brother's turn to level his eyes at the sisters. Phobetor had learned his lesson the hard way during his imprisonment in the Underworld. He once allowed his beast to seek vengeance. He learned from that experience to wrangle his self-control and find more creative means to get his way, and the sisters knew it.

"We pose the demi no harm," Clotho said. After she declared no harm, Phantasos noticed her eyes cut to her middle sister. Again, they were acting shifty—more so than was usual.

"Why do you not want me to seek a relationship with Amanda? She is of the royal line," he directed his question to the eyes of Atropos. She lifted her chin.

"We only gave you warnings. Nothing was ever said that was untrue," Atropos dodged his question.

"I did not ask you what you told me. I asked you why you do not want me in a relationship with her," he repeated.

Atropos glanced at her sisters, then stood and walked to the back of her chair. Laying her forearms across its back, she cleared her voice and began to speak.

"Every mortal and immortal has a thread of life woven and maintained by us—destroyed by us. Clotho is there at the birth of each being. Deciding the significant points of each one's life while spinning their thread. Lachesis then pulls the thread the length of that soul's lifespan. For immortals, there may or may not be an ending. Zeus has a say in these events, and my sisters are to consider his wishes as they spin and pull the thread. It is I who cuts the thread that ends the being's existence. The Almighty gave free will, so each thread contains extra time for free will to play into their life. If Clotho said a person was to marry, then the person would marry, but it would be up to them who and when unless Zeus told us who, and that person was woven into their thread. Collectively, my sisters and I know everything. We may not know when or who, but we know the outcome *if* those things were not woven into the thread at birth. There is one thing that is always for certain, though." Atropos lowered her arms from her makeshift podium and returned to stand directly before Phantasos. "I know when to cut the thread, *Death.*" He heard her voice in his head.

"We know this. What does this have to do with Amanda?" Phantasos asked, not giving her the knowledge that her mental intrusion caught him off guard, making him uneasy.

"I weaved Amanda's thread with popularity, intelligence, beauty, marriage, and three children," Clotho said.

"And a lifespan of eighty-seven human years, by me," Lachesis said.

"We always watch and call for threads, especially as individuals begin to insert their free will. We examine those threads and see where Clotho's major events land along the timeline. We do it to pass the millennia," Atropos circled around the Oneiroi, who stayed planted in their chairs, waiting for answers. "It is entertaining to watch as fate wars with free will. Of course, fate always wins," Atropos grinned and sat back down on her throne.

"For the lives that have fewer major events assigned to them at birth, the more freedom they have—Amanda was granted a lot of freedom. She was not assigned a partner or a specific career. Those were for her to decide upon," Clotho said.

"When she became friends with Kallisto, we began to observe her timeline carefully, wanting to see how their threads fit together throughout their lives. All looked fine until Amanda turned eighteen," Lachesis said. "It was right after her birthday that Morpheus met Kallisto, and then you met her, and Ares found her. At that time, her thread started to lengthen and—fade."

"You see, if her thread continues to lengthen, or worse, it fades completely, I will not be able to cut it. I have always been able to cut a thread; even if the immortal's thread is *never-ending*, it can still be cut," Atropos' turned-down lip twitched.

"What does her thread of life have to do with me being warned against her? You knew she was a demigod," Phantasos' voice echoed throughout the room. "Before we knew of her true lineage, you warned me away from her because she was mortal. Then, you came to my home and warned me away because I would bring immortals to her. It was all lies. Why?"

"Where the demi is concerned, we know little. Her thread is fading," Atropos said.

"What does that mean?" Phantasos asked.

"Heed our warnings or do not. In the end, it will be you who must pay for your choices. Now, my sisters and I have things we need to do. You may take your leave," Atropos said, then stood and left the room. Her sisters stood and looked between the Oneiroi and the door their middle sister had gone through and proceeded to follow suit without comment.

"Something is up with Atropos, and I will find out what it is," Phantasos said. "Fading threads. What the fuck?"

Chapter XXXVI

Anaheim was a large city with so much fun to be had. Determined to get out of her apartment, hell, get out of her bed, Amanda dragged herself to the bathroom, washed her face, and brushed her teeth. She needed a full bath, but first, she needed food. Ten days. She had been cloaked for ten days. So far, it worked. Well, she supposed it had. She had only seen the four walls of her studio apartment since that day, and no one from Hawaii or Olympus had popped in. If she was going to survive this, she needed to live life. That meant getting a job. Between online courses and a job, hopefully, she wouldn't have time to dwell on those she missed. She rolled her eyes at her thoughts. It would take her a lifetime to be happy again, if not longer.

Her refrigerator held eggs, milk, and yogurt. Those were the only things she purchased the day she arrived. Out of a dozen eggs, she had four left, and the yogurt was almost gone. Scratch that: three eggs and no yogurt. Yep, she'd survived for ten days—if you could call it that—on just about nothing, and finally, her stomach decided to call the shots. This was the first morning she'd woken with an appetite. *Scrambled eggs it is.*

After eating, she made her way to the shower, *damn, the warm water felt good.* Then she took a pair of shorts and a T-shirt from her shopping bags. Yes, the same ones that she had purchased when she went shopping with her grandmother.

They were still in the bags, tags attached, taunting her with memories.

Now dressed, it was time to search for a job and some groceries. Luckily, her father had set up a bank account in her name with a couple of thousand dollars, and a burner phone sat on the counter of her apartment. She had no idea how her dad pulled everything off, but he had. It had taken him only two weeks to set her up with a new life. She supposed years of helping students follow their dreams gave him the inside connections. How she wished her good fortune had come with a job, too. *Okay, now I'm just being a brat,* she thought.

A quick Google search for part-time jobs told her that Angel Stadium, home of the major league baseball team, needed ticket takers and ushers, a local theme park needed a princess, several members of its cleaning crews, and one of its resorts needed a fitness instructor. Off to Angel Stadium, she went. Being a ticket taker would be okay, but an usher sounded more like it. She wanted to stay in crowded areas where any altercation would stand out, and even an immortal creature would think twice before confronting her. Or that was what she told herself anyway.

Uber dropped her off at the stadium, where a quick scan showed a sign to the main office. After an hour of filling out the application and a lengthy interview with a rather young-looking HR guy, Amanda called for another Uber. She had gotten the usher job and would start in two days.

She was finally back at her apartment after quickly stopping at the grocery store to pick up the food she'd ordered online. She handed the driver his money and tip and sighed at the building. She'd needed to stay out of bed and do something, but her pillow with its tear stains was calling her name.

"What the actual hell?" she said aloud, standing outside her apartment and looking inside through the door she did not leave open to where Annika stood.

"Hey," Annika gave a nervous wave. "Glad to see you're okay."

Walking to her kitchen without acknowledging the Satyress, Amanda sat the grocery bags on her counter. She felt anger from the pit of her stomach rise up her body. She was sure your neck was on fire. Thirsty, hungry, and now betrayed, Amanda tried counting backward from ten. Slowly, she turned toward her unwelcome guest and stared.

"Are you not going to say anything?"

"What would you like for me to say, Annika?"

"I know how this looks, but your grandmother did not do this. I swear," Annika eased toward her, hands out in front like she might get attacked.

"Then how?" Amanda raised her voice.

"Well," Annika began to fidget while biting her nails. She'd never seen her do that before, so Amanda knew this was going to really piss her off.

"Well?" Amanda parroted.

"Your dad and your grandmother both know. So, Kellie begged Nicole to, uh—"

"To uh, what?" Amanda's neck started to heat up again.

"To get Phobetor to take Nicole into their dreams. Ironically, your grandmother's dream state was the only one he could penetrate. From her dreams, they found out where she took you."

"That doesn't explain how you are in my apartment. My grandmother took me to LA, not Anaheim. She doesn't know where I landed."

"Once I arrived in LA, I felt you. The concealment didn't completely work. I'm unsure if all creatures can sense you, but I could. Maybe that's because we're friends, I don't know. But—you're not concealed from everyone. Your essence led me to this apartment. I just arrived no more than a couple of minutes before you did."

Amanda pulled a stool out from the bar and sat. Everything she was trying to do had failed. She had put her family, her friends, and herself through ten days of hell for nothing.

"Did you or anyone else tell Phantasos where I am?" Amanda's voice was barely audible.

"Uh. Well. He already knew where you were. He, too, would not tell us."

"What?" Amanda was back on her feet, accidentally kicking the barstool over.

"The only reason he hasn't visited is because he knows you are right. You deserve better. You deserve your freedom from the immortals and all our bullshit," Annika said.

"How did he find out?" Her heated cheeks were now wet with tears. What had she done?

"You and he are bound. On your third night missing, he found you in your dream state. He's been watching you through your dreams."

"Bound beings can find each other, even when concealed by magic?" Amanda asked, staring into space with the bar stool still at her feet.

"Apparently," Annika answered.

"Does he hate me?" Amanda sniffled, trying hard to hold back the onslaught of panic and sobs she wished she could unleash.

"He could never hate you. And when I say never, I mean in his lifetime. For three days, he was angry and broken. I only saw him from a distance, but from what Kallisto said, if he could have died, he would have. Once he could see that you were safe, he started training again. He's still heartbroken but relieved."

"Before I pack up and go back, I need to know if all creatures can sense me," Amanda said, working to calm her racing heart by setting the stool upright. "Also, will others not sense your signature and find me?"

"Once your grandmother discovered what was done, she concealed me from the gods as she did herself for a thousand years. My signature is easier to hide than yours for some reason. It must have something to do with you being a Demi doppelganger," Annika explained.

"So, why are you here?" Amanda crossed her arms over her chest.

"Just because your location has changed doesn't mean my job to watch over you has. When Hermes learned they had found you, he made me come."

"Why didn't Phantasos tell him since he knew?"

"Because he watches over you all the time—he just does it without you knowing it. He's concealing himself when he does. Me being here will help him, even if he refuses to admit it." Annika's shoulders had relaxed a little.

Being the messenger had to be hard, Amanda thought.

"Are you mad?" Annika asked.

"No. At least you guys found me, not Ares or his minions. So—I suppose it's for the best. Do you think you can sense me because we are close friends, or am I just a sitting duck for all immortals?"

"I'm not sure. It could be either," Annika answered.

Amanda put the groceries away and started making dinner for herself and her unwanted but much-needed house guest. Her mind drifted to Phantasos. He had known but not shown himself for seven of her ten days away. She was uncertain if she should be upset or happy that he let her make her own decisions.

"I just got a job as an usher at Angel Stadium. I start in two days. You should see if you can get a job there too. That way, you don't have to hide," Amanda grinned.

"A job? I have a job—you."

"And how much easier it is to do your current job if you are working with me," Amanda arched her brows.

"Fine."

"You and I on hideout may be fun," She grinned at her beautiful friend.

Two days later, both had a job at the stadium as ushers. Amanda was excited, Annika, not so much.

Chapter XXXVII

For the next three days, the Los Angeles Angels had home games. Her first day at work had been a lot of fun. It was easy to get lost in the ambiance. Amanda adored the screaming fans; most of all, she loved the Rally Monkey. It was so damn cute.

The first night, they were together, learning the ropes of ushering. It was their second night to shepherd the baseball patrons, each given their own section to guide and look over. Unfortunately, the sections weren't close together, making Annika overly anxious. This was evident as soon as the assignments were handed out, and Amanda saw the outline of horns on her head. The Satyress was losing her composure. She looked wide-eyed at her friend, hoping she would get the hint.

Leaning toward her, Annika whispered, "What in Hades' name? I got this job so I could watch over you better."

"Put those away before someone notices." Amanda chided, glancing at Annika's head.

Amanda couldn't help but grin. They had gone the whole day without incident during training. In fact, not one immortal graced the stadium out of thousands of fans. She felt safe for the first time in a long time. *Maybe this was the right thing to do,* she thought.

"I'm calling for Phantasos to watch you," Annika continued her whispered tirade.

"No, you won't. I'm fine. He needs to train. There will be almost forty-five thousand fans. No one, not even the devil himself, would dare confront me. And by the devil, I mean Ares. Now, go. I'll be fine," Amanda turned Annika by her shoulders toward the opposite side of the massive stadium. "Go," Amanda grinned at her friend. "Have fun for once."

It was the fourth inning, and the Angels were up by two runs. The fanatics were having fun. Amanda had no idea how she got the short straw, though. A group of ten or more frat boys in her section decided they needed to take turns asking her to show them to the bathroom, back to their seats, to the concessions, and back to their seats—over and over. Every inning, the fraternity brothers became increasingly boisterous. Catcalls and lude comments were becoming louder and more frequent. The actual touching started when the group leader, who had a few too many beers, asked her to join him in his car and proceeded to grab her ass. When she turned down his advances, that's when it happened. She spun so fast and pushed him off her. Only he went backward over several seats, which was saying a lot since it forced him through his friends when she did it. She could have chalked that up to adrenaline, but the next thing she heard from the unruly twenty-year-olds was—

"What's wrong with her eyes?"

"What the fuck?"

"What's up with her?"

"Bitch, what's wrong with your—"

"Man, we didn't mean anything by it," said one of the guys, but she could see their collective looks above her head and the fear in their eyes—and she knew.

Phantasos. She braced herself and turned around to find—*No! It can't be. Please, God, no!*

Ares towered over her head, snarling at the frat boys. The sound was animalistic. His eyes swirled blood red, and his fists pumped at his sides until he braced her arms and turned his eyes to her.

"No! Let me go," Amanda pleaded.

"You know I cannot do that," Ares's back stiffened, and he shook in anger, but not at her. At that exact moment, she felt a shift in the air.

The arrogant college boys had gone completely quiet, and Ares' eyes were now on the bleachers above them. Amanda had two thoughts: Phantasos was here, and the sounds of the stadium had grown silent.

"Please, no. Please, no," she cried. *This can't be it.*

Ares bent to her ear and whispered, "You allowed him to touch you. Might I remind you that you are mine? He," Ares' eyes stayed trained on Phantasos, who she couldn't see behind her, "will die for killing my son. It will be a slow death because he touched what is mine. Are you ready to play?"

She felt his grin against her ear. He smelled of Olympus, and when he licked her face, his tongue wasn't rough; it was gentle, sensual, and it made her stomach churn. Bile rose in her throat.

"There are over forty-five-thousand mortals in this arena. If you do this here, not even your father can help you," Phobetor said.

Where did he come from? Unlocking her eyes from Ares, behind the war god stood the god of nightmares. His eyes were swirling just like the devil who had ahold of her.

With a roguish smirk, Ares let go of her arms. "I will be coming to claim what is mine." He leaned down and pressed his mouth to hers right before vanishing.

She remembered hitting the steps and the world going black.

❖━━━━━❖

"Why is she not waking?" Phantasos held Amanda in his lap on the couch of her Anaheim apartment. She felt like a child in his arms. This was all his fault. She would have been safe if he had shown himself to her and made her accept that running would not work. *Amanda, please wake up.*

"What she just went through was a repeat of the trauma she endured at Ares' and Phobos' hands. This is her way of keeping herself safe. Not waking means she does not have to confront her monster," Hypnos answered Phantasos' frantic pleading.

Once they got Amanda back to her apartment, they called on the only ones who could help her. In the middle of the studio apartment stood Thia, Hypnos, his brothers, Kallisto and Annika. Morpheus called their father to help heal his mate; the rest were for protection. Since Thia was Ares' half-sibling and just as strong, she was the first called.

"How long?" he asked his father. He was too upset and worried to notice his father conversing with him for the first time in decades.

"That is up to her," Hypnos said. "Once she wakes, it will be safe to take her somewhere besides the middle of a very crowded mortal city."

"I will lie with her on her bed and see if I can find her in her dream state. Maybe I can pull her back," Phantasos said as he lifted her from the couch and took her to her bed.

With an audible swallow, Phantasos soaked in the beauty before him. Her golden hair fanned over the pillow. Her thick pink lips formed a natural smile. His heart ached. If he failed, Ares would take her. *I cannot fail—not at this.*

⟡————⟡

She sat on the pier where she had met Kallisto almost ten years ago. It was a place that held good memories. Wrapping her arms around her legs, drawn to her chest, made her feel safe. The calm water relaxed her and helped her think. There, next to the slip, was where she and Kallisto first saw each other. Of course, her ten-year-old self was sizing up the beautiful girl with a gold bow in her hair. She had never seen another kid who looked like Kallisto. She remembered thinking she was some child movie star.

Kallisto was shy, so Amanda did what she did best. She forced her friendship, and the two became inseparable.

The next memory was of the two of them at fourteen. They sat on the deck, feet dangling in the water, waiting on her father. He was talking to some of his students and assigning work. They had just returned from a glass-bottom boat ride where he told them about each creature they saw. Her dad always took the girls out on excursions with his students. He told her mom it was for educational purposes. She supposed that was true. She and Kallisto knew more about water creatures than any of their classmates. But she also knew that her dad loved her more than anything else. If he could be with his daughter, he would.

"My ἄγγελος, are you okay?"

Where is he? She thought.

Here, behind you. I did not want to frighten you. Phantasos returned telepathically.

Without turning to see him, Amanda continued without speaking aloud. *He's back.*

Yes.

He touched me.

"He did, and he will pay for it," Phantasos sat beside her on the dock.

"I'm scared," Amanda said, placing her chin on her knees without looking at him. If she looked at him, she would break. She needed to think, not break.

"I know. We all are."

That got her attention. "Are you telling me the great god of fantasy fears something?" She relaxed a little with the banter that came naturally around her arrogant Oneiroi.

"I now have something to fear." She could feel his eyes on her.

She couldn't help it. It had been over two weeks since she looked at him. Lifting her chin and lowering her legs, she turned to the god beside her. Even now, his muscled arms, broad chest, sculpted jawline, full lips, and dark blonde hair lit her libido. Not to mention those eyes. He was so beautiful it hurt to not be in his orbit. What was she thinking, leaving this man?

"Really? What's that?" She smiled as if she didn't know.

"Losing you," he said with a sweet smile. Before she had time to think, his mouth was on hers, erasing where Ares had forced his lips on her. He leaned her back on the pier and made her forget about the evil she had just faced.

"I should have never left," Amanda admitted.

"You were trying to save everyone. You get a pass. But from here on out, we stick together. No matter what," Phantasos said as he kissed her nose.

"No matter what," she agreed.

"We need you to wake up. After the incident, you blacked out. Hypnos said that you are protecting yourself by staying unconscious. We cannot move you any further until you wake."

"Where am I now?"

"In your apartment with my father, brothers, Thia, Annika, and of course, Kallisto. She refused to leave."

"Sounds like a party," Amanda made herself smile. She needed Phantasos to think she would be okay. No matter if it were true or not.

"What happened at the stadium? Was it televised? What are people saying about it? I remember everything going quiet in that large arena," Amanda asked several questions without a break to be answered. She knew she sounded a little crazed, but damn, there had been a lot of humans in that stadium.

"The only thing the mortals are saying is that a bright light flickered in the stadium. Ares must have made sure they did not see or remember anything. He would not want Zeus to know about his trip to the human realm," Phantasos said as he rose to his feet.

"I made it ten whole days. Of which I was only alone for three. I'm such an idiot," Amanda giggled.

"From what your grandmother said, the concealment had a high chance of not working. It worked, but not well enough to keep those desperate to get to you away from you. The only thing that will help you is me, your family, and your friends. Nothing more. Now," he held out a hand to her. "Let us go home and watch out for each other."

She took his hand and woke up in his arms on her bed at her parent's house.

Chapter XXXVIII

Sacrifice

Everyone decided Hawaii was the best place to go and discuss Ares' return and their next steps. Amanda refused to go to another realm where her worst nightmares had come true more than once. So, everyone went on high alert, and Amanda carried on with her days with Phantasos and the rest of the crew at her side. The days of one or two deities guarding her at a time were long gone. There were never less than three at any given moment—Phantasos refused to leave her side. The Oneiroi weren't taking chances with Kallisto or Nicole either. You never found them without their bonded.

She added hours at the Gallery since she had already changed her classes to online. This allowed three of her bodyguards to continue with their lives without much change. Surrounding herself with the faces of so many deities, especially after being taken from the gallery floor just a few months ago, wasn't her first or second choice of things to do, but with so many looking out for her, she needed to make things as easy on them as possible. The exception was Annika. She was in and out. Amanda questioned where she went, but they were constantly interrupted, or the subject changed, making Amanda curious about her hooved friend.

Anxiety filled the air, making her parents as uneasy as her friends. They stopped by the gallery several times a day when she was at work, sometimes together, sometimes separately. Her mom wrung her hands all the time, and her dad looked like he could single-handedly take on the entire Greek Pantheon. She had never seen him so protective. And to make everything a little stranger, she could have sworn she saw Hades outside the window one night before closing. She knew it had to be her imagination getting the better of her.

To her chagrin, this meant she and Phantasos never had time together. When she went to California, she resigned herself to never having sex with the god again but having him corporeal—Every. Single. Day.—Kept her hormones on edge. Every touch sent jolts of pleasure through her veins. Every night, he sat vigil by her bed and, sometimes, in her bed, but he never touched her where she needed him to, even though she could feel his need against her. Not that she hadn't tried. Damn, his will was strong as iron, but he refused to succumb to his basic needs if that meant her having fewer to watch over her.

A week and two days had passed since the stadium incident, and no Greek gods or creatures that weren't part of her entourage showed themselves. The longer they went without a confrontation, the more anxious the crew became. She and Nicole jumped when the door chimed. They had been dusting the pictures, and no customers had been in for over an hour. They were conversing about what their grandmother had endured and the intricate politics of her Pantheon. The subject matter had both of them uneasy, so the chime caused a little yelp from her and two Oneiroi to appear at their sides. Luckily, a customer from the prior week needed to pick up a sculpture they had set back.

"I'm not sure my nerves can take much more of this waiting. It sucks," Amanda said, tossing her dusting cloth into the bin behind the counter.

"It's better safe than sorry," Nicole responded to her cousin while hugging Phobetor's middle.

She watched Phantasos circle the room, looking around every corner and out the windows. She hated how uptight he was. She knew this wasn't her fault, but knowing and feeling were two different things. If she hadn't gotten herself taken by either deity, he wouldn't be about to fight for his life and her freedom.

"I'm so sorry, Phantasos," Amanda said once the eldest Oneiroi had finished his trip around the gallery. She hugged him and kissed his cheek. He returned it with one to her nose.

"This is not your fault," he tilted her chin so he could look her in the eyes. Having her think the abuse she endured at the hands of demented beings was her fault made him irrationally angry, not at her, but at Zeus. He could have stopped all of this from happening a millennia ago, but no, he chose to believe his piece of shit son instead of his granddaughter.

"I know that in here," Amanda pointed to her temple, "but here," she laid her hand over her heart, "I carry the blame. I can't help it."

"I love you," that was all he could say. If he allowed his anger to take over, he would be irrational and unable to protect her as she deserved. He already carried an arsenal around with him. He had an Atlantean dagger strapped to his chest, a short sword sheathed on either side, and a long sword across his back. He may be visible to her and other immortals, but to the humans coming and going, they saw nothing. If they did, they would be calling the authorities.

She raised on her tiptoes and kissed his cheek again, "I love you, too, you barbarian."

He and Phobetor watched the girls as they locked up. His thoughts drifted to what-ifs and how he would never survive without her. He met her eyes across the gallery, and his heart skipped. Once in his immortal life, he thought he was in love. Come to find out, he had not been. This, what he felt for the blonde beauty across that gallery, was so much more. Could he win this fight against the god of war? Could he save her? *I have to. There is no choice.*

"Let's walk along the beach before going home. I need the fresh air and saltwater," Amanda said, making her way to him.

"Only if we ask for more guards," Phantasos answered.

"Fine, if we must. I feel guilty with everyone at my beck and call. I can't wait until I'm not everyone's pain in the ass anymore."

⁂

Ten minutes later, with a small group of immortal gods, they walked the beach under the full moon. Phobetor and Nicole walked ahead, and Morpheus and Kallisto were behind them. She felt more deities watching, but they weren't visible. The salt air went a long way to soothing her nerves. The stars were bright, and the water was cool against her feet as the surf rolled in.

"Did you see that?" Amanda asked.

"What?" Phantasos asked, smiling at her.

"It was a falling star. Make a wish."

"Make a wish?" his brows scrunched.

"You're supposed to wish upon a falling star."

"What was your wish," he asked.

"If I tell you, it won't come true," Amanda giggled. It was the first freeing moment she had felt in a long time. They continued their stroll, laughing and telling each other stories. It was just before they were to turn around and make their way back up the beach when the air began to shift. Sand started to swirl around them. Everything happened at once. In a flash, faster than her brain could process, Phantasos pulled his dagger, simultaneously pulling her behind him. Three giant white wolves surrounded them, separating them from their friends. Snarling and snapping, they stalked. She could hear her friends screaming for her and Phantasos. Then the unthinkable happened. Ares appeared right before Phantasos with the most crazed grin she had ever seen. With no time to think, Amanda pushed Phantasos to the side. From the corner of her eye, she saw him fly several meters, but she was focused on Ares and the look of horror on his face. *Why?*

"No!" the god of war bellowed.

Amanda looked between them to see why her body was on fire. A dagger stuck out of her chest. She gripped its hilt, and blood flooded her hands from around the blade. She looked from the sticky red hilt back up to Ares' eyes. The bastard had a tear rolling in slow motion down his face. She slowly followed that tear. When it dripped from his chin, everything sped back up. She could hear Phantasos' frantic screams and saw Kallisto's lightning streaking above them. Ares grabbed her when her knees buckled and laid her on the sand. Pain. So much pain. *It burns.* Metal. She tasted metal.

"This is your fault, Oneiroi," Ares' eyes flared, and he stalked toward Phantasos.

⬥▬▬◦▬▬⬥

A bright light flashed between him and Ares. When the brightness subsided, a celestial being with large white feathered wings, long golden hair, and the look of a man about to execute those in his path crouched like a tiger, ready to pounce.

Phantasos blinked. *It cannot be.*

The angel who had just fallen from somewhere above them wore leather around his chest and vambraces engraved with symbols, all religious in nature, on his forearms. His chest heaved with anger, and what were once blue eyes shined like white lights. Alaric stood from his crouch and growled so loud the earth beneath his feet shook. Wind started spinning around them, gathering sand and saltwater. Everyone was in the eye of the storm created by the angel's wrath.

Alaric went straight for Ares' until his daughter called for him. The second he faltered, Ares vanished.

"Amanda! Amanda! Fuck, someone help," Phantasos screamed and rocked her, not sure how he had gotten to her with all the commotion going on around them. Blood covered them both as it dripped from the wound where the Atlantean dagger was buried in her heart. The sand and water under them turned pink. She was trying desperately to say something, but blood leaked from both sides of her mouth, keeping the words from forming. He leaned his ear to her lips and tried to make out what she was trying to say. When her breath ceased and her eyes glazed over, he heard a gut-wrenching roar of pain, then realized it was coming from him. She was not breathing even though her mouth was opened slightly. Her eyes stared up at him. Lifeless. He felt the blood pumping through his veins. His heart cracked—

"Back away, son," the angel—*no Alaric*— said, placing a hand on his shoulder.

"No! I will not leave her. No!" He wiped his eyes with one hand, trying to see the angel who told him to let her go. *No fucking way. She is mine.*

"Listen to me. Lay her on the sand and back away from her," Alaric's voice was not that of the man he knew. It was so deep it reverberated around him.

Angered at her father's demand, Phantasos pulled his short sword and told Alaric to go fuck himself. The next thing he knew, Hades held him by one arm, and Phobetor grasped his other.

"Do as he says," Hades commanded.

They watched as the waves continued to wash up just under Amanda's body. The air was full of sobs, and he swore death to everyone in the royal line of the Greek Pantheon and the bastards keeping him from her.

His mind raced, trying to make sense of what he was seeing. *This cannot be.* He wanted to die. She looked so broken. Alaric looked like an avenging angel but did nothing. That cannot be right. The only angels allowed in this realm were guardians, not warriors. They were banished from this realm thousands and thousands of years ago. *What in Hades' name is happening? Am I hallucinating?*

The water retreated and stopped; time stood still, and a flash of the brightest light burst from Amanda's chest. Phantasos heard himself scream for her. "Amanda!"

He caught sight of her body through the glow, levitating and convulsing just above the sand, when another burst of light erupted from her.

"What the fuck is going on, Alaric?" Phantasos yelled at the angel. "What is happening to her?"

This time, the brightness did not subside; it grew unbelievably powerful. Heat radiated from the light to where he was being held by his brother and the god of the Underworld. It was so bright he had to close his eyes, but through his lids, he could still see the illumination, white and pulsating.

"Alaric! Answer me, you bastard. Help her!" Phantasos screamed at the angel as his body shook violently. He was unable to see, and because of his brother and Hades, he could not get to her. "Wake her damn it!" The force before them pushed him to his knees, both gods holding onto him on theirs, keeping him from completely falling forward.

The heat from the light dissipated as fast as it had come, allowing him to open his eyes. From remnants of the light walked the most fantastic creature he had ever seen. Amanda was alive, dressed in a stark white gown with a thin golden crown around her head and large white wings flaring from her back.

He looked around to see if he was the only one seeing her. Everyone was on their knees, staring.

"Nephilim," Phantasos cried.

Chapter XXXIX

Nephilim

Her body felt unbelievably amazing—strong, light, and full of power like she'd never experienced. However, shock continued wreaking havoc on her mind. She looked over what parts of her body she could. Instinctually, she flexed her shoulder blades, and large white wings flared from her sides. Looking down, she noticed she was radiating a soft white light. She turned her hands over and looked at her palms. In their center, a bright light rested. Mesmerized, she flipped them from back to palm two more times.

Looking up, she registered that her friends were watching her. Tilting her head slightly, she took in Phantasos and her father. Her father also wore wings with armor. *I'm dead, and this has to be heaven.* Her dad was dressed like an angel, and Hades was on the beach with the rest of the crew. *No, he wouldn't be in heaven.* What is going on?

Her senses were overloaded. Colors were more vibrant than ever. She smelled salt water and blood and heard the breaths coming from everyone who stood meters from her. Friends who were otherwise wholly silent, on their knees, and transfixed on—her. She said nothing but watched as they all slowly rose to their feet, unmoving from their knee prints in the sand.

When she took a few steps forward, everyone but her father retreated the same number of steps. *Are they afraid of me? Hell, I'm afraid of me. Same inner dialogue at least.*

Now, scared to approach her friends, she had no choice but to continue to stare. They looked both in awe and fearful. *Should they be?* She needed answers, so she turned, facing only her father. "How?"

Her father walked toward her, his hands out in front of him as if she were going to attack. "Come with me so we can talk," Alaric said.

"Not until you tell me what the hell is going on," She looked him up and down and continued. "And with you."

❖━━━◆━━━❖

Hearing Alaric tell Amanda that she needed to go with him snapped Phantasos out of the shock he had been in since the dagger was buried in her chest. Finding his arms free, he stood and ran to Amanda, stopping inches before her. He hit his knees once more, with red tears dripping from his eyes, bowing to her and begging for her to stay. He could not lose her again. Answers to his questions would come, but what he needed the most was for her not to go with the angel. *What if she never returns?*

"Phantasos, you need to back away and let us go," Alaric voice was calm, but the tightness of his jaw muscles and his clenched fists told a different story.

"There is no way I am letting you take her from me," he replied, not moving from his knees at Amanda's feet.

"If she and I don't leave now, we might never return. As it is, I have much explaining and groveling to do. Say your goodbyes," the Angel said to him and Amanda.

Phantasos, still on his knees, something he had never done before, said, "Please come back to me. If you do not, all of this was for nothing."

⟡

Amanda knelt, facing Phantasos, "None of this makes sense. I need answers." She cupped his face in her hands and said words she knew might not be true: "I promise to come back. But what my father is saying is true, and I have no clue how I know that—it's in here," she said, laying her hand over her heart. "Trust me."

Amanda stood and dared one glimpse at Kallisto before her father took her hand, and they disappeared.

⟡

"Where are we?" Amanda turned in a complete circle to gauge her position. There was greenery for miles, and she could see a waterfall and hear the splashing of more in the distance. "This is beautiful."

"I didn't want to take you too far, so we are on the Na Pali Coast of Kaua'i. Very few humans come here. It's too difficult to reach. We need privacy, and I hope to explain everything to you before we are brought before our maker," Alaric said as he led Amanda to a spot where they could sit and talk.

"What does that even mean?" She was overwhelmed, and after finally figuring out how to tuck her enormous wings, she felt like she could concentrate on what her father was saying.

"Have a seat, Amanda. I'm about to tell you my story," Alaric gestured to two beautifully made bamboo chairs that he conjured with a wave of his hand. She felt her eyes widen.

"First. Are you really my dad?" She asked before he started his tale.

With a slight chuckle, he replied, "Yes, you are my blood. You are a Nephilim. Now, let me get all this out." He smiled at her enthusiasm and patted her hand. And with another wave, he became her human father without the wings or armor; his eyes returned to blue, and his blonde hair was just below his ears instead of past his shoulders. He transformed from a warrior to a scientist in the blink of an eye.

"I have no words," Amanda said, awe-struck.

He chuckled again. Her eyes were the size of dinner plates. He knew her senses were overloaded. She should be able to hear insects buzzing at least nine meters away and see tiny particles no human could see. A sense of pride swelled in his heart as she took everything that had happened in stride—no passing out or inconsolable tears.

"After my story, if time permits, I will teach you how to return to your human form. This," he pointed to her wings, "is your natural form. You are a half angel, half demi-god."

Amanda looked at her arms and legs again. "Ethereal, just like Annika said."

"In the beginning, when God made man, many angels followed the unholy one to earth. They began to mix with humans and destroyed the bond our maker had created with mortals. Angels were never meant to procreate. We are a completely different race of beings. We are made as humans were, in His image, but that is where the similarities end. There are many categories of angels, and they function in a hierarchy: guardians, warriors, and worshippers are allowed to cross into the human realm to help mortals. The rest are bound to the heavenly realm," Alaric said.

"I thought all angels worshipped God, except fallen ones, of course," Amanda interrupted with a furrowed brow.

"We do; they are categorized as worshippers, meaning their primary job is to lead a mortal to worship our maker," he answered, proud she was engaging in what he was saying.

"Okay. Sorry I interrupted," Amanda said.

"That's okay. This is a lot to grasp. The warriors, which I am part of, have only been sent a few times—ever—and only once in a large quantity.

"Anarchy began after the fallen angels had fathered many children with humans. Those children were referred to by man as giants and were predominantly evil beings, wreaking havoc on the mortal realm. We were sent in to fix the problem. We banished and imprisoned as many fallen angels as possible. Our maker then sent floods to remove the Nephilim—the proper name of the children created by the fallen and mortals."

Amanda gasped, "They were all killed?"

"No. Many survived, and the blood of angels runs through the veins of both mortals and immortals to this day, however minuscule. The unruly and evil were removed in one way or another. Once our job was done on earth, the warrior angels were to return to heaven. We had a limited window of time to get back, and because I was helping children by eliminating several nasty demons who thought they would torment innocence while the world was under siege—I missed the window. I'm not a *fallen* angel. I was sent to banish them; however, I am a *trapped* seraph."

"Why are you still here? That was thousands of years ago. It's more time than I can comprehend." Amanda shook her head, confusion all over her face as she blinked rapidly.

"The short answer is, I don't know. I've begged, prayed, and have done many other things, but God has not taken me back to the heavenly realm. He is the only one who knows why. I have kept my head down and helped mankind, never striving for power, just working to improve this world from the moment I entered it. I have spent so many millennia protecting mortals. It wasn't until I met your mother that I veered off course, and still, my maker never punished me or removed me. When I met Kathryn, I knew she was mine. I've always known she was a demigod. I could sense her power under the concealment," Alaric continued. "She captured me like no other before. I remained celibate for thousands of years, never even tempted, but one look at your mom and I saw a life with her and our unborn. She is my other half. The only one I would forsake my lineage for."

"If you are all about protecting people, why didn't you stop Ares from taking me?" He could see the hurt and anger on his daughter's face.

"Unlike what most people think, angels are not all-knowing. No being but our heavenly father is all-knowing."

"What about The Fates Three? Aren't they?"

"When they are together, they can predict more correct outcomes than most. However, due to free will, not even the infamous Moirai know everything as they would like you to believe," Alaric answered.

"So, you were not supposed to be with Mom?" Amanda asked.

"No. For that reason and for making a child with her, I have stayed under the radar, not causing trouble and trying to keep from catching the eye of our maker."

"What will happen to you? To me?" her voice shook, and her hands trembled. This revelation was scaring her, and he felt horrible about it.

"I don't know. That's where my begging and explaining comes in. I'm more concerned for you. God removed Nephilim from this world because they were using their gifts for nefarious reasons," Alaric said. "God knows all, but because of his gift of free will, I chose to marry, love, and bear a child with a demigod. He knows our hearts, and I pray He judges us for what's within them."

"When will we know?" She asked, still shaking. Alaric wrapped his arms around his daughter, trying to calm her trembling body.

"I don't know. Soon though. I have tried not to get involved with Phantasos' and Ares' feud. I assigned Hades to protect you. He was not happy when I showed up to reprimand him for Phobos. Then he promised Phantasos, for a price, to help watch over you. That's why creatures have been in abundance. Plus, you give off an otherworldly signature that only they can sense. Like mortals, the gods believe in only what has been set before them for centuries. They have forgotten that playing with the lives of mortals is what got them sent away thousands of years ago."

⟡━━━━⟡

"I have so many questions; I don't know where to start."

"We can talk more about the past later. What do you want to know now?" Alaric asked.

"Okay," Amanda stood and paced, the tips of her tucked wings a mere half inch from the ground. "I'm half angel, half demigod—but what does that mean exactly?"

"You're the first of your kind. You weren't showing demigod abilities when your grandmother lifted her concealments because my suppressions are far stronger and undetectable by anyone other than angels. Your mother doesn't even know," her father looked shamefaced at the admission.

"Are you kidding me? She has no clue you naturally have wings?" It was a question. "Holy shit, Dad," Amanda stopped her pacing and stood slack-jawed in front of her father. She couldn't believe her ears. Her parents were so close, and until his admission, she had never sensed any deception in their marriage.

"I'm not proud of the secret I've had to keep. I do so to protect her. When Angelia's lineage was learned, I almost told her. But too much was going on for me to tell her, and if I did, I would have broken another vow. She would be another being to know a warrior angel walks among you. The only ones who know of me are you, your friends, and Hades," Alaric stood up and looked her in the eyes. She saw her father looking back at her, not an angel. But she could see the light in his eyes when she looked closely. "Before the night is done, the only ones who will know are you and Hades. Once Ares is taken care of, the only other person who will know is you. Your friends and Hades will forget."

"How?" Amanda could feel her forehead tighten as she tried to understand what he said. "You can do that? Make them forget so easily?"

"Yes, and I suppose you can too. That is something we need to figure out."

"What?" Amanda's head felt fuzzy.

"What abilities you possess," Alaric smiled.

"I'm not going to get my hopes up. So, if I continue with Phantasos, I will have to keep my lineage a secret as you have with Mom?"

"Yes," Alaric gave a pained whisper. "Unless we are told otherwise by our maker."

CHAPTER XL

HADES

"It has been a week, Hades," Phantasos stood before the dark king, weak from days of looking for Amanda and nothing else. She had become excellent at blocking him. His mind was consumed by what happened on the beach. The memory of Amanda shoving him out of Ares' way made bile rise in his throat. She took his spot and placed herself in direct line with the god's dagger. Nightmares assailed him every night, always of her dying in his arms and never waking. One would think being a dream god, he would be able to stop the horrific visions or get Phobetor to, but for some reason, he felt like the torture was necessary. He should not have been so easily shoved.

Nothing could have prepared him for when she rose from one being into another. She walked out of that bright light as an angel. He supposed the reality of her being half-seraph played with his mind since he had not been able to see her since that evening. To make things more unbelievable, not one of their friends remembered anything that happened that night, not even Kallisto. They thought Amanda had left again without wanting to be found, and he was going mad. They had no clue that she left with her father, who was a warrior angel, and she was not just a doppelganger, but a Nephilim.

There was only one other who witnessed Amanda's return from the dead on the beach a week before. Only one other knew the truth about her and her father—Hades. And he was the one Phantasos needed more answers from.

He had gone to everyone on the beach the night Ares took his demigod, and when Hades confirmed his knowledge of angels and Nephilim, Phantasos latched on to him. This was his third time, in so many days, to beg the dark god for answers.

"It depends on the Almighty now. Alaric has walked the mortal realm longer than most gods have existed. God has allowed this, but only He knows for what reason. Alaric feared the Almighty might feel differently if anyone learned of him or his child since God destroyed the Nephilim once before. The angel is afraid the Almighty may not be welcoming of Amanda now she has wings."

"There is not an evil part of her. The half-angels, half-humans of long ago, were immoral creatures," Phantasos defended his bonded. "She is all good and kind. Loves with her whole heart."

"The Almighty is all-knowing and will do what is best. If my brother finds out about her, he may try to use her. If her powers are half as formidable as her father's, Zeus will be unstoppable," Hades rose from his throne and hopped from the dais to stand before Phantasos. "Whatever the decision is, it will be the best for the masses. Now, you look like death. Go to the cave. Get cleaned up, sleep, eat, and meet me in the training area when you can hold a sword without falling over."

"How do you know Alaric?" Phantasos asked.

"That is a long story. When you meet me to train, I will indulge your curiosity, but for now, you need to take better care of yourself. If my nephew were to come for you at this moment, you would not survive," Hades turned and left him standing below the dais where his gorgons stood guard. He was once again alone with his thoughts, this time with the hissing sounds of life-sized snakes to keep him company.

Hades was not acting like himself. In fact, he had never witnessed the god concerned for anything other than revenge and power. Phantasos left the throne room and did what the lord of the Underworld suggested—one step at a time.

❖———❖

Over the last week, Amanda trained incessantly with her father. She finally had control of her wings—sort of. She could flare them out, tuck them in—one wing at a time, even. However, she couldn't lift herself off the ground.

Flight was not as easy as one would think. There was a balance to her body that she had to learn and make muscle memory. It would do her no good to learn to fly but to have to tell her wings to flap constantly. *Ugh!*

She balanced on a fallen tree about two feet off the ground. This had been going on for two days. She had fallen off the tree dozens of times, pissed she wasn't further along in her week of *Angel 101*. Fall off, hop back on, fall off—the cycle frustratingly continued.

On the other hand, they figured out she possessed much more power than her father expected. On her first day, she learned to conjure things made of natural materials. Her father told her that was normal since human-made materials felt different, whatever that meant, and were more challenging to wield. She had enough on her mind without mentally arguing why her abilities had limits. She was ecstatic that being *godly* beautiful wasn't her only *skill set*.

She also had unreal strength. The tree she was currently balancing on was lying on its side because she had pushed it over.

Controlling her strength when she needed a light touch proved harder than pushing a large tree down. With great power came the need for even greater control. Power needed honing—control required learning.

"Lift your right foot and count to a hundred. Then switch to your left one and do the same," Alaric commanded from the ground. He was a great teacher, as he should be since that was his profession. He taught her how to handle her new normal. Unfortunately, returning to her human form had been out of reach, and the pinch of her father's forehead every time they worked on it worried her.

"This is getting easier," Amanda said, lowering her arms to her sides and using only her wings for balance. Yesterday, she kept falling because she tried to use her arms instead of her wings. She had to rely on body parts she had never had before, which wasn't easy.

"Good. After you finish staying still, walk back and forth across the tree while keeping your arms at your sides." Amanda nodded, letting her father know she had heard him.

She counted loudly in her head. If she concentrated on nothing but balancing and numbers, her mind wouldn't drift to the shit storm they were in. Neither of them had been summoned, which had them both on edge. The not knowing and waiting were far worse than just getting it over with. Plus, the look on everyone's faces when she came out of that blinding light haunted her memory. Especially Phantasos'. She shook the invasive thoughts from her head. *Ninety-eight, ninety-nine, one hundred—Now walk.*

She was halfway back across the tree when she realized she and the massive log under her feet were levitating. She glanced at her father, who was smiling ear to ear at her.

"Keep walking, Amanda. The height is irrelevant. Stay the course."

"That's easy for you to say. You can fly," She wobbled slightly.

"So can you," he replied. "You have to be confident in your wings."

"Well, considering I've only had them for a few days, that's easier said than done. You never had to learn to use them. You always had yours," she said. It happened when she looked *down* and saw the tops of the trees. "No, Dad. Too high." Her legs began to shake, so she instinctively flung her arms out, forgetting to concentrate on her wings. She fell. Luckily, her dad caught her just before she hit the forest floor. "Damn it! Why would you do that?"

"Because it will take your instincts kicking in for you to learn how to fly. You aren't confident yet."

"I lived nineteen years with arms and legs as my appendages. Now, I'm to use my wings like I've had them my whole life. One week isn't long enough for me to have instincts of confidence," she scowled at her father. She knew why he pushed her so hard, but heights had never been her favorite, and now she was expected to soar above everything like a damn bird.

"Let's work on something else," Alaric said.

"Only if I can keep both feet firmly planted on the ground." He chuckled, "Okay. Come with me."

She followed her father to the table he had conjured on their second day. On the table sat three glasses. One was full of water, and the other two were empty. With a thought from her dad, the full glass was now a third full, and so were the other two. However, she had not seen anything happen; it just was.

"I want you to use only your mind." She looked back, and the glasses had returned to one full and two empty. "Make the water equal in each glass.

"How?" Amanda looked between her dad and the challenge before her.

"You've learned to use your hands to conjure. Your hands have nothing to do with it. I don't want you dependent on hand gestures because you believe it helps. Use only your mind."

Amanda stood in front of the table and the taunting glass of water. Again, she placed her arms at her sides and stared at it. Surprising herself, it took less than a minute before the water in the two empty glasses appeared, and the third one emptied to a third full.

"That was easy." She beamed up at her father.

"Flying is no different. It's between here," tapped her temple, "and here," he tapped one of her wings. "Faith in your new body."

She worked on her mental strength for the rest of the afternoon and controlled the world around her without touching it. She felt like a badass.

◆——··——◆

After a shower, food, and a couple of hours of sleep, Phantasos went to the training room, searching for Hades. The dark god had taught him a lot of battle moves over the past several months but had never talked to him about anything other than fighting. He was curious how the god of the Underworld knew a warrior angel. He was even more curious about why Hades agreed to tell him how they met.

The hole in his chest was still raw. His cleanliness and full stomach had not helped with his despair, but his mind was definitely sharper. The days taken to search for Amanda had his muscles tight. It would take a while to work the stiffness out.

The training room was empty, so he began with his usual warm-ups and continued working with his daggers and the practice dummies. He had worked up a sweat before Hades sauntered into the room with a smirk spread over his lips.

"I see you did as you should and cared for some of your basic needs. How does it feel to beat the shit out of inanimate objects?"

"Since you were not here, I had to improvise," Phantasos used the hem of his shirt to remove the sweat from his brow. "How about joining me on the mat so I can beat the shit out of you instead?" He knew better than to taunt the king of the Underworld, but like his bonded, he could not resist the temptation of pissing the god off.

Hades narrowed his eyes and, with a thought, donned black training leathers with no shirt. The arrogant ass still wore his thin obsidian crown, suggesting he would not be the loser in their sparring match.

"Short swords, daggers, and your powers are all you need to fight the god of war. Your power is your main weapon. No training swords during this round. We will use the real thing, except for the daggers—no Atlantean daggers." Hades smirked. An Atlantean dagger was the only weapon capable of killing a god as powerful as either of them. "First, use your powers to subdue; next, get in close for a kill shot; do not let up. A stab wound with these will not kill either of us. I expect to need healing after this young Oneiroi. Now fight."

Hades lunged at him faster than he had expected and sliced diagonally down his chest. Blood pooled at the waistband of his leathers. With a thought, he closed the wound and began the deadly dance of survival.

The ability to use power and physical strength while fighting for your life came easily to Phantasos. However, when paired with a god older and more experienced, it became unpredictable who would succeed as the victor. Hades was physically a mountain of a god, had millennia more experience, and his powers rivaled most, if not all, the gods; therefore, besting him would be a feat.

After both gods experienced several flesh and a few muscle wounds, they switched to daggers. Phantasos was proficient in Katāri and confident he would win the round against the King of the Underworld. However, practicing with the small blades would help work his muscle memory since he knew Ares had an Atlantean dagger—the one he had used on Amanda. Where he got it was beyond him. The question was, did he have another?

The mini battle ended with a dagger sticking from his forearm, one plunged into Hades' last two ribs on his right side, and a room destroyed from the wielding of their powers.

Hades handed him his drink after taking two long drags of the liquid. Phantasos did the same and found Ambrosia in the waterskin. All of their wounds began to heal.

"How do you know, Alaric?" he asked the king while setting the room to rights.

"He came looking for answers to what had happened to Kathryn and Kellie. He knew they had concealments on them. Since I control the dead. He thought it was more likely someone in my realm would have his answers than Olympus. Plus, he knew my integrity was greater than my brother's,"

Hades replied.

"How did that lead to him having you watch over Amanda?"

"We met before he introduced himself to Kathryn. He was in awe of her and watched her for weeks before he came to me. Of course, who was I to deny a war angel answers to his questions? I had him meet Priapus."

"Why did you never tell anyone about the angel?" Phantasos asked.

"No lesser gods or beings of any kind go against an angel. There may be different degrees of angels, but all angels are second to the Almighty. The strongest of us have immense power, wings for flight, and strength far greater than any mortal, but angels are a league unto themselves."

"What about Nephilim?"

"I have never known one, except for Amanda—who is no regular Nephilim. She is not part angel, part human; no, she is part angel, part demigod. The only Nephilim that could be any stronger would have to be part angel, part god—and to my knowledge, there has never been such a creature," Hades looked worried as he spoke of Amanda's lineage.

"Does Alaric make you nervous?" he asked, knowing that asking this particular god may not be his best idea.

The twitch of Hades' eye gave his irritation away, but he answered his question, "Alaric is as old as time. He's been in the mortal realm for almost as long as mankind and is a skilled warrior. It would be stupid of me if I were not nervous where the angel was concerned."

Chapter XLI

Rules

THREE WEEKS HAD GONE by in both slow motion and a flash. Amanda spent her days learning how to use her new body and learning about her heritage as much as possible. Still, no one had hauled her dad and her off to berate, torture, or execute them. They had heard nothing from the Almighty, not that she thought God would deign to present himself to her. Around the two-week mark, her father had stopped, literally looking over his shoulder. However, over the last two days, he started fidgeting again. When she asked what was wrong, he changed the subject. She could tell he was trying to protect her, but he didn't understand that her not knowing played with her head, and her imagination was running rampant.

While lying in her tent, Amanda thought about her life, taking a much-needed break from wielding exceptional power and learning mind-boggling information. She missed her friends, especially Phantasos. Their relationship had been a whirlwind of ups and downs. They mostly had downs, not because of them but because of the circumstances they found themselves in. She couldn't help but wonder what would have happened if The Fates Three had not interfered and not warned him against her. She still didn't understand what their issue with her was. They knew damn well she wasn't all human. They knew she had god blood running through her veins, but from what her father said, they didn't know she was half-angel. She guessed they suspected she was something nefarious. Would Phantasos and her friends forgive her for leaving right after their interaction with Ares? *After he stabbed her. After she turned.*

She needed to get back to them, so she worked hard to learn everything quickly. She couldn't help but wonder when the warlord would strike again. *When would he go after Phantasos?* She was pretty sure he wouldn't come after her, not while her father was nearby. Ares would definitely hunt her Oneiroi down, though.

One thing her dad taught her in their short time on the beautiful Na Pali Coast was about all the different Pantheons and their gods and creatures. Shocked at how many there were, she saw her world in a completely different light. In South Africa, she found that not only Greek gods and Greek creatures existed but also an elf from the Norse Pantheon. Her father informed her of hundreds more, which opened the floodgates to a universe beyond anything she could have fathomed possible. She felt small and relatively insignificant in the grand scheme of things. Having her newfound knowledge and knowing her father was the only warrior angel and she was the only Nephilim on earth was even more daunting. Of all the millions of deities, angels, and creatures, the knowledge they were the only ones of their kind in the human realm and she, the only Nephilim in existence, was beyond mind-blowing.

"May I join you?" Alaric asked, standing at the entrance of her home away from home.

"Of course. You, okay?" His hair stood on end like he'd been running his hands through it. Onc of his signs that something was amiss.

"I'm good. I received a message today about meeting a messenger offshore." He ran his hand through his hair. Yep, he had something worrying him.

"I'm going to unpack that statement and say by messenger, you mean someone sent from Heaven. And by offshore, you meant—I'm not quite sure what you meant."

"Yes. A messenger angel, and by offshore, I mean not over land. High in the sky. Where no one would see us," her father said as he sat by her.

"What did the messenger say?" She heard her voice crack and felt her hands grow clammy. He was nervous and had heard from their maker. Now, she was a few seconds away from having a meltdown.

"He left me here to help balance the world. There is so much evil. He wanted a fierce protector fighting for mankind. Meeting your mother was not all by coincidence."

"What does that mean?" Amanda scrunched her forehead.

"As long as you do not marry and reproduce with a mortal, you may live in the mortal realm. You were very much meant to be here as a protector. If you procreate with a mortal, your destiny will be that of all the Nephilim before you," Alaric rubbed his other hand through his hair.

"I don't think that will be an issue, Dad. If Phantasos continues to have me, I'll be with him," Amanda smiled at her father's worrying face. "Besides. I'm not sure I could keep my heritage a secret from my partner."

She watched as her father closed his eyes in shame. He had kept his lineage from her mother. He wasn't proud of it but determined to protect her identity no matter who he had to keep in the dark. "I'm going to tell her."

"Did the messenger say anything else?"

"Your lifespan is the same as any other angel, with one difference. You are capable of dying from other means than by angelic hands or by the Almighty. This may sound crass, but—your head would have to be severed for that to happen."

Amanda winced, "That's rather disturbing but good to know."

"You may have children, as long as they are by a god or an immortal of heavenly choosing. You can never tell anyone who is not approved of beforehand."

"By whom?" Amanda asked.

"By me," Alaric answered.

"Well. Can I tell Kallisto, Phantasos, his brothers, Mom, and Nicole?"

"You and I will speak with your mother together. You may tell Phantasos and the rest after this situation with Ares is rectified. Until then, you may not tell anyone else,"

"But—"

Alaric held up a hand. "Before you argue—The Greek Pantheon does not need to know anything until this mess is cleared up. If something happened to you before then, I'm not sure I could keep from leveling Olympus. I almost did before. It was the concern I had about your future and how you would be judged for existing that stopped me. Now, get changed, and let's work on your flying."

Her father put a halt to the conversation. She didn't have the chance to ask the hundreds of questions running through her head. Like everything else, it would have to wait until she could take care of herself if Ares came looking for her. She was a little unsteady and unfamiliar with her body at the moment, but every day, she became stronger and more confident.

No matter how he said it, one month—four weeks—twenty-eight days—it might as well have been forever. He felt like it had been. That was how long it had been since Amanda left the beach with her father, just minutes after she returned from the dead *with fucking wings*. The connection between them was quiet. *Is she alive?* Each day made Phantasos more anxious. He finally had his brother watching over his sleep due to the nightmares from that night on the beach. Now, there were three from that night who knew the truth. When Phobetor witnessed Amanda's death and reawakening into an angel through Phantasos' nightmares, he was stunned to have forgotten such an epic event. Phantasos swore him to secrecy but was relieved to have someone he could talk to about it.

Marissa's death had caused him over a century of pain and a divide between him and his father. What happened on that beach a month ago had cost him what felt like his soul. There will never be another after Amanda. He knew that for certain—no matter the time that passed.

Amanda had managed to lift herself off the ground using her wings and a lot of willpower when a booming voice made her drop a meter she had accomplished. The voice surprised her, but not her father. Poseidon stood knee-deep in the water, and her dad stood between her and the Earth Shaker with his arms crossed in his God-given form—the warrior angel.

"What brings the god of the oceans here?" Alaric asked, not turning around.

"Things are making more sense now," Poseidon looked between her father and her. "Seems Hades has friends in *high* places,"

"He and I have known one another for a while. What does that have to do with anything?" Alaric wings remained tucked behind him, but Amanda knew how fast her father could move. After the weeks she'd been training with the angel, she knew the gods were no match.

"No need to fret, Angel. I am not going to harm your offspring. She was given access to my horses—something I have only allowed one other in all my days. I knew if my broody brother had an interest in the demigod, there was a reason. I am just stating that the reason is a good one. If I were to come across an angel of your station and asked to protect his child, I would move mountains to do so, as well."

"Good to know," Alaric smiled. "Just understand, if another god of the Greek Pantheon ever harms my daughter again, I will demolish every single one of you. No matter if you were part of her pain. I sat back too long. She will never be harmed again."

"If she were mine, I would do the same," Poseidon looked at her as she walked to stand by her father.

"I want you to help protect Phantasos," Amanda raised her chin, waiting for the god to refuse her.

"I can do that. But you should realize that he would be agitated if he found out you asked me or any god to protect him. Oneiroi are powerful. They do not take kindly to being thought of as weak."

"I'm not weak. I'm actually more powerful than you, and my father has you and your brother looking over me. Weakness has nothing to do with it," she stared at Poseidon.

"He will not take it that way," the king replied.

"Then say nothing to him. If he is near the water, protect him if you can. That is all I want," she turned, returning to where she had been training.

"You need to get your daughter in the air, Angel. Even I can see that she has not mastered her new body," Poseidon said. "I wanted to meet my first warrior angel. I will now bid you goodbye. All she has to do is call my name," Poseidon vanished into the water.

Alaric turned to her and raised one brow. "Do you trust him?"

"I don't trust anyone." Amanda closed her eyes and concentrated on levitating.

Chapter XLII

Passion

Amanda knew her father would hear her when she lifted her tent flap and exited. She also knew he would let her do what she needed to do. Another week had passed, and she could finally take flight and defend herself enough to outperform any mythos or human. The ones able to render her powerless would be someone of her origins, heavenly or fallen, and to her knowledge, only the heavenly knew of her existence.

Only Poseidon had found them. Unfortunately, he wasn't among the top ten she wanted to see. Desperate to see her friends, she had to leave Angel 101 for a little while. If she were honest, she was desperate to see Phantasos. Her father had her conceal their connection so she could learn without distraction, an ability given with her wings. She could conceal any signature or bond between herself and another being or creature. Amanda closed her eyes and opened the bond between herself and her Oneiroi. She took two steps and leaped into the air.

He felt her before he heard her land. Phantasos sat on the black sand, watching the waves, when a jolt shot through his body. The bond was back. Just as the thought went through his head, Amanda landed in front of him in a flowing lavender dress, bare feet, and snowy white wings. Before she could speak, he was on his feet and had her wrapped in his arms.

Maneuvering around these wings will take getting used to, was his first thought. "You are alive!" He buried his nose in her neck and took a deep breath. "Thank the gods, you still smell like you. I missed you."

Amanda giggled and returned his embrace with as much enthusiasm as he had shown her. Her laugh gave him the entry he had been craving. He covered her mouth with his and growled when his tongue found hers. *Fuck!* He could feel her and what she was feeling.

He picked her up, and she wrapped her legs around his waist, neither letting go of the all-consuming kiss. He stood ankle-deep in the water, devouring her. It took his brain a minute to figure out her wings were gone.

Reluctantly, he let her lips go and stared into her brilliant blue eyes. He registered that they were more vibrant than before, as impossible as that seemed. "Never do that again. Please." He pressed his forehead to hers, "I need you."

He felt her nod. Then he flashed them to the cave.

⊰•—••—•⊱

Amanda looked around at her new environment with her legs still wrapped around Phantasos' waist; his erection pressed to her center. While his in-the-moment arousal felt beyond amazing, she couldn't help but notice the dark circles around his eyes. Guilt sent a pang through her. She knew she had put them there.

"I'm sorry. I *had* to leave. I needed to learn, and shock had me captive for the first two weeks. Not only did I gain wings, but

I also had to realize that I'm not human. This isn't my normal body. Wings are my norm now."

"Did you figure everything out?" He kissed her between each word—the first word to her forehead, the second and third to each eye, and the last two to her lips.

"Not everything," she giggled under his loving caresses. "That will take years. But I can fly," she raised her chin for easier access to her neck. *Damn, that feels good!*

He kissed from her chin down her neck, then back up, "I saw. Impressive. By the way, I like wings. I should be grilling you, but right now, I need to bury myself inside you and feel your heat all around me."

"Yes, please," Amanda closed her eyes as he continued nibbling and licking her neck.

With no more preamble, both their clothes were gone, and he tossed her onto the bed. "This will not be slow or easy, my άγγελος. I am afraid my desire, mixed with relief that you are here and well, has me ravenous."

He clasped her wrists in one hand over her head, and with a push of his hips, he was buried deep inside her. She, just as frenzied, matched him thrust for thrust. It was the fastest and most powerful climax she'd ever had, and they reached it together with the intensity of each other's orgasm, leaving them sweating and panting.

"Thank the gods I'm a Nephilim, or I might have died just then," Amanda breathed heavily with Phantasos' comforting weight still on her.

"Give me a few minutes, and we will do that again slower so I can enjoy every inch of this glorious body," he pushed up on both forearms and looked into her eyes. "I was so scared that I had lost you, Amanda. I cannot go through that again, ever."

She pulled him back down to her chest and whispered, "I'm sorry. I love you."

"I want you to tell me everything you went through, but first," She felt his erection against her. He smiled mischievously.

"That didn't take a full minute," Amanda giggled.

"I have never needed someone so bad. Thousands of years of existence—it only took a Nephilim to bring me to my knees." With a slow lick, tracing the seam of her lips, he sunk back in, and for the next several hours, they sated their need for one another.

Amanda tucked herself against his side, laying her head on his chest. She could hear his heartbeat as they lightly stroked their hands all over each other, unable to stop touching.

"We had to wait until we found out what would happen to us?" She spoke quietly, just above a whisper. "Nephilim were eradicated not long after creation. Dad didn't know what God would do. So, while I learned about my new body and gifts, he waited for a messenger. Finally, one came."

"And?" She felt his body go rigid.

"The messenger said I had to help mankind and could never procreate with a mortal. If I obey, I will live the lifetime of an angel," Amanda looked up to see Phantasos' reaction. She was pleased to see they were turning back blue as he calmed. Knowing he would worry, she kept the whole head rolling for her to die, quiet. He didn't need to know there was any chance of death.

"Thank the gods," Phantasos pulled her tight and kissed the top of her head. "I would have had to go with you. Like I said, I cannot live without you again."

"How is everyone?" Amanda asked.

"Worried. The only ones who know what happened on the beach are me, Hades, and Phobetor. My brother knows because I needed help with the nightmares I was having. When he visited my sleep, he saw it play out. I have sworn him to secrecy, which he is unhappy about," Phantasos answered.

"What does everyone think happened to me?" There it was again. Guilt. She felt it to her bones.

"They think you decided to leave again. Your mother thinks your father left with you. They are all heartbroken," Phantasos rolled out from under her and pulled on his pants. He stood facing the wall, not looking at her. "I know there are reasons you and your father have chosen to keep everything quiet, but I believe it is unfair to your friends and family. They love you." He rubbed his hand through his hair and went to the en-suite bathroom, leaving her filled with shame.

✦━━━━━━✦

Phantasos closed the door and leaned the back of his head against it. Having Amanda back healed his soul. The last several weeks had been the longest and most difficult of his existence. Every moment was exhausted with worry and longing for the only woman to consume him, body and soul. Unfortunately, during that time, he had allowed his heart and mental state to undo a lot of his hard work preparing for the fight of his life. Knowing Amanda was more than capable of protecting herself went a long way in calming the anxiety surrounding his inevitable battle with Ares. Now, he needed to get back to training for the fight of his life. Then, he needed to figure out how to take the fight to the god of war instead of waiting for the bastard to make a move.

Chapter XLIII

Battle

Amanda walked into the gallery with her father by her side. Both were masked in their human forms, looking bright-eyed and ready to enter the world they belonged to, the mortal world to which the Almighty blessed them with rules to live out their lives. Alaric was given the gift of staying married but would never be allowed to marry or procreate with another—Kathryn would be his only mate. If she were to pass, he would live out eternity alone. Amanda would never be allowed a carnal relationship with a mortal, which suited her just fine. No one could ever hold a candle to her Oneiroi.

"Amanda!" Kallisto all but tackled her. They clung to each other, both shaking and crying. "Of all that has happened to us—you being—"

She pulled back to look her best friend in the eyes with a warning not to finish the sentence.

"You are the biggest surprise. No. I take that back. Alaric is the biggest. I mean—just wow!" Kallisto was awe-struck. Amanda could see it in her eyes. The literal goddess standing before her was star-struck by her dad.

Before she could think beyond Kallisto's visible fascination, she was almost bowled over by three more immortals who materialized in a semicircle around her—Morpheus, Phobetor, and Nicole. She found herself in the center of a large group hug.

Looking through a small fissure between everyone's arms and legs, she saw Phantasos standing just outside the huddle with his arms crossed over his chest, grinning. His bright sky-blue eyes showed just how happy he was.

The decision to tell the crew and her family everything was made, and the night before, she and her father sat her mother down and told her everything. While her mother absorbed the news through many stages of shock, sadness, and eventually anger—she and Phantasos spent the night in the cave. He opted to tell his brothers via their Oneiroi link, and they spent the night exploring the many different things her body could do in its natural form.

Walking into the gallery was the first time she, as a Nephilim, faced her friends. Before, she was the lesser of the group; now, she bore more power than all of them combined. Granted, most of that power was yet tapped, but she was now the strongest, and strangely enough, she only felt equal, not superior. When she turned to tell her dad she would be okay, he wasn't there. She smiled to herself. He still had much groveling to do with her mother and must have felt she was in good hands.

Will I ever get her out of there? Phantasos loved seeing her surrounded by their friends and family, but he had something he needed to do.

"Good thing you don't have customers," Amanda said, followed by her equally muffled laugh from the middle of the huddle, which had more occupants. John and Annika had joined the cluster.

"If they had, we would have gifted them with new memories," Phobetor winked, pulling away from the group to look

Amanda over. "Seeing my brother's memories was hard. Seeing you standing here is a blessing."

"We missed you so much," Nicole hugged her one last time before he decided she had enough smothering.

"Could you watch over Amanda while I care for a few things?" He asked the group of his excited brothers and friends.

"Where are you going?" Morpheus squinted at him. There was no getting past his youngest sibling.

"To get a few items to take back to the cave. We," he nodded toward Amanda, "will be staying there for the foreseeable future."

"We have her, brother. Be quick, though. Nicole ordered pizza," Phobetor winked.

"Does your shirt say what I think it does?" Kallisto held Amanda at arm's length and read the t-shirt he had given her that morning.

Amanda rolled her eyes. "It does." She glanced at him with a mock, astounded expression.

"*Property of the god of Fantasy*. Are you serious?" Kallisto laughed.

"I am," he pulled Amanda from her friend's grasp. She rolled her eyes. "She loved it when I popped it on her this morning," he smirked.

"It was this, or he threatened to pee on me," Amanda laughed. "According to him, everyone needs to know who I *belong* to."

"Everyone will know you are mine, whether they feel my signature around you or not. Now, have fun. I will be back in less than an hour. Save me some pizza," he flashed to the atrium of his Olympian mansion.

His home was quiet, which was not unusual. What was strange was that when he called for his house nymph, there was no answer. This was it. What he hoped for. He could feel the tension in the air. As he walked from the door of his atrium to the main sitting room, his t-shirt and jeans faded with each step into the leathers and weapons he had donned in his cave. Being the god of fantasy, he could make anyone see what he wanted them to and not just while dreaming—an ability he honed the century after losing Marissa. He refused to go into dreams—he never stopped granting fantasies. Something not even his brothers knew he could do.

With a smirk, he sat on his sofa, arms resting on either side, with one ankle propped on a knee, and waited on his nemesis.

The air shifted before the god who appeared behind him said, "You have kept me waiting, Oneiroi."

"I was busy. I had an ἄγγελος to show how her body could feel in its new form. Did you know that wings are an erogenous zone all unto themselves?"

Ares growled and rounded the sofa to stand directly in front of him. He, too, was in fighting leathers—neither god in their true battle form—yet. "So, the rumors are true. She is an angel?"

"A Nephilim, to be exact. The child of a πολεμιστής Ἄγγελος and a demigod. She is my bonded, and you will never touch her again."

With a roar of unbridled anger, the god of war struck, and suddenly Phantasos found himself on what would be their battleground—the valley between the mountains where Zeus once fought and imprisoned his father, Cronus. Each god crouched in full battle form.

Phantasos felt his eyes swirling, and he saw crimson. His wings and fangs were fully displayed. The obsidian feathers, so small from a distance he knew they looked smooth, flared out behind him. This form had made lesser gods tuck tail and run.

Unfortunately, the god before him stood equally impressive, with his black eyes, red tattoos across his face, and neck swirling with each pump of blood through his veins. He wore leather and metal armor over his forearms and sternum, weapons sheathed down his chest, and two broad swords crossed at his back with hilts waiting just above his head to be drawn.

On the hill, to Phantasos' right, stood Zeus and Hera. "Are you going to face me alone, or do you need your parents?" He cocked a brow, asking Ares if he was that big of a pussy.

"Oh no. They are here to enjoy me removing that beastly head from your shoulders," Ares answered and began sidestepping.

Phantasos grinned, "And it begins."

⸗——⸗——⸗

"Did you feel that?" Phobetor looked from his pizza to his brother.

"Yes," both Morpheus and Amanda said in unison.

"I'm not sure what I'm feeling. I just know he's in trouble," Amanda continued.

"Who?" Kallisto asked.

"Phantasos. He's in trouble. I can feel it." Amanda began to shake. Keeping her human form while upset was not on the short list of abilities she had acquired. She went from the beautiful doppelganger to the formidable Nephilim in a breath.

"Nicole," Phobetor turned in mid-transformation to the dream bender. "Get everyone, and once you have them all, touch this." He handed her a bracelet like the one on Kallisto's wrist. "When you do, you and the ones you gather, will come to wherever I am."

"Can you find him?" Morpheus asked Amanda.

"Yes. He's on Olympus. Can I enter that realm like this?" She looked down at her glowing body and to her side, where a wing stretched, ready to fly.

"You can go anywhere your bonded is," Morpheus answered. Then, he reached for her hand, and Kallisto's hand. Phobetor grabbed her other hand.

"How do I do this?" Amanda asked.

"Close your eyes. Think about Phantasos. Allow your bond to take over. Smell him, feel him, hear him. Once he consumes you, you will open your eyes, and we will all be where he is," Phobetor answered.

Amanda closed her eyes and began to think about the man she loved. Memories of the first time she saw him entering the gallery with Morpheus. His smartass, arrogance. Him lifting her off the floor of the dilapidated house after she'd been beaten. The kiss against the wall at the gallery. Arguing outside the cemetery. When he pinned her in Nicole's bathroom. Sweaty, dirty dancing at the club. Killing Phobos and stopping her from making a mistake with Mark. Her body pressed to his as she clung to him on his motorcycle. His hand splayed across her stomach, showing Poseidon who she belonged to—kissing her on the ship and making love to her for the first time in the cave. Possessing her body and soul. The look on his face when she emerged from the light glowing with wings. The memories ran in a loop. She could smell his body, hear him whispering his devotion as he pressed his body to hers.

When she opened her eyes, she, his brothers, and Kallisto stood on a small mountain overlooking a valley where Phantasos and Ares circled one another. She took a step to intervene and was stopped by Phobetor's hand on her arm.

"No. If you do, they," he nodded to the slightly larger hill across the valley, where Zeus, Hera, and The Fates now stood, "will join the fray."

"I can stop this. Let me," Amanda jerked her arm free.

"No, you cannot. Yes, you are stronger than any being here. But you cannot outmaneuver the king of Olympus and everyone he would bring to the battle if you so much as think about interfering. You are not ready for that."

Chapter XLIV

Underworld

"Are we going to dance or fight?" Phantasos grinned at his opponent.

"In a hurry to die, Oneiroi?" Ares smiled back at him.

"No—in a hurry to kill," Phantasos stopped. He smiled as wide as he could then and with a smirk and a mere thought he watched the god of war grab his head with both hands and fall to his knees.

He stepped toward the god writhing on the ground, clutching his temples, and heard a bellowing sound coming from the mountaintop, followed by lightning streaks in the sky. When Phantasos looked up at the Greek king, he knew he was about to die by Zeus' hand. After all, he had his beloved son seeing fantastic dreams of himself and his sons in horrific death scenes playing on a loop in his head. Ares had no way out of the mind fuck Phantasos was putting him through. Watching his precious son Phobos and his other children die in graphic detail. Ares was a horrible being, but he did love his children.

Phantasos stood above the god of war. He could end the divinity at his feet and die simultaneously from the lightning wielder with just a step and a half. *Amanda would forever be safe from this asshole. Would such a death be so bad?*

In the seconds he contemplated killing Ares, Phantasos watched Hades and Poseidon appear before their brother, blocking his lightning bolts and intervening when they said they would not. *Their change of heart must be due to Alaric showing himself*, thought Phantasos. *Zeus is no longer the one to fear.*

While his gaze was on the three enormous gods, Ares had gotten to his feet and, with as much power as he had been dealt, had Phantasos' mind seeing Amanda's fixed dead eyes and a dagger in her chest. He knew the images were all in his mind, but he had seen her like this before, and it had rendered him frozen then, just as it was now.

That was all Ares needed. Phantasos felt a deep slice across his upper right arm, then a sharp, hot pain in his left side, just below his ribcage. *Stabbed*. He took two stumbling steps backward, and his vision became clear. He no longer saw Amanda's death; he was now seeing his, as Ares stood over him with his sword arm reared back seconds before taking his head.

✤•——••——•✤

"No!" Amanda screamed, and with the emotional outburst came tornadic winds. She flashed between the god of her nightmares and the god of her heart. She could feel her eyes burn and the strength in her body expand beyond the physical. The look on the bastard's face before her was between reverence and fear. He had not seen her with the wings of an angel. She cocked her head to the side and grinned at the hulking god. The one who had held her captive multiple times. The one who swore to own her body and soul.

"Put down your weapon, Ares," Amanda's voice sounded strange to her own ears—far off and deeper than her norm.

"Hello, my beautiful. Have you come to give yourself in his place?" Ares' sword arm hung above her dream god.

"I've come to give you a choice," she grinned at the god. It was that moment when she felt it—what her dad had told her, but she had just now grasped—superiority over her tormentor. She knew he was no match for her. Ironically, he didn't seem to have the same revelation.

Mentally, she called to her bonded. He went from writhing on the ground to standing.

"Let me guess. You are ready to submit to me if I allow him," Ares pointed at Phantasos with his free hand, who now stood directly behind her, "to live."

She could feel him so close and smell the copper scent of his blood, which angered her even more. He bled for her. He killed Ares' son to save her. He held her heart, which Ares wanted. She was the reason Phantasos was here. The reason he had captured the ire of the warlord.

"No. I'm here to stop you," she allowed herself a slow grin.

Ares returned her grin. Then, he frowned and squinted his eyes.

She felt a flutter at the edge of her head. *He's trying to use his mind fuckery.* Did he believe the wings on her back were her only change? *This is going to be fun!*

Phantasos stepped from behind her and glared at Ares. "You will submit and end this. You cannot have Amanda, and you are wasting time trying to win a game that you have no clue what the rules are."

Ares threw back his head and laughed. "Are you going to hide behind a half-angel with no power, or at least only the power of wings, if she can fly? I at least thought this would be worth the fight. Watching the life drain from your eyes will be much less dramatic."

The god of war pulled his other sword from his back and took a warrior's stance.

Amanda heard the growl, and they were gone before she realized what Phantasos was doing. He dove toward the warlord, and when he touched Ares' arm, they vanished.

Spinning around, Amanda yelled every god's name she could think of. Before she made a third turn, Hades, Poseidon, Kallisto, and the Oneiroi stood in the valley with her.

"Where would he have taken him? Morpheus, where is he?" She screamed, unable to calm the fear and fury raging up inside her.

"I have no idea. His mansion, maybe?" Morpheus answered.

"Go look," Kallisto said.

Amanda could hear the fear in their voices. Closing her eyes, she thought, turning over every conversation she and Phantasos had.

"They are not there," Morpheus returned as fast as he had vanished.

"How about the realm where he found me with Phobos?" Amanda asked anyone who would listen.

"I will check," Phobetor left in a flash.

It took him longer than Morpheus to return, but he didn't find them. "Why would he leave here? Where we are. It doesn't make any sense," Amanda paced around the gods.

"To get an advantage and keep you safe," Hades interjected. "I believe your brother took Ares to the Land of Dreams. Think about it. His power is stronger there, and Ares has never stepped foot on Oneiroi land. Phantasos has the upper hand."

Amanda put her hand in the crook of Hades' arm, Kallisto grabbed Morpheus' hand, and Poseidon and Phobetor followed as they faded from the Olympian valley.

Amanda found the air was cooler outside the Oneiroi's cave. If she hadn't been to the Elysian Fields, she would never have guessed they were so close to them. Here, fog hung low around their feet, and the trees were bare of foliage. The birds made ominous sounds, not the pleasant chirps of songbirds.

Hades pulled from her grasp and pointed to a hillside. "If he brought Ares here, they would be over that hill."

"If you are not armed, stay behind," Phobetor said in his commander's voice—the one his brothers talked about when they tried to rile him. The memory of the six of them hanging out laughing at one another brought a smile to her face.

Kallisto raised a brow. "If you suggest Amanda and I stay back because we aren't wielding swords and daggers, you must be kidding."

"Follow, Hades," Amanda ordered the gods as if she were in charge.

"I knew I liked you," Poseidon winked.

"Out of curiosity," Amanda turned her head to speak to the huge god behind her. "If I need Polemistís, would he come? I mean—since we are in the Underworld." She didn't think she would need the beast, but you never know what could happen.

"He would. For me, he would not breach the barrier; for you, he would," Poseidon answered.

Well, that was interesting.

She heard the sounds of metal against metal and the grunts of pain and exultation before she saw them. They all stood on the hill and watched the dance below. If the amount of blood and speed had anything to do with who was coming out on top, it was clearly Phantasos. He looked like an avenging angel. His wings were spread wide, and his muscles stretched and bunched with each swing and parry. She could see the dried blood trails from the wounds he sustained on Olympus. She allowed herself a moment of adoration as she watched his skill.

Ares was equally skilled. However, he was actively bleeding from his right temple and his shoulder. It seemed they had both decided on hand-to-hand instead of being mind-fucked, or could they do that down here? She had so many questions.

"How long will it take my grandfather to figure out where we are?" Kallisto asked Morpheus. Amanda turned to hear his answer. She hadn't expected Zeus and the rest of the Pantheon to be able to find them. She figured since they were in Hades' realm, he couldn't enter. Poseidon was here, so what would keep Zeus out? Hades had gone to the oceans and visited his brother. *Damn.* Now that she really thought about it, nothing would keep him away from making sure his son survived this battle.

"I am surprised he has not already," Morpheus responded.

"Hopefully, Phantasos will end this before he figures it out," Phobetor stood with his arms crossed and his legs shoulder-width apart.

⁂

It worked. Bringing Ares here had given him the advantage, just as Olympus gave Ares one. Here, Phantasos' wounds healed faster, although not completely. They had at least stopped bleeding, and his energy had increased. Here, Ares' mind control was minimal. If he had not wanted to watch the evil bastard bleed so damn bad, he would have used his mind and killed him as soon as they entered the Underworld. He had not trained so hard for nothing.

"Why her?" Phantasos asked as they sidestepped each other.

"She is just like her grandmother and my second chance," Ares grinned. "I can smell her on you. If you are not dead when I take her, you will feel how I make her body sing through that special little bond you have. Then, you will understand why."

"Fuck you!" Phantasos felt red-hot anger. With a growl and the additional strength the Land of Dreams gave him, Phantasos launched himself at Ares, taking him to the thick grassy terrain. He locked eyes with the god of war and burrowed through his mind, giving him the memories that would lead to his undoing. Phobos held Amanda against her will. Blood and tears streaked down her face, and then, in slow motion, he made the god watch as he buried the Atlantean dagger through the beast's chest. Through his beloved son's heart. Instead of fantasy, he showed the warlord the truth.

Ares began to scream a pained, guttural cry for his son. Phantasos continued his psychological onslaught. Amanda smiled up at him, not Ares, as they made love—when she told him she loved him. The feeling he had when he felt her orgasm as if it was his own.

"She will never be yours," Phantasos hissed in Ares' ear. With Thia's dagger, the same one he used to kill Phobos, Phantasos drew back his arm to plunge it through the tormented god beneath him.

"Get off my son, Oneiroi," Zeus's deep voice echoed around him, and the king's hand squeezed his forearm.

Phantasos stilled and closed his eyes. This was it. The memories he had given Ares were the last ones he would remember. He was about to die by the hands of Zeus. He waited for the blow, but it never came. His arm was released, and he still straddled the warlord's chest—without the blade. Opening his eyes, he saw pandemonium all around him. He jumped off the god and pulled the only sword he had left. But he and Ares were both in shock at the chaos. Poseidon was toe-to-toe with Hera, Hades against Zeus, and his brothers and Kallisto stood before The Fates Three, daring them to join the fray—where was Amanda?

Chapter XLV

Jar

Phantasos spun around, looking for her, when he landed face-first on the ground.

"You are still going to die today. And today—she *will* be mine." Ares kicked him in his kidney so hard he knew he would be pissing blood. Before he could do anything more than vomit, Ares landed another kick to his spine.

Closing his eyes, which made him more vulnerable, he planted an illusion of Harmonia, Ares' daughter, in Angelia's place the day Ares raped her. It was sick and twisted, but he had to get off the ground.

Ares body began to convulse. Phantasos held on to the imagery, forcing him to watch the sickness playing in his mind's eye as he struggled to his feet. When the god of war kicked you in the kidneys, and you lived, it was miraculous.

Keeping his hold on Ares' mind, Phantasos looked for Amanda. He saw Hades and Zeus in gridlock and briefly remembered the power Hades had that Zeus knew nothing of. Poseidon had Hera by the throat. Oh, how he wished he could watch that play out. And hate them or love them, the Fates knew when to stand down. But where was Amanda?

"What in Hades' name is that noise?" he thought as he continued to look for Amanda. A breeze started, and the noise grew. Everyone stopped and looked around.

Songbirds? Beautiful music from the beaks of doves and cardinals. The wind came as thousands and thousands flew over the warriors. Behind them, two brilliant lights followed. The closer they got, the larger they became. He knew those lights. They were the ones from the beach when Ares returned—the day he killed Amanda. With those thoughts, his forced imagery on Ares ceased.

The two lights landed in the middle of the stunned gods. When their glamour faded, Amanda and Alaric stepped forward.

"Angels?" Zeus spoke the question they all had—all but the few who already knew.

"Those are not demi wings." Ares finally got it.

"No. They are not. You, Ares, will never possess me. Nor will any of you," Amanda looked from her nemesis to each king, Hera, and the bitch sisters. "I'm done with this. You abused my grandmother in the foulest ways. You tormented me. Your son tortured me. I want you dead. But that would be too merciful for you. Your father would pull for you to go to the Elysian Fields, which is unacceptable. I've been there, and you don't deserve the beauty. So. See this?" Amanda waved her left hand over the palm of her right hand, and a large bronze jar appeared.

"No!" Ares shouted and began to back away. With a wave of Alaric's large hand, Ares froze.

"Poseidon was gracious enough to tell me the story of you and the giants. When I discovered how scared you were of being trapped again—I decided your fate." Amanda smiled sweetly at the motionless deity. "You will go into this jar for a thousand years. Once released, if you ever so much as think about laying a hand on another woman, I will return you to your imprisonment for life. Your jar will be held in Tartarus behind Hades' unique bars."

"You cannot do this to my son," Zeus thundered. "He is of the royal line."

"And he touched my daughter. She is of the angelic line," Alaric flared his wings and narrowed his eyes at the king. "My daughter is merciful. If I were doling out his sentence, he would die a painful death and be banished to the three rings of hell, where he would be tortured for all eternity. So, it's my way or her way. Decide, Zeus."

Zeus glared at Alaric and nodded once in resignation. When Alaric walked toward the sisters, he noticed Amanda tilt her head. Apparently, her father was going off script. Amanda followed behind him, and Phantasos stepped to her side. "Because you meddled, my daughter was put in danger and kept from her bonded," He looked directly at Atropos. "Isn't that so?"

Atropos lifted her chin, "We knew she was not of our world."

"That may be so, but you must understand that I refuse to allow any being to put her in harm's way," Alaric's grin grew slowly.

That is where she gets it. Phantasos thought.

"I have something special in mind," the angel said.

"And that would be?" Atropos spoke for all three of them.

"Where would be the fun in telling you? The anticipation will be part of the enjoyment for all of us."

"How will I see my son?" Hera asked, nose in the air as if she had control over the situation.

"You will not, just like Aphrodite and Hermes have gone without seeing their daughter," Amanda answered. She then walked over to the frozen god, and with another wave of her hand, he faded into vapor and entered the jar. With a pop, the lid sealed. "Hades, may Phantasos and I place him in his cell?"

"Yes," Hades turned to Zeus. "Since you cannot keep your son on a leash, I will."

❖━━━━❖

Amanda placed the jar on the pedestal that Hades and Poseidon had arranged in the cell. Once the base of the jar touched the stand, a yellow light flashed, and metal fingers locked onto its sides.

She stepped back and looked at the vessel. Her eyes stung, and she felt safe for the first time since the day Ares came into her life. It was finally over. "The seal and those metal bands are charmed to stay locked for one thousand years. He's not going anywhere."

"I love you, ἄγγελος," Phantasos winked, then enveloped her in his arms and held her while she shook with relief.

"I love you, too, Phantasos. I have since the first time you saved me."

Epilogue

Seven Years Later

"Not over there. I told you; those flowers go on either side of the altar," Nicole scolded the florist for the third time in the span of twenty minutes. She wasn't sure who was the most stressed, her or Amanda. "No. Amanda is anxious—I'm stressed." She spoke to herself as she draped white clothes over tables in the vestibule.

"Talking to yourself, again, my έξυπνος ομορφιά," Phobetor leaned down and kissed his wife on the cheek. "Tell Mommy she is beautiful." He held their daughter, Amabilia, down to kiss her mother as he had. Amabilia was almost three. She and her cousin, Arcas, the four-year-old son of Kallisto and Morpheus, kept their parents on their toes. Unlike their mothers, each child came into the world with their abilities. Needless to say, parenting them had been a challenge and the best part of life. Challenging because their fathers were pushovers who spoiled them.

"She's not dressed. I thought Kallisto was dressing her when she dressed Arcas. We only have thirty minutes," she said, tapping her watch. She felt sweat dripping down her back. She had gotten to the church four hours ago and hadn't stopped running around since.

"Kallisto will have her dressed with a wave of her hand. Have you forgotten she's a god?" Phobetor laughed at her. She gave him what he wanted—a smack on his shoulder and a glare promising pain.

"Hit me again," he waggled his eyes.

She rolled hers. "Stop aggravating me, you scoundrel," she tried hard not to smile at her hot *nightmare* of a husband, but he was absolutely delicious.

"I figured if you are a little riled up, I would get some hate s—

"Do not finish that sentence. You know she repeats everything we say," Nicole smirked. "Now go. Take her to her aunt."

⋇———⋇———⋇

Phobetor walked away laughing, carrying their beautiful daughter to the dressing room. When he got to the kids' room, Kallisto was nowhere to be found. Morpheus sat watching his son and laughing at the rogue's antics. His nephew was what the southern American mortals called—a fine mess. He had the vocabulary of an adult—an adult sailor when he was mad. When he heard his uncle Phantasos say fuck for the first time, the boy ran with it. Now, when he visits, Kallisto places a verbiage charm on Phantasos' mouth. It was hilarious to hear him use random childish words in place of his everyday four-letter ones.

"I was told to bring Amabilia to Kallisto so she could get her dressed. I see Arcas has already been put into his penguin suit."

"She's in with Amanda. She told me to tell you to put that," Morpheus pointed to a light baby blue dress, "on her. Once done, take her to the bridal suite, and she will do her hair."

"Okay." Phobetor began to dress his baby girl. "Did you ever think while on battlefields that one day we would be dressing our children in the human realm for Phantasos' wedding? All while wearing tuxedos and controlling our foul mouths?"

Morpheus snickered, "Brother, I never imagined life could be as beautiful as it turned out for us."

———

Kallisto stood transfixed. Kathryn and Kellie were getting Amanda ready for the wedding, and she was supposed to be dressing the children, but she couldn't stand it any longer. She had to see her best friend. After giving Morpheus his instructions, she left her husband in charge of himself and the kids and went to see Amanda. No matter who she married or where in the universe they lived, Amanda would always be hers. Closer than sisters.

"Oh, Amanda! You look gorgeous. Look at my arms. I have goosebumps. I've never seen someone as beautiful as you are, standing there in the window. That dress—wow! If Phantasos stays around for a reception, it will be a miracle. In fact, I'm not sure he will make it through the wedding. He will have you swept up and gone."

"Stop it. You're going to make me cry, and Mom had to fix my makeup twice already," She watched Amanda blot her face with a tissue. "I need one of those."

———

Ten minutes later, after her mother fixed her makeup one last time, Amanda was alone in the bridal suite, waiting for her father. Standing in front of the full-length mirror, Amanda smoothed her hands down the bodice of her wedding gown. This was it. The day she became the wife of the eldest Oneiroi. She allowed a moment to think about the man she was about to say *I do* to and the story of their love. After all the hardships of their first year knowing one another, the last six had been the epitome of amazing. It had taken her several years to become skilled at being half angel, half demigod.

Phantasos was patient when her father took her back to the beach so she could learn without interruption. Being an angel came with unbelievable skills. There wasn't a language she couldn't speak or read. She was faster and stronger than any of the gods and was confident in that assessment since she and her dad had visited every Pantheon together. Angels were meant to help all beings, not just mortals.

Her father had known Mark was an elf of the Norse Pantheon. Apparently, her father employed many gods and creatures from different Pantheons when at sea. He was helping others when Ares and Phobos had taken her, and he had never gotten over that. To this day, her dad held a lot of guilt for what had happened to her, another reason he made sure her abilities rivaled all. Still, to this day, he didn't know everything. Kallisto and Hypnos were the only two who knew her story, and Hypnos didn't know it in detail. That was a story she had only shared with her best friend.

Phantasos made her laugh and was the only one who could rile her up in seconds. Something he enjoyed doing from time to time. No matter what, over the last six years, he made sure she knew how precious she was to him. He treated her like his angel, like his queen.

"It's time," her father said, standing in the doorway of the bridal suite. "Darling, you look—" Alaric closed his eyes, then looked back at her. "I thought your true form was the most beautiful sight ever, but looking at you today, in that gown. Well, you're about to knock his socks off."

"Oh, Dad," Amanda walked to him, and he wrapped her in his arms. "No matter what, you will always be the first man I loved. Thank you for loving me so much."

"Let's go, baby girl. You have a destiny to get to," Alaric kissed her forehead and placed her arm in the crook of his elbow.

✦━━━━✦

Watching the love of his life walk toward him down that long ass aisle was the most exhilarating experience ever. She looked like the angel she was, the one he had always called her. She was so magnificent that he was unsure if touching her was possible. They had chosen to write their own vows, and since the gathering was a mixture of gods, demigods, and mortals, they had to be careful with what they divulged in them. When the priest asked her for her vows, Phantasos lost it. Standing before over two hundred people, he cried like a baby. It took him several minutes to compose himself so he could recite the vows he wrote. When the priest said he could kiss his bride, he lost it again. Bride. Wow. She was his. Not only bonded but his in every way possible.

After a barrage of photos and pleasantries from people not staying for the reception, Kallisto and Nicole pulled Amanda from his arms and took her off to change. He had to admit, he was aggravated. He wanted to help his wife slip into something more comfortable for the reception. Kallisto told him that she didn't trust him to come back out with her. So, he conceded, knowing she was right. If he had gotten her alone and his hands on her, they would be on Olympus in their bedchamber instead of making small talk and eating cake with their guests.

"Well, brother, you did it. You are no longer the most eligible bachelor on Mount Olympus. How does it feel to be a married man?" Phobetor handed him a glass of amber liquid.

He assumed it was a mixture of ambrosia and whiskey. *Yep.* "It is surreal. I wanted to do this six years ago. She is the one who made us wait, insisting on getting her college degree after learning everything she needed to be the best of her kind. To me, this was the step that meant the most. She was raised mortal, and this ceremony is what mortals do to claim each other."

Amabilia ran up to him about that time, saying, "I love you, Uncle Phantasos." He picked his niece up and swung her around. He had no idea how much he could love children until his brothers made him an uncle. This was what he could not wait for to make the love of his life the mother of his children.

People began to part to let someone through close to the double doors. He assumed Amanda was making her grand entrance. So, he handed Amabilia over to her father, and when he looked up, he saw his amazing wife standing halfway across the room looking at him. She wore a T-shirt that said, *Property of Phantasos. My fantasy came true—D.F.O.*

Before he realized he had moved, he was grabbing her and kissing her—the rest of the evening they spent dancing and enjoying their wedding bliss.

◈■──■──■◈

"Have any of you seen Atropos?" Clotho asked. She stood on her tip-toes, looking over the ballroom, acting strangely.

"We haven't," Amanda said. "Have you checked outside on the terrace?"

"We have looked everywhere. She was there one minute, talking with Apollo and me. He went to get us drinks, and I turned for no more than a second and said hello to Hermes. When I turned back around to resume our conversation, she was gone."

"I'm sure she's around somewhere. If she's not here, maybe she went back to," Amanda lowered her voice and looked around, "Olympus."

"Already checked," Clotho said. "I will keep looking."

Once Clotho was out of sight, she turned to her father and squinted her eyes. "Dad?"

He took a sip of his wine, "Yes, darling."

"Where is Atropos?"

"Finally learning a lesson." With that, he finished off his glass of wine and smiled. "I love you, Amanda. Don't worry. All will be as it should." He replied as he sauntered toward the dance floor with his wife.

Amanda sat there with her mouth agape.

What has he done?

Acknowledgements

I WANT TO THANK God for giving me the gift of gab and perseverance; it definitely took both to finish this book.

Second, who knows where this trilogy would be if Joanna and Kellie had not helped so much. It takes a lot to tell a friend "no" that won't work while keeping up their spirits, but these two women have done a phenomenal job at it.

Third, Joanna, thank you for the awesome merch and inspirational words.

Fourth, Rowan Magennis for the best cover art an author could ask for.

Fifth, my daughter, Allison—she is my biggest fan.

Last but not least, my husband—Ty, thank you for putting up with me for the last year and a half as I race to the finish line.

Thank you for helping make my dream come true!

L. W. PHILLIPS IS a businesswoman who figuratively wrote all day for years. She went through each day thinking of her life and those of others as scenes and scenarios in books. Finally, she wrote her musings down—well, she typed them out. She woke one morning with a full-length novel—actually, it was four months later, after much hard work, she woke up with a very raw, full-length rough draft of Dream Divine.

She is married and has three children—two grown and one teenager. She breeds crested geckos and runs a dental company. Not to mention all of her dogs, cats, and fish. When does she sleep, you ask? She doesn't.

Her escape is the world of fantasy. Reading and writing relax her. Young adult fantasy is her favorite, with adult fantasy and historical fiction following close behind.

Her motto is never to give up and always to follow your dreams!

Thank you for reading Dream Sacrifice!

Book III of the Oneiroi Trilogy

Sign up for L. W. Phillips's author newsletter. This is where she finds her ARC and BETA readers; there are always giveaways!
http://eepurl.com/ii9BAb